Territory

MISSOURI

Franklin

UNITED

Santa Fe

NEOSHO

VERDEGRIS

Osage village

36°

Three Forks

CIMARRON

OF ARKANSAS

NEOSHO

Vance killed by a bear

ARKANSAS

Fort Smith

WASHITA

Stock lost

NO. FORK OF CANADIAN

CANADIAN

RED

RED

Spanish

Territory

100°   98°   96°   94°

EX LIBRIS

A. Clifford Abbott, M.D.

VOYAGE TO SANTA FE

VOYAGE TO
SANTA FE

by Janice Holt Giles

HOUGHTON MIFFLIN COMPANY BOSTON

To
OLIVER G. SWAN
who is
honorable in his dealings, wise in his counsel
and
warm in his friendship

More valid than the instinct which would have kept him innocent, which would have trained and civilized him, was the instinct which moved her to love, and so moving, provided her with the courage and the strength to love wholly, nothing kept back, nothing reserved.

from JOHNNY OSAGE

I

Husband, she thought, and would have left it there, comforted. But he rode across the head of the wagon train shouting at one of the drivers. Her eyes followed him.

Her hands, her skin, her bloodstream, knew every angle and bone of the dear body. Her ear knew every inflection of the loved voice. Her eyes knew in the smallest detail every inch of the cherished flesh. Her heart knew the utter commitment of its devotion to him. But—and a barb of fear wounded her—her mind did not know his mind. No more, she thought, than if he were an Osage Indian. He says this thing or that. Why? By what processes does he arrive at those firm determinations? What does he think and how does he think? What does he want? What drives him? What divides him? Where must he go and where must I go to follow him? And where is the habitation of his spirit?

She closed her eyes. Husband, she said aloud, trying to recover the heart and the flesh and the voice and the bones and the comfort, and again, more slowly, she said it—husband. But the image was gone.

A panic seized her.

Her eyes flew open and she chattered the word rapidly and with a finger she spelled it out on her knee trying to capture it solidly, to force the word into its commonplace context. Appalled, she lost her grasp of it. It was gibberish in an alien tongue, two syllables newly coined and meaningless—tall, upright sounds standing strangely separate and unjoined.

Husband. What was a husband?

Her mind skittered back. The word had an origin. It had to have an origin. It had to begin somewhere. It had a meaning, if she could only recall it. Painstakingly she traced it back, down the paths of her learning. Anglo-Saxon, yes—the word was hüsbonda; in the old Norse it was hüsbondi. Saxon or Norse, it meant a householder. But my husband, the blade of her mind bit grievingly, does not like a house. A tent, a tree, an Osage lodge, a sheeted wagon, his saddle on the ground, the open sky, will do as well for him. His house is everywhere and nowhere. But where shall the house of his wife be? How shall she accustom herself to such vastness? How shall she room with a householder whose house is the earth itself? How shall she grow a rooftree on her back?

Her eyes fled to the man on the horse and something torn and lonely cried to him, husband—Johnny!

The wagon jolted over a stone.

As though it jolted her soul back from a cold and windless plain she seized the moment and pinned her mind to the real and the sensible and the necessary immediate.

She was Judith Fowler—wife, beloved wife, united in lawful wedlock to Johnny Fowler. He had been her husband for ten months. What woman knew her husband after ten months? Or ten years? Or a lifetime? What human being ever wholly knew another or was meant to know? No man is an island—she knew her Donne—but each grain of earth which makes a continent is separate and different of itself.

She laughed shakily.

She had fallen once more into an old and childish trick of letting the sounds of speech entrance her so that she had lost the meaning, that was all. When she was only a little girl she had learned that she could enter at will a world of cloudy trophies, a self-hypnosis, by watching a drip of water, the woven pattern of a rug, the pendulum of a clock and, much more swiftly, by saying over and over and over one word. There had always been, she remembered, the feeling of leaving the house of her skin and her mind and the accompanying feeling of chill and fear. She had long ago disciplined herself never to do it, for it reached too near, she thought, to the hand of God. She had no wish to explore the realms of mysticism and she feared to feel too often that brittle chill of homelessness.

Her identity returned, her fear explained, she felt lighter hearted and she shook out the reins briskly and shouted, "Gee, there," to the off mule who was bridling archly. "You know that's only a bush, Pedro."

She was Judith Fowler. She was twenty-two years old. She had thick, reddish-brown hair and brown eyes to match. She had a pale but not thin white skin which darkened evenly and freckled a little every summer. She was small and slender, but as tough as a willow switch.

She was Judith Fowler, she thought, riveting it consciously, and she was young and healthy and strong and she was driving a team of mules hitched to a light wagon which was to be her home on the road for she knew not how long. Sometime in August, Johnny had said. Sometime in August, they would arrive in Santa Fe.

They were Spanish mules and her wagon was part of a train made up of three more wagons, heavier, freight wagons, twenty men, forty-seven mules, thirty mustangs—but not another woman. In the entire train she was the only woman. Her husband was sole owner of this wagon train, and outfitting it had cost him every penny he possessed and all he could beg or borrow. They were traveling from their home at Three Forks, in the Arkansas Territory, to Santa Fe in Spanish territory.

She was Judith Fowler, and it was the thirtieth day of April in the year of our Lord 1823. The sun was shining and, three days out from home they had made good a distance of forty-five miles. There were seven hundred and fifty more to go. No matter. Johnny knew the way.

He rode up beside her. "We are coming to the Deep Fork."

She looked. "That line of trees?"

"Yes. We'll cross before making night camp." A smile cracked the dust on his face. "Are you tired?"

She smiled back at him and shook her head.

His horse sidled off. "Shift from the wagon to your horse day about. It'll ease you."

"Yes." She measured the sun with her hand. "Isn't it early to make night camp? Two hours of traveling time yet."

"Not by the time we make the crossing. It's a mean creek and a mean ford. Be dark by the time we're over." He nodded toward the trees. "We'll halt this side of the timber. Pull up behind the other wagons. Legette will take care of your mules." He grinned. "You'll have time to stretch your legs."

She nodded. He nudged his horse with his heels and rode away. She gave her full attention to driving.

Here, in the first easy days, on the known prairie, her own light wagon was pulled by a single team of mules. She could drive herself. Later it would take four, perhaps six or eight mules to haul the wagon through the bog and mire, the sand and rivers, the foothills and mountains. Later, her strength would not be sufficient. Legette would have to drive.

She looked ahead at the white-tilted freight wagons which required eight mules already. They were big, heavy, lumbering and very deeply loaded. Take the name you pleased, Conestogas or Pittsburgs, they were enormous. They had high prows and sterns and high wheels with iron tires a good six inches wide. Because she had heard Johnny Fowler talk about them interminably she knew they were built with curves, like a ship, so that goods could be stowed tightly and would hold steady no matter the jouncing and bouncing they must take. She knew that the beds were as nearly watertight as possible so that silks and satins, easily rusted iron goods, cottons and woolens, would not handily be wetted in river crossings. She could say over to herself the woods that had gone into their construction. White oak, hickory, bois d'arc, all well seasoned, for singletrees, tongues, hounds, bolsters, felloes, hubs and spokes.

Stay chains and traces were of iron with short, heavy links.

The sheets were of osnaburg, two thicknesses, with Mackinaw blankets between for added protection. The bows followed the curve of the prow and sterns and it occurred to Judith Fowler, following them, that the white tilts looked remarkably like sails and the curved wagons looked remarkably like ships. Instead of the blue they sailed a new-green, tender sea of grass.

Johnny Fowler did not like foofaraw so his wagons were not painted. They were oiled down and left drab. He did not care about their appearance. His only concern was with their utility. Lashed beneath the beds were two extra tongues for each wagon. Inside, along with twenty-five hundred pounds of cargo, were extra wagon spokes, extra links of chain, extra pigs of iron, extra anything which his fertile and practical mind could think of being needed. However far his dreams led him on an endless road toward pale and western distances, Johnny Fowler's caution made him take pains that all things should be done with foresight and care. The dream and the necessity perfectly balanced, the one forever beckoning, the other carefully acting.

She was Judith Fowler. And she was following a man's dream to Santa Fe. And what was Santa Fe? And where was Santa Fe?

Behind her a whip cracked and she heard a voice raised in Spanish imprecation. She laughed. The pack mules followed in her track. Manuel, she thought, was restless under the slow progress. He was going home. "I wish I had wings," he had told her, "so I could fly to the mountains."

She flicked her mules with her whip. She wanted to reach the shade and the Deep Fork and she wanted to walk about and stretch her legs.

2

W HEN she drew up behind the freight wagons the black man, Legette, appeared so quietly to take her mules that he startled her. He is like a cat, she thought, like a big, soft-stepping, midnight-colored cat. She smiled down at him.

He helped her over the wheel. "The captain says if you would like to take a look at the creek, ma'am, just follow the trail. He has gone ahead." His voice was as soft as his step, with a hint of thickness, but he spoke precisely and without the erosion common to his race or to the frontier.

"Yes. What about the mules, Legette?"

"The captain says they are to be picketed. It may take some time to make the crossing."

She watched him as he went about unhitching. He spoke to the mules, rubbed their heads, kept them standing without skittishness. He was good with animals.

He was taller than her husband, who stood six lean feet in his stockings, and the breadth of his shoulders was greater. He was big, very big, without being hulking, and the black skin was as glossy and smooth as satin. "Healthy," Johnny said. "When a Negro's skin goes dull he is sick."

They did not know his age. He was young enough that his joints were still loose, his muscles still supple, his teeth still good. He was old enough to have learned many skills. He was an excellent cook; he was a good blacksmith; he was a better-than-average carpenter, and he admitted to having barbered some. He could doctor a sick horse or break a wild one. He could read and write and he was reasonably quick with figures. "Somebody trained him well," Johnny said.

They did not own him. He was not their property.

Judith pondered again the circumstances of his coming to them and felt, as she had before, a sense of unease. Morally they had done right, but legally? Six months earlier her husband had been in Fort Smith, as he frequently was, on business. He had brought the black man home with him. "You didn't buy him?" she had asked quickly. She did not hold with owning human beings.

"No. The *Natchez* came in. He was deckhand on her. Said he didn't want to go back downriver with her. Wanted me to buy his contract with the captain and let him work it out."

"Johnny, what do you know about him?"

"Nothing. Except he is big and strong and healthy and I can use him."

"Is he free?"

"He is now."

"He's a runaway, then."

Her husband had shrugged.

"But, Johnny . . ."

He made an impatient chopping motion with his hand which stopped her. "You want me to send him back to the boat? Send him downriver? Legette! Come here." The black man came and stood mutely before them. "Drop your shirt and turn around."

His back was corded with welts. They had healed but they were still so new that the scars had gray, tender edges. She had shuddered and covered her eyes. "No. No, Johnny."

"Then never mention it again." He dismissed the Negro. "And never ask him any questions. What's behind him is behind. I am taking him to Santa Fe. He can make his own way then. Nobody can touch him once he is over the Spanish line."

He served them competently and with a quiet foresight which made them comfortable. But with as much integrity as he observed with the rest of the men Johnny Fowler had given the black man a contract for the journey. He was signed on as blacksmith to the train and as cook and general servant to themselves.

He led the mules away to be hobbled and picketed. The Mexican drover came to meet him, laughing, reaching for the ropes. "Qué tal, amigo?"

She could not hear the black man's reply but the Mexican yelped with glee and clapped him on the back. The two were excellent friends already.

She turned about and went trudging past the parked wagons. The men near her path spoke as she passed, quietly and decently. She spoke in reply, smiled pleasantly, and kept on.

Johnny had gathered together such an odd assortment of men for this journey. Where, for instance, had he found the Mexican, Manuel, and under what circumstances? He did not say. He only brought him home from St. Louis. "He is from Santa Fe. He wishes to go home. He knows horses and mules. He will drive the herd."

He was a slim, dark young man who spoke English badly and was given alternately to gay laughter and such deep fits of melancholy that his dark eyes melted with sorrow. "Homesick," Johnny said. "He'll be fine when he sees the mountains again."

Judith said, "He's like an Indian, grieving."

"Exactly. This is not his land."

It pleased her that since the train had started his spirits had lifted considerably. He took his meals with them and he gave her lessons in Spanish. If she was going to live in Santa Fe she wanted to be able to speak the language.

She did not know how long her husband had been dreaming of this journey to Santa Fe. He said so little of his dreams and longings and yearnings. But even before their marriage she had known he was restless and unhappy with the situation in the Arkansas Territory. He had been a trader to the Osage Indians for many years and a way of life he liked was ending. The government was moving eastern Indians into the territory and pushing the Osages out. Johnny Fowler was as powerless as the Osages to prevent it. He did not like what was happening and moody and restless he prowled the trading post, made journeys, went on long hunts.

She had wished she knew how to be of help to him, but she felt that only some great change, some fine new adventure could offer him hope.

Last year the chance of change had come, the great, fine new hope had been born. He had traveled to St. Louis, as much to ease his restlessness as to buy for the trading store, and he had come home excited, his eyes bright with a new interest. He brought with him the news that the revolution in Mexico had been successful. Iturbide had accomplished the impossible and freed Mexico from Spain. All the old proscriptions would be lifted now. No longer would American traders in Santa Fe be thrown in the calabozo and their goods confiscated.

"William Becknell told me," he said, "the new government will be friendly to American traders. He was there. He was in Santa Fe. He took three wagons over the road this year and he was there when the news came through. He says American traders will be welcome. The people have had nothing but shoddy goods from Vera Cruz and they are hungry for goods. And the proscription is lifted on trapping, too. A man could take goods for the Santa Fe trade, say three or four wagons to start, and he could take traps and men to trap, and he could . . . for years I've believed wagons could be taken on a more southerly road. You could leave from here, keep within the latitude, get an earlier start . . . Of course there would be the dry plains this side the mountains, but Becknell got in a water scrape on the Cimarron cutoff. You've got those plains on any route unless you go as far north as Bent's Fort, and you can't take wagons

over the Raton. You could spend the season in Santa Fe and work the
trappers out of Taos . . ."

He talked on and on. He was like a boy, she thought, thrusting his
hands through his hair, talking rapidly, the words tumbling and flowing
and going off in all directions as he explored one idea after another. He
paced the floor, his eyes lit with pleasure and excitement, his body swift
and taut. "Keep the party small . . . allow for the Indian trade . . . follow
the Osage path through the Timbers . . ."

He was a man galvanized now. As though this news released him, the
restlessness was channeled into tremendous activity and he was filled with
quick purpose and power. First he must ride north again to talk more
with William Becknell. "He knows the trade best. He's been taking pack
trains through for years and he took wagons lately. I want to see his wagons
myself."

He was gone a month and he returned with all his plans matured and
hundreds of notes which Judith must decipher and copy in her clear fine
hand. Johnny despised to set pen to paper so she made his lists, wrote his
letters, abstracted information from the replies and indexed it for easier
use. With him, she went over the shelves of the trading store to discover
what could be had and listed the items carefully:

> *Axes, mattocks, picks, shovels, spades*
> *10 doz. point-four blankets*
> *50 gross blue and white beads*
> *Brass work*
> *Needles, awls, mirrors, shells*
> *Stroudings and super blues*
> *Coarse cambrics*
> *Domestics*
> *Cutlery*

She made another list of things to be bought in St. Louis:

> *Fine cambrics*
> *Cotton, wool and silk shawls*
> *Handkerchiefs*
> *Shirtings*
> *Cotton hose*
> *Pelisse*
> *Bomazettes*
> *Crapes and silks*

When he finally determined to keep the party to twenty men, including
himself, he set about recruiting them. "I want Jesse Cooper for my second."

"Who's Jesse Cooper?" she asked.

"Fellow I grew up with back in Kentucky. Steady as a rock. And I'll go to Pittsburgh for the muleskinners. Not many had much experience here in the Territory. Those fellows been driving freight wagons over the Alleghenies all their lives. Know their business."

There were ten of them, finally, and they had come in by the first steam packet this spring, arriving only a few days before the departure date set by Johnny. They all knew each other, personally or by reputation. Judith thought them an odd assortment. "They're strange men. They seem to have ways all their own."

"Yes. But they have one thing in common, besides itching feet."

She looked at him questioningly.

"They are all good muleskinners. Best I could find."

He had then organized the train. "We'll have three camps of five men, one to each freight wagon, the wagon to carry its own provisions and cook outfit. There'll be four at our wagon—ourselves, Legette and Manuel.

"The Indians?"

"They'll take care of themselves."

He named on his fingers and she made the list:

> For each wagon, One skillet
> One frying pan
> One iron kettle (medium)
> One coffeepot
> Five tin cups (pint)
> Five tin plates (deep rimmed)
> One butcher knife

She added knives, forks and spoons to the outfit for their own wagon. Men on the trail might spear meat with their knives and sop stew with their bread but she meant to keep a little civilized.

Johnny worked a long time over the amount of provisions to take. He wanted no discontent over shortages but neither did he want space taken up by an excess of rations. Meat they would kill. What he had to have was enough dry rations. The list he finally handed her was worked out per man for the journey:

Flour	50 lbs
Bacon	" "
Coffee	10 "
Sugar	20 "
Meal	25 "

He read aright the look of dismay on her face and added, "Take some extra things for yourself if you want, but keep it light."

She added beans, rice, tea, and some dried food to their own necessities.

Much of the time those months of preparing, he was away. He went to St. Louis and was gone for three months. He went often to Fort Smith and oftener to the Osage village on the edge of the prairie. He was trading for mustangs with the Indians, learning more from their warriors about the Comanches and Kiowas, consulting with the Osages about the road through the Cross Timbers. He had lost all his excitement now and had become painstaking, patient, methodical, and thorough. He neglected nothing which might add to the safety or the comfort of the train. But it was February before he set a departure date. "The last of April, if the weather is fit."

The fine down on her arms felt strangely alive. She glanced at it curiously.

He saw her. "Are you afraid?"

"I don't know," she said slowly, and honestly.

"Don't be. It'll be all right."

"Of course. You'll be there."

He laughed and went away.

She did not think she would be much afraid of the usual things. She did not like snakes but she did not have hysterics when she saw one. She would not like crossing rivers high and swift with flood waters but she did not think she would panic if it was necessary. She did not enjoy thinking of being attacked by Plains Indians, but she could not believe she would faint or scream or lose her head. Johnny would be well prepared for such an attack if it came. She knew she would grow weary of riding day after day in a wagon or on a horse, but she was young and strong and she knew she would grow accustomed to it. What made her shrink a little when she thought of the journey was the leaving, the uprooting, the going into the unknown, even into a foreign land, for . . . how long? The rest of her life?

The trail she was following went into the woods which rimmed the Deep Fork and she looked up with pleasure. The sun had been bright all day and the shade was welcome. She picked out the trees she knew—elm, pecan, hackberry, oak, cottonwood. Many of them were twined with grapevines and poison oak. There was a brushy undergrowth of greenbriers and scrub, thicketed in many places, and the trail was rough with their sprouts. She found her husband and Parley Wade looking at the creek and she knew from their thoughtful expressions that this stream presented special difficulties. Mean creek, mean ford, Johnny had said. Without disturbing the two men she studied the water herself. It looked sullen and cold and it flowed very quietly. The banks were steep and the soil was shaly. When she moved she started a small avalanche of pebbles and loam. Her husband looked at her quickly. "Don't go near the brink. The bank caves easy."

It was not a very wide stream, not nearly as wide as the Verdigris at home, or the Neosho, and it was only a gully compared to the broad but shallow Arkansas. What problem did it hold?

She did not ask. A chattering woman was a bother when a man was thinking. She tried to determine for herself.

That quiet flow of water meant the creek was deep. And the banks were steep and caved easily. Suddenly she noted the narrowness of the stream and it came to her that there wasn't room to maneuver. Wagons would careen down one bank, sink into the deep water, and almost immediately have to begin the heavy pull up the other bank.

Johnny Fowler swung about, his mind made up. He took off his hat, wiped his face, settled the hat back on his head. "Cut the banks down, Parley. We'll start 'em in here, angle downstream, come out on the far side by that cottonwood."

Parley squirted tobacco juice and pulled at his whiskers. "Yon side the cottonwood?"

"Yon side."

"Yep. Gives ye as much room as ye kin git."

Johnny Fowler nodded and left down the trail through the woods. Parley dug his bootheel into the gravelly soil and shook his head.

Judith watched him.

He was the last man in the world she would have expected herself to be drawn to. He was admittedly and unashamedly an old renegade and reprobate. "He even tries to steal from me," Johnny had told her.

"Why do you put up with him?"

"I like him. And he's loyal in his own way. He won't sell out. In a pinch you can depend on him. He's shrewd and crafty and smart and I'd rather have him with me than against me."

He was happily dirty, profane and almost totally lacking in what she understood as morals. When she married Johnny Fowler she was prepared to put up with him but not to like him.

He had come out of the shade the day Johnny brought her to the post to live, to take their horses. She had known him by the black patch he wore over his left eye. It was said the Osage woman he lived with had put it out with a firebrand one night when he beat her harder than she thought necessary. He was of indeterminate age and moved without hurry, a ragged hat askew on his head, his scanty beard split with a grin and his good eye squinted with good humor. That much of him resembled the man Johnny had told her about, but from the neck down nothing about him squared with Johnny's tales. "Puts on a new suit of buckskins every two years or so and don't take 'em off till they fall off," he had said.

They must have fallen off, Judith thought, for he was resplendent in a linen shirt which was spotlessly clean but unironed. Over it he wore what must surely be the gaudiest and fanciest waistcoat ever made for man. Wild red roses climbed recklessly on green vines from his paunch to his shoulders. Buttonless, it was latched together loosely with a watch chain of heavy gold links. His black cloth pants were dusty and green with age and a rent had been patched with striped blanketing.

She looked quickly at her new husband and found him staring, his eyes wide and his mouth gone loose in amazement.

It was Parley who spoke the first word. "Shet yer trap, boy, 'fore it traps a fly."

Johnny passed a hand before his dazed eyes and peered from behind it. "Well, if you ain't something to behold. Just plumb dazzling. The spitten image of a peacock with his tail all spread. And it couldn't be more gorgeous. My, my, cover your eyes, Judith, or he'll blind you and put 'em out."

Parley's grin stretched a little wider. "Ain't I elegant, though?" He fingered the tabs of the waistcoat. "Ever see one brighter or purtier?"

"They don't make 'em no brighter," Johnny admitted. It was the first time Judith had ever heard him slip into the speech of the frontier. It came easily to him, she thought. He had draped a knee over his saddle-horn and was staring fondly at the old man. "Nope," he shook his head, "they sure don't make 'em no brighter. Where'd you get it?"

"Offen a riverboat gambler. Feller hadn't learned his trade too good." He gave Johnny a sly glance. "I give him a lesson," he added.

"'Twouldn't surprise me none if you didn't," Johnny said. "Watch chain his, too?"

"Yep." The old man scratched an ear. "Come to think of it, Johnny, the feller was right poverty-struck fer any kind of clothes time the game was done."

"Leave him his skin?" Johnny flung himself off his horse.

"'Twas wuthless to me. No use fer it. Never begrudged it to him. Howdy, ma'am. I'll take yer reins."

Confused, a little breathless and more than a little giggly, Judith handed him her reins.

Johnny was still eying the old man. "Didn't get that shirt off the gambler, though, did you?"

"Nope. One of yore'n. Swiped it from Becky's washline." He was not perturbed.

Becky was Rebecca Burke, Johnny Fowler's sister. Her husband was Stephen Burke and a partner of Johnny Fowler in the trading business.

Judith's husband grunted. "Thought I recognized Becky's stitching. That's one of my best linen shirts."

"Ain't hurtin' it none. Jist took the loan of it. Good as new when she washes it ag'in. Had to make my respects to yer lady, didn't I? Wouldn't want me to appear unmannerly, would ye?"

Johnny was peering closer. "Is that *white* skin I see? That little streak on your neck? You mean you *washed?*"

"Tuk me a whole bath," the old man said. "Doused in the river an' scoured with lye soap."

Johnny fell back against the hitching rail, overcome. "Judith, feel honored. Greater love hath no man. He has not ever had a bath before. Not ever in his whole life. He won't even dabble a finger in water. Says it's only fit for animals to drink. He has risked his life for you. He'll doubtless come down with pneumonia."

Old Parley grinned. Coming toward her, his laugh chuckling out, he said, "Now that ye've married up with the boy, ma'am, the fust thing ye've got to l'arn is he's got a monstrous misconception of the truth. Fact is, he ain't got none at all. He's not even got a speakin' acquaintance with the truth. The gift of gab passed him by, but when his tongue loosens up a mite, which it does oncet in a while, half whut he says is made up out of his head and the other half don't make no sense whutever." His shoulders shaking he stuck up his hand. "Welcome, ma'am, to Three Forks. I'm old Parley Wade and yer sarvant, ma'am."

The banter between the two men had made plain their affection for each other. Judith put her hand in the bath-streaked paw and said, warmly and impulsively, "I've heard of you. You are Johnny's good friend and I hope you will be mine."

She was surprised when the gap-toothed mouth closed and there was a tremor of the straggly beard about it. What had she done? What had she said? Had she hurt his feelings? She put her hand on his shoulder. "Parley, will you help me down?"

He bowed slightly. "Hit'd be an honor, ma'am."

Gently, as if he might hurt her, he disengaged her stirrup foot and when she bent lifted her out of the saddle and set her carefully on the ground. He stepped back and turned to Johnny. "Why, she ain't no bigger'n a leetle girl. Ain't she the leetlest thing? She don't weigh more'n a feather."

"Oh, come now," she protested, "I'm not that small."

"Not more'n a feather," he insisted, "not a mite more'n a feather. But she's bonny, boy, she's real bonny." He added, his good eye twinkling, "And I'm on her side from this day forrard. He don't treat ye right, ma'am, jist tell ole Parley and I'll whomp the daylights outen him."

"I'll remember that," she promised, laughing. "I'll remember it."

He never made a nuisance of himself, but he had been a little like a big shaggy watchdog from that day on. As she learned to know him better she came to have great respect for him. He was wise in the ways of the natural man and he had a vast knowledge of this country still so new to her. He was a great talker and though he didn't burden her with stories and tales, a question from her, which always pleased him, would set him off. As her respect for him grew, so did her liking. He had a hard core of plain sense and a shrewd instinct about people. He treated her, with a glint of fun in his eye, as if she hadn't an ounce of sense, as if he couldn't understand how anyone could be as ignorant as she, as if she tried his patience beyond bearing. Knowing it was his way of showing his affection, and that any other would have embarrassed him, she cemented their relationship by adopting Johnny's bantering way with him. She scolded him, scoffed at him, and ragged at him. He loved every bit of it and, looking at him now, digging his bootheel in the gravel, she thought how there was almost nothing she could not take to Parley and almost nothing he would not do for her. She felt a flush of gratitude for him.

He had his hatchet out now and was hacking at small sprouts and saplings which he piled to one side.

"Why are you doing that, Parley? To clear the way?"

He cracked a sapling down before answering her. "That's a dang-fool thing to ask. Got eyes, ain't ye? Kin see fer yerself, cain't ye?"

She pecked back at him. He would have been disappointed if she hadn't. "As foolish as you are, my eyes might deceive me."

"Kind of eyes you got," he retorted, warping his tobacco into the other cheek, "'twouldn't be hard to do."

Her footing with him was so easy she could even quip about his empty socket. "At least I've got two of them."

"And still blind as a mole." He spat and chopped three more thickset bushes.

She waited. This was merely skirmishing.

He piled the scrubs on the saplings, gave her an oblique look and said, "Ever see anybody try to make bricks without straw?"

"No."

"Tryin' to make a road down this bank 'thout packin' it tight with brush'd be worse'n that. Wouldn't hold. Wagons'd sink and slip."

She contemplated the bank a moment, then nodded.

Parley sighed. "Reckon ye'll git some sense in time." He ran his thumb over the hatchet edge and frowned. "Ain't much of a edge on it. Ort to brung my axe."

"Shall I get it for you? So you won't lose time?"

He gazed at her sadly, shaking his head. "Now, thar ye go ag'in. Not thinkin'. Not usin' yer head. What good would it do? Men is halfway here from the wagons. Bringin' plenty of axes. Ain't ye ever," he asked plaintively, "goin' to l'arn to think?"

She laughed. "Doesn't look like it."

"It shore don't. Now, git out of my way and quit jawin' at me so's I kin git on with this. Ort to had a pile twicet this size. Would've, too, you hadn't come pesterin'."

She hooted derisively. "You couldn't cut that much in a whole day."

"You," he said, pointing with his hatchet, "go set down on that log and don't say nothin' more to me. Git!"

She threw him a last retort. "I *meant* to knit you some stockings on this journey but you're so cantankerous I don't think I will."

"No skin offen my nose," he grunted, "don't wear 'em."

But he would be delighted when she had finished them, as she would, and he would wear them proudly she knew.

She marched away from the bank, found the log and seated herself upon it. She had sewed big pockets on her traveling skirts to carry her knitting, the small pouch holding her few valuables, a handkerchief, and other necessaries. From her pocket now she took out the list of Spanish words and phrases Manuel had made for her the night before: *por favor*—please; *a sus órdenes*—at your service; *hacienda*—country house; *haciendada*—ruler of a house; *cómo está usted*—how do you do; *gracias*—thank you; *adiós*—farewell; *un momentito*—just a moment; *padre*—father; *por qué*—why; *alma de mi alma*—soul of my soul.

She stared at the last phrase in astonishment. How odd that Manuel had included it. Why had he? When would she ever have any need for such a phrase? Soul of my soul. She thought about it and smiled. Manuel must be homesick for more than the mountains. It was surely his need he served here, not hers.

What a graceful language it was and how much it lost in translation. Soul of my soul had a ridiculous and self-conscious sound in English. Not even in transport would one dare use such words. They would be stiffly embarrassing and singularly out of place between reticent and modest persons. But anyone, just anyone, could breathe *alma de mi alma* to the beloved and never blush or stammer. It was simply a sigh, a caress, a heartbeat, a question, an answer. It was anything you wanted love to say. *Alma de mi alma.*

3

THE MEN, with axes, spades, mattocks, picks and shovels, poured down the track through the woods. Pointing, Parley Wade dispatched them. They stood bunched for a moment, looking at the stream and speaking together. Two of them stepped off the length of incline and width of the road to be made, then all spat on their hands and fell to work.

Mattocks and picks gouged loose great chunks of the loamy soil and spades and shovels threw it aside. Men with axes went to the woods, and saplings and bushes fell before them, were dragged up and packed as the road took shape. Dirt was shoveled in, tramped down, and more shrubs and bushes were laid on.

Johnny Fowler rode in, leading four mustangs. With only a glance at the road, he tethered the mustangs, then rode his horse down the slope. The animal stepped flinchingly into the water, throwing his head up and sidling a little at its coldness. Johnny gave him time, then spurred him lightly to make him take the water and angled him firmly downstream. The horse, feeling the tight reins, moved steadily. Judith stood to see better.

The slope of the creek bed was not gentle. The water rose quickly up the mustang's legs, to his belly, and then onto his flanks. Johnny put his feet up, his head bent studying the water. Judith found herself gripping the Spanish list and she thrust it into her pocket. Would it be swimming-deep? Swimming-deep meant unloading the wagons and rafting the freight over. She knew this might have to be done many times on the journey, but this early? Johnny and Parley Wade, hunched over the winter fire, had talked about the prospects, studied Johnny's rough map closely. "Here, and here, and here," Johnny had said, stabbing the map, "there may be deep water." She recalled that they had hoped to catch the Deep Fork low. Was it? Or was it running fuller than they had expected? She didn't know. They hadn't said. Was it going to be necessary to unload all those bales and kegs and boxes Parley had fitted so economically and carefully into the wagons? And lose all that time?

But Johnny's mustang was heaving up the opposite bank, water sluicing off his flanks. Johnny pulled him round and brought him back across. He grinned cheerfully. "Footing all the way."

Parley grunted, swung about, and chopped another sapling.

Judith sat down again. This time she took out her knitting. A stocking was shaping on the needles but the wool and the tools were so well known to her fingers that she did not need her eyes. They were free to observe what was going on.

The men finished the road on the near bank and four of them mounted the mustangs Johnny had brought up and tied in the bushes.

The black man rode up. "Ma'am, I have brought you some water."

Gratefully she took the cup he poured. "Thank you, Legette. I didn't know I was thirsty."

She drank but stood to keep her eyes on the men Johnny was leading down the incline and into the creek. "He says it is a mean ford, Legette."

"Yes, ma'am. The captain will manage."

"Of course." She smiled at the Negro. He was devoted to the man who had rescued him, believed him to be, she thought, a sort of half-god who could do all things well and nothing wrong. And small wonder, she reflected, remembering the welts on the black man's back. There would be no more of that for Legette, and no more of the hopelessness of a slave's future. Johnny Fowler had given him his manhood and a living life and all the years of it to make what he would of it. Of course, to help a runaway . . . her chin came up. No one had a right to abuse another human being. It only served such an owner right to lose his property.

Her eyes went back to the men crossing the stream. They were nearly halfway, now. Tig Vance, a scrawny, catlike little man, was immediately behind Johnny. They were in the deepest part and all was going well. But even as she felt relief for it, Vance's horse slipped, threshed awkwardly, and lost its footing. At the same time the animal's hindquarters skewed crazily around. The scrawny little man yelped a string of oaths and began beating the horse with his hat. The mustang screamed in terror and floundered and was swept downstream by his struggles.

Judith's cup clattered to the ground. The creek did not look to have that much current. What had happened? She swung about to Legette but the black man was already on his horse and the horse was already moving. Johnny was wheeling his own horse downstream and Parley Wade was shouting. All the men were shouting, running down the bank, following the drifting horse to which Tig Vance clung.

Frozen, Judith saw Legette jump his horse sheer off the cliffy bank below Vance's floundering mustang. She saw them disappear beneath the surface, then churn up, the Negro blowing the water from his nostrils, shaking the water clear of his eyes. His horse swam strongly but before he could reach Vance, Johnny had got there.

The men gave a cheer, then were utterly quiet, watching. Judith, still tense because this man rescuing Tig Vance was, after all, her husband and not yet out of a dangerous situation, was also quiet. No one was prepared for what happened next. With one long sweep of his arm Johnny Fowler swept the scrawny little man off the back of the mustang, grabbed the bridle of the terrified horse, and bent his muscles to holding it until Legette could come alongside and take the animal from him.

Vance, who had gone blubberingly under the water, bobbed up like a cork, cursing and screeching. "I can't swim! I can't swim! Goddammit, I tell you I can't swim! I'll drown!"

Shifting her eyes to her husband's face Judith saw that it was dark and contorted, and his voice when he spoke to the man was dangerously quiet. But all could hear it in the absolute stillness. "Then, learn, my friend," it said, biting the words off. "There's no better time. Swim, or drown."

Unbelievably, then, he swung his horse about and left the man. Judith felt the water she had drunk rise hotly in her throat and her hands clasped to frame it. Johnny! Johnny! You can't leave a man to drown. But he could, and he was.

There wasn't a sound from the men now. The creek was narrow. Vance threshed about, some kind of sense quieting his panic. He made slow headway, with frequent dousings, chokings and splutterings, but with no more screeching, toward the opposite bank, which was nearer. A handy limb grew out over the water which his dog-paddling finally brought him near enough to grasp. He hung on, heaving, until his breath got easier, then he slowly dragged himself out of the water and collapsed on the bank. There was a long sigh, as though it came from one great chest, from the watching men. Then one of them, a stocky, blocklike man whom Judith knew to be Bullitt Trice, said growlingly, "By God, what a sonuvabitch that Fowler is!"

Other men took it up. "Didn't care for nothing but his horse!"

"Would of left old Vance to drown."

"Never seen nothing like it. Pure cold-blooded."

Parley Wade rounded on them. "Shut up, all of you. Vance lost his head. Hat-whipped his horse when he ort to handled him firm. All his own fault. And they's no place on this train fer a man loses his head. The cap'n was giving him one more chance."

"But he was leaving him to drown!"

"You think so?"

Trice spoke loudly. "By God, I know so! I seen for myself."

"All I seen," Parley said mildly, "was Vance learnin' to swim. Trice— O'Toole, bring the first wagon up. They'll have the bank cut by the time you're up with it."

Her knees suddenly weak, Judith sat on her log again. She fumbled for her knitting. Dear Lord, dear Lord, help me to know that he knows what he is doing, that he knows what is best, no matter how it looks. He is not a cold-blooded man. He would not have left the man to drown. But wouldn't he have? She shivered a little. Better than anyone else in the world she knew exactly how steel-strong, how inscrutably nerved, how coldly implacable he could be. Better than anyone else, for it had concerned her. Knit two, purl two—knit two, purl two, furiously. Vance *did* lose his head. He yelled and beat his horse and frightened the animal. And he endangered all the others crossing. Johnny can't have that, she told herself. Too much depends on strong nerves on this journey. This is just the first test. A man has to control himself. He can't let fear loose to infect others, to infect the animals. He has to swallow down his fear and sit it out. There will be more dangerous times than this. Parley is right. He was teaching Vance, and all the others, what they must do if this train is to get through. Knit two, purl two—knit two, purl two. Her hands moved less rapidly now, and her heart quieted.

Legette came. "I hope you were not upset, ma'am. It was nothing."

"No," she said steadily. "Thank you, Legette."

The first wagon came lumbering and swaying down the woods track. Twelve mules were hitched to the big wagon. Bullitt Trice, the blocky muleskinner, rode a mustang on one side, shouting and cracking his long whip. The redheaded Irishman, O'Toole, was on the other side. But the man who rode the leader, who drove the twelve-mule team, was Jesse Cooper, Johnny's neighbor from Kentucky, his second-in-command. He had been with the wagons, strapping down cargo, readying them for the crossing. Judith did not yet know him well but he seemed as steady, as nerveless, as inarticulate as Johnny himself. Did Kentucky grow nothing but these strong, sometimes ruthless, men of few words?

She shifted an empty needle into her right hand and picked up the first stitch on the next needle.

The wagon came on without faltering, Trice and O'Toole cracking their whips. Jesse Cooper sat the lead mule as lumpily as a sack of meal. He looked boneless and muscleless, slumped and easy. Astride his mustang, Johnny Fowler looked on, himself and his horse as motionless as statues.

The lead mules reached the ramped road to the water, felt delicately for footing. There was suddenly a quickening. Trice and O'Toole strung out curses and flicked the mules, drawing blood with the lead-weighted ends of their bullwhips. Jesse Cooper leaned forward and the sack of meal was gone. He thinned before Judith's eyes, became as taut as one of the bullwhips. He added his shouts to those of the muleskinners', his oaths to theirs, his prod and whip to theirs. "You'll have to shut your ears to profanity, Judith," Johnny had told her. "Apparently mules only pull well when cursed."

"I have heard men curse before," she had retorted.

"Not, I think," he had grinned, "the way a muleskinner does. They are especially inspired."

Watching now she hardly heard the words. She was aware of a solid, steady, fluent flow of sound, but she was more aware of the heavy feeling inside her of having to pull as hard as the mules. She leaned forward as if against a trace, felt the tightening on her chest, the pull on the muscles of her legs.

Johnny was ahead of them now, leading the way.

Judith put her knitting in her pocket.

The mules, plunging, prodded and bitten by the whips, entered the water. They were given no time to flinch. The whips snapped, drew blood, the oaths crackled about their ears, and every man on the bank added yells to the noise. Awkwardly the mules sank into the water, but the whips cracked faster, more keenly, the yells and shouts rose, and the forward momentum was sustained. The mules sank and sank, the water reaching their bellies and flanks. They kept lunging, needled by the whips, urged on and excited by the shouts. Steadily Johnny led the way. Steadily they followed.

Midstream was reached. Now, now came the hard pull. With the wagon still on the ramp, not yet wholly in the water, the mules must bend to the pull. The whips cracked faster and faster. The curses thundered, and all the men leaned forward, driving, herding, urging. The mules dug in, reached for footing, found it, held it somehow, pulled gut-stretched and leg-strained as the heavy wagon hit the water and lumbered, helplessly, into the stream. Belly-down, flat to the earth, stretched as on a rack, the mules clawed at the opposite bank, the whips flaying their flanks, the curses of the men flaying their ears. They lunged and heaved and slid and lunged and heaved again. Inch by inch they hauled the heavy wagon out of the creek, up the bank, onto safe land.

Judith took a deep breath and sat again on her cottonwood log. One wagon was across. Three more to go. She felt utterly used up, but already her husband was crossing again. The next wagon was coming up.

She looked at the sky. There was still, incredibly, an hour of sun. How swiftly they had actually done what had to be done. How surely Johnny had known. Like a woman sorting her wash he had handled the familiar garments of decision. Oh, her husband never placated any gods. He had his own will and he was never afraid to pit it against man or nature. There were no terrifying mysteries to him. There was simply the purpose and the strength of Johnny Fowler. They were like iron in him. The encroachment of white settlements with their veneer of civilization might irritate and divide the inner man, but in the role of trailblazer he was in his natural element. He was pre-eminently suited for it, and he was whole, now.

Was she?

Her mind flinched away from that question and restlessly she took out her knitting again. Wryly she thought Parley and Johnny were going to have a dreadful lot of new stockings by the time they reached Santa Fe if this kept up.

4

A SIMPLE errand, the need of salt, sent her searching for Parley
that night. Parley rarely made an error, but even he was not infal-
lible. In her own housekeeping wagon he had forgotten salt. They had
been eating food brought with them from home until now, so the lack had
not been discovered. When Legette, cooking for the first time, told her
she had laughed easily. "I'll find Parley. Isn't it wonderful that he should
forget something as simple as salt?"

In the firelight Legette's white teeth glittered against his satiny skin as
he grinned. "I hope, ma'am, he didn't forget to bring any at all."

"Oh, no, he wouldn't do that. He just mislaid the sack for our wagon."

It was full dark. It had been dusky when the last of the train had got
across the Deep Fork and by the time camp had been made there had
been no light left. But now the men's fires, ringed like ritual fires, glowed
warmly in the rich, deep night. She traced them round, seeing not the men,
for she did not know which men were where yet, but seeing their names
as they had looked in her neat hand on a page of blue-lined ledger paper.
"Make me a list, Judith," Johnny had said, "for the custom house in Sante
Fe."

> *Members (and their duties) of an expedition*
> *to go on a Voyage to Santa Fe:*
>> *Party of 20 men, three freight wagons, one light wagon, with full*
>> *teams, 17 pack mules, 30 spare mules, horses to seat all hands with*
>> *10 extra.*
>
> *Johnny Fowler, sole owner and captain in command (and his wife,*
> *Judith)*
> *Jesse Cooper, second in command, charge of all wagons*
> *Parley Wade, third in command, charge of cargo and supplies*
> *Asa Baldwin, fourth in command, carpenter*
>
> *Manuel Garcia, Head Drover, charge of all stock*
> *Pete Shelley, Pack drover*

Hull Archer, *helper*
Legette, *the Negro, Blacksmith (also cook & general servant to Capt.)*

Muleskinners & Wagon drivers:
  Bullitt Trice
  Nathaniel Butler
  Terence O'Toole
  Wm. Day
  Washington Craig
  Tig Vance
  Joshua Brand
  Ben Spring

Indians:
  The Beaver (Osage fullblood) *chief scout*
  Auguste Suard, *hunter*
  Baptiste, *hunter*
  Crowbait, *hunter*

Johnny had set Parley Wade, Jesse Cooper, and Asa Baldwin, as wagon drivers, over their own wagon crews, to eat and to sleep and camp with them and to be, under himself, responsible for them. They were lieutenants to his captaincy. So Parley would be with his men. But where? At that farthest fire? She asked Legette.

"Yes, ma'am. Mr. Parley's wagon crossed first. Mr. Cooper brought them all over, but it was Mr. Parley's wagon ahead."

She trudged away in the dark.

It was a very simple and feminine fear which stopped her within earshot of Parley's fire but out of its light. She stepped on something which gave under her foot softly, seemed to ooze away, and made her catch back a small squeak at the thought of a snake. She shrank back against a tree and when she had called up nerve enough looked more closely at the thing that was still lying across her path, had not crawled away. She gave a small chuckle. Someone had thrown away a short length of old rope. It was probably frayed beyond further use, for otherwise it would have been saved. Just the same she gathered up her skirts. No use asking for trouble with their dragging length. There might be real snakes about, though it was early for them yet.

A man's voice grew loud, and she hesitated. "It's plain lunacy, if you ask me. Taking her along. If I'd knowed a woman was going . . . hell, a woman on the trail!"

Four men were in a knot near the fire, their backs turned. Only Parley

Wade faced her. Judith dropped her skirts. Why, they were talking about her.

Another man grumbled in a less loud voice, but just as plain. "Jist plain stupid. What's he want to bring her for? Can't he do without . . ." The voice bumbled and the knot of men laughed lewdly.

"His bizness," Parley Wade said, turning the meat on the spit, "and they's been women on the trail before. Injun women live on the trail."

"She ain't no Injun."

"Been Spanish women on the trail. Come clean from Santy Fee to Saint Louie. She'll not be the first woman to cross the prairies, nor the last."

"Don't make me like it no better, her being along. My opinion, she'll not bear up. She'll come down sick 'fore we git through the Timbers."

The fire was small and smoky and Parley Wade squinted through it. "Lay you ten to one she don't."

"What makes you so sure?"

"I know her."

"Well, you'll see. She'll be skeered of the least thing, allus vaporin' and faintin'."

"She'll not."

"She'll hold us up, Parley. The cap'n will lay over ever' time she gits a pain. Be lucky if we git to the mountains 'fore the freeze-up."

Parley turned the spit again. " 'Tain't May yit. Never heared of a freeze-up 'fore October. Plenty of time. You'll git yer traps out."

"I've heared it freezes in September in them high places."

"Still plenty of time."

Then a man muttered what was perhaps the fear of them all. "Bad luck," he said, "havin' a woman on the trail. Like havin' a woman on a ship and ever'body knows that's bad luck. It ain't enough the captain has to foller a new trail don't nobody know and nobody's ever traveled before, he's got to fetch his woman along. Bad luck, and we'll have it, you'll see."

"Especial," Parley said, "if ever'body commences lookin' over his shoulder fer it." His voice suddenly became sharp and strong. "Now, you listen to me and pay heed. This woman you're so almighty afraid of. She come to the Territory from Connecticut with a party of missionaries two year gone. Hit was a long and tejious journey she made, better'n ten months on that boat with death and fever ridin' it with her. She never had the fever but she nussed all that did. She didn't do no vaporin' or faintin' then. She's knowed a hard trail before. She'll do, I tell you. She looks leetle and soft, but she ain't."

"How long her and the captain been married?"

"Close to a year."

"No young'uns?"

"Nope."

Someone laughed. "And no sign of e'ern. Mebbe the cap'n ain't . . ."

Parley thrust a cut of meat in the man's mouth. "Eat, and shut up. Ye kin jist recollect you got no say about this here wagon train or who goes with it. Kit and caboodle the cap'n owns it. Hit stops and starts when he says. Hit follers the road he picks. Hit'll git to Santy Fee and the mountains when he gits it thar. And he carries who he wants with it."

Judith was horrified to be listening but she felt paralyzed, rooted to the spot where she stood for fear of being discovered. It wouldn't do now. She had heard too much. The salt must be forgotten and when the fire died down . . . it was a wonder Parley hadn't seen her in the shadows before now. She pressed her skirts close. If she turned very carefully and slowly? But her first step dislodged a stone, which rattled in rolling. A man turned his head. She froze. That was Bullitt Trice. He listened a moment, then fell to eating again.

Someone spoke again. "Hope the captain knows this new course he's follerin'."

Parley, whose gapped front teeth had been tearing at a bone, tossed the remnants to his dog. He swiped his hands on his buckskins. "How many times you crossed the prairies?" he asked.

The man hesitated. "I been up the Arkansas . . . oncet."

"Anybody else?"

"Not me. I been drivin' freight from Philadelphy to Pittsburgh."

"This is as fur west as I been."

"Then why don't ye leave the decidin' to somebody knows how."

The man's voice sounded sullen. "Ever'body knows the old trail is best."

Parley Wade grunted. "Cap'n don't think so."

"Who's he to know? He ain't never been before, and all the rest of 'em that has, Becknell, McKnight, Chouteau, all of 'em, and the fur trappers, they all go from Franklin up the Arkansas. You reckon they don't know the best road?"

Parley threw another bone to his dog. He didn't eat, Judith thought, he just tore and swallowed. "Nope," he said, "they jist ain't give no thought to ary other way. Folks is critters of habit. One man follers the Arkansas, ever'body else follers the Arkansas. Cap'n ain't like that. Uses his head, Johnny Fowler does. He's figgered how fur outen the way it takes a train headed fer Santy Fee. Now, Santy Fee is might' near on a straight line west from Three Forks. Makes sense, don't it, seein' as the cap'n lived in

Three Forks to head straight west from there. Hit's a heap further south, too, and ye kin git a sooner start. Grass greens a month earlier."

"Yeah, but it ain't marked . . ."

"You got ary notion how many times the cap'n has been over these prairies? Got ary notion at all?"

"Several, I reckon, but . . ."

"Well, I'll tell you. He warn't much more'n a boy when he come to the Territory nine year ago. But he ain't missed a spring or fall hunt with the Osages sincet. He's roved plumb up the lakes north and beyant the Spanish boundary west."

"How fur beyond the Spanish line?"

Parley grinned. "Don't matter. Where he ain't been, the Beaver has. The Beaver has been plump to the mountains. You ain't gonna git lost with Johnny Fowler leadin' ye. He'll git ye thar."

"It's an awful big country."

"If it'll set yer mind at ease a leetle more, the cap'n has got a compass and sextant with him. Knows how to use 'em, too."

There was a brief silence before the next comment. "Right good to know that. He sure ain't a very talkin' kind of man. Feller don't rightly know how to figger him."

"Ye'll find him a tough bone to gnaw," Parley said. "You been signed on as hands and skinners to git this train through. Ye'll git along if you do yer job. Ye don't . . ."

A rough voice jeered and Judith thought it was Trice's, "Yeah. What then?"

"I seen him set a man afoot oncet, on the prairies."

"Afoot! Whyn't he jist kill him and be done with it?"

"Well, he give him a gun."

The rough voice was raised again, after a snort of laughter. "Reckon his bones is bleachin' on the plains to this day."

"Nope." Parley wiped his fingers through his beard. "He's settin' right here, hale and hearty, though I don't mind sayin' I was a mite ga'nt time I got back to the settlemints. No more'n I've been after a bad hunt, though. When they warn't no buffler."

The voice got rougher. "I'd a killed the sonuvabitch. How come you work for him after such a thing?"

Parley stretched his blanket on the ground. "Had it comin' to me. Fillin' my belly with rotgut whisky ever' night and went to sleep on guard. Let the Pawnees steal ever' damn horse we had but two. They was me and the cap'n and Suard on the hunt. Cap'n said if one of us had to walk back, stood to reason it was goin' to be me. Had the right of it, too. Man's got no call to be keerless." He lowered himself onto the blanket and rolled it about him.

"How long you been with him?"

"Nine year."

"That's since he come?"

"Since the day he tied up at the landin' in Three Forks."

"I've heared," the voice was curious, "I've heared he is a blood brother to an Osage chief."

"Ain't no blood brother. Been initiated with the blood rites is all. B'longs to the Wolf's clan."

"I heared," the next voice was eager, "that he had a knife fight with another Indian—ripped him plumb open and scalped him."

"You heared that right. Him and the Blade fit with knives. Johnny cut his guts out and lifted his skelp fer the Beaver."

"God, he's no better'n a Injun hisself!"

Parley raised on one elbow. "Now, you listen. The Blade was a murderin' halfbreed that led the Cherokees skulkin' after the Osages on their fall hunt that year. Whilst the braves was away they fell on the camp and massacreed 'em. Warn't nobody in camp but a bunch of women and kids and old men . . . jist a handful of warriors to guard 'em. Suard was one of 'em, Johnny's friend. He was tromped to death by their horses. The Blade took some prisoners to march back home and show off. He warn't named 'The Blade' fer nothin'. With a knife he was right fancy. What he done to a young girl prisoner warn't purty. She was the Beaver's woman."

"This same Osage that's scoutin' fer the train?"

"It's him."

A thin, scant-framed man stood and stretched. "Back where I come from a man does his own fighting. Whyn't this Injun, this Beaver, go after the Blade himself?"

"Where do you come from?" Parley asked.

"Kentucky."

Parley Wade's voice was very soft when he spoke again. "Friend, Johnny Fowler comes from Kentucky, too. He had his reasons fer goin' after the Blade and they ain't none of yore'n. But he picked a knife on account of it was the Blade's own weepon and he fit him fair. He gutted and skelped him and that ended it. Now, git to bed."

The men stirred about noisily and Judith fled in the dark.

He had his own reasons for going after the Blade, and they are none of yours.

Parley Wade might have been saying those words to her, for neither then nor now did she know why Johnny Fowler had been compelled to fight that duel to the death with the halfbreed Indian known as "The Blade." All she knew was that neither the sweet wiles of love which she had tried, nor her angry, ultimate threat not to marry him if he insisted, had prevailed with him. The deed must be done. The iron had been in his soul then, too. In the end, brought to her knees in a travail of terror and agony, she had prayed that since one man or the other must die, *must* die, it would not be Johnny Fowler.

It had not been.

But from that day, eighteen long months ago, to this moment in the dark, she had never let more than the first hurting spear of thought concerning it enter her mind. When, like forked lightning, it lanced the night as she lay beside her husband, or as she went about the work of the house during the day, she resolutely and with great discipline put it away.

She had married this man. Of her own free will and wish she had married him, knowing what he had done, but not why. She asked him why when she pled with him. But his face had been stony and his only answer had been, "It has to be done and I must do it."

Perhaps she had forfeited the right to the answer now. On her knees, in love's weakness, despite her failure to understand, she had been compelled, by love, to accept. On her knees she had learned how frail was truth, or right—as she saw them, oh granted as she saw them, but no man was absolved from forming principles—beside love's strength. In the end she had been able only to pray, let it not be Johnny Fowler, let it not be love's hostage. There was now no answer to the question that would serve that weakness.

She fled in the dark, stammered an excuse to Legette, gave thanks that Johnny was not yet in camp, and went to bed without touching the food Legette set before her.

5

THE WAGONS are loaded too heavy. This crossing has proved it."
Jesse Cooper kneaded the chill from his hands before the fire. With
the sun had gone the deceiving warmth of the day. The night was cold,
and damp from the quiet, deep creek lay heavy over it. The heat of the
fire was good. "You'll have to cache part of the load, Jonathan."

Jonathan. She had not known it was his name until she heard Jesse
Cooper call him by it. Jonathan. She liked it. She wished she had known
it before she became too accustomed to Johnny. "It's a pity," she said to
him one day, "you were ever called Johnny. Who began it?"

"Don't know," he had said. "Nobody but Jesse ever called me Jonathan."

"But it *is* your name."

"Oh, sure. Ma has got it written in the family Bible that way."

"I like it."

He had studied her soberly for a moment. "I expect you do." Then suddenly he had smiled and put his hand against her cheek. "Maybe someday
I'll turn into Jonathan for you. Leave off buckskins and wear a fine coat—
get me some learning. You'd like that, too, wouldn't you?"

The heat rose in her face. "I didn't say it, you did. And you've got plenty
of learning. Besides I like Johnny fine."

"That's good," he said, turning about, "for I wouldn't like you to disapprove even if I was called Fool."

Sometimes he knew her so well . . . sometimes, he didn't know at all.

He was shaking his head, now. "I know they're overloaded, Jesse. I
didn't see what else I could do. We'll be doing some trading with the Plains
Indians farther on—bound to meet 'em and bound to trade. They won't
let wagons get by, nor pack mules. They know they mean goods and they'll
pester till they get some. Anyhow, they'll have horses we'll be needing by
then, maybe Spanish mules. I'd hate to cache any goods right now. Like
to carry 'em a few more days."

From her wagon, where the sheet had been raised, Judith studied the
man across the fire from Johnny Fowler. He was of middle height with

a brush of dark hair, deep-set dark eyes, blunt, unhandsome features which by their bluntness and irregularity gave his face a strong look. Like her husband he had a body built for action with lean tightness, controlled movements, good hands, good shoulders.

From the day he arrived at Three Forks she had liked this boyhood friend of her husband's. She felt he could be trusted and, without defining it, she sensed that Johnny felt strength had been added to his own strength, like patch on patch, because this man had been cut to the same pattern, from the same cloth.

Jesse Cooper was silent now, chewing a great cud of tobacco. "Well," he said finally, "I don't know the country. You know what you've cut out for yourself. I wouldn't say you'd try the impossible."

Johnny bent for a twig and fiddled it, grinning crookedly. "I've done it and may be doing it now. But I'd rather not own it yet."

Jesse Cooper nodded. "Try to get 'em as far as you want, then. But you saw the way the mules had to pull today."

"I saw. Thing is, Jesse, they pulled and they made it."

"They're fresh now."

"We got a big head of 'em."

Jesse grinned. "And it may take the whole danged string."

"That's what they're for. Time they're wore out we'll be meeting the Comanches or the Kiowas." He poured coffee and handed a mug to Jesse.

Jesse eyed the steam silently, blew it away, sipped, and said, "Expecting any trouble?"

"Always expect it. Not been disappointed very often, either. A good swap is one way of avoiding it."

Judith stirred on her bed in the wagon-dark. It was Johnny's invention, ingeniously designed to provide a maximum amount of room inside the wagon. It was hinged, with folding legs. During the day it was strapped up against the wagon frame. At night it was let down. It was comfortably wide for one, but as crowded as a cot for two. Johnny had laughed at her raised brows. "You'll be glad to be that close to me. It's cold at night on the prairies."

She had slept a little, then their voices had wakened her and she had pulled a blanket around her and propped herself with pillows, leaning against her folded hands on the wagon side.

As Johnny Fowler and his friend sat silent now, her eyes traced the low-burning cook fires around the camp. They glowed and blinked and above the feathered tops of the trees the stars blinked too. The sky was far away, an unreachable tent of rich, deep, dark night, scattered with star-pricks of light. She did not know those men who sat about those fires under the tent of night. They were all unknown quantities as yet. Time and the entering iron of the journey would prove them loyal and faithful or weak and faithless. Weather, wagons, the trail . . . mud, sand, and the rivers . . . sky, thirst, and the deserts . . . space, emptiness, loneliness . . . they would separate the strong from the weak, the straight-backed from the spineless, the brave from the cowards, the men from the images of men.

Whoever they were, whatever they were, if they were not sleeping they would be talking now. They would be talking about the crossing today. They would be talking about Tig Vance and the way the captain had swept him off his horse and left him to sink or swim in the Deep Fork. They would be saying the captain was as cold as a wedge left out in the frost. They would not, she was certain, be saying what Parley Wade had said, that the captain was teaching a man not to lose his head and frighten his animal and endanger the lives of others. "Nothing," her husband had told her once, "is more certain than the discontent of hired hands. There is no pleasing them. So you'd best please yourself."

They would be talking about the wagons. They would be saying, as Jesse Cooper had said, they were too heavily loaded. They would be talking about the mules and how the pull had stretched them belly-flat to the ground. They would be saying, "We'll never make it." They would be saying, "Wait till we get onto the plains and into the sand. He'll find out. He'll learn mules can't pull their guts out. The hell with his goods. What I want is to git to the mountains alive."

Johnny had told her, "A man sets out to lead, he's got to lead. It's his job. If he's soft the hands will find him out. He might as well quit right then."

She didn't think the hands would ever find Johnny out. He had shown them today, the first test of his hardness.

Parley Wade slouched into the firelight. His old buffalo hat drooped over his eyes and his Mackinaw was hunched about his neck against the cold. He kicked the fire into blaze and warmed his hands. Judith winced. Some of the men would be talking, also, about a woman on the trail, declaring it lunacy, thinking it bad luck, running their bawdy tongues over her wifehood. There was nothing she could do about it. You can't still men's tongues. But she could disprove it . . . and she would.

Parley said, "The Beaver has come in."

Her husband poured another mug of coffee. "Ba'tiste with him?"

Parley took the mug and slurped noisily. "Nope. They split up. Ain't much game yit."

"What'd they find?"

"Nothin' but some turkeys."

Johnny Fowler shrugged. "They can eat fatback and johnnycake till we get past the North Fork. Be good hunting then."

Old Parley chuckled. "The hands'll be cussin'. They think they ort to be eatin' off fat buffler cow aready."

"Let 'em cuss."

Judith pulled the blanket closer about her shoulders. The cold was deepening. She wished Johnny would come to bed—if he meant to. He hadn't spent a night in the wagon yet and he might intend to prowl the horse string and the fringes of the camp again tonight.

Parley heaved a log toward the fire and sat upon it. There loomed behind him suddenly a figure, half naked, half shadow, only a little lighter than the night. "Come to the fire, Beaver. Warm yerself. Cap'n'll give ye some coffee."

Her husband stood. "What the Beaver needs is something stronger than coffee." He rummaged in a goods chest and found a jug. "Here."

The Osage drank deep.

Parley Wade said plaintively, "I've earned my keep today, too."

"Then drink. But only once. You don't know when to quit."

"Who says so?"

"Me."

"Fine, then. Fine. Whatever you say."

The Osage spoke then, in his own tongue, low and rapidly. Her husband replied, his hands rising and falling like birds with his voice. The Osage listened, then answered as gracefully. Her husband grunted.

She had tried to like this Indian, by blood a member of the Wolf clan, her husband's brother by his initiation, long before she knew him, into the same clan. She knew Johnny held him in deep affection, and respect, and trust. But it had been to him Johnny had brought that other Indian's scalp when he had killed him, and it had been the Beaver's woman the Blade had murdered. He was too associated with that time of hard testing of her love, which her husband had risked. A residue of resentment could not be erased. She was too fair to blame the Osage wholly, for Johnny had admitted the Blade was his own enemy, too. But he was a part of the circumstances which she wished to forget. She did not think she actively disliked him. What she felt when Johnny was with him was an uneasiness. What the Osage thought of her she could not even guess, for he never spoke with her or noticed her. Sometimes she caught him

staring at her, his eyes obsidian and expressionless. But that was a way
of all Indians. They meant no rudeness.

She watched him in the firelight. He was as straight as one of his arrows. He was dark. His profile was pure, his roach was handsome and
proud, his nose beaked, his chest deep, his stomach lean. Above the waist
he wore nothing. Below were buckskin leggins. About his shoulders a
blanket was draped, one arm ornamented with a wide silver band, free.
His roach sported an eagle feather which told that he had killed his enemy.
Had he? Or had Johnny killed him for him? He wore moccasins which
tinkled when he walked. He wore the bells which only warriors might
wear. "Osage men are the handsomest and proudest Indians in America,"
Johnny had told her.

Yes. And this was one of the handsomest and the proudest. He was
also, if not the best scout and guide among the Osages, one of the best.
From the moment the journey was decided it was foregone that he should
accompany Johnny Fowler. "I'd think twice before setting out without
him," he had said. "I need him."

Johnny was translating for Jesse Cooper. "He says not much game.
Hunting no good."

"Reckon we'll lighten the provision load a little, then," Jesse said, laughing. "Pick up when we pass the North Fork you said?"

"Ought to. Ought to be deer and plentiful turkey in the Timbers before
we get to the North Fork, though."

"Nothing to swivet about, then."

"Nothing to swivet about. To be expected."

"How far to the Timbers now?"

"Six, seven days. Little more or less, depending."

Jesse nodded. "Heard some talk in the settlement before we left. Seemed
nobody thought you could get wagons through 'em."

Parley Wade laughed and reached, surreptitiously, for the jug again.
Without seeming to notice, his eyes on Jesse Cooper, Johnny's long arm
stretched and the jug was set between his own feet. "Why, it'll be troublesome but I figure the Beaver'll mark us a road we can follow."

"Pretty bad?"

"About as bad as could be, I reckon, but if we're lucky with the weather
we ought to do it."

"If we're not lucky?"

"Take longer but we can still get through. We'll be following the North
Fork through. If it's a bad season we can take to the river on rafts."

Jesse Cooper nudged the coiled bullwhip which lay at his feet. "Poles instead of these."

"Might be."

Jesse dangled his hands between his knees and picked at a clump of grass. "Reckon Bull Trice'll like giving up his whip for a pole?"

Johnny was tamping his pipe. He did not look up. His long, lean fingers worked away at the tobacco, taking unhurried care with it. When it suited him, he said quietly, "You mixing it with Trice, Jesse?"

"No. He don't trouble me none. Just thought you mightn't of noticed he was right fond of that whip of his'n and real good with it."

"I've noticed."

Jesse looked up at him, held the look a moment, then nodded. "Just thought to mention it."

"I'm obliged."

Johnny turned to look at Parley Wade, then. The sandy hair, too long and curling on his neck and behind his ears, looked red in the firelight. Judith's hands moved involuntarily. It was rough to her palms, as rough as straw, thick and thatchy, but it was an immeasurable pleasure to feel it under her hands, a somehow sensuous delight to grasp it in play, tug or smooth, or tickle her nose in it.

The smoke haze from his pipe cleared as he took it out of his mouth. The jut of his jaw was clean in profile. His face was as angular as his body, the bones edged under a thrifty skin. She knew how he looked as he faced Parley Wade. His eyes would be squinted a little; they usually were. She guessed it came from his years in the wind and sun and maybe the wind and the sun had faded their blue a little, too. When he was angry their color darkened, but not much. His mouth would be incisive. It was long, and it could be sweet, but now, not searching her eyes or her lips or her throat, it would be a little thin as he habitually held it. He was speaking again. "Trice making any trouble in camp, Parley?"

She had known that Trice was one of the men at Parley's fire. She had felt that that roughest voice, and the loudest, went with the burly, solid muleskinner. He was a bruising hulk of a man, chunky and blocky, with short solid legs which he planted in a spraddle when standing and spread with a swagger when walking. She remembered his papers. He was from Pennsylvania. He was thirty years old and he had been driving mules over the mountains to Pittsburgh for ten years. Muleskinner by trade, never done anything else, or never admitted he had.

She bent a little forward, willing Parley to say nothing. Don't do it. Don't make a bother of it. Don't tell him Trice and some others don't like a woman on the train. Don't lay something else on him to trouble about. You and I will do the troubling. You talk it down and I'll prove it down.

As if hearing her, Parley shook his head. "No trouble."

She sighed against her hands. Good. Good.

Johnny was smoothing the bowl of his pipe. "Five of them men," he said, nodding toward the other fires, "come with good recommendations. Trice is one of 'em, though I was warned he's a rough un. Others I took because I couldn't do any better. They can handle mules, though . . . all of 'em. But most of the good ones are too well satisfied to take chances on a long journey like this. Too uncertain for 'em."

"That figgers," Parley said, grinning.

Johnny grinned back at him. "Reckon it's up to us to handle the ones that come. A long road makes changes in a man. Some it betters, some it worsens. We'll see." He swiveled around. "Legette—make another pot of coffee."

As richly black as the night, the Negro came into the light. "Yes, sir." He took the pot away to fill.

"That one," Parley said, "is one you can count on all the way, Johnny."

"He's beholding."

"Not beholding enough to jump a horse in the creek like he done today."

"No. Not that beholding." Johnny blew down his pipe. "The man who laid a whip on his back was a fool."

"Any idea who he is?"

Johnny straightened and put his pipe away. "Not the least. Rather not."

Legette came back and set the filled pot on the coals. "Manuel says if the captain likes he can play his guitar and sing some music for him now."

The Negro had sensed that the evening was growing old, was passing into that slow tempo and mood this side of sleepiness but nearing it, a half-drugged comfort of hot drink and warm fire and a bed calling but not quite yet.

Johnny looked a question at Jesse Cooper and Parley Wade. When they nodded Legette raised his hand and Manuel came out of the shadows, his guitar slung by a thong from his shoulders. His teeth gleamed as he broke into a smile. He bowed slightly and sat beside Johnny.

The Osage rose and strode away into the night.

Johnny chuckled. "White man's music hurts his ears, he says."

Parley struck his knee. "Well, by God, ain't he the one to judge! Ain't nothin' hurts a body's ears worse'n theirs."

"Ever hear the Beaver's flute?"

"No, and I ain't hankerin' to. I've heared plenty others. Ain't nothin' but a wailin' and a whinin'. Ruther to hear a coyote howl, myself."

Johnny's shoulders lifted and fell. "A man hears what he wants to hear. Play, Manuel."

Grinning, Manuel spanked the guitar like a drum until he had got a rolling beat going, then he whacked the strings into a pick and chord rhythm, shouted "Hola!" and went pelting into a song of "Gee! Haw! Whoa, there, mule!"

It was fast-paced and reckless. Judith could not understand the Spanish words, but it was funny and full of fire and mildly sprinkled with an Americano's profanity. At the end of every stanza the chorus took off with the repeated, "Gee! Haw! Whoa, there, mule!" A mule driver's song, she guessed, that would not bear translation.

She arranged her pillows and settled back against them. They had let the fire go low and she was cold. She pulled the blankets to tuck about her neck. Manuel was singing something soft and slow and sad, now. Something about three Marys—Mary, the mother; Mary, the sister; and Mary, the wife. Tres Marías. It had a simple melody, sweet and sorrowful, full of tears, full of longing, full of love. Briefly, her eyes closed, she wondered why there was no in-between in Spanish music. Either it was madly galloping or it was slow and tear-welling. Johnny said once he had never known a Spanish who didn't love sorrow. "It's a virtue with them. They enjoy being sad."

Manuel's song was soothing and lulling. Her tired body loved the bed and she slept.

Johnny waked her stumbling against the bed. "Sorry," he said. "Were you asleep?"

The cold had penetrated her blankets and she shivered. She was stiff from being rolled into a ball. "I'm freezing, Johnny."

"It will be my pleasure, ma'am," he said thickly, "to come into your bed and warm you."

Startled into full wakefulness, she stared into the dark. There was nothing to see but much to hear as he blundered about, knocked into things, swore, dropped his garments and sat heavily on the hinged bed. "Johnny! Are you drunk?"

"No." His breathing was rough but his voice was jaunty. "No, I'm not drunk, but I'm as near it as I ever allow myself to get. Especially," he emphasized, "when I'm going to sleep with a lady."

She had a fit of the giggles suddenly. "Come on, Johnny, I'm cold."

He was beside her at once, and heavy in her arms, boneless and nerveless, and almost instantly asleep. Her nose wrinkled at his breath but she held him lovingly. She so seldom saw him helpless.

6

MOSES in the wilderness, she thought, and most of the children of Israel are not happy. Manuel was one of them. Four days in the Timbers had reduced him to a state of dumps and melancholy. She was riding with him, trailing the slow-moving, often halted wagon train. For the twentieth time in an hour he looked up at the green ceiling and mourned, "The sky—she has vanished, for good, I think."

"Ah, no, the sky is there. It's always there. It's only that we are here."

"Which I wish we were not."

"But the Timbers must be passed, Manuel. There is no way around."

"But, sí, Señora—if the captain followed the Arkansas . . . the old trail which all other men use. No forests there."

"It's too late now."

"Sí." His sorrowing eyes gazed gloomily at the swaying rumps of the horse and mule herd plodding before them. "Is good road, that one."

"I suppose. But not direct, as the captain wishes to go. You've been over it many times?" She was not really much interested. It seemed to her that every man with the train, except those in command, was afraid of this new route Johnny was taking. Certainly they had not her faith in a husband to sustain them, but they had known the train would take this route when they signed on. It ill behooved them to complain.

"One time," Manuel said, "but one time is enough, Señora, to observe."

"Why did you leave Santa Fe, Manuel? Why did you go to St. Louis?"

"In a moment of weakness, Señora, I allowed myself to be persuaded to accompany Señor Becknell when he return to United States. I think I wish to see these United States. Which I wish now I had not. If God wills it, Señora," he added fervently, "that I should see the mountains and my home again I shall never have such foolish thinkings any more."

"You didn't like St. Louis?"

The Mexican lifted his shoulders. "Is good perhaps for Americanos, but not so good for Manuel García. Is too much rain and mud and dark. Is bad for Spanish." The boy hunched into his gloom and shivered his shoulders higher. "Is bad, this place . . . is very dark and bad."

"Oh, come, now. All dark isn't bad. There's the night. And these Timbers have their own peculiar beauty. Look at the trees and the bushes and all the colors, the green and brown and . . ."

"You look, Señora. I wish not to see."

She gave up trying to cheer the boy. It was no use. He was steeped in his gloom and hugging it to himself, in some miserable way luxuriating in it.

This belt of timber interested her, but then she had seen it sketched on Johnny's map. She remembered how he had roughed it in and laid it flat, across the waist of the prairies sixty, seventy miles at its deepest, narrowing to ten or twenty at either end, and a full four hundred miles in length. Even on the map it looked a formidable barrier. Johnny's route followed an ancient Osage hunting road, angling across a fairly wide strip but following the North Fork of the Canadian. Admittedly the Indians had not taken wheeled vehicles with them but whole villages had gone on these hunts and the Osages with whom he had talked agreed that wagons could cross—with some trouble perhaps, with a great deal of trouble maybe, but it could be done.

The belt of timber was not majestic, for the trees were neither tall nor especially fine; but it excited Judith's interest because they were small and tough, ironhearted, undaunted by drought, wind, storm, sun, cold, or fire. In the face of nature's unfriendliness they had persisted and thickened and grown into this perplexing maze, which ruffed up like a dog's hackles on the rolling land all about. In the face of man's unfriendliness, the prairie fires of the Indians, the axes of white men, how much longer could it persist?

For four days they had been penetrating it making very slow progress. The halts were so many that she found them tedious and decided to ride with Manuel where she could occupy herself. She nosed out new things, weeds, flowers, grasses, which she plucked and sniffed and tasted. She stored her finds in her big pocket and brought them back with her, tried to interest Manuel in them. "This piece of sour grass is very like one of our eastern herbs. If boiled it would surely reduce a fever."

Manuel eyed it with indifference. "It would give you a big bellyache, Señora."

"Poison?"

"That I do not know. I only know if the *mulas* eat it they roll on the ground in great pain. Sometimes they die."

She cast it aside. "But look at this, now. See the leaves? This is a kind of cress. It makes a good salad to thin the blood."

"Salad? What is salad? And who, Señora, wants to thin the blood? Mine is too thin already. If it gets thinner I will die of it. What my blood needs is the good meat."

"We shall have it in time, my friend." She laughed helplessly at his stubborn woe. "Do take cheer, Manuel. Today, tonight, we will reach the river. There will be a piece of sky then."

He refused to smile. "I do not know if this Beaver know the way. He lead us four days in these woods." He shuddered. "Is maybe a trap."

"Manuel, that's nonsense. The Beaver is the captain's good friend. He knows the way. He has crossed here many times. The captain also knows the way. We are not lost. We are making for the river."

"That river, she keep running away."

It was impossible to give him heart. It was as Johnny had said. He loved sorrow. The green shade, which gave her rather a sense of shelter, tried his soul. She saw him now claw at the neck of his shirt and open it, as if he were suffocating, to give himself a deeper breath.

"You have crossed the prairie. You know that rivers don't run away."

"But they do, Señora. Sometimes they go down in the ground and leave nothing but sand."

She laughed helplessly. "You will see. Whether there is a river or not there will be a riverbed and it is wide. There will be stars tonight."

His mouth drew down. "I do not think so. Tonight I think it will rain."

She gave him up. "Oh, Manuel. You are purposely being gloomy. You *want* to be gloomy."

He sniffed the air elaborately. "My nose, she tells me."

"Fiddlesticks."

He slid his gloom off and smiled at her. "Perhaps not, Señora. Maybe I only smell the sourness of this place."

He knew as well as she that they did not want rain just now—not, at least, the hard, soaking downpour the country often got in the early spring. What they most needed now were the packed sandbanks of the North Fork to give them a faster and easier road. These first probing miles into the Timbers had been worse than Johnny had expected. He had not thought to spend more than a couple of days reaching the river, but the old Osage trail had grown up badly. Sprouts throttled it and shrubs and saplings choked it. It was passable but not without axe work. "If the Osages use this trail . . ." she had wondered aloud last night.

"Haven't used it for several years," he said. "Been hunting up north."

"But the Beaver said . . ."

"All the old men said it was passable," he interrupted, "and it is. Slow, is all. But we'll be out of this tomorrow. Even with another bad day we'll hit the North Fork by tomorrow night."

There were so many anxieties. She wondered if there would be one single day of this journey when he would not be faced with difficulties which lay largely beyond his control. You could not remove whole forests from your path. You could not hold up your hand and order rains to abate. You could not command rivers to be shallow and give no problem. You could not predict the moods, the abilities, the willingness of the people you depended on. All you could do was drive ahead on your own nerve and will and borrow no trouble. You had to take each day as it came and each event. But Johnny was gifted that way. He didn't look back and though he took care for tomorrow he didn't use his credit on it. And he wanted to make this journey. More than anything in the world he had wanted to make it. She didn't think anything, short of his own death, would stop him now that he had started.

They were making no noon stops in the timber. It wasn't necessary because they were halted so often every man could eat his cold fare when he was hungry. Judith felt hungry now and she went ahead to her wagon to find bread and meat. She set some out for Legette, who was driving, and a portion for Manuel. She sat beside the black man to eat. "The captain is up ahead?" she asked.

"Yes, ma'am."

"Did he say how much farther it is to the river?"

"No ma'am, but I haven't seen him since early this morning. There are signs," he added, grinning, "that it isn't far."

"What signs?"

"The team is hard to hold. I think they smell water."

"I hope so." She munched on the cold bread and wished for a cup of hot coffee. Here where the sun never shone the days were not as warm as they had been in the open. "Manuel says he smells rain. Maybe that's what the mules smell."

"It could be, ma'am, but I don't think so."

They ate silently until they had finished. The wagon moved very slowly, jolting over small logs and into potholes, creaking at the twisting and heaving of its bed and axles. It was impossible to find comfort on the wagon seat. She had to hold with one hand and feed herself with the other. At least her horse didn't shake her up so badly. She shook the crumbs from her skirt and wrapped Manuel's food in a napkin.

As Legette pulled up to let her down it occurred to her that this was the first time they had halted since she had joined him. They had been moving steadily. All these days in the Timbers they had not gone so far without stopping. She looked about. "Legette, does it strike you the forest is thinner, not quite so dense?"

He held the mules steady. "Yes, ma'am. The last hour, I'd say."

She felt wonderfully excited. "It must mean we are near the river. There is less underbrush to be cleared. The men are working faster." She made a quick decision. "I'll take this food to Manuel and then I believe I'll ride ahead and find the captain."

She found Bullitt Trice first. Leading the road choppers, he stopped, took off his hat to her, and leaned on his axe. "Ain't seen him, ma'am, but him and Jesse is up ahead."

Though his voice was easy and polite he had a forward eye, a bold and sizing eye. It met her look then slowly traveled down, pausing over her bosom and waist, moving on to the trim ankle in her boot. She felt herself flushing and hated the telltale color in her face. "Thank you, Mr. Trice," she said curtly.

"Nothing, ma'am."

This time his eyes traveled from her boot upwards to her bosom and remained fixed there. They were set very close together and almost hidden by the thick-boned brows that bulged out over them. Pig eyes, she thought, little pig eyes. His nose was flattened as if it had been broken at some time and it was broad and almost obscenely open at the nostrils. What could be seen of his mouth under a brushy black beard was unpleasantly moist. The hand holding the axe was big-knuckled and broad, fleshy and hard-palmed. He was a brute of a man, a brute, and he was arrogant and insolent. A cold anger filled her. She would put this man in his place. She leaned forward. "Mr. Trice, are you not in Parley Wade's crew?"

"Yes, ma'am." His eyes lifted slowly.

She met them straight on. "Yes. I understand that you do not like women on the trail."

"Then you don't understand correct, ma'am," he grinned slyly, "I like women anywhere—specially pretty women." His eyes dropped to the rounded front of her blouse. She caught her breath at his audacity.

"Mr. Trice," she said, clipping her words acidly, "I should like you to know that I will not vapor or faint or hold up this train in any way. Please understand that *you* will sicken on this road before I do, and remember it."

The man spat and nodded, wiping his beard with the back of a beefy hand. "You got more spirit than I reckoned. I ain't likely to forget, ma'am."

"See that you don't." She kicked her horse and rode rapidly away.

When her anger died her satisfaction with herself faded. She didn't know whether she had come off best or not. She didn't really know what the man meant. She felt shaky and a little sick inside. She ought not to have stopped and spoken to the man at all. She didn't know what had come over her. What had possessed her to let him know that either she had overheard his opinions of her or Parley Wade had talked? It was probably very unwise. But the sight of him, and his insolent eyes licking through her clothing, had determined her to put him in his place. What she had most resented, she thought, what had made her flame with color, had been the knowledge that this man watched her and Johnny, thought about their intimate times together, laughed about them, made bawdy remarks about them. When his eyes had fixed on her bosom it was as if he saw them together, stripped her of clothing and saw what no man but Johnny had ever seen. Wanted, and her face flamed again, to see for himself. How could any woman misinterpret that kind of look? You couldn't allow it! But, how could you stop it with a brute like that?

She reined up and wiped her flushed face. She'd just put it out of her mind and she would avoid the man. She sat a moment looking uncertainly at the path. It was very old and dim, not easy to follow. Maybe she ought to go back. She could lose her way and cause trouble and further delay. But she didn't want to ride back past that man again. Not alone. As long as the plagued path didn't play out entirely, she'd rather keep to it.

Her eye caught a small green lizard basking in one thin line of sun on a log. He flicked out his tongue at her, as if chiding her for her folly. She broke into laughter. "What did you expect?" she addressed him. "I'm only a foolish woman."

A crashing in the underbrush startled her and she swung about, her hand going to her throat. Had Trice followed her? Would he be that bold? But it was Jesse Cooper's horse that broke through the green screen. Relief surged through her. "Goodness, Jesse, you scared me."

His horse danced sideways a little and he reined him around. "You kind of startled me, too. It's so thick in here I couldn't see you till I was right on you. Looking for Jonathan?" He took off his hat and mopped its sweatband, mopped his forehead and face, held the hat in his hand then.

"Yes. Have you seen him?"

"Just left him. He's reached the river. I was going back to pass the word to the boys."

She was delighted. "What good news that is! Manuel has been ready to lie down and die. Can I find Johnny? Is he far ahead?"

"Not more than a mile and a half. Trouble is, the trail's grown up pretty bad. Little hard to follow." He scrubbed his hand through his hair. "Tell you, whyn't you wait a minute and let me give the boys the word, then I'll guide you there."

"I'll wait right here."

When he returned shortly he rode in front, finding the way and pushing the worst of the limbs out of her way. Over his shoulder he said, "You'll eat good tonight. The hunters have been. Left some carcasses in the trees and a note for Jonathan."

"Any deer?" she asked.

"Some—mostly turkey."

"Plenty?"

"Plenty, for several meals."

"Good. We can all use some meat."

For a little way the road was thick then, almost abruptly, the sprouts and bushes thinned, the earth grew more sandy and packed, the trail was plain, and the sky could be seen overhead. She looked up at it. "Manuel will love that sky," she said, "and the road-crew will love this stretch of road." She drew alongside Jesse Cooper.

"It's like this to the river," he said.

She found that she was enjoying the opening out of the Timbers, too. She hadn't felt particularly oppressed by their thickness but it was good to have a wider road and to see a higher sky. The air seemed lighter somehow. It wasn't difficult to imagine how the thick canopy had pressed down on the Mexican boy. Well, he could breathe freely for a while now.

"Was the note from Suard?" she asked.

"He wrote it for the Beaver."

"Yes. The Beaver understands English and can speak it a little but he can't write or read. What did he say? Were all the hunters together?"

"Had been. Said they'd waited a day and night and were going out again. Said they'd meet us farther up the river."

She had heard Johnny tell the Indians to meet him on the North Fork, nothing more than that. To her it seemed very indefinite. It was a huge range of country to find one's way in. Where on the North Fork to meet? It was a big river and a long one. How would the Indians know the exact spot Johnny meant? She would have said, pinpointing the place, meet me where the old Osage trail crosses the river. But they had understood that without words. She laughed at herself. Well, naturally, there was no other way for the wagon train to go. It was following the trail. And meet me on the North Fork meant, of course, where the trail met the

river. Men were so economical. They didn't waste words. What seemed
haphazard in many of their understandings was perfectly orderly to them.

Their horses were walking easily. Judith looked at the man riding beside
her. She didn't know him well, yet. He had arrived at Three Forks only
a week before the train left. She didn't even know if he was married.
Johnny had never said. She asked him.

He laughed. "Lord, no. Would I be off traipsing if I was?"

"Johnny is," she said.

"Jonathan's different. Besides, he's taking you along."

"Haven't you ever thought about marrying?"

"Not enough to bother."

"You will," she predicted, "when you meet the right girl. You'd make
a good husband, Jesse. At least," she amended, "I think you would."

"I've not thought of it." He laughed again. He had a nice laugh which
shook him gently. "Why are women always hankering to marry a feller
off? Seems the minute they see a man free and easy they've got to get him
tied up."

"You think Johnny is tied?"

He looked at her. "Some ways, yes," he said slowly. "Can't help but be.
Man that's wed has got to think of somebody besides himself. But," he
added, "he was luckier than most." He smiled at her. "Find me one like
you, Judith, and I'll wed her tomorrow."

She answered his smile. "I'll remember that and keep my eyes open."

He swung a knee over his saddle which turned him more toward her.
"Jonathan tells me you've not been in the Territory long."

Her own saddle, the sidesaddle women used, faced her in his direction.
Her knee rested loosely in the crook, her long, full skirt amply covering.
Her horse, plodding comfortably, needed no direction. She gave her at-
tention to what Jesse Cooper had said. "A little over two years," she said.
"Sometimes it seems longer, sometimes a lot shorter."

He nodded. "It's puzzled me some. Why'd a girl like you come out to this
rough country?"

"There ought to be a simple answer to that," she answered thoughtfully,
"but there isn't. I suppose you mean I was too young, and I had no rela-
tions, was alone in the world. And I ought to have shrunk from such a
venture . . . stayed safely at home. That's what *anyone* would think, on
the face of it." Her voice was slow, pensive, as she sorted out her thoughts.
"What anyone would think who didn't know me well, or the sort of parents
I had. The truth is, Jesse, I didn't have a very conventional upbringing.
My father and mother were . . . I expect they would be called free think-

ers. Not that they flew in the face of traditions, or didn't see good in them —but they believed, and taught me to believe, that you must think about things for yourself and do what you believe is right and best even if it doesn't fit . . . or suit . . . the generally held opinions."

He still looked puzzled though he nodded.

A skirling breeze, strengthened briefly, disarranged her hair and she smoothed it absently. "My parents died within a week of each other the winter I was sixteen. There was a particularly virulent fever prevalent that winter. They caught it and died very quickly. Except for some distant relatives of my father's, I was left alone. The entire village gathered around to advise me. It was generally thought," she smiled, remembering, "I ought to go into service, though the minister very generously offered me a home. He had an ailing wife, you see, and I would be most helpful in tending her and overseeing his brood of young children. Many counseled marriage, as soon as possible." Her smile went wry and a small tooth, set a little crookedly in the otherwise even row, showed briefly. "It wasn't difficult to see that what was weighing heaviest was the possibility of another burden on the township. The idea was to get me placed quickly, simply, so that no monies need be spent on me." Her horse lifted easily over a sunken log. Her body gave to the lift and swayed gracefully. "I had other ideas," she added, a little primly.

Jesse Cooper, squinting under his hat brim, nodded again. "I see."

Judith laughed. "I doubt you do. But I had been well taught and I believed I could teach others. And my mother was an herb woman and I knew all her arts and believed I could continue her healing works. I saw no reason why I should not be self-reliant and support myself. I began a small school in my home, which thrived, and I packaged and sold herbs. I never needed," she said simply, "one penny of public monies or any private aid."

Jesse stripped a leaf from a limb as he passed under and put the twig end in his mouth. "That took some doing," he said.

"Not especially. I did what I thought was best for me, right for me."

"I can see that. But then you come to the Territory with that bunch of missionaries."

"Yes. Well, that, too, seemed best, seemed right for me. Three years after my parents died a man with great missionary zeal visited our village. He had dreamed of a mission among the western Indians for many years and he had what seemed a splendid plan." She frowned a little, seeing again the thin frame of the Reverend Epaphras Chapman, hearing again his rich, deep voice, listening again to his well-laid plans. "He believed these western Indians must learn the ways of white men if they were to survive. Oh, he was concerned with the state of their souls, with saving them, but he went much further than that. He wanted to teach them and their children, educate them, show them better ways of living, teach them to till the soil, tell them about disease and how their sicknesses might be healed. It was truly, Jesse, a beautiful and splendid idea. And he was right about so much. If they are to survive, they really *must* give up their old ways. The Cherokees are already doing that, and some of the Choctaws and Creeks. But the Osages," she shook her head, "aren't only western Indians, they're Plains Indians, and proud and stubborn. That's where the difficulty lay . . . but that's nothing to do with me. I was asked to join Mr. Chapman's party, come to this country with them, be part of the community. I could teach, it was felt, and I could tend the sick. I expect," she said dryly, "I was caught up in a fine dream of my own. I thought it an excellent idea to join Mr. Chapman's party."

"You don't think it now?"

"Oh, yes. I still think the idea was excellent and I still think the dream splendid. But what I learned is that dreams must be tempered with truth and ideas must be tinctured with facts."

She did not say that her own disillusionment had begun during the voyage when clear eyes and plain sense saw the ignorance, ineptness and bad management. It had taken the Union Mission party ten long months to drift down the Ohio to the Mississippi, down the Mississippi to the Arkansas, then up that silty, stubborn, shallow stream. Fever and death and endless delays had lodged with them and she had witnessed the havoc fanatic but ignorant fervor could wreak. She had seen their leader, Epaphras Chapman, with utter selflessness expose himself recklessly, worry and fret, come down ill, lade onto himself the burdens of every member of the group, and drive himself to the point of emaciated exhaustion. She had also seen him, with utter selfishness, willing to sacrifice the last of them, even his own wife, to serve his tranced and self-centered dream. It was a learning that came too late.

Arrived, she saw too clearly that this mission family could teach little until it had learned much. She saw that it was not, nor ever would be, that perfect community envisioned; that instead it was fraught with all the frailties given to human beings. There were jealousies, bitternesses, strained nerves, errors, pain and suffering. But there was also great courage and dogged endurance and persistent hope and never-failing effort. And besides, whatever she saw, she had to answer for her own duty and it remained steadfast.

So much so that her marriage to the Indian trader, whom the frontier called Johnny Osage, was burdened a little with some sense of guilt at leaving the small band so early. Not much, because she was a person taught all her life to be honest in her thinking, even with herself, and she knew that no one is absolutely essential. If she stayed, she would make her contribution and she did not belittle it. But if she married, and went, the ranks would close over her absence and the work would be done equally well. That was honesty speaking. Love told her that she was young, she was a woman, and he was lean, tall, beautifully straight-muscled, disarmingly reticent, and he was also everything the men in the mission were not. He was physically healthy where they were forever racked with fever; he was quickly decisive where they were vacillating; not quite respectable where they were, oh, without any doubt at all, inexpressibly respectable and, to herself she confessed it, inexpressibly dull. Even now she blushed to remember that more than any other way Johnny Fowler was different from the mission men was that he was wholly, powerfully, urgently, male.

"Never been sorry you came, then?" Jesse Cooper asked.

"Oh, no." Her eyes twinkled with humor. "I would never have met Johnny if I hadn't."

Jesse chuckled and chewed on his twig. They rode silently for a while, then Jesse slung his leg back over the saddle, slid his foot into the stirrup, straightened, and looked about him. "You like it here? Like this country?"

Judith thought about it. "Mostly, yes. You have to get used to it. The climate's hard . . ."

"Lot of rough characters about, seems to me."

"That's to be expected," she said, and he guessed she was quoting her husband. "There's always that kind in a new land. Johnny says they've got a nose for new country and are always the first there." She lifted her shoulders and smiled. "But it doesn't matter much now, we're leaving the Territory."

"Think you'll not be coming back?"

"To Three Forks? No. Johnny doesn't like to retrace his steps. Besides, he hasn't been very happy there lately."

"Think he'll be happier in Santa Fe?"

She felt a sudden vexation with these questions. What business was it of Jesse Cooper's, even if he was Johnny's good friend? She said, shortly, "That's for him to say."

"Yes. Well . . ." he pointed ahead, "there's the river and there's Jonathan."

7

THE STORM broke at dusk, with streaked lightning and long booming drums of thunder. The sky was very dark and there was some wind.

A prairie storm was so different from the kinds she had known all her life. With nothing as a barrier the thunder clapped loud and sharply, reverberating endlessly, rolling noisily into distance. It hit the ear like a cannon shot, suddenly, deafeningly, and then clattered on, dying away by slow degrees, leaving one stunned, the ears dulled. Its shock rocked the earth. The lightning forked in the sky, seemed to branch, grab the ground, burn and leap upward, blue and white, red as the devil, crackling and vivid, dangerous, fire-leaping, simmering, inimical. It was constant and seared the eyes. While the thunder boomed and deafened, the bright streaks blinded and burned.

Then the rain came in a solid sheet, an unrelenting curtain, dense, gray, rattling, thick, and flooding.

Judith sat in her wagon and watched. She wondered about her husband and Parley Wade and the men. Where was Manuel? And Legette? Where were the horses and mules? This storm seemed to have scattered them all. She had seen Johnny only a moment when they camped. "Stay close to the wagon, Judith, it's going to storm."

"Will it cause the river to rise?"

"Not if it's soon over. But you stay in the wagon. Those clouds are ragged and that means a little wind. Few trees may be uprooted."

"I'll stay," she promised. "Don't worry."

She had stayed and raised the sheet to watch and it was swift and violent and beautiful. Something in her always responded to this violence of nature. Something forgot danger and exulted in all the noise and blinding light, the force of the wind and the driving rain. I must be part witch, she told herself, thrusting her hand out to feel the stinging cold pelt on her palm. In a storm I ride a broomstick. Some day I shall be dunked in a pond or hanged in Salem Square. Her humor moved ahead to the Spanish town. Do they dunk witches in Santa Fe? Or hang them on the Plaza? No, they only throw them in the calabozo. I would pine away in a calabozo. I would get thin and lean and hagworn in a calabozo. I'd better mend my ways. I'd better forsake my New England broomstick. But where were they all? Where had they gone? What were they doing?

Legette came out from under some trees, a blanket hooded over his head. He called to her. "Your supper is ready, ma'am."

She wrinkled her nose. "Cold bread and meat again! It's bad luck, this rain, just at camping time. I wanted hot coffee tonight, Legette, and some of that good deer meat roasted."

He grinned. "That's what I've got, ma'am. Built a little fire here under the thick of the trees. The meat's on the rare side, but it's hot."

She scrambled up and shouted, "Dish it up, Legette, I'm coming."

It was wonderfully good, half raw as it was—deer meat, the breast of a turkey, hot bread, black coffee. And she was so hungry for hot food. She ate quickly, clawing the meat off its bones, chewing and swallowing hastily like the men about their fires, gulping down great swigs of the hot coffee. She picked the bones clean, drank down half a dozen cups of the hot liquid, scrummaged the plate of bread bare and finally felt a glutton. "Is there plenty, Legette?"

"Plenty, ma'am."

"Then eat. Where is the captain?"

"Don't know, ma'am. Nobody in camp but me. The captain rounded up all the hands."

She stood and hugged her arms across her bosom. The rage of the storm was lessening but the rain still fell heavily. She wished he weren't out in all this wet. He'd be soaked to the marrow. "The storm has spooked the herd, I guess," she said.

"Might be," the Negro replied. He was eating heartily, swabbing the meat juices from his plate. "He didn't say."

No, he never said. He just did . . . whatever must be done.

The rain was beginning to penetrate the leaf roof over their heads. She shook a cold drop from her forehead. "I'll be in the wagon, then, when he comes," and thought immediately what a silly thing it was to say. Where else would she be, for heaven's sake?

The rain had slanted around to the other side now and she had to put down the wagon sheet to keep the bed from being flooded. It made the tiny room under canvas seem cooped and stuffy, and even smaller than it was. She lit a candle and stood, her hands loosely clasped before her, and thought what she should do with this piece of idle time she had inherited.

She felt at loose ends with Johnny gone and the camp empty and no good, homely sounds of men closing up the day and fixing for the night. There were no sounds but the rain, dull on the canvas, and the growling of thunder. She thought how dreary it was, when you had got used to being married, to be alone. A man filled such a *lot* of space even if he wasn't a tremendously big man, as Johnny wasn't—tall, but not run to size otherwise. There was something about him, slumped in a chair, that filled a room until it was crowded—the deep rumble of his voice; that hard leanness of his brown hands; the mixed man smell of tobacco, leather, sweat, and rum; the good, tight look of his bones; the comfortable stretch of his legs, over which you stumbled or stepped high; the clutter he made so recklessly and so surely in his knowledge of possession. Oh, there was certainly no man so un-neat as Johnny Fowler. She spent half her time she did believe picking up after him. With his own affairs finicky to the point of fussiness, the moment he stepped into a house he shed order as a duck sheds rain. Shirts, boots, jackets, hats, fell where he dropped them. But when he went to find them again he could go unerringly to the proper peg or shelf, certain she would have picked them up and put them away. She pretended to mind and scolded him in the way only wives know is not scolding but loving. She wondered, smiling fondly, if time would ever stale the quick, small lurch of joy she always felt simply at touching something he had worn. A shirt, still wrinkled at the armbands, could assail her with such a swelling of love that she could bury her face swiftly in it, so much more immoderately than she allowed herself very often with the flesh. Oh, she loved him, she loved him so. He was her whole world. And where was he? Where was he? Why didn't he come home?

She puttered about, filling up time, then facing the fact that she was dithering she undressed and settled herself in bed to read until she was sleepy. First her Bible chapter and then, she thought, the *Gazette* instead of a book. There were at least a dozen copies of the paper which came to them irregularly, but always eventually, from Little Rock. Neither she nor Johnny had had time to read the paper for a long time before they left so she had folded them neatly and flatly and made room for them in their chest.

She had not organized them by dates and did not read them so. When she came across the advertisement and recovered a little from the stunning shock she looked quickly to see the date of publication—April 5, the last issue to reach them before they left! She caught her breath at the implications. The paper went all over the Territory, it was the *only* newspaper in the Territory and it was widely read. Someone surely must have recognized the description, remembered the deckhand on the *Natchez*. She snatched at the paper to read the description again. It didn't mention the *Natchez*. The owner didn't know how he had got away, then. Her eyes scanned rapidly, only the salient facts—stands six-foot-two—full black—answers to name Prince—aged twenty-five—no disfigurements. No disfigurements! She thought of the lash marks on his back which would be there as long as there was flesh on his bones. Answers to the name of Prince—like a dog, she thought, and a dog's name. But the thing which stuck in her mind was the last sentence—handsome reward for information concerning this man, or for his return to owner. The owner was Dolphus Perrault, Houma Parish, Louisiana.

She flung the blankets back and felt for her dressing gown and slippers. The bed was impossible now. Did Johnny know about this? Had he seen it? Had somebody told him? His friends would have warned him and if men came looking would have denied, lied, helped hide but, she swallowed painfully, there were always those who for any paltry sum—and the reward wouldn't be paltry, certainly it would not be—would inform and pad their consciences with duty done.

She paced back and forth. Oh, they were breaking the law, no doubt about it, and she believed in law . . . but it was an inhuman law and she did *not* believe in slavery. No one with an ounce of humanity in him could have sent Legette back to that whip or back, if she was consistent, to being owned even by a benevolent owner. But that didn't wipe the law off the books. If they knew, if they had learned, men might even now be following . . . what could they do to Johnny? Would he be taken away? Harboring a runaway slave was bad enough, but to take him out of the United States . . . to *try* to take him out of the United States, her mind amended, for if they were caught up before they reached the Spanish boundary . . . Oh, what kind of person was she, to be thinking only of their safety? There was a right and wrong to this, but she had never been able to find it clearly and she could not find it now. The *law* said a slave was property and if you didn't return a runaway it was just the same as stealing. It *was* stealing something valuable, something for which the owner had paid a great deal of money. But it was a *human being*, not a mule or a horse or a cow. It was someone who, like yourself, had feelings and thought and wept and laughed and hungered and thirsted and believed in God and heaven and sweated and slept and conceived children. How could that be property? How could it be justified?

But they had broken the law, and how could that be justified? Oh, she was all mixed up. Where was Johnny? Why didn't he come? She swerved about to find his hammered gold watch in the pouch of valuables she carried in her skirt pocket. The night was surely almost worn away! She dug in the pouch until she found it, her fingers shaking so that she almost dropped it when she drew it out. She released the catch of the case and held the black-numeraled face near the candle to see. It must have stopped. It had to be later than eight o'clock. But its tick was clear and steady, and Johnny wound it faithfully. She had never known him to forget. Only two hours since they had made night camp and the storm had swelled and faded, she had eaten, she had been abed . . . only two hours. The watch was never wrong. It did not lose time or gain time. "You could bet your whole life on it," Johnny had told her once, "to the second." Slowly she closed the case and slowly she put the watch back in the pouch. Johnny might be out until midnight. He might even be out until morning. She might have the whole night alone with this new knowledge.

She drew in a deep, long breath and prepared herself to think calmly . . . and the first thing to do when one is to think calmly is to act calmly. She took off her dressing gown, slid her feet out of her knitted slippers, and got back in the bed. It gained nothing and lost both courage and nerve to waste time walking the floor. She made herself lie still though her legs, wishing of themselves to move, twitched a little. Now, think, she told herself. In the first place this is not new knowledge, it is only new to you. This issue of the *Gazette* was widely circulated before we left home. And nothing occurred, did it? No one came searching. No one troubled. If, in the first flush of the announcement, no one troubled it isn't likely they will now. It is known everywhere, it was even printed in the *Gazette* months ago, that Johnny Fowler intended making a voyage to Santa Fe and by now it is generally known that the Johnny Fowler train has departed. So . . .

In the second place, and this caused another deep breath, it is bootless to ponder the right or the wrong. What is done is done. We made that choice long ago and it is only treading a wheel of worry to consider it again. Even if Johnny would consider it she did not suppose, and she faced this flinching a little but sturdily enough, she could bring herself to insist on it. On yet sending Legette back. No more than she could do it earlier, when she had first known, could she do it now. So—her mouth twisted a little, it was a humbling position for Judith Lowell Fowler who had been taught, and who believed, that freedom lay only under the law and order—let there be no more fuss and bother about the right and the wrong. Their position was taken. "Woman's mind oft shifts her passions, like th'inconstant wind . . ." John Gay—she identified the poet immediately and

thought how like a ragbag was her own mind with its odds and ends of
stuffings, all of nothing and a deal of bits. She must some day learn the
whole of a poem if for nothing but its discipline.

She brought her mind sternly back to its purpose. In the third place,
yes . . . in the third place, and in this matter, at this late date, she knew as
well as she knew anything on earth that she could not possibly have the
slightest influence on Johnny Fowler. When he first brought the Negro
home, perhaps—yes, then. But not now. Nothing this side of catastrophe
would stop him taking this wagon train through to Santa Fe.

All these things being so, and they were, it was out of her hands and she
might as well put it out of her mind. She would show the notice to Johnny,
in case he might not have seen it or heard about it, so that he might be
forewarned. That was all she could do, except go now to sleep.

Sometime in the night she roused, a little, and knew that he was beside
her. In the dark she smiled and turned to huddle her head between his
shoulders and lay her arm across him. He was so warm, so warm.

8

IT WAS full daylight when she next wakened and Johnny's place was so long empty his pillow was cold.

Horrified to be late she scrambled about with her dressing. It was a set rule of Johnny's that sunup should find the train ready to travel. He should have called her. He shouldn't have let her sleep. But if she hurried—if she ate in the wagon after the start—she buttoned up quickly, shivering a little in the chill, and gave her hair only a brush. How could she have overslept? She had never done it before. The first morning sounds always waked her. There would be the clump of wood dropped, and the pop and crackle of fires, the grumpy voices of the men still rough with sleep; and there would be the ring of an iron kettle, the splash of water in a coffeepot, the sizzle and smell of meat frying. These were the sounds which always wakened her.

She gave her dress a twitch to settle it over her petticoat and stopped, her hand arrested. There should be, there always was by this time, a great clatter and clamor of men shouting and cursing as they caught up the mules, of cook boxes rattling as cooking gear was thrown in, of trace chains banging about, of animals whickering and blowing. There was always this hurry and bustle, for each crew wanted to be first hitched and set. Bets were made each day. Winners crowed and jeered and losers went sullen and grim. But there was nothing this morning. The camp was as quiet as it had been last night. What was wrong? Why weren't the hands working?

She came down from the wagon.

The camp straggled up the river in a single line. The wagons were edged into the woods but the men had made their cook fires on the riverbank. She guessed they were sick to death of woods and meant to enjoy while they could the open sky above them.

She had already, this early on the journey, got into the habit of looking quickly at the whole camp when she came out of the wagon in the morning. It was Johnny's way of taking in, in one brief glance, the well-being of the train, the mood, the order, the health, the safety, the readiness, as though these things might have altered during the night. The men, she saw, were gathered about the farthest fire doing nothing. They were simply loafing. Puzzled, but knowing they wouldn't have dared except on Johnny's orders, she looked for her own breakfast fire. There was not one. Last night's fire under the trees was a draggle of wetted-down ashes. No one had cooked here this morning, and none of them, Johnny, Manuel, or Legette, was about. She set a pin more neatly in her hair. Well, wherever they were and whatever they were doing, three men would be coming back to the wagon eventually and they would be hungry men. She built a fire, sliced bacon into the skillet, put water into the coffeepot and ground fresh coffee beans. She mixed bread and set it to baking, and was warmed as much by her energy and bustling as by the fire.

She walked then to the brink of the riverbank and was astonished. Good Lord, it wasn't a river . . . it was a sand flat. Half a mile away was something that resembled an opposite bank, but barely. Narrow channels of red water snaked about on top the sand, like a red ribbon dropped by a careless child. Upstream the channel was on the far side. Nearer it crossed a spit of sand to flow on this side. There was so little water for all that space, and in between nothing but sandburs and willows and bleached, drifted logs. It could be a devil in a high tide, Johnny had told her, a real witch of a river. But it was hard to believe, seeing it so low.

The bacon smell came to her and she went back to tend it. She kept glancing up the river hoping to see Johnny, wishing he would come when the meal was ready.

It wasn't Johnny who came, however. It was Jesse Cooper and Asa Baldwin. Jesse was smiling. "So you're up."

"I'm ashamed to have been a slugabed."

"No need to be. We're not traveling today. Jonathan said let you sleep."

A puff of breeze blew smoke in her face and she fanned it away. "Not traveling? Why?"

"The rain softened up the sand. Be heavy hauling through it. Jonathan says the sun will bake it hard by tomorrow. Said we'd camp here . . . give the hands a rest. Let Asa and Legette make and mend a little. Wagons need tightening some and the mules can stand seeing to."

She moved the coffeepot back from the fire. "Where is Johnny?"

"Him and Parley have gone upstream. Looking out the road."

"Without food?"

"They took something cold."

She broke into laughter. She had cooked enough to feed ten men, a woman's common failing, she thought. Come mealtime a woman had to cook and more than ample. Well, if she couldn't feed her own man these two would have to do. "You and Asa sit down and eat. And don't tell me you've already fed."

"I don't aim to," Jesse said, "for I've not and this smells powerful good. I'm purely ready for it."

Asa, a silent man, took his seat without a word. She filled plates and handed them around, poured coffee, and sat on the little campstool Johnny had made for her comfort. A log or the ground would do for him, he'd said, but he wanted her to sit easy. She was hungry, too. "Where are Manuel and Legette?"

"Breaking out the critters to be shoed. They'll be on."

"I'll put something back for them."

The men ate quickly, emptying their plates before she had scarcely begun. She filled them again. "What will the hands do today?"

Jesse sopped bacon grease with his bread. "Most of 'em think to go hunting. They've been hurting to get a shot at something. Reckon some'll sleep, laze around, tidy up their gear. Won't bother you, though."

"I didn't think they would. Just wondered how they'd occupy themselves."

"It's a free day. Jonathan just told 'em we'd travel tomorrow. Said anybody not present at catch-up'd be left behind." He grinned. "Reckon there's some wouldn't believe that."

Briskly Judith gathered up the plates and cups. "They'd do well to. Johnny doesn't say things he doesn't mean."

"Any of 'em getting a snort too much today or wandering too far in the Timbers will likely find it out."

Asa left, but Jesse lingered. "If I was you, Judith, I wouldn't go into the woods today."

Surprised, she looked at him. "I don't mean to, but why not?"

"Liable to be some pretty wild banging around in there today and somebody might mistake you for a deer."

She stared at him, then laughed. "I don't think that's likely but I've had enough of the woods for the present. I'm not tempted by them. I think I'll houseclean. You wouldn't believe how quickly a wagon can get cluttered."

"You do that. And I'll be around if you need anything." He added ruefully, "I'm told off for camp guard."

She paused, her hands full of dirty dishes. "You'd rather go hunting today yourself, wouldn't you? I'm sorry, Jesse."

"I could do with a little time to myself, but Jonathan will see to it. Him and Parley both gone, falls to me to see to things."

When she came back from washing the plates and cups she saw that he had joined Asa and they were taking a wheel from the lead wagon. A spoke was cracked, perhaps, or the rim needed tightening. Asa was carpenter for the train and on a day of make and mend he would go over every inch of each wagon looking for weaknesses and strengthening them.

She saw, too, that Legette had set up his forge now and Manuel was bringing up a string of mules. The sight of the Negro reminded her of the notice in the *Gazette*. Well, telling Johnny would have to wait. She called to the two men that food was ready. Legette answered her. "We have eaten, Miss Judith."

"You call that eating?"

Manuel laughed. "Save some coffee, Señora. It will hot up the cold bread and meat."

She left them to their job and went about hers.

Inside the wagon she decided to do a washing before cleaning. The clothes could bleach all day in the sun if she got them spread early. She was really pleased, she thought, to have this day of rest from traveling. If she took advantage of every stop to keep their clothing washed, and to sweep and tidy the wagon, she wouldn't have such a grimy feeling of making do. If she could find a secluded place, it occurred to her, she might even get a bath and wash her hair. There might be tasty fish in the river, though she doubted it. If there was time left over she might try her hand. She liked to fish. It was a thing she had done as a child with her father. And at this time of year, before the water grew warm, small fish might be sweet and good.

Happily, she sorted out her wash. Johnny had dirtied three linsey shirts and several pairs of socks, and she had changed her waist and petticoats as many times. She also stripped the bed. There was no way they could cleanse themselves well at night and they took dust and sweat into the bed with them. The sheets were dreadfully dingy.

Clutching her bundle she climbed down the back step again. As she passed the forge Legette looked up. "Miss Judith, if you will leave those things I will wash them for you."

"No, thank you, Legette." She added quickly, "I'm sure you could do them better, but I like to wash."

Manuel was holding a mule for the black man to shoe. "You go to wash the clothing in the river, Señora?"

"Sí." She laughed. "I thought I would. Where else?"

"You look at that river yet?"

"Oh, yes. I know it's muddy but there might be a backwater pool some place handy."

"No pools." He shook his head. "No pools. But is a little creek that way. Small río." He pointed. "Is clear water there."

She looked where his finger pointed. The woods came down to the river in that direction, leaving only a narrow bank for a path. "How far?" she asked.

"Not far. One mile, maybe."

Legette jerked at Manuel's arm, muttered to him and silenced him, then spoke to her. "I can do the washing for you in that creek this afternoon, Miss Judith. It's more than a mile, ma'am."

She hesitated, not because of the distance but because of the woods. But it wouldn't actually be going into the woods to follow that little path. Still . . . she swung about. "I'll just see about the river, Legette."

"Yes, ma'am."

She slid down the sandy bank and began her search for one small pool where the silt, unroiled, might have settled and left clearer water. She deposited the clothing and went wandering up and down the sandbar, stepping gingerly in her fear of quicksands. For half an hour she went probing about but she had finally to admit Manuel was right. There were no clean pools. Wryly she looked at the sheets and her white petticoats. To dip them in this water would be to dye them red. They were better off as they were. There was nothing for it but to leave them for Legette and the clear creek this afternoon.

She kept busy for two hours tidying the wagon, hanging the blankets to air, sweeping and then scouring the floor and raising the sides of the wagon sheets to sweeten the air. When eventually she had done everything there was still time left on her hands. What to do with it? The closer look at the river had convinced her it was useless to do any fishing. The flesh would be flavored by the mud and too coarse. She could knit, but it would be mere make-work. Knitting was for those times when she could do nothing else and there must be some way she could more usefully occupy herself.

She had already studied her Spanish list and knew it perfectly. She felt frustrated of her desire to make the most of this day made to order for catching up on things. Legette might do the washing this afternoon but white clothing needed a full day of sun. And nobody could rid her body and hair of grit and grime but herself. She did want a bath so badly.

She wandered outside. Legette and Manuel were not at the forge and the fire had died down. They had finished, she supposed, and were gone to some other task. Asa and Jesse were busy with another wagon. Oh, drat!

The whole day was wasting. She would just go ahead and do that washing. What was a mile, or a little more, of walking? And what possible harm could there be? It wasn't as if she would actually go into the woods—only follow along the riverbank at their edge. And she didn't believe the men would be as careless with their shooting as Jesse said anyhow. The shots she had heard all morning sounded well into the Timbers, very far away. It might be two weeks before she had another opportunity like this. She was just going to find that creek and do her own washing the way she liked and have herself a good bath.

Her spirits rose as she left the wagons behind. The sun was bright and hot and it glazed the sands of the riverbed into a fine glittering dazzle. The willows on the sandbars were green and the sky was high and cloudless and blue. There was a good wind from the south to cool, and a sand crane, motionless on one leg, was fishing in the shallows. It was a lovely day. She felt a great delight in it and began to sing an old song her mother had used to sing to her when she was a child.

It wasn't so far to the creek, she thought when she found it, or else she had lost all sense of time. And it was a beautifully clear little stream. The floor was lined with smooth slatestone and there was a small waterfall inland, only a hundred yards or so from the river, which made a perfect little pool for her purposes.

She washed the clothing first, soaping them well, then rinsing them, watching the suds wash down the current as fast as she made them. Then she took the washing to the riverbank and laid it in the sun to dry.

Her first chore done, she had a feeling of luxury as she peeled off her own clothing and plunged into the pool. It was so cold it took her breath at first but she struck out to swim briskly the length of the pool. She did not remember when she had learned to swim. Her father, she supposed, had taught her when she was still too young to keep it in memory. Their village had been near the sea and she had been taken often and allowed to play in the surf. As she grew older it became a lost freedom, for women did not swim, did not display themselves. It had been years, she thought, floating on her back, since she had done more than douse in a tin tub. How good it was, how wonderfully good it was to swim again, to cut through the water so strongly, to feel it all over. She had forgotten how fine it was to bathe like this.

She kicked over and swam the length of the pool twice more, then she let down in water to her armpits near the rock where she had left the soap. She sudsed her hair well and ducked it a dozen times until it sang with cleanness as she shook it out. It was too long, troublesome to arrange, too soft and not curly enough, but Johnny would not let her snip so much as an inch off. He liked to see it down to her waist when she undid it at night. It spread out on the water now like a silky brown patch of seaweed.

With a feeling of sensuous pleasure, a great joy in being alone and being clean and being once more wholly immersed in running water, she ducked under, stayed long, and came up winded and gasping for breath. She shook the water from her head and mopped her face. It was so cold, so pure, so clear. She must do this every chance she had on this journey, for once in Santa Fe she would be condemned to a tub again.

She opened her eyes and looked straight across the creek into another pair of eyes staring at her from the bushes.

Panic shot through her and she froze for a moment. Indians, she thought without much coherence, Indians! Instinctively she backed a step and threshed with her arms, opened her mouth to scream. Only a gasp came out for she remembered instantly that there was no one near enough to help. She forced herself to be steady and something made her look away from the bushes quickly, as if she had seen nothing. What shall I do? What shall I do? Her mind went scurrying like a frightened squirrel. What shall I do?

Instinct served her better than reason and without knowing why or thinking consciously she reached for the soap, sudsed her hair again and went through the motions of washing it. Her heart was thudding and she felt choked and panicky but she made herself move slowly, leisurely, as she had been doing. He might, she thought prayerfully, go away if he thought he hadn't been seen. But how long had he been there? How much had he seen? She doused her face under water, feeling its quick heat, as she thought how much he might have seen.

But her mind began to work more clearly. Indians were friendly here. Johnny had said so. Hostile Indians didn't cross the Timbers. They came no farther east than the western edge. If it was an Indian, then, it could only be some wandering Osage . . . or, the Beaver? Suard? Or was it an Indian? There had been only the frame of the eyes, nothing of the lower face. And all the men were brown from the sun now.

From the screen of her hair she darted another look at the bushes, then sighed with relief. The eyes were gone. She had to get out of here quickly. She shouldn't have risked it. She scrambled out of the water, making of herself only a bright flash of white flesh, then she was in the shelter of the saving bushes herself, breathing hard. Her hands shook as she slid her shift over her wet skin and tugged it down, then more easily slipped the dark cotton dress over her head. She took in a deep breath. Whatever happened now, if anything did, she would be decent. It made her flesh crawl to think some man, any man, had seen her . . . why not even Johnny had ever seen her without anything at all on! To go the rest of this journey knowing that one of the hands. . . . She felt like crying with shame. How could she bear it? And Johnny would be furious. What would he do? Haul every man before him and threaten and punish? And expose her, she thought shrinkingly, with his questions and threats. Oh, it was dreadful and she ought never to have risked it. She ought to have stayed in camp and read or knitted or slept, anything but this wandering off alone and getting herself into such a scrape. Johnny would kill the man! He would, she knew he would. It wouldn't be enough to banish him, to turn him out, he would be so murderously angry he would choke him with his bare hands, choke the truth out of him. If he only didn't have to know. She was winding up her hair and having trouble with it, it kept falling down and the pins kept slipping out of her hands. She had never kept anything from Johnny. But how could she tell him this? That his own wife had been spied on and spied on when she was . . . and by somebody with the train, she was convinced of that now. One of the Indians wouldn't be so bad. They didn't look on a white woman the same way white men did. They didn't covet them. But one of the hands . . . ? Oh, it would shame Johnny, shame him to the quick of his soul. He would never forgive her or forget it and things wouldn't ever be the same . . .

She got her hair done up finally. What should she do? What should she do? She looked about as if the woods themselves could tell her the answer, then her mind lit on the one wise friend she had. Parley. She would tell Parley and he would tell her what to do. She felt immediately comforted. Parley would know best. He would scold, but it wouldn't be like Johnny scolding, or going cold and not speaking and holding his anger deep and quiet. Yes, she'd tell Parley.

She walked quickly, running a little in the clear spaces, down the creek toward the river. She would gather up her clothes and finish drying them at the camp. She only wanted to get back as soon as possible. She wished she had never left it.

She had almost reached the river, was within sight of it, when a shot rang out from the woods across the creek. She swung about, one arm going up as though to ward off whatever threatened. There was a shout, which turned into a scream, and a great crashing in the underbrush. She flung herself onto the sandy ground beneath a bush.

There was another shot, more shouts and yells and screams. The woods thinned here and from her bush she watched, fear closing her throat and breaking her into sweat. It mounted to terror as Tig Vance came into view, a great black bear on his heels. She crammed her fists against her mouth. The bear was so close, so close! She crouched on the sand under the bush, unable to tear her eyes away. Run, Vance, run . . . make for the river!

At every step the little scant-framed man was screeching, looking back over his shoulder, stumbling, yelling, "Kill him, Trice! Kill him! Shoot! Shoot him, Trice!"

Trice bellowed back, "Make for the water! Run for the river, Tig. I've got to reload!"

Yes, yes, run for the river! It was unbelievable how fast the huge beast could cover the ground. Vance was running swiftly in mortal fear, but the bear closed up more swiftly and in three more great bounds she saw it swipe out with its paw and, horrified, she saw the paw rip the jacket and shirt off the man's back and lay it open in broad strips that must have torn through muscle and nerve to the bone. The whole back was red and dripping immediately.

Vance screamed and stumbled, then giving up the river, ran up a slanting tree. The bear behind him made nothing of the ramp and followed.

Trice appeared in the clearing and she saw him take quick aim. She heard the gun fire but the climbing animal must have been a poor target. He was hit—there was no doubt about that for he made a hideous, growling noise—but he was not stopped.

Judith had never felt so helpless in her life. There was nothing she could do but lie where she was, her chest tight and her stomach roiling, a cold sweat of horror freezing her. What she was seeing was like a nightmare from which she ought soon to awake.

The tree gave beneath the man and the bear and as he came close the bear swiped again with his paw and laid the man's arm and shoulder open. Poor Vance, wild and screaming, dropped from the tree and ran again. The great beast, so awkward looking, so lumbering, but so amazingly swift for all his seeming clumsiness, dropped to the ground, too. It was Tig Vance, now, who looked more clumsy. He was weaving and stumbling instead of running, as if the sand hung on his feet and slowed him. But he was still screaming, "Trice! Trice! Shoot him! For God's sake . . . for God's sake, Trice!"

The desperate screams died away—the bear had reached him again. Vance stumbled and the bear caught him. The massive arms clutched and clawed and pawed but, worse, the great jaws opened like maws and when they closed Vance's head was under the teeth.

There was one more shot and, slowed so that each move seemed to take an eternity, she saw the huge paws let go, the great jaws loosen, saw the muscles go slack, the instinct to kill dim, the will and nerve fade, the organism begin to die. Slowly, very slowly, the giant beast slumped, sitting first like a pleading beggar, growls of pain coming from his throat but slowly choking off. Then the tremendous frame, helpless to hold itself upright, toppled and tottered and lay finally in a heap beside the man he had felled.

Trice came out of the woods. He went forward cautiously, one step at a time, his gun at the ready. Carefully he approached the fallen animal. When he reached him, he stood over him and prodded with one foot and made certain he was dead. Then she saw him take his familiar stance, his spraddled, arrogant, proud, mighty stance—the stance of man, the conqueror, the killer.

But Tig Vance looked as dead as the bear . . . dreadfully mutilated, horribly still, terribly silent.

Painfully Judith pulled herself up. She watched as Trice knelt beside Tig Vance. An oily slime rose in her throat and she forced it down. Her legs held her though they were as weak as water and she took a step or two. Then seeing what Trice was about, the nurse in her rose to consciousness and she called, her voice croaking, "Don't move him, Trice. Let him lie. I'm coming."

The man looked across the creek at her, studied her a moment, then nodded. "Wait there, ma'am. I'll help you over."

She waited and Trice waded the creek and lifted her as easily as if she had been a child and carried her across. "Is he dead?" she asked.

"Don't know. If he ain't he's mighty bad hurt."

"Yes. Put me down."

She knew the claw rips would be deep and mutilating, probably cripple the man for life, but the wound she feared was the head wound from the bear's great jaws. It was almost terrifying to have Vance open his eyes as she went down on her knees beside him and recognize her and say, weakly, "I'm killed, ma'am. I'm killed. I felt my skull crushed in his jaws."

Quickly she looked.

Every tooth had left its mark, raking the skull from the temples over the ears to the crown of his head, plowing deep furrows. But for some reason the animal had not been able to close his jaws for the huge, crushing blow which would have made mincemeat of the skull cage, the bones and the soft matter of the brains. "No, Vance," she said, "you are not killed. The teeth have not broken the bones."

The little man moaned. "I felt the bones crack, ma'am."

He lapsed into unconsciousness then.

Judith was quick and curt. "Trice, I did a washing today. Find a sheet. They're spread on the sand. Tear it into strips for me. These wounds must be sewed but that must wait until we are back at camp."

He was quick and unquestioning. His strong hands were ripping the sheet as he brought it. "You want some water?"

"No. I'll bind the wounds now. We can wash them and sew them up later. Turn him and hold him, please."

When she had finished, she said, "Now, you'd better go for help to carry him. I'll stay with him."

Trice stripped her authority from her. "No, ma'am. That won't do. If there's one black bear in the woods, there may be several. 'Twouldn't do to leave you alone. I'll carry Vance. He's a light load. You get your clothes, ma'am, and take my gun. I'll be as easy with him as I can."

He waited until she had gathered up her wash and taken his gun, then he cradled Vance effortlessly and led the way. If the long mile tired him he didn't show it. Judith was hard put to it to keep up and her own burdens seemed very heavy. They made no conversation. Trice walked ahead, with a spring in his step which made the sand fall away as if he spurned it. She sank and felt weighted and there was soon a stitch in her side. Her legs were numb when they finally reached the wagons.

Men came running. Someone took the gun from her and someone else took the clothing. A man took her arm and another threw down a blanket for Vance. Someone set a stool for her, touched her hair, knelt beside her and held hot watered whisky to her mouth. She choked and sputtered and looked and it was Johnny. "See to Vance," she said, "he's badly hurt."

His fingers bit into her shoulder. "Are you all right?"

"You're hurting me, Johnny." She nodded, and coughed again from the drink. "No harm to me. No danger. I was across the creek. Trice killed the bear."

Johnny stood. "Legette!"

"Yes, sir."

"Help Mrs. Fowler into the wagon."

She pushed up from the stool. "No. Those wounds must be sewed and poulticed. Truly, Johnny, I am all right . . . just winded."

Trice spoke. "I set a hard pace for her, sir, and the sun is hot."

She flicked him a look.

"We will care for Vance," Johnny said gently.

Resolutely she took charge. "Legette, get my satchel. Then build a fire and set water to heating."

The black man looked uncertainly from his captain to her. Johnny searched her face, finally nodded. "Do as she says, Legette." He laughed, then, and before them all laid his arm about her shoulders and tightened it. "She is very good with this kind of thing. She says no harm has come to her and she will give me less trouble if we humor her than if we don't."

The men laughed with him, then scattered to bring up wood, get a fire going and bring water. Legette brought the black medicine satchel from the wagon.

Johnny left her and went to the wounded man's pallet where Trice stood beside him. "How'd it happen?"

"We wasn't expecting to see no bears that close to the river, sir. We was looking for turkey or deer. Come up on this 'un unexpected. Vance seen him first and takened a shot at him. Missed him, and the bear kept coming at him and he didn't have no chance to reload. He throwed his gun down and commenced running. I fired but only wounded the beast. Time I could reload and shoot again he'd got to Vance. I done the best I could, Cap'n."

Johnny's face was grave as he looked at the figure on the pallet. "I warned you men this morning there were black bears in the Timbers."

"Yes, sir," Trice nodded, "but it was open where we was . . . not much underbrush and we figured to see any game a good ways off. This one, he just riz up from back of a log."

Johnny looked around, his eyes going from one man to another, resting on each in turn, letting his look bear its weight of somberness. Finally he spoke. "I told you this morning there were black bears in the Timbers. I warned you then to leave them alone unless you had a good shot at the head. There's only one vital spot to hit in a bear—the brain. You can pump a dozen shots into the body and it won't stop them. They just keep coming. And once you've emptied your gun, you're helpless. I told you then, don't fire. Get away. You've got a good chance unless you shoot and wound a bear because they're stupid, bumbling animals until they're hurt, short-sighted and not curious. But if you hurt one, he's deadly and I told you this. Now, Vance is bad hurt for not listening and heeding. I don't want it to happen again." His hand chopped down. "The train will stop here until we know how Vance fares. We don't move tomorrow. I feel for Vance, but you see how one man's carelessness upsets the whole works. God knows how long we'll be delayed here." He turned to Trice. "Is the bear young?"

Trice shook his head. "No. He's so old he's beginning to grizzle."

"Useless for meat, then. Parley, take six men with you and dress him out for the fat. Rest of you men get back to your own affairs. We'll take care of Vance."

Reluctantly the men moved away in small groups, talking together, looking back, sobered by the accident, feeling the firm strands of the rope that tied them all together suddenly frayed and giving. Vance was hurt bad, no doubt about it. He might die. And it might have been them. And on their faces, along with their shock, was the relief that it hadn't been. Too bad about Vance, but thank God it wasn't me! Judith saw it and interpreted it and held no blame. It was always present, the mixture, when death clawed its way into one's life—the very real grief and the guilt of relief.

Trice still stood beside the pallet.

Johnny barked at him, "That means you, too, Trice."

"Mebbe I can help."

"You've done what you could. It's my job, now."

Trice stood with his eyes down, his gaze on Vance. Suddenly he looked up, across the body of the man on the blanket, at Judith, and just as suddenly she knew whose eyes had watched her bathing in the pool. It had left her mind. The dreadful and appalling accident to Vance, accompanied with its terror and horror, had swept the watching eyes out of her mind; but with his head a little bent, his eyes confident and possessive and gloating under the bushy brows, she knew he meant to recall it to her and meant her to know he was the one. How bold and insolent he was and how loathsome he was. It made her feel all hollow inside to know it had been he who had seen what no man before had ever seen . . . herself wholly unclothed.

She met his look unwaveringly but she moved quietly to her husband's side and put her hand on his arm. Look, the gesture said, look if you will. In spite of what you have seen, I belong to this man. Nothing you have seen alters that. You have violated me with your eyes, but I am his.

Her proud stare gazed him down and he bent for his gun and walked sullenly away.

Johnny watched him go, thoughtfully. "Don't much like that man. He pushes a little close. Best muleskinner of the lot, though. Can't fault him there." He rubbed his chin, still watching the blocky figure making its way down the string of wagons. Then he shook his head and turned about. "Got your medicine bag?"

"Yes. Legette brought it."

"Let's get on with it, then."

With Jesse Cooper and the black man they worked over the wounded

Vance. He stayed mercifully unconscious as Johnny sewed up the head wounds. It wasn't a very good job and Johnny admitted it. "Needs a surgeon's hands," he said.

"And tools," Jesse said. "You've done as good as anybody could with what you've got. Wonder them teeth didn't make mincemeat out of his skull, ain't it?"

"Reckon Trice's shot was in time."

The head bandaged, they turned the man over and Johnny tried the shoulder. "Out of joint," he said, "no break. Grab hold, Jesse." With one quick jerk they put the arm joint in place again. Then they bathed and stitched and bandaged the deep claw marks on Vance's back.

They made him as comfortable as they could and Johnny gave him, finally, a pill of opium, forcing it into his throat and making him swallow water to take it down. "That's as much as I know to do," he said, then, stepping back. "Fool," he said grittily, wiping his hands down his pant legs, "the man's a fool. There's some like that. Can't ever do nothing right, and he's one of 'em. Ought to've sent him back after the Deep Fork crossing. Ought to've known he'd never learn and he'd just blunder into something worse. Now, it's done and we'll be held up for days on his account."

Jesse was thoughtful. "How much delay can you afford, Jonathan?"

Johnny shrugged. "Rather have none. Like to reach Santa Fe early for the best trade. Have to allow for more delays farther on. Some are bound to come. Depends how long we have to hold up for him, how little leeway'll be left. I'm not aiming, though," he said, "to hold up overlong. When he mends, if he does, we'll get on. Suard can stay with him and bring him on when he can travel." He swung about to Judith. "And now, my girl, I'll have the story of why you were so far from camp."

She had been burning the discarded bloody strips of sheet and packing her satchel again. The tone of his voice, stern, vexed, irritated, made her stand and face him. She felt guilty about it, but she told him without hesitation what she had done and why. She kept back only the eyes in the bushes and as she deliberately withheld that she knew she would not now tell anyone, not even Parley. It was too shameful and she could not bear for another living soul to know.

"I asked Jesse to tell you not to go into the woods," Johnny said, when she had finished.

"He told me," she said, "and I didn't go into the woods, Johnny. I only went to the creek."

"Same thing. What I meant was for you to stay in camp."

"Then why didn't you say what you meant?" she flared. "And why didn't you say *why* I was to stay in camp? I'm not a child!"

"Act like one. Think your judgment is better . . ."

"I don't! Jesse didn't say why . . ."

"Didn't need to."

"I suppose you told him *not* to say there were bears . . ."

"Sure."

From the corner of her eye she saw that Parley Wade had come up, but suddenly more angry than she knew she could be, shaking with anger, she set the satchel on a stump and whirled on Johnny. "We may as well have this out right now! There are going to be dangers on this journey. This is just the first of them and mercifully no harm was done to me. I know what's bothering you and I know I'm a woman and I know you want to take care for me. But say so! Whatever I am, I'm making this journey. Don't try to play ring-around-the-rosy with me! Don't treat me as if I were an idiot! If I'm strong enough to make this journey with you, I'm strong enough to know what's in your mind and what the dangers are. I'll fare better and you'll be less uneasy if you *tell* me, Johnny. But don't try giving me orders as if I were ten years old. I might have been killed by a bear today because you just don't talk! You act as if nobody had any sense but you!"

"And you are acting," he said dryly, "hysterical. Since you want to get things clear and have things out, remember this. I give the orders on this train and you'll obey same as the men. Is that clear enough?"

She stared at him unbelievingly. He had never spoken to her so sternly before. And he meant it, he meant it. But she was too angry to heed. "If I don't?"

"Then, by God, you'll go home. Right now!" He was suddenly as toweringly angry as she was. "I'll send you back tonight, understand?"

Her hands fumbled as she picked up the satchel but she made her voice coldly steady. "Very well. I'm ready to go. I'm not one of your hired hands. I'm your wife and if you haven't any confidence in me I'm not prepared to go one step further. Good night."

He watched her march to the wagon and wondered that someone as small as she could suddenly look so tall. He swung about and glared at Jesse Cooper and Parley Wade. "What the hell do you do with a woman like that?"

"Give thanks to God for her," Jesse said, shortly.

"Whomp her," Parley said, chuckling. "Woman gits too big fer her britches ain't nothin' to do but whomp her. 'S whut I do with my woman."

"There's not," Jesse Cooper said slowly, staring at Parley, "not much comparison, is there?" Then he turned quickly and walked away.

Parley watched him, scratching his beard. "Now, whut in Sam Hill's wrong with *him*? Don't he know joshin' when he sees it? God damn, he ort to know if you ever laid a finger on Judy I'd whomp the livin' daylights out of you."

Johnny rubbed the back of his neck. The muscles felt stiff and sore and there was a small headache forming at the base of his skull. Absently he said, "He'll be all right. Little upset, I reckon. Seeing a man clawed up by a bear's right new to him."

Parley batted his hat brim back and blinked, spat tobacco juice and hitched up his pants. "Better git the jug out, Johnny. Hit's gonna be a long night settin' up with this feller."

9

H E DID NOT send her home, of course. Instead they made their peace.

When his vexation and anger died away he went to her and haltingly spoke the words that eased her hurt. Seeing tearstains on her face he wondered ruefully what other men did with rebellious wives. He had handled her before but then she was not his beloved burden. It was his right, then, to walk away. He no longer had that right, and she was so brave and she was so willing and she was so uncomplaining. And maybe he ought to have explained and maybe he ought to explain more, but it came so hard and new to him. He hadn't ever owed explanations to anybody before.

He couldn't help feeling she ought to be willing to take his word. He wasn't an unreasonable man, she knew that—or she ought to know it. Some of this he said.

"I can't read your mind, Johnny. Sometimes, if you'll tell me . . ." Her mouth looked so soft and tender and sweet, and as she tried to smile the little crooked tooth, almost the first thing he had ever noticed about her, showed. He moved his big shoulders restlessly, as if the shirt bound them. He grinned wryly. "I guess I'm still new at being a husband. Don't know how to treat a wife. Reckon you'll have to be patient."

She flung herself into his arms. "Johnny! Don't let me be a bother. I'll not be a nuisance, I promise. I'll not. But don't let's ever quarrel again. Please, not. The whole bottom falls out of my world when you're angry with me."

"What do you think happens to mine?" He soothed her. "We'll not. Not any more. Hard words are something we can't *ever* afford."

They talked together for an hour, a quiet, good hour when he told her much that was on his mind—the load it was to be responsible for every human being hired on for this venture, every piece of property, the risks taken with all the money he had in the world and a great sum borrowed, invested in the train. He told her he did feel bad about Vance being hurt but he had to think, too, what effect a long delay would have on the general plans. Some of the men, most of them, meant to trap this winter. Part of his job was to get them west soon enough they could find the parks and streams and be settled in before freeze-up. He said how it was that there were only a few with the train he didn't have to nurse along. Talking slowly, almost as though he was thinking aloud, mulling things over, he said Jesse could be trusted and Parley, and to do his own job, Asa Baldwin. The Negro, Legette, was a stout man, and for tending the stock Manuel did fine. But the others, he shook his head, "You've got to spell out everything. Like today. I told 'em, warned 'em, but I reckon I oughtn't to've turned 'em loose in the woods without somebody along."

"They have to learn, Johnny." The immense hollow inside her was filled, now, and she wanted yearningly to be of comfort to him, to help him, to drain nothing of his strength away by fret and worry over her. She vowed she would do her part, let him put her, at least, out of his mind. It was too much to worry about his wife, too. He mustn't.

"Yes," he said, "they've got to learn. I can't cosset 'em like young'uns." He stretched wearily. "Lord, I'm as limp as a last year's cornstalk."

"Sleep," she said, eagerly throwing the blanket down. "Sleep a while. I'll watch with Parley."

But they had to call him within an hour. As the opiate wore off Vance became restless, though not conscious, and it was plain that he was in delirium and once more fleeing from the bear. His screams waked the whole camp and two men were needed to hold him down. He appeared to be in pain only from the head wounds, for he kept clutching his head and moaning and, threshing about, he repeatedly raked the bandages on his back against the blanket slipping them out of place.

All the men not on guard gathered about and Johnny let them. Sleep was impossible and there was some comfort, he knew, in letting them see for themselves what the commotion was about. He was glad he had because it wasn't long before they were needed. So great was the wounded man's strength in his seizures that two men were quickly worn out trying to hold him and had to be relieved. Trice could handle him longer than anybody but as the night wore on even his bull-like strength began to wane. "I never seen nobody heave as quick and powerful," he said, coming to the fire and rubbing his arms. "He keeps this up, Cap'n, there ain't nothing to do but tie him. We'll all be give out."

Judith poured coffee for Trice but she spoke to Johnny. "Why not give him another pill?"

"He's not hurting. He's just having these nightmares."

"He ought to be kept quiet, Johnny."

He looked at her quickly. "Brain fever?"

She nodded.

"All right. Get the pills. Trice—Jesse, I'll need both of you."

It was appalling to watch the thin little man, who couldn't have weighed more than a hundred and ten pounds, struggle against them. Jesse Cooper held his feet and did it only by sitting on them. Trice had to straddle his middle and by sheer weight keep the skinny, birdlike body from lunging. When Judith bent to give Johnny the pill a flailing arm, twitched loose suddenly, struck it from her hand and she had to fumble to find it while Johnny clutched the arms and hands again. "Two more," he bellowed, "to hold his head. When they have a good grip, Judith, cram the pill in quick."

She knelt, the tablet ready, a cup of water to follow it. The men holding the poor, ceaselessly moving head were too gentle, too afraid of hurting. "You'll have to be cruel," she told them, "you'll have to forget his wounds."

Grimly they took hold and held tightly. But Vance's teeth were so clenched she could not force the tablet between them. Half a dozen times she tried but the jaws wouldn't open. They were clamped like a vise. "Hurry, ma'am," one of the men at the head said, "this bandage is so bloody it's slipping."

"I can't," she said, fumbling with the pill. "Johnny, it will take somebody stronger . . ."

"Legette!"

"Here, sir. Yes, sir."

"Where've you been? I need you."

"On guard, sir. Just come off."

"I forgot. Make him take that pill, Legette."

"Yes, sir."

Judith handed it over and stood back.

The Negro straddled the injured man and slowly, relentlessly, his strong hands forced the clenched jaws apart, held them open and forced the tablet deep into the throat. "Water, ma'am, quick!"

Judith handed the cup and the black man poured it in a flood into Vance's mouth. He choked, gurgled, spit some of it up, but he swallowed enough to take the pill down. "There," Legette said, suddenly gentle and tender, "there, now, sir, just lie still. Forget the bear and the bad dreams. It will be better, now. The pain will be better. Just lie still, sir, just lie still. Sleep. Sleep. Sleep like a baby, sir. Friends are with you. Friends will care for you. Just sleep. Forget the bear. Forget the nightmare. Forget the pain. The pain will go away now. The pain will disappear. All will be done for you that can be done. Nothing is as bad as your dreams. Sleep, now. Sleep, sir. Sleep."

The words were as soporific as the drug, soft, slumbrous words murmured and repeated. The black hands that soothed and smoothed and rubbed and quieted were gentle. As the Negro stayed by, talking and soothing, keeping the fretful hands quiet, easing the convulsive jerks, the drug began to work and soon no one was needed to hold down the twitching legs or the restless shoulders. Vance slept.

The men, watching, sighed and slumped and began to melt away to find their own beds.

Johnny touched the black man's shoulder. "Legette, thank you."

"Nothing, sir. I am only glad he sleeps and rests from his pain."

Vance was conscious the next morning and though he was suffering he no longer threshed about in the nightmare of delirium. He lay quietly bearing his pain. Judith fed him hot tea and broth and then, making no trouble, he took another pill and slept away the day.

The men made work to occupy their time. Judith slept a little.

When she woke, around noon, the camp was quiet and the men had scattered. Only Parley was present. He sat slumped against a log, dozing near the sick man. He wakened when he heard her moving about.

"How is he?" she asked, pouring herself a mug of coffee.

"Asleep yet." Parley pushed himself up and stretched and yawned, twitched his shoulders and grimaced. "Gittin' old. Plumb stiff. Pour me a cup, will ya, honey?"

She handed it to him and pulled up her campstool. Parley leaned loosely against a tree.

She felt stiff and sore herself. Too much had happened yesterday and she'd had too little sleep. She sighed. "Will Vance pull through, Parley?"

"Mebbe," he said, shrugging away from the tree. He guzzled down his coffee and dashed the dregs on the ground. "I've seed men hurt worse make it fine. Seed men not hurt as bad die. No good reason either way. Jist depends, an' they ain't no way of tellin'. He's doin' as good as he could right now."

"I suppose we'll have to be satisfied with that. But it's too bad, Parley. If we're delayed long . . ."

"Jist have to lay up, that's all. You wearyin' 'bout Johnny's luck, don't. Ye do too much of that."

She sat up straight. "I do not!"

"Let him do the wearyin'. Hit's his job. Jist see you don't weary him none."

"Well!" she exploded, starting to rise.

He stayed her with his hand. "That leetle piece o' bizness yestiddy, fer instance. An' them strong words last night." He eyed her shrewdly. "Know whut's wrong with you?"

"There's not one thing wrong with me. Johnny and I . . ."

"I seen it. An' I heared it. An' I know he follered an' spoke sweet words to ye. Whut I'm sayin' is he ortent to had to. You got gumption. You know he's got things on his mind. Don't lay no more on fer him."

"Just to satisfy you," she snapped, "and not that it's any of your concern, I've already . . ."

"Shore," he interrupted, "when ye've had her say an' eased yer temper." He stopped and grinned at her. "All's wrong with ye, though," he went on, his voice softer, "is ye're a *leetle* mite trip-sick."

"I've told you, there's nothing wrong with me."

He ignored her. "Hits ever'body, some. An' it ain't a natural way of livin' fer a woman, though I never seed nobody do finer'n you. But it's hitchin' up ever' day an' ridin' on. Ain't no place fer a woman to put her belongin's . . . makin' out with a campfire . . . beddin' down nights in a wagon. Man makes out purty good on the trail. Free an' good fer him. But it goes ag'in the grain fer a woman. Woman wants four walls around her an' her own bed at night . . . things nice to cook with an' to keep herself clean. Hit's her nature an' she cain't he'p it. Reckon it hits her, like it done you yestiddy, she's jist *got* to git her washin' done an' git herself clean. A body as tidy as you is bound to think so. Trouble is . . ."

"The trouble is," Judith said angrily, "you're a nosy old busybody and I'll thank you to keep out of my affairs." The anger came because her eyes were suddenly moist with tears. He was a kindly old man. He meant well. But he hit hard at the truth and no better than most she didn't like to be exposed. She scrubbed at her eyes.

"Go on an' cry," he said.

"I'm not crying. There's something in my eye."

"Shore. Gimme yer hankcher."

He squatted in front of her and peered and wiped with the big, white square. "Cain't see e'er thing."

She studied him carefully, then she grinned and gave him a shove that sent him toppling backward. "You smell like a polecat. Why don't *you* take a bath?"

He scrambled up, laughing cheerfully. "Be the death of me. Where ye goin'?"

She was swishing purposefully away. "To iron my clean dresses, that

I took such a notion to wash yesterday, all because I was just a *leetle* mite trip-sick!"

Grinning foolishly Parley watched her mount the wagon steps. She was a minx, that one, a real minx. Took a smarter man than old Parley Wade to flummox her. She stuck her head out, raising the side canvas near him. "I almost forgot. Here's something I want you to see."

She handed him the *Gazette,* folded to the notice about the runaway slave. She gave him time to read it. Then she said, "I don't think Johnny's seen this. Ought I to show it to him?"

Parley handed back the paper. "He's seen it. Seen it 'fore we left out. Didn't bother him none."

"Oh. Well. I wondered." She gazed at the old man thoughtfully. "He's not worried about somebody following?"

"Nope. Nary bit. 'Twouldn't be sensible. Don't mind sayin', though," his grin was mischievous, "hit was the reason we left a week early."

"I see. He didn't tell me . . ."

"He don't tell nobody ever'thing he knows. Make do with that, Judy. Jist put that paper away, or burn it. Fergit ye've seed that notice."

All right, she thought, lowering the canvas, I will. She laid the paper in the trunk. I'll burn it first chance I get. It was a relief to know that Johnny knew.

Late in the afternoon she went to change Vance's bandages. She was pleased to see that his back showed improvement, but she was horrified when she took the wrappings from his head and she ran for Johnny at once. She kept her voice down but what she had seen had been dreadful. "His brains are oozing out," she said. "He was right, Johnny. The bear did crush his skull. He said he felt the teeth crack it, remember? He was right. The brains are oozing through."

"They can't be, Judith, Parley brought the head in and the bear was so old half his teeth were missing."

She clutched his shirtfront. "But they are!"

Johnny walked with her. "Probably pus or matter."

"It isn't! The man's brains are seeping out!"

There was no mistaking what was oozing from the toothmarks. The old gap-toothed jaws had sunk deep, far deeper than any of them had realized. A gray viscous matter was spreading slowly from the wounds. As they watched, Vance sighed and opened his eyes. He fixed them on Judith. "Ma'am, will you write to my mother?"

She started. "Why, yes, Vance. But you can write to her yourself, later . . ." Her voice dwindled away.

"No, ma'am, I ain't gonna git well enough to write. I never married, but my old mother will be worried. Tell her how I died."

Judith felt inexpressibly sad. "Vance, you mustn't give up hope."

The wounded head moved wearily. "No, ma'am. There ain't no hope. I knowed from the time he caught me I was a goner. I felt his teeth crackin' my skull. Write my mother. And tell Trice," he raised up unexpectedly on one elbow, "tell Trice he is to have my rifle."

"Yes, Vance," Johnny said, "we understand. Trice will have your rifle."

Letting himself down, the man kept his eyes on Johnny. "I am sorry about the Deep Fork, sir. I didn't mean to make trouble. I've allus been skeered of water."

"No matter, Vance. No matter at all."

Vance grinned crookedly. "I learnt to swim, didn't I?"

Johnny's mouth twisted into an answering grin. "You sure did, Vance. You learned to swim."

The man's eyes wandered. "I'd of liked to finish the journey. I'd of liked to see Santy Fee and them mountains. Ain't ever traveled much. That was why I joined up. Allus had a hankerin' to see them mountains. Wish I could of glimpsed a sight of them. I would of died easier. I would of died easier."

His hands picked fretfully at the blanket. Judith bent over him. "Vance, don't give up. Don't give up."

But he couldn't hear her now. His mind went into its dark recesses and he mumbled weakly, "Ain't never had no luck. Not ever. Ain't had no luck in all my life."

Johnny raised Judith up. "Come away."

She rested against his chest. "I can't bear it. He's such a pitiful, scrawny little man. And to die away out here. Never any luck."

"It's no use."

She pulled away from him. "We have to try. Get hot water, quickly."

She bathed the man, his face and hands and arms and his body and his legs, rubbing him, trying to keep the life in him. When she grew weary, Legette spelled her. Trice spelled him. Jesse spelled Trice. Johnny spelled Jesse. Caught by the fire of Judith's determination none of them gave up. They did everything they knew to do. All night they worked over him. They bathed him and rubbed; they put hot stones to his feet; they put cold rags to his head; they forced whisky down him. Judith tried poultices to stop the oozing and the men gathered about, as they had done the night before, willing to help, offering to help, needing to help. The whole camp centered about Vance's pallet. Nothing in the world existed for them but him. Every thought was for him, every effort in his behalf. Twenty men and one woman stopped time to try to snatch back from death one life. And failed.

At daylight he died.

There was no warning. The chest was rising and falling as it had done all night, no weaker, no less sustained. There was only a sudden choking, a rattle and gurgle, a long, deep breath held and never let loose. Judith was at his head. Johnny was working over the chest, rubbing. Legette was stroking one leg and Trice was rubbing the other. They all waited, their hands stopped, for the caught breath to sigh out. A trickle of bear oil Johnny had been using on his palms ran down the chest and he wiped at it. As if his touch had caused it, the chest collapsed and that was all. Judith went limp. "He's gone. He's dead."

They had tried so hard, but the bear had had his way. Vance was dead. They covered him with his blanket and went away to sleep, exhausted.

They buried him on the North Fork of the Canadian, the first casualty of their westing.

No man said what it meant to him or what it did to him, and there was no way of knowing how it affected any man. They gathered, gravely, about the open pit and consigned him to the earth. No one wept. No one sighed. But all were somber and grave. One of their own had given his life as a first expense of this crossing. Not one man gathered about that dark pit could have failed to feel it yawning for him, Judith thought, watching their faces. Precarious enough at any time, in any place, the thin line of life was stretched a little thinner, and each man was a little diminished by this man's death.

Johnny read the service from Judith's Bible. At its conclusion, on impulse, Judith started up a hymn in which, at first, no one joined. The men shuffled awkwardly, looking at her then at each other, not knowing what to do. Then old Parley lifted a quavering tenor and the rich bass of the black man joined in. Johnny, completely voiceless, stood with his eyes fixed on the blanketed figure, the hooded lids hiding whatever responsible sadness he felt, whatever personal sternness with himself. But his mouth was a drawn line and Judith thought he took on himself the blame for this death. Luckless Vance knew no better than to join a wagon train going west, but Johnny Fowler ought not to have let him.

The hymn died away. The grave was filled and mounded. Then Johnny announced that the train would not move until the next day. "In keeping with the custom of this country," he concluded, "an auction of the dead man's effects will be held this afternoon, save for his rifle which he wished Mr. Trice to have."

It was not possible to tell how much of heart or sentiment went into the purchases. In Judith's ledger, which kept a fair account of the journey, she made only the entry:

> Held today, an auction of the effects of one Tig Vance, killed by a black bear in the Cross Timbers. The captain has marked down to the debit of the men listed the following items, to be deducted from their wages at the end of the journey. To wit:
>
> One short rifle, gratis, to Bullitt Trice, as per the dead man's
> request, at worth $15.00
> One musket barrel, to Ben Spring 5.00
> One blanket to Wash Craig 10.00
> 2 vests to Legette, black man 2.00
> Sundry small articles to Jesse Cooper 1.75

That was all Tig Vance possessed and it was valued at a paltry $33.75. But who was to say what his dreams were worth? Who could put a value on his wish to see the western mountains? Given small courage, given a small frame, given, even, a small brain and no luck, how much was a man's soul worth? Granted he had panicked at the Deep Fork. Granted he was foolish to fire his gun at the black bear. Granted he was little and of not much account and troublesome. What was the spirit of any man worth? Had he lived would Tig Vance have overcome his panic and his lack of judgment and his cowardice? Would his soul have grown to match the mountains he wanted to see? There was no telling. By the small act of circumstance, by the little act of firing off his gun too soon, the future was forever veiled in the past. No one would ever know.

Judith helped Jesse Cooper stow the small articles he had bought in a basket. Johnny, his unpleasant chore done, was already riding away. "What do you mean to do with these things, Jesse? Why did you buy them?" she asked.

"Don't know. Just seemed a good idea." His mouth twisted. "Here's a knife, and a piece of hide, and some things to mend with . . . what'll Jonathan do with the money?"

"Send it to his mother, I expect."

"Yes. Is there anything here ought to be sent to her, you reckon?"

Judith looked at the small heap. "What would it be?"

Jesse fingered over the things. "The knife, maybe?"

Judith shuddered. "Oh, no. No. Let Johnny send the money."

"It's best, I guess. He didn't collect much, did he?"

"No."

The auction had been held at the first wagon where Tig Vance had slept and where his few possessions were collected. Judith walked silently beside Jesse Cooper as they made their way down to her own camp. They stopped beside Jesse's wagon where he emptied the small trash and handed her the basket. "Judith . . . I didn't like to hear Jonathan speak to you so the other night. He oughtn't to . . ."

Her hands closed over the basket handle. "It's no matter, Jesse."

He spoke more strongly. "It does matter. A man's not called on to use such words to his wife."

"I've forgotten them," she said.

"I've not."

There was a strain and a tension in his voice which caught her attention. She smiled at him. "Husbands and wives do have words, Jesse. It was unfortunate that we forgot ourselves in front of you and Parley."

"But he accused you unfairly . . ."

"No. I worried him unfairly. The fault was mine."

"I don't see it that way. He ought to have warned you . . . if I'd known . . . he said it might frighten you to know there were bears . . ."

Judith's head went up. "He was right. It would have frightened me."

"He ought to have told you," he said stubbornly.

"I ought to have obeyed."

"Jonathan has changed since I knew him . . ."

"He suits me as he is," she said brightly. "Put it out of your mind, Jesse. I don't need your sympathy."

He stood aside to let her pass. "If you ever do, Judith . . ."

"I won't. Good day, Jesse."

They moved on at daybreak the next morning and listening to the shouts and the curses and the laughter and the hubbub and uproar, Judith thought how quickly the most solemn moments are put behind. These men had done what they could for Tig Vance. They had worked over him faithfully as long as he lasted. Dead, they had given him a decent burial. But this morning it was as though he had never existed. Briefly he had been one of them. Now the necessity of moving on, the urgency of rolling wheels, had thrust him from their minds. He had lived—he was dead. It was that simple.

She saw not one man visit the grave before they pulled out, and looking back at the lonely cairn she herself felt a sense of fate in the occurrence. It was an achingly relentless land. There was no room for weaklings and the faint-hearted. They were culled by this accident or that, made usually of their own folly. Only the strong, perhaps the ruthess, could ever inherit this strong, ruthless land. No, she did not much think Tig Vance would ever have reached the mountains. He was too gifted with footless foolishness. If it hadn't been the black bear in the Timbers, it would have been a flood on the Washita, thirst and sun on the plains, losing his way in the desert, or a lonely, chance encounter with a hostile Indian. He would have blundered constantly, and how many times could he have been rescued and saved? She set her face forward and took up her own necessity, to ride, horse or wagon, the distance for the day.

She saw Pete Shelley, the drover, approach her husband; saw Johnny's head incline, listening, then shake.

When he came beside her later he said, "Shelley wants to turn back."

"Why?"

"Says he's ailing."

"What did you say?"

Johnny flicked his horse ahead. "Told him nobody could turn back now."

Nor could she. Nor did she want to. The wheels rolled on, and with every mile they neared the Spanish town that was their goal.

IO

THE DAYRISE was slow and sweet-smelling and as innocent as a child's clean face. Judith sat on the step of the wagon and watched its coming.

The land at first was only a loom in the darkness, dim and vague and shapeless and formless, a sense of pulse and deep breathings and distance, felt but still unseen.

So gently did the night leave that each slow-shaping feature was born lonelily and for a time stood forth in its loneliness. In the beginning there was only the darker darkness beneath the shine of stars. Then, like a low cloud, a bulk of distant timber heaved away from the bleach and stood massed solidly, a brooding, textureless clot against the sky-pale.

Slowly, very slowly, the light rose. Now the earth itself began to take on form. The grassed swale around the creek became the oval of the camp and as the night slipped away there swelled up from the floor of the valley long riches of flowered grassland, rumples of low ridges, crests of rock, troughed ribs of gullies and stripes of sandy wastes.

The sky-pale rose and swallowed the last of the stars and the bulk of timber became a spine of trunks and sprockets and feathered spires of trees.

Judith leaned against the tailrib of the wagon and felt hungry and a little sad and cool and rested and at peace.

The strongest sense now was the sense of smell. They were unweighted and fresh odors. Dust, laid by the dew. Grass, crushed by the wheels. Spring flowers trampled by the stock. There was a minty smell—betony? And the faintest smell of sour—cress, in the creek?

He had said it would be like this.

Yesterday, the last hard day in the Timbers, Johnny had promised her this lovely valley. "It's a long rich piece lying between the North Fork and the Canadian, with high grass and good trees and dozens of springs and creeks all full of trout and perch and bream. It's the prettiest lie of land I ever saw, the richest in the country. And there's game." He had smiled at her. "It's a restful, peaceful place."

She had been so weary she was dull. "Are you sure?"

"I've spent many a camp there."

"Are you sure we will reach it today?"

He touched her hand. "Certain. I promise you will sleep in that valley tonight."

In the middle of the afternoon they had come out of the Timbers.

They were all, she thought, lunatic with joy at being out of that dark prison. No one could know how two weeks of its gloom would affect the mind and the senses. Especially when it had been believed, as she believed and the hands believed, they were through with it at the North Fork. Johnny had known different, and old Parley, and the Indians, but they hadn't said there was more and worse. The very day they had driven away from Tig Vance's new grave they had been plunged into all the old difficulties again and uneasiness and foreboding companioned the train.

The men grumbled. "Thought when we hit the North Fork our troubles'd be over."

"Thought there'd be a road along the bank."

"Thought it was plain sailing up the river."

The river was there and they followed it, but the banks were crossed with ridges and gashed with ravines and sponged with swamps. The wagons jounced and shook loose their parts on the ridges. They had to be unloaded and roped down the ravines, then hauled up the far sides and loaded again. They bogged in the swamps and mired in the quicksands. Occasionally there was a good, clean, hard, level road, but it never lasted far, a mile or two at most. And often they were pushed deep into the Timbers because of the mazes of drift washed up by old floods. They inched forward so slowly.

There was one nightmare of a day when they moved only two short miles and it had taken every mule they had to haul the four wagons that far. That night Judith said, "Did you know it would be so bad, Johnny?"

She had stewed some dried apples, as much to lift her spirits as to tempt their appetites. He cleaned his plate before replying. "I knew it might. I hoped it wouldn't be."

"Will we get through?" She was ashamed for asking, but the road was so bad, the work so hard, the progress so slow, she felt a shaken need for reassurance.

He looked at her, surprised. "Sure. Sure. You've got doubts?"

"I don't know. Not really, but . . . it's so much worse . . ."

"Takes time," he said, "but we've not come to anything there's not a way around or over or under. Troublesome, that's all."

"What if it gets worse?"

"It won't." He grinned. "Can't. Look, honey, you don't think I'd have started wagons through here if I didn't know I could get 'em through, do you?"

Her loyalty and faith answered instantly. "Of course not."

"I've been through here many a time," he reminded her.

"Oh, Johnny, I'm just tired. Pay no heed to me. It's the gloom, and the hands grumbling, and . . . two miles . . . only two miles today!"

He had been filling his pipe as they talked and he lit it now, squinting at her through its smoke. "I was right proud of that two miles," he said. "Would have been satisfied with half."

She gazed at him, too astonished to speak. Then she laughed, the small crooked tooth flashing. She felt immensely better, somehow. Her spirits lifted. She had felt so downcast over two miles. Johnny had been pleased. Her gauge had been fifteen miles on level land. Johnny's had been what was possible over impossible surface. It made a difference.

Jesse Cooper had loomed into the light then and looking up at him from his log Johnny had said, "Something on your mind, Jesse? Sit down."

Jesse had glanced at her and sat, taking out his knife and picking up a twig to whittle. "Ben Spring," he said, "has come down sick."

Johnny took his pipe from between his teeth. "What with?"

There was again a quick look at Judith. The knife snicked against the dry wood. "Well, it's a . . . it's a kind of a flux."

"Bloody?" Johnny's voice was sharp and Judith's own nerves tightened up.

"Well . . . no. Figure he's just et too much game meat." Jesse's voice was very low and he kept his head bent.

"What are you mumbling about? Has he just got the trots or is he bad sick?"

Jesse cleared his throat and mumbled again, but Johnny laughed and settled back against his tree trunk. "For God's sake, Jesse, you had me scared. The bloody flux'd run through this train like a fuse of powder that'd been sparked. Be about the worse thing could happen to us. But the trots is just inconvenient. Been eating a right smart of game meat, you say?"

Jesse nodded. "All of 'em has been. Change from salt pork."

"Yes. Well, I don't reckon it sets good on him. Some, it don't. Let him ride a wagon a few days. When we hit buffalo a bait of good hump'll put him right and Judith's got some powders that'll ease him a little till then."

"Goldenseal root," she said and stood immediately. "You want me to dose him, Johnny?"

Johnny took his pipe out of his mouth and grinned slowly. "Better let Jesse, honey. Man don't much like a woman biding near when he's got a flux of the bowels."

It was nothing, only the slightly coarse but easy thing a man might comfortably say to his wife about something innately gross but a little funny, too, and she laughed. It surprised her that Jesse didn't join in. Instead his face went splotchily red and his look toward her was imploring. It dawned on her that he was embarrassed. For her sake he was embarrassed. This whole conversation had embarrassed him, because of her. Oh, for heaven's sake . . . A kindly impulse made her say, lightly, "If I don't mind, why should he? I've tended more flux than Ben Spring ever saw."

Johnny said, proudly, "Judith is a herbwoman."

Jesse Cooper's face paled and he took in a deep breath. "I didn't know. But I'll tend him, Judith."

When she returned with the cachets of goldenseal root they were talking about mules. "Have to turn four loose in the morning," Jesse was saying. "They've gone lame."

"First Indians we meet," Johnny said, "I've got to do some swapping. We'll lose plenty before we're out of these woods."

"You counted on it, then?"

"Sure. Had to. But we'll meet up with a band of Comanches or Kiowas other side of the Timbers. They'll have mules. These four gaunted, Jesse, well as lame?"

"Some."

"If they can stay on their feet and pull, Jesse, better hang on to 'em. Only mule I'm ready to turn loose is one can't get up when he's down."

Jesse flicked him a look. "That's punishing, Jonathan."

"We'll be punished if we run short of mules before we meet the Indians."

"It ain't human," Jesse said stubbornly.

"They ain't human, either. It's us or them, Jesse."

Jesse's mouth had become a thin line.

Judith had been waiting till they finished but she decided to interrupt. She stepped into the light and handed Jesse the medicine. "Stir it in a spoon of molasses, Jesse, and have him swallow it down."

Jesse fingered the folded papers of medicine. "All right. Pete Shelley wants to talk to you," he said to Johnny.

Judith saw a muscle in Johnny's jaw tighten. "Send him along. You'll remember about the mules, Jesse?"

"I'll remember."

Judith dug her knitting from her pocket. "What ails him, Johnny?" she said when Jesse was out of hearing.

Johnny puffed a last time and knocked the dottle from the pipe bowl. "Dunno. He's not like I remember."

"He said the same about you."

Johnny flicked a look her way. "He did?" He tapped the empty pipe bowl in his palm, reflecting. "Reckon we've both changed some. Ought to've thought of that. Been fifteen years. Well," he added, putting the pipe in his pocket, "here comes Shelley. More trouble."

Pete Shelley was tall and lean, droop-shouldered and droop-faced. All his features hung downward, as if listing. He wore clothing too big for him which hung about him, torn and flapping, adding to the look of droop and drape. He slouched up to the fire and Johnny stood to talk to him. "What's your trouble, Shelley?"

The man's voice was a whine. "Cap'n, I hate to tell you, but I jist cain't go no further. I jist cain't keep up. I know I signed on but I'd jist be a drag to ye . . . jist hold ye back."

Johnny's voice was as cold as the ice on the Verdigris in January. "Nobody's going to hold me back. You getting cold feet?"

"It ain't that, no, sir. I'd be the eagerest to go on if I could. But I got the rheumatiz in my laigs an' shoulders, an' a misery in the back so's I c'n hardly sleep of a night. Don't b'lieve sleepin' on the ground is good fer me. An' I got a weak stummick, too. The grub don't agree with me."

"You eat enough. Nothing weak about your appetite."

"Don't seem like it does me no good, though. A man's got to eat to keep up his stren'th. But you wouldn't b'lieve it, Cap'n, how bad the pains is when I've et. Jist wretch me. Don't hardly see how I c'n make out to stand 'em no longer." The voice was as shambling as the man, slow and whiny but dreadfully insistent.

"What do you propose to do?"

"Well, I've give it a lot of thought . . ."

Johnny cut in. "I'll bet you have. I'll bet you've laid awake nights giving it thought. How you can turn back." His cold scorn lashed at the man. "Who's going to do your job? Who's going to drive the pack mules? You hired on to do that."

"There's them that could be spared," the man said, droning on. "I know I hired on, an' I meant well, Cap'n. A body don't know whut's goin' to happen to him. I don't rightly see how I c'n go on, but I feel beholdin' an' I've did the best I could to figger what would be right."

Johnny snorted. "What would be right is to keep to your bargain."

"Yessir, but, I'm owed a month's pay, wouldn't ye say? If it'd be agreeable, I'd be willin' to take it in a good horse an' gun an' jist fergit my end of the bargain if you'd fergit yore'n. I do believe I ort to turn back, sir. I shorely do. Way I feel, an' if it gits worse, which it likely will, I couldn't be no real he'p to ye. Like I said, I'd jist be a drag."

Johnny's hand chopped down. "You aren't owed anything yet. The bargain is you get paid in full when we reach Santa Fe. Same bargain as the others. You're no different."

The slow eyes lifted and the slow voice whined on. "A mule, then, sir? Jist one wore-out mule? An' a gun? I'd jist have to have a gun."

"Nothing," Johnny said, "not a damned thing. You don't get nothing from me unless you go all the way to Santa Fe." He was so angry Judith saw his hands shaking and she thought he would surely throttle the man. But he controlled himself, only his voice rising to the upper register giving him away. "And recollect this, Shelley. You don't keep up you'll be left, afoot and *without* a gun. That's certain death in this country."

"Ah, Cap'n, ye're hard . . . ye're hard."

"I've got to be. There are too many like you. Get back to your camp."

But Shelley didn't give up easily. He was like a ball of dough. You could punch and it would give, but it rose back up again. From that night he grew droopier and droopier. He groaned and complained, he fell, he stumbled, he cut his hand and couldn't haul on the wheel of a bogged wagon, his heel blistered and he limped when he walked. Slowly he won the sympathy of the hands. When Ben Spring came down with the flux the captain sent him to the wagon. But he didn't like Shelley and he abused him. "That black man could drive the pack mules," they said. "A man with as much misery as Shelley ought to be let turn back. The captain don't like him."

"He plays favorites."

"He's got it in for ole Pete."

"What can you expect? He don't like nobody don't haul their guts out for him."

"Ben Spring got next to 'im."

"He don't like Pete."

Judith thought of all the men as she watched the dayrise mount. The Timbers crossing had been a hard test of all of them. Few had been unaffected by the long gloomy time. It had been almost worse than the road to watch their slow silencing, the growth of their weariness, the leak of darkness and doubt into their minds. Except for Bullitt Trice, who remained as granitic, as bulking, as bruising, as durable and impervious as ever, the others had manifested some inner uneasiness which showed up in irritability or sullenness, in staring inattention and general loss of energy. Some had stood it better than others but there were none, save Johnny and Parley and Bullitt Trice and the Indians, who hadn't been a little affected. Oh, she had learned these men during that dark fourteen days of the Timbers. She knew now where each belonged and she knew something of the kind of man he was. The Timbers had taught her.

The light began to penetrate the green glade with a pale, sea-water shine, and as the white tilts of the wagons loomed like bleached mounds, she thought of the men sleeping like wheel spokes around the hub of their embered fires. Little of the light reached down to them and they were yet only dark rounds, feet to the ashes, heads wrapped against the damp.

Apart from her own wagon, but next to it, was Jesse Cooper's. In his crew was Nathaniel Butler. He was a heavy, shaggy, straw-haired man with a pocked, doughy face. He was a strong man and unvocal, seeming dull and a little stupid until you saw his eyes. They were quick with intelligence. It was a native intelligence, because he could neither read nor write. He was taciturn to the point of sullenness and he was what the men called a "loner." He never sought out anybody and he appeared to have no need for companionship. Johnny said he talked to his mules. Nate, he said, thought mules had more sense than people. He was not one of the grumblers but he didn't like the hard way Johnny used the mules.

Also with Jesse was a limber switch of a boy, the youngest man with the train. His papers said he was twenty years old. He had red hair and freckles, pale eyes, pimples on his chin and a liking for using his trigger finger. He had signed on as a hand and he had fallen heir to so many chores that he went sulky the first week. He had the curiously nice-sounding name of Hull Archer. He had a bad case of hero worship for Bullitt Trice. Trice could get any amount of work out of the boy but he was morose away from his idol.

When he bedded with the train, the halfbreed hunter, Ba'tiste, was with Jesse's crew also. It happened so seldom that it was always a surprise to find him in camp.

And finally, with Jesse, there was the Irishman, O'Toole, who gave no trouble, sad or merry. His spirits rose and fell like the tides but if he gloomed or sang he did his part.

The wagon parked beyond Jesse Cooper's was Asa Baldwin's. The man Shelley fed and bedded there. The drivers were the two rough, tough-looking individuals, Wash Craig and Josh Brand. They were bearded, dirty, slouched and bullying, but they were competent muleskinners. In the Timbers they had been morose and sullen and muttering. Like Hull Archer they had become admirers of Bullitt Trice.

'Guste Suard, the nephew of Johnny's great good friend who had been killed in the Osage massacre at Turkey Creek, ate and slept at Asa's fire when he was in camp.

The lead wagon was Parley Wade's. Bullitt Trice was head driver and the invalid, Ben Spring, had been the other driver. When he came down with the flux a man so mousy looking, so inconsequential that he was easily overlooked and forgotten for whole days at a time, William Day, did a better than passing job of it. Tig Vance had belonged with Parley's crew and his death had left it one short.

Judith's eyes followed round to the dead ashes of their own fire. Here, there was herself, Johnny, Legette and Manuel. Of the whole train, she thought, theirs was the most uncomplicated camp, the most pleasant, the smoothest running and it was owed, largely, to the black man. If the Timbers had bothered Legette he had showed no signs of it. She thought it had something to do with his devotion to Johnny. Where Johnny Fowler led, the black man followed without question and in complete faith. It was enough for him that this man who had showed him kindness led.

But Manuel . . . ah, Manuel. In the Timbers Manuel had sorrowed to the point of sickness. His stomach refused food for days at a time and he grew thin and sallow. From some depth of will, however, he managed to forge on and do, capably, the work for which he was responsible. Retching and miserable he even continued to hear Judith's Spanish lessons each night. "Manuel," she had said, "it isn't necessary."

"But, sí, Señora. This is a sickness of the soul. It will pass. What is the word for governor, Señora?"

She remembered the night Bullitt Trice had visited their fire and Manuel had been lying with his blanket wrapped about his head. Trice had grinned wickedly. "Want to see some fun, boys?"

He lashed that long bullwhip across the blanket and Manuel came howling and screeching out of it.

Young Archer's whinny rose in appreciation. "Give it to him, Bull, give it to him!"

But Trice, slow in his pleasure, was still coiling in his whip when Johnny reached him. He caught the man by the shoulder and sent him sprawling. As Trice went down, Johnny jerked the long whip out of his hands. "By God," he said, and his voice was sizzling, "if you ever do a thing like that again, Trice, I'll take your own whip to you! Hear me? Don't you ever use this whip on anything but a mule!"

Trice fished for his hat, put it on, and dusted his hands on his pants. He looked at Manuel and touched the empty blanket roll with his boot. "He's gone granny," he said. "Little touch of the snake won't hurt him."

"I'll decide that," Johnny said. "And I'll do it without your help." Judith knew from the tight control of his voice how terribly angry he was. "Don't take the running of this train into your own hands, Trice."

Trice didn't truckle easily but he was stared down finally before a clutch of men who came running at the uproar. He held out his hand. "I'll thank you for my property, Captain."

"In the morning."

Trice widened his spraddle and bristled. "No man takes my whip . . ."

Johnny roared at him. "*I said in the morning, Trice!*"

Silence, heavy with tension, hung in the air as the men waited. This was a showdown between Bullitt Trice and the captain. Eyes shifted from the swart, blocky, bull-like muleskinner to the tall, taut leader of the train. If they fought, who'd be the best man? Faces were still, except for a tongue or two that licked out nervously. Was Trice going to call the captain's hand? They waited, and then they sighed as Trice backed down. The man shrugged as if it didn't matter. "You're the boss, Captain."

"Don't forget it again."

Trice walked away, laughing, rolling heavily in his swagger between the men who parted in a wave to let him pass. Johnny's hands worked on the whip, coiling it, but his eyes followed Trice. Parley watched the man, too. He said, softly, "He'll hate yore guts fer that."

"Yes." Johnny gave him the whip. "I don't like his much, either. Give it back to him in the morning."

Parley nodded, and Johnny strode away.

These, then, were the men of the wagon train and this was the way they were situated. It could have been better but it might have been worse, wayfaring men being what they were. They had come this far together and all had learned something, for better or for worse, of himself and his fellowman. She wished it might all have been for the better, but it was not. What was good and what was decent and what was generous in a man stood forth for all to see, but what was mean and what was deceitful and what was evil also stood forth in the public view. A wagon train, she thought, had all the parts of a village. There was the good, and there was the bad. There was the sublime, and there was the dregs. And mixed in every man was both, for no man was wholly good or wholly bad. He could rise to great heights or he could descend to the lowest depths, and nobody knew what he would do until his time of testing.

She put her thoughts away from her.

The rim of the sun crept above the horizon and the sky was stained red.

She was conscious, suddenly, of a tinkling, splashing sound which came from the narrow clear little creek. Curious, she climbed down from the wagon and followed the tiny chiming sound.

She found the creek boiling with fish, hundreds and hundreds and hundreds of fish, breaking water, leaping, skipping in some kind of wild excitement. She stood for a moment watching their silvery sides flashing in the early sun, stunned with pleasure and delight. Fish after fish broke the surface, and the water drowned back, a wet rainbow, across their arched backs and fins, making the tinkle she had heard. She was so absorbed she couldn't think; she could only stand and watch, her heart thudding, until, her excitement abated, she began to wonder. What was urging them? What was exciting them? What was driving them? She had never before seen such a school of fish. They were moving by leaps and swift finny flashes up the shallow, rock-bedded little creek as if harried by enemies on their tails. She did not even know what fish they were; she hadn't seen their kind before. The water was almost solid with them. She wondered where they had come from and where they were going and why there were so many.

A foot crunched the gravel behind her and Johnny said, in her ear, "Did you ever see anything like that before?"

"Never." She spoke as softly as he. "What are they, Johnny? And why are there so many?"

"Suckers," he said, "and they're shoaling to spawn. They're sure frenzied, aren't they?"

"They're wild!"

"I reckoned they'd be shoaling this morning. Saw flying ants around an old stump late yesterday. It's a pretty good sign. Used to watch for flying ants back home when I was a kid. First one saw 'em gave the word and we'd all light out for the river to see who could catch the first sucker."

"Shall I try to catch a mess for breakfast?" she asked.

"If you want," he said, "but they're not much good to eat. Too bony. Besides," he hesitated, "they're full of eggs."

"Oh."

"Kids are little rogues, you know," he said. "Never made any difference to us they were spawning. But I kind of hate to interfere with their instincts now." He put his arm about her and leaned his chin on the top of her head. "Sleep good last night?"

"Wonderful. Can we stay a few days? The valley is as pretty as you said."

He rumpled her hair. "Just a few. Wagons are shook a little and Asa's got to mend but then we'll have to get on." He was quiet then and she felt his chest rise with a deep breath. "I've always liked this place. Be a pretty place to live—someday."

"Why not now?"

"Indians use it." He waited a moment before going on. "We're west of the Timbers now. Few hostiles come around here."

Her shoulders stirred under his hands.

"Scare you?" he asked quietly, "knowing it?"

"I'd just as soon not think too much about it," she said lightly, "but of course I've always known we'd reach this point sooner or later. I know we're ready, if there's need."

"Yes. Don't trouble about it." He swung her about and kissed her. She clung to him a little, then pulled away. "Hungry?" he asked, letting her go.

"I hadn't thought about it."

"Legette's been stirring some time. Expect he's got some grub hot by now."

"Then let's go eat it," she said, and tried to match her step to his.

II

THEY STAYED in the glady valley three days and these were days of pleasure for Judith. It was a beautiful place floored with spring flowers, new-ripe strawberries, and every sort of wild greens. She walked much, exploring, and gathered the wild lettuce, dock, lamb's quarter, poke sallet, cress and dandelion. She washed them clean and boiled them with bacon and tried to get everybody to eat them. Parley Wade looked at his askance. "Ain't much of a greens-eatin' man," he said.

"You should be," she told him, "they're good for you. Best tonic in the world."

The old man grunted. "Reckon I'm the best judge of what's good fer me. Been eatin' whut I pleased longer'n you've lived, an' it ain't included weeds an' sprouts."

"They aren't weeds and sprouts, Parley, they're wild greens."

"Same thing. I jist as soon eat hay."

"Parley! You have to set an example for the hands!"

"Why?"

"Because . . . well, if you don't eat them, they won't."

"Don't see no cause they ort."

"They'll be *good* for them!"

"You eat 'em, honey. Let 'em be good fer you. Man don't like sich truck."

"But men . . ." she sputtered. "Parley, I *know* about herbs and wild greens and such."

"Sugar, you jist keep whut ye know to yerself, less hit's yarbs if somebody's sick. Man c'n keep healthy on buffler hump."

Johnny came up and grinned wickedly at the old ruffian. "You do what she says. If I got to eat the danged stuff you ain't too good to do it."

Parley gulped and looked at his heaped plate. "All of it, Johnny?"

"Ever' damned bite. It won't do no more than give you the trots."

"Johnny!" Judith said sharply.

Innocently he met her eyes. "Well, ain't that what wild greens are mainly for? A purge? Never saw one yet that didn't act like one."

Judith let out her breath in exasperation. "They thin the blood."

"Thin the bowels, too," Johnny said.

The men ate the greens obediently. She was, after all, the boss's wife, and Judith ignored the uncommon seeking of the bushes for the next two days. Only Parley had the courage to say in her presence, "Good thing this train ain't moving. Ain't a man but's so weak he'd have to ride a wagon."

Judith went hmmmph and said, "Good for them."

The old man said mournfully, "I've done fergot whut it feels like to have my pants up."

"Parley!" Scandalized she stuck her nose in the air and walked away.

There was a happy day when a small herd of buffalo wandered down the valley. Few of the men had seen a buffalo before, but all had heard much of the Great Plains animal. They went as wild as all greenhorns when the big, shaggy, humped beasts hove into view. Johnny gave the word to drop all work and kill meat.

With a great deal of zeal, and much less skill, they obeyed. They chased many, killed a few, and, watching, Judith thought nothing could have revived their Timber-flagged spirits more.

Johnny and Parley stood on the sidelines and grinned at each other as the men dashed about. They could have told them that this little herd was nothing compared to what they would see farther on, but they didn't. These were the first buffalo for the men, and there would never be this time again. Let them have their fun.

Judith was with them when suddenly Manuel charged past. He was astride a good horse and beside himself with excitement. He pulled up to shout at them, flinging gravel and dust in their faces, "Señora! Señores! I go to kill the cíbolo! The buffalo, she is many . . . no?" He dashed on. "I kill," he shouted over his shoulder, "I kill a big one!"

Judith stared. "But he had no gun! Johnny! He's forgotten his gun!"

Johnny and Parley were pounding each other, splitting their sides. "The dang fool don't even know he's got no gun!" Parley spluttered, and sat suddenly, holding his stomach. "He's done gone loco!"

"Oh, Johnny, call him back!"

Johnny wiped his streaming eyes. "Honey, he wouldn't hear you. He's gone clean balmy with buffalo fever. He wouldn't hear if you fired a cannon."

"Poor Manuel. Oh, what a shame. What a pity!"

"Lord, honey, he's out of his mind. No need to feel sorry for him."

They watched, until even Judith laughed, the amazing sight of Manuel, without a gun, giving chase to every buffalo that stampeded out of the herd. He was delirious and wild. He didn't even miss his gun. When a beast ran past him he humped his mustang into a gallop and took off after him, yelling and whooping, following as far as he could. When the buffalo left him behind he turned and took off again after the next animal, just as wildly, as madly, and as ineffectually. Johnny and Parley laughed until they rolled on the ground and even Judith got a stitch in her side. She had never seen anything funnier in her life.

Of course he never did kill a buffalo, but as she told Johnny, "He sure chased more than anybody!"

When the hunt was over he came back to camp with the others, just as exhilarated as the most successful. "Señora, you see me! You see me chase the cíbolo? Ah, nobody chase the cíbolo like Manuel, Señora!"

"No," she agreed, smothering her mirth, "nobody chased the cíbolo like you, Manuel."

He was joked unmercifully but nothing could damp his joy. It didn't matter that he hadn't killed. He had seen, he had chased. He was finally a cibolero!

They had tongue and hump for two days. Judith finally understood what Johnny meant when he said there was nothing that satisfied like buffalo meat. "With coffee," he had said, "it's all you need. You'll never miss salt or bread or potatoes or beans. And you'll never weary of it."

She had eaten it before, mostly as jerky, but she had had little experience of the lush richness of the fresh fatty parts. She found you could eat until your craw was full and never feel glutted. Three hours later you could begin again and eat your fill and the gorging would not make you sick. The fires were kept up those days and a roast of buffalo meat was always broiling. The men would visit the fires, hack off a chunk and go away, tossing the hot meat like a potato from hand to hand until it was chewed down.

Judith's stomach was a little turned when she watched the halfbreed hunters eat the liver raw, and it was turned completely when she saw them gulping down the intestines, squeezing the excrement away only a foot or two before their mouths. But she was too hungry for meat herself for it to affect her for long. She put the long loops out of her mind and the next meal of hump or tongue tasted as good as it had ever done.

It was a miracle what the meat did for the ailing Ben Spring. His flux was checked within twelve hours and his strength returned so rapidly that by the time the train was ready to leave the glade he was able to take his place again.

The only man with the train not tempted by the fresh meat was Pete Shelley. He had taken to his pallet when the valley was reached. He said he was a lot sicker than Ben Spring. He said his stomach had the heaves. Johnny went to see him. "You can rest while we're laid up," he said. "Legette will do your work. But when this train moves, you move, or you'll be left behind."

"Cap'n," the man whined, "you wouldn't do that. I'm a sick man, Cap'n."

"You try me and see," Johnny said, and walked away.

Shelley wouldn't eat the buffalo meat. He turned his face away from it. "My stummick is too weak," he said. "I ortent to eat nothin' but stew or something easy to swaller."

Judith heard of his wish and because she felt so rested and so well and so happy that the Timbers were behind them and so hopeful for the rest of the journey, she had compassion for him. She made a good broth of buffalo marrow and rice. She added a dish of stewed dried fruit and she sent it to the man by Legette. She had to answer to Johnny for it. Looking like a thundercloud, he said, "Quit it."

"But it was only kind, Johnny . . ."

"Let him starve. Nothing wrong with him but laziness and cowardice." She handed him coffee. "Johnny, you're tired."

He pushed his hat back, sipped the hot black drink. "No. But I don't like Shelley's kind."

"What is Shelley's kind?" she murmured.

"Four-flusher."

"How do you know?"

"Saw 'em in the Army. Seen 'em in the Territory. They're easy to spot."

"I'm sorry, Johnny. I only meant to help."

"I know. But don't interfere. Please. The hands are my job."

"You're sure he isn't sick?"

"I'm sure."

The ghost of Tig Vance rose before her. Johnny owned he should have sent Tig Vance back at the Deep Fork. Was Pete Shelley another Vance? This is his choice, she told herself. He decided to take these wagons to Santa Fe. It isn't my duty to question. My duty is to make him as comfortable as I can, and to be cheerful, to be no trouble to him, and to soothe him. I can't take on his burdens. Though I would. Though I would. She looked at his big shoulders, slumped. Ah, Johnny, Johnny. This wagon train is your heaviest burden. Without it, and without us who drag at you, you would have ridden halfway to Santa Fe by now. You are used to your freedom on these prairies and with us you are moving like a winter-cold snake and it troubles you. Though you keep steady, it troubles you. It shows in your shoulders that slump, and it shows in your voice that is short, and it shows in your eyes that keep looking ahead. But this is the way you took and you have to abide by it.

On the morning of the fourth day when the train pulled out, Shelley was in his saddle astonishingly cheerful. "That rest done me good, Cap'n," he said as Johnny passed him. "B'lieve I c'n make it now."

Judith saw Johnny look him over and nod. "Fine. Expect you to do your work, now."

"Yes, sir."

They did an easy twenty miles that day and made their night camp on the western edge of the beautiful valley. "Ten miles to the Canadian," Johnny told Judith. "We'll get an early start in the morning so we can make our crossing before dark."

"After the Canadian?" she asked.

"The start of the plains," he said.

They didn't get their early start.

It was still black dark when Manuel roused Johnny. He stood outside the wagon and called softly, "Señor? Señor! Please! Las mulas . . . is trouble, Señor!"

Johnny scrambled up, awake at once. "Where are my boots, Judith?"

"Under the bed." She leaned up on an elbow. "What is it, Johnny?"

"Something about the mules. Manuel?"

"Sí Señor. They are gone . . . las mulas, los caballos . . . all gone. The picket, she is cut. They have scattered themselves."

"God damn!" Johnny had found his boots. "Somebody's cut the picket line. The stock's got loose!"

Judith reached for her wrapper. "I'll build up the fire and make coffee."

"Keep it hot." And Johnny's back disappeared.

She could hear him talking to Manuel. "Who had guard tonight?"

"I do not know, Señor. Señor Cooper, he is boss. He is good boss. I slept."

"Sure. Sure. Not your fault. Get Jesse for me, Manuel."

"Sí. I get."

Judith had a fire smoking and the coffeepot filled when Jesse came up, his pants sagging, his hair on end, his eyes sleep-drugged. "Trouble?"

"Trouble. Plenty. Who had guard on the picket line last night, Jesse?"

"Ben Spring. Trice. Pete Shelley."

"In that order?"

"In that order."

"Legette!"

The black man sprang from the shadows. "Sir?"

"Rouse Ben Spring and Trice and Shelley. Pete ought to be at the outpost. He had last guard. Tell 'em I want to see 'em. Now!"

"Yes, sir."

"That will leave the stock without a guard, Jonathan," Jesse Cooper reminded him.

"There ain't no herd," Johnny said. "Somebody's scattered it."

Jesse was shocked awake now. He secured his pants. "All of it? You sure? Who did it? Indians?"

"Maybe. What I want to know is how Indians got past the guard. How anybody could cut that picket line." His voice was tense and curt.

"Jonathan, I set the usual guard . . ."

Johnny chopped him quiet.

Ben Spring and Bullitt Trice came, still yawning but hurrying. Johnny pivoted to face them. "Spring. You had first guard on the herd last night. Anything happen? Hear anything unusual?"

"No, sir. Everything quiet."

"Did you walk the herd?"

"Yes, sir. Every hour. They was peaceful."

"Test the line?"

"Yes, sir. Ever' time I walked it."

Ben Spring's face was anxious but he asked no questions. He kept his eyes on Johnny's face and answered steadily.

"Everything all right when you turned over to Trice?"

"Ever'thing all right, sir."

"Trice?" Johnny turned to the blocky, short-spraddled man.

Trice cocked his head. His close-set eyes were splintered in the light of the fire. "Trouble, Cap'n?"

"I asked you a question."

"Yes, sir. Herd was quiet when Ben turned over to me. Quiet as I ever seen 'em."

"You roused Shelley when you went off?"

"I roused him."

Johnny grunted. "Where's Legette? Legette!"

The line of wagons was coming alive now. Men poured up from their blankets and gathered together. Judith saw Parley Wade kick his fire into flames and hurry toward Johnny. The water in the coffeepot boiled. She dumped in fresh-ground beans. Parley came up, his mouth working on a chew of tobacco.

"Johnny?"

Johnny waved him off. "Keep still. I want Legette and Pete Shelley. What the hell's taking that nigger so long?"

Parley warped his tobacco into his cheek. "He's lookin' fer Shelley."

"Looking for him! Sure, he's looking for him. I sent him to find him, but why's it taking all night?"

"Simmer down, Johnny. Shelley warn't at his post. Legette's askin' around."

Johnny stopped his pacing to freeze facing the old man. "What did you say?"

"Said Shelley is missin'."

Johnny swore and smacked a fist into his palm. "Damned sonuvabitch! Sure. Sure, he's missing. It figures." He made a circle around the fire. "He's the one cut the ropes. He's made off. Hell . . ."

The Negro came up with the pot-bellied Josh Brand. "Sir?"

Brand spoke up. "Cap'n . . . Shelley sleeps alongside me. I come awake when Bullitt roused him out and I seen him turn out. He acted sleepy like and he waited a while till Bullitt had went to his blanket. Then he got his gun. I never thought nothin' about it, natural. I seen he taken something besides his gun but it gits chilly 'fore daylight and I figured it was his coat or a blanket. I wasn't real good awake and like I said, I never thought nothin' about it. Looked like a blanket roll he wropped up and takened. I went on off to sleep."

"Sure," Johnny said. "Sure. Anybody seen Pete Shelley since?"

Nobody spoke up.

"Then he's gone. He's cut the picket line and scattered the stock. He's cut the rope and made off. The mules and horse are scattered to hell and gone. And there's no way of following him. Time we get the herd caught up he'll be across the North Fork and back in the Timbers."

The men were silent. Johnny's right hand chopped down. "All right. We'll not be traveling today. Parley, Jesse, Asa. Orders are for every man to eat and pack rations for two days. We'll send 'em out in pairs. Half will work up the valley and across. The other half will work down and across. I'll take Manuel and we'll comb the middle. Legette, you'll stay with the camp. We'll work crisscross, but everybody's to come in by tomorrow night. What we don't find by then we'll have to leave. They'll be too far scattered."

The men left on the run. Judith sat, voiceless, on a log. "The sonuvabitch," her husband muttered, "the goddamned sonuvabitch."

"Johnny . . ."

"Oh, hell, Judith, I hate to be took in. It's my job *not* to be took in. The feller's hooked me."

"That's not true."

Johnny took a great swig of coffee and sprayed it out. "God! Whyn't you say it was hot? I've scalded my mouth!"

She restrained her impulse to remind him that coffee which came directly from the fire was usually hot, and that she usually served it directly from the fire because he had told her at least a hundred times since they had been married that boiling coffee was the only kind fit to drink. She kept her silence instead. It was no time for reminders. It was no time, she thought further, for a woman to speak at all. He was too exasperated and cross. She busied herself putting up rations for him and Manuel.

The men left on foot, in pairs, as ordered, fanning out in all directions from the camp. The earliest began to trail in around noon the next day, riding now, and driving little bunches of horses and mules ahead of them. By nightfall every man was accounted for and the herd had been recovered except for three mules and two horses. "He never tried to stampede 'em," Parley told Judith, "jist cut 'em loose an' driv 'em ahead of him a piece an' let 'em go, savin' the ones he taken with him."

One of the missing horses was Johnny's own big roan. It put him in no better humor. "Shelley took him," he said bitterly.

The Indian hunters were sitting by the fire. They had been waiting for the train at the Canadian and when it didn't catch up they had drifted back on the trail. They had helped with the search. Impassive, unconcerned, they sat by the fire and waited, belching now and then from the gorging meal they had eaten. Suard and Ba'tiste looked sleepy, but the Beaver kept his eyes on Johnny, who was brooding into the smoky fire. He spoke to them, finally, in their own language, and the two halfbreeds took their guns and left. Parley was trying to help Judith find the end of a tangled hank of yarn. He peered after the departing Indians. "He's sent them on to the river ag'in. Told 'em to go ahead an' mark the crossing. Said we'd be on in the mornin'."

Judith nodded, her fingers following a strand of wool. "That looks to lead to the loose end, Parley."

"If it does," the old man said, "hit's in the worst imbranglement I ever seen. How'd ye git it in sich a mess?"

"There it is!" She pulled the end free. She found a twig, broke it off small and began winding the yarn into a ball around it. "Got it tangled in my pocket," she said. "Ought to have balled it first."

The Beaver was standing now and Johnny was speaking to him. It took only a few words, then the Beaver grunted and faded into the twilight. "Where's *he* going?" Judith asked Parley.

"After Shelley."

Judith's hands paused, then, more slowly, went on with their winding. "After Shelley? I don't see . . . Why doesn't he let Shelley go? He wouldn't be any good to Johnny now."

"Hell, honey, he don't want Shelley. He don't give a damn about him. Jist good riddance of bad rubbish, him leavin' out. What Johnny wants is his horse. He ain't gonna let nobody steal that roan."

The camp was dark early that night, and quiet. The men didn't gather around one fire to listen to William Day scrape on his fiddle and to clog and jig to the reedy, whiny tunes. They were too tired after foot-tramping the valley. The blanketed figures were like logs around the dying fires soon after dark. Judith, a little glad the fiddle was silent, slept quickly herself.

The train moved at sunup and before noon had reached and passed the Canadian. It was a twin of the North Fork, wide, shallow and red. Manuel said his people called it the Río Colorado, because of its color. Like the North Fork, it was also dusted with long islands clumped with willow and pitted with quicksands. But they made a good, safe crossing following the stakes the Indians had set to guide them and made their night camp eight miles farther on.

That night Johnny called Parley Wade and Jesse Cooper to look at the map with him. He spread it on the ground and Judith set a candle to light it. They hunkered about it, following Johnny's finger tracing their course. "Here's the way we'll go. Swing west to the False Washita."

"Commencin' when?" Parley asked.

"Tomorrow."

"You ain't aiming to foller the Canadian, then," Jesse said.

"No. Canadian bends too far north. We'll head for the False Washita . . . hit it about here and hang on till we get to the Spanish line."

Jesse nodded. "Don't reckon there's much risk, leaving certain water in the Canadian to head for that other river."

"No," Johnny said, "we've not hit dry country yet. Parley and me have hunted this piece. Plenty of grass and plenty of water. I know that. I've been there. But this," he pointed, "is the Spanish boundary, and from there," he added quietly, "it's all new country to me."

The three men stared down at the rough map, studying it. Judith watched. Parley Wade's face was untroubled. He had long acquaintance with this map. He had studied it with Johnny Fowler all winter, had helped draw it. Jesse Cooper's brows were knitted and his fingers fidgeted his mouth a little. He was going on blind trust, she thought. He had no long acquaintance with anything about the venture except his old friendship with Johnny Fowler. The map, the country, the men, the purpose, were all strange to him and new.

She studied her husband's face. His eyes seemed to drink up the map as though it could unroll for him the land itself, the long, broad sweep of it clear to the mountains, the whole lonesome, empty, unspotted stretch that waited for him.

To most men, she thought, it would appear a cruel land, inhospitable and hard, and for most men it would hold no lure. Most would be glad to leave it alone and never think of it, stay safely behind their fences and their bricked walls and their store counters, behind the lace curtains their wives had put up at their windows. Most men liked the comfort of their ways and days. Not her husband. He had had a long love affair with this western land. It pulled at him like some great magnet and he could no more resist the pull than he could change the color of his eyes. It was as if the needle of his compass could only settle west and point, undeviating, in that direction. He ran his hand over the map, now, as though touching the soil his feet were so eager to tread. "Out there," he said softly, "out there it's all new." She saw his hand tremble a little, reaching to make the newness his.

That, she thought with a swift understanding of the truth, is really why he hates these delays. There is time, there is all summer for this journey— but he can't wait to see that new country and to wear off its newness with his own eyes and feet and hands. His mind has left these slow wagons and hurried on ahead.

Jesse Cooper looked up from the map. "How far," he said, "is it to the Spanish boundary?"

The spell broken, Johnny rolled the map into a cylinder. "From here? Four, five days travel maybe. Little better than sixty miles."

They stood and Jesse Cooper dusted his hands down his pants. "After that," he said, "just the Beaver knows the way."

"Just the Beaver," Johnny said. He grinned wryly. "He's crossed once, but I reckon he can get us past the dry scrapes and the canyons." He straightened. "Parley, you and me'll look out the road tomorrow. Jesse, you keep the wagons rolling."

"Reckon I can do that all right," Jesse said, laughing, "but you'd best not count on me to do no picking out a road. It's all been new to me, ever' last mile of it."

"Don't figure to," Johnny told him. "Reason I asked you to come was because you're used to wagons and teams. We'll find the road. You keep the mules pulling and the hands working and the wagons moving."

"Do my best." He left, then.

Parley, watching him go, pulled at his beard. "Seems a mite nervy, don't he? Got the wind up about the Spanish territory, reckon?"

Johnny pinched the candle out and handed the rolled map to Judith. "Put that in the chest, will you, honey? Jesse," he said, turning to Parley again, "was always one to take care. Even when he was a kid he tried to figure ahead. A little cautious, maybe, but he's a good man . . . good and sound and you can put your dependence in him. He's knowledgeable with teams and heavy wagons."

"What's he do back whur he come from?"

Johnny chuckled. "Got a freight line from Louisville to Nashville. Twenty wagons hauling for him."

"Well," Parley said cheerfully, "I'd say that'd make him right knowin' 'bout the peculiarities of mules. Not," he added, "that e'er man in a lifetime could predict *all* their cussed ways, but I'd say Jesse's been exposed a right smart." Parley's nose pointed west and sniffed. "Wind's gettin' up." He clapped Johnny Fowler's shoulder. "Right outen the west an' thar's whur she'll blow from plumb to Santy Fee. Smells good, don't she, boy . . . that west wind."

Johnny faced the wind and breathed it in deeply. "Smells better'n anything in the world to me. God, Parley, we're getting there! We're getting there!"

"We shore air. Let's us push 'em, Johnny, an' git to that boundary soon. Let's us make 'em stretch out. Whut say?"

In the wagon, opening the chest to put away Johnny's map, Judith heard the eagerness in their voices and she smiled. They were like two little boys, she thought, ready to jump the mark and light out in a footrace.

Her smile faded. Here was that newspaper with the notice about Legette. She'd forgotten to burn it. Her hand hovered and hesitated. Well, it was too late tonight. And besides Parley had only wanted her to make sure nobody else got hold of it. It was just as safe in Johnny's chest one more night. It had been safe there since they left Three Forks. But she'd try to make a chance to burn it tomorrow night, sure.

12

WHAT'S GOOD about it, she thought, fretted into vexation within an hour of taking to the saddle the next morning—this west wind those two think so highly of. Just blows your hair and burns your skin and chafes your lips and blinds you with dust and if there's any sweet smell to it I can't smell it. Smells! All she could smell was mule sweat and man sweat and rancid bear oil and greased leather and horse droppings. There were enough smells, all right, but none of them sweet.

She flicked her horse and rode rapidly around the wagons, catching up Jesse Cooper who was riding out in front picking up Johnny's trail. There was still the wind but she'd be ahead of the dust and smells. He welcomed her with a smile and then looked up at the sun, which was already like brass. "Going to be hot today."

Though he shouted the wind tore his words aside and she barely heard them. She nodded to show she had. She wasn't going to fight the wind by trying to talk.

He sidled his horse nearer and leaned toward her. "Days been getting hotter for a couple of weeks, I noticed."

She nodded again.

"Nights ain't so cool as they was, either."

She fought down irritation. Of course the days were growing hotter, and of course the nights weren't so cool. They were six weeks out from home now, and it was early June. Time for hot weather. And it would get hotter, if he but knew it. This sun was going to beat down on them, and it was going to get drier and dustier and the grass was going to get thinner and thinner, and this wind was going to blow right on to eternity. She was tempted to tell this man from Kentucky that he hadn't seen anything yet. But it would take too much effort and besides he was just trying to be pleasant. She wondered why so many people backed and filled all around the weather to open a conversation. She'd heard Johnny do it, with strangers. It was safe, she supposed. A kind of probing until you knew how much to say, or what else to say.

She groped in her pocket for a bandanna and tied it about her mouth. Jesse, watching her, nodded his approval and drew his horse away. At least it would save her from rudeness, she thought, and it might keep her lips from drying too much.

She rode beside him all morning, wordless and braced against the wind. After the nooning, however, she crawled into the back of her wagon. She felt slack and lazy-limbed and more tired than she usually was at the end of the day. There wasn't room to let the bed down in the daytime; too many things were stored about. But she threw down some pillows and curled against them and nodded and dozed and was jerked awake and nodded and dozed again. She must have slept soundly, finally, for she came to with a start and realized the wagon had stopped. She crawled to the tailgate and stuck her head out. Johnny was giving his horse to Legette.

She yawned and stretched. "Are we making night camp?"

"Yes. Made good twenty miles today!" he said exultantly. "Best day we've had. Good road." He slapped the horse's rump and said to the black man, "Give him a good rub, will you, Legette? He's pretty hot." He turned about and looked at Judith, started to say something, but hung his mouth open, staring. "Good God, what's wrong with you? You got a fever?" He took half a dozen quick steps and laid his hand against her cheek.

She winced back. "Don't do that! It hurts!"

He let down the step and reached for her. "Come out here where I can get a good look at you. You're as red as a boiled lobster!"

She stumbled out, groaning. "I'm so stiff! And my face is so sore, Johnny!"

He tilted it and peered closely, then began laughing. "I reckon it *is* sore. You've got about as bad a case of wind and sunburn as I ever saw. Don't know as I ever saw worse. Lord, Lord, I bet that's tender. Honey, you're just plain fried! You didn't *ride* in this wind today, did you?"

Her fingers left off exploring the sensitive skin. "Well, of course I did! I can't ride the rest of the way to Santa Fe in the back of the wagon!"

"You don't have to, but when it blows like it's blowed today you'd better stay inside."

"I heard Parley say myself, last night," she said indignantly, "and he was standing right here, that it would blow clear to Santa Fe!"

"Blow?" Johnny broke into laughter. "Sure, there'll be wind, honey. Always is on the prairies. But not like today. That one today come near being a duster."

"Well, why didn't you say so!" she snapped.

"Now, look, Judith," he took her hands, "go on back inside. It's still blowing. And rub plenty of grease on your face right now. I'm afraid you're going to blister and peel anyway, but the grease'll take some of the fire out of it. Don't try to help with the cooking tonight, either. Let Legette do it. A cook fire'd be a misery to your face. I've got to give Manuel a hand with the picket line, now." He gave her hands a little shake. "I'm sorry, honey. It'll be better tomorrow."

Feeling as miserable a greenhorn as Jesse Cooper, she waited till he had gone, then pulled herself up the wagon step again. She'd put a pot of goosegrease in the chest, she remembered, at the last minute. It was good to cut a croup. She'd rendered it out herself and strained it through fine cloth and it was clean and white. Thank heaven, she thought, it had come to her to tuck it in. She didn't know if she could have stood bear grease on her face. It was dim under the wagon sheet and she rummaged about, feeling more than seeing. She'd stood it in a corner, she recalled that, but which corner? And there was that bothersome newspaper again. She flung it out onto the floor. Ah, here was the jar of goosegrease, wrapped about with brown paper just as she'd tied it up, not overturned or spilled. She closed down the lid of the chest. Under her foot the sheets of the *Gazette* crackled. Drat! She swooped one hand down and swept it up. She'd burn it right now and be done with it.

The wind whipped smoke in her eyes as she approached the fire and the heat set her face to burning as though a thousand nettles had stung it. Awkward with the pot of grease in one hand, she struggled to thrust the newspaper under the weight of the wood. She saw its corner catch and then, blinded by the smoke, her eyes streaming, her face on fire, she retreated and turned her back to the heat and the smoke. She didn't see a piece of the paper, caught by a gust of wind, swirl up lazily, then spiral higher and higher in a whirling dustdevil and blow away.

She was so uncomfortable that she slept uneasily that night. The sheets felt coarse and rough against her face and she wakened a little each time she turned. She guessed Johnny was sleeping outside, for she had the whole bed to herself and was grateful for it. It was too hot for two in the narrow space.

The heat wakened her fully, eventually, and she got up to raise the wagon sheets. The wind had died, now, and the air inside had become close. And she was thirsty. She wanted a long, cold drink of water.

She didn't trouble to find her wrapper. The water keg was just outside, on the ground near the wagon step. She dipped a cup and drained it down. Legette had filled the keg that night from the water hole and the wood was still wet and cool. She rested her hand against it and wished she could bathe her hot face. But it would only take the heat out momentarily, she knew that. It would burn worse when the dampness dried. Best leave it greased.

She moved to a new patch of dew-wet grass and wiggled her toes in its coolness. It felt so good. Everything was cool but her face. Neither Manuel nor Legette was rolled by the fire embers tonight—too hot, she thought, but she guessed the blanket roll on the far side was Johnny. She listened. He didn't snore, he never did, when sleeping out. In a house, safe at home, he might, a little. But he had trained himself out of it when he had to take care. "Osages taught me," he had told her. "A snore can give you away to your enemy." But there was a sound . . . something. . . .

She turned her head and cupped her ear to hear better, and identified the sound. A horse, or mule, coming. Broken loose from the picket line? She ought to wake Johnny . . . but the cocoon on the far side of the embers was already shedding its skin. Johnny was sitting up, his head bent, his ear turned to the sound. He threw aside the blanket, then, and reached for his rifle. He did not look her way or see her in her white nightshift, but she remembered it suddenly and fled into the wagon. But she knelt on the bed and peered over the side to see. It dismayed her to find her heart beating hard. Could it be, she thought, her mind fleeing to the first danger she could conjure up, could it be that man from Mississippi, following Legette so far? Don't be foolish, she told herself, trying to breathe easier, it's only one of the hunters coming into camp, one of the Indians. Johnny isn't alarmed—he's just ready, and that's sensible. He hasn't wakened the camp, and he would if he thought . . . the horse was walking steadily, coming nearer, but very slowly, as though he or his rider was tired, had come a long way.

The night was not wholly black, there was a starshine over the prairie, and her eyes used to it now, she saw the horse almost at once when he loomed into view. He was carrying a rider but not until Johnny put his gun down and went to meet him did she recognize the Beaver on Johnny's own big roan. The men spoke and the Indian leaped off. The mustang whickered softly and brought his head up and nuzzled Johnny's shoulder. The Indian stepped aside while Johnny walked all around his horse, looked him over well, rubbed his flanks, then came back to his head and smoothed the nuzzling nose. He said something to the Indian and the Beaver took the saddle and bridle off the roan, side-hobbled him, then Johnny turned him loose to graze. He watched for a moment as the mustang nibbled grass, then led the way to the embers of the fire. With his boot

he stirred the embers into a glow but he did not lay on more wood. He set
the coffee to heat and motioned the Indian forward.

Judith sucked in her breath. The Beaver was wearing only a breech-
clout and his naked body was painted. He had striped himself with black
and red and his face was daubed frighteningly. He carried his gun but
over his shoulders was slung a quiver of arrows and a bow, and pressed
against his ribs under his right arm was a pouch of some kind. When he
walked, the feather tied to his roach whirled and danced spinningly, and
the tiny bells on his moccasins chimed. The scout's buckskins were gone
and the warrior's paint and eagle feather and moccasin bells were proud
tonight.

They sat and when Johnny bent into the fireglow to set the coffee over
hotter coals she saw that his face was very still, carefully impassive. He
would have asked his friend, she knew, if he had eaten and since he did
not offer food the Beaver had already fed. They did not speak while they
waited and Johnny kept his eyes on the fire. He felt of the pot from time
to time and finally he poured their cups and they drank. When they had
finished he spoke briefly, asked a question, she judged, in the Indian's
own language. The Beaver set his mug aside and folded his arms and began
to talk in the guttural monotone the Osages used to tell a tale. He spoke
at length, beginning, she knew, at the beginning. As he worked into his
story, he became more excited and he used many gestures. Johnny listened
quietly, but when the Indian had finished he made that quick, chopping
motion with his hand which she knew so well meant impatience or the
beginning of anger. He faced the Indian, now, and his mouth was tight
and his face was grim. He harangued the Osage and though she could
not understand the words there was no mistaking the tone. He was very
put out with the man.

When he had got through the Indian stood and drew something from
the pouch under his arm. He flung it on the ground at Johnny's feet. He
made a gesture of abandonment, of disavowal and then he strode away.

They had quarreled. Johnny and the Beaver had quarreled. That was
plain. But what about? What had the Indian done? How had he displeased his friend? And what was it the Beaver had flung at Johnny's feet?

He stared at it a long, long time, not moving, keeping his seat. Then
he leaned over and picked it up. She saw him handle it, turn it in his
hands, and when the light struck against it she saw long, reddish hairs
hanging down limply, as a man's hair hangs from his head. Her breath
hung in her throat. It's a scalp . . . a man's scalp . . . he's brought Johnny
a scalp . . . a red-haired scalp . . . Shelley had had red hair!

Her hands gripped the side of the wagon until the knuckles cracked and she didn't feel the pain. Dear God, the Indian had killed Pete Shelley and scalped him and then he had brought the scalp to her husband! It was ringed on a hoop and it was red and it hung limply in her own husband's hand. A shudder took her and shook her. She leaned her forehead against the hard wood rim and pressed it into her flesh, and felt sick at her stomach. Her mind took hold again and she gulped and raised her head. He hadn't ordered it. He wouldn't have ordered it. He couldn't have. Parley said, all he wants is his horse back. He don't give a damn about Shelley. He'd told the Beaver to get his horse back and the Indian had taken it into his own hands. That was the way of it. That *had* to be the way of it. Johnny *couldn't* have wanted Shelley's scalp!

He was angry, she remembered. He was very angry. He had harangued the Indian and the Indian had flung the scalp down as if he despised it, had walked away from it. Her mind clutched the memory. Yes, Johnny had been so displeased that he had scolded his own blood brother and he had angered him. He *hadn't* told the Beaver to kill Shelley. Oh, there was so much she didn't understand. The Beaver was all mixed up in that time Johnny had gone to fight the Blade and wouldn't listen to her and there was such a long time he had lived with that old man that was head of the Wolf clan, before she knew him, that he wouldn't talk about, and the Beaver was mixed up in that, too, and she would never understand why . . . she found her fist in her mouth and bit the knuckles. The Beaver meant trouble. He always meant trouble, to her . . . and now he'd brought trouble to Johnny. She wished he'd go away and stay away. She wished Johnny had made him so angry he'd never come back! She wished she would never have to look on that stolid, dirty face again!

The hair-ringed hoop still hung from Johnny's hand. Poor Shelley. Poor, poor Shelley. All he wanted was to go home. This wild land frightened him and he wanted to go home. He oughtn't to have cut the picket line, of course, and he oughtn't to have stolen a gun and horses. But he'd begged and Johnny wouldn't let him go, and he'd been too scared. Like Tig Vance he'd got in over his head, not knowing. It wasn't a country for everybody. He'd come to the same end, finally. She wondered if the Beaver had buried him, and knew he hadn't. He'd left him for the wolves to eat and the buzzards to pick. You didn't bury an enemy. You left him for the ulti-mate humiliation.

With dull eyes she saw her husband kneel and she watched as he raked away the live embers of the fire. She saw him dig deeply with his knife. Then he placed the scalp in the hole he had made and covered it. When he had done, he raked the coals back over it, brought wood and laid it on, building the fire into flames. Then he sat and looked into the blaze, dreadfully, dreadfully alone.

She began to cry quietly. What armor did you buckle on against the turnings and twistings of life? How did you live with its secrets and its remorses and its sournesses and its necessities? By chance she had come by this knowledge tonight. Johnny would say to her, put it behind you and forget it. But forgetting came hard, hard, to her. There were such pockets and recesses in her mind to hole up memories. And their tendrils escaped her, no matter her will. One more now—one more. She sobbed lonelily. And she slept. And then the sounds of the waking camp came to her.

Legette was speaking and Johnny was answering. His voice was level and calm and quiet. Last night might never have been.

She threw back the covers and stood out of the bed.

When she stepped down from the wagon she wore a fresh cotton dress. One armor a woman could wear was pride, simple pride . . . and today it was clothed in a clean dress. It said she did not know her husband's affairs or understand them. It said she did not need to. It said she was utterly loyal though she did not understand. It said she might look at the bed of coals under the breakfast fire and know what lay hidden there but not even the torture of the Comanches would make her reveal it. It said she was a wife, cleanly and proud and faithful and discreet.

13

A ND SO it was they passed the False Washita and came out finally onto the great western plains.

Now, Johnny Fowler's trail organization took on the look of an Osage hunt. Now the line of march was tighter. Now a spearhead of riders, the Indians, rode point, like sentinels of the road. Flankers fanned out on either side and a guard was kept to the rear. The wagons, cumbersome, bulky, lumbering, were protected and moved forward two abreast. Each night they were formed into a crude square with the mules and the horses staked inside. When they camped, Judith looked at the formation and thought how they forted themselves in every time they halted.

A stricter guard was kept, also. Men were posted on all four sides of the square. "Danger from hostiles?" Bullitt Trice asked.

It was as though he wanted Johnny to admit the danger. "Sure," her husband said, "we're in hostile country. You want to live safe forever?"

And now the country itself took on a different look. Everything familiar had been left behind. It was a long land but not a level one. It rose in slight swells and dipped and it was marked with little growth save the rugged shin oaks, the skimpy lines of cottonwoods on the watercourses, and the bunchy, clumpy grama grass. To Judith it looked like a land that had fallen asleep, each rising swell a billow that had been frozen into numbness. As with the sea, it had its currents, currents of wind that bent the grass and flowed it ripplingly. It was such a vast land, she thought, such an empty land. It was endless with sand and clumpy grass and sun. It had the look of long endurance and age, of long dryness, of long pointing to something forever beyond. You wanted to hurry over it and get wherever you were going. It led on. It promised nothing now. It was something to travel over.

There was no end to the line of sky and it stood above them high and blue and hot and cloudless. It beat the brains, this bright blue sky. It numbed you and clubbed you and turned your mind into a simmering stew.

Beneath the wheels was an ocean of grass. Wagons had never traveled it before. Looking back, Judith thought their tracks were puny and amounted to nothing. The grass bent, but tomorrow it would spring up again and hide their passing. Who, in all the world, would ever know they had passed this way? Who would remember? Who would look and keep them in mind?

Nobody. Her heart told her no one would remember, or no thing. There will be nothing to remember. We are going beyond the limits of memory. We are going where no one has ever gone before and where no one would seek us. We are venturing onto the rim of the earth, the rind of the planet itself and we are going into a foreign land, among foreign peoples. Never in her life had she felt so lonely, not even when she had journeyed to the Territory from Connecticut. Then there had been some things, a few things, that were like home. Now, there was nothing. The land and the sky were too big, and she was too small. She felt an aching yearning to cry out to someone, to some thing, we are here—we are passing this way— we are walking this earth. We are under this sky and these stars. Take notice of us. Remember us. She wanted to make a mark some place. She wanted to build a cairn, or cut her name on a tree, say to someone Paso por aquí.

At the same time she felt this intense loneliness, she felt also an immense exaltation that puny as they were, tiny on the face of the prairie, pygmies under the domed sky, they dared, driven by their wills and their own human pride, to pass this way, to cross this pathless desert. It took guts, she thought coarsely, just plain guts to do it and we've got them, and it's a thing to be proud of.

The nights were beautiful. The stars were the brightest, the most sparkling ever sprayed across a midnight sky and the air was the lightest and the purest. The sounds were the sharpest and the clearest. The clink of a bridle bit was like a bell gong. A man's whistle was a flute note. The bark of a coyote was a fractured drum roll. And the howl of a wolf was the wail of a lost soul. She slept each night soundly. She woke and fought back the sense of smallness with the wonder of each new morning.

For two days they followed the False Washita through sandy hillocks and the gypsum that lay so heavily deposited north of them.

The third day they halted early and as soon as the stock was picketed Johnny called a meeting of all hands at his wagon. "We are now in Mexico. At noon today we crossed the hundredth meridian. The hundredth meridian is the line between the United States and the Spanish territory."

She hadn't realized, and at his words Judith felt a queer sinking away of her stomach. Never before had her feet stood on alien soil. Now, they did. Since noon, she had been in Mexico. There had been nothing to tell her. It had all looked the same—mesquite and scrub oak; tumbleweed and grama grass; greasewood and cactus; sand and sand and more sand. Something, she thought, should have warned her she was leaving her native land; but nothing had. Her horse had plodded on and she had ridden, unknowing.

From the rear of the men there came now a long-rising, joyous whoop and Manuel leaped to his feet. "Ay, Dios de me vida! Thanks to God's grace my feet touch my own land again! María Santísima, it has been so long!" He stamped and patted the sand and laughed and danced excitedly. "Soon, soon the mountains! Soon my people and La Ciudad! Señor Captain! Señor Captain, you are sure?"

Johnny was grinning. "I am sure, Manuel. I took a sight with my sextant at exactly noon today. We are on Spanish land."

Judith looked at the sand. One man's wasteland, she thought, another man's home.

The Mexican boy broke into sobs. "Then I am a man again, Señor, and no longer a piece of stone." The men turned away from him in embarrassment. Americans didn't weep. American men didn't show their joy or pain and grief with tears. This Mexican, their turned backs seemed to say, was womanish . . . a girl, whose tears flowed easily. They were ashamed.

But Judith had been homesick once. When the hard and unlovely fact of Arkansas Territory had had to be faced she had longed wistfully for gentle grass and flowering shrubs and clean brooks and white houses. She made her way to the boy's side. "Manuel, I am so glad. I am so happy for you."

The boy choked and snubbed his sobs, dipping his head in a dozen quick nods. "Sí, Señora, sí." He began to beam through his tears. "Is good, no? Is good to be home. Thou knowest."

"Sí, Manuel." She patted his arm. "Es bueno."

He swiped at his eyes with the heel of his hand and smeared the dust around them grotesquely. "These are tears of joy, Señora, tears of gladness. Manuel does not weep in sorrow. Some things are so happy one must also weep. Is it so, no?"

"It is so."

He was all heart and radiance and glow now. He flung his arms wide. "Is it not beautiful? Mexico?"

Obediently she looked about and smiled, seeing only what she had been seeing for a week . . . the greasewood and stunted cactus and the patchy grass and the long, long miles of sand. The sun was low, and the land ran into it and was stained by it, turned gold with the dark stripes of shadows in the troughs. The sky was gorgeous and violent, dripping with red and orange and yellow. Against the backdrop of sand and sky the stunted and twisted little trees stood out clean and clear, shaped fantastically, writhen by wind and the scour of the sand. And it all went on and on and on, as far as the eye could see. Why, she thought, surprised, if you didn't look for what you knew, if you just looked at what you saw, it did have a kind of beauty . . . a kind of starved, stark beauty, a kind of terrible, desolate beauty. It was so empty. If you forgot, she thought, about the clutter and closeness of thick trees, and the humps of hills, and the nearness of houses . . . and when your eyes had to look so far, that long stretch that looked to meet the sky and never did, did sort of pull you on. It made you feel puny, but it sort of made you feel proud, too. To be crawling across it and not to be too afraid of it. It wasn't a friendly land and, her eyes following around the endless horizon, she sensed somehow that it would either give a person some of its own grandeur or break him into bits. It could unnerve you, if you let it. If you let the wind and the dust and the sun and the distance bother you, it could unnerve you easily. You could get to feeling like a piece of naked skin crawling across eternity, with no place to hide. But if you looked at what was there, if you paid heed to the colors and the bigness and the changing lines and the light, dry air . . . Manuel was right. But you had to see with different eyes.

He was whispering, but she cautioned him, "Sh-sh-sh. The captain is talking. Listen."

Johnny was saying, ". . . we're in a foreign country now. It's the first time for most of us and it goes a little queer, maybe. Thing I want you to keep in mind is, we don't want any trouble. No trouble of any kind, with anybody."

Judith and Manuel were behind Johnny, facing the knot of men gathered in front of him. He stood easily before them, one foot propped on the hub of a wagon. Bullitt Trice and his friends stood a little to one side, away from the rest of the men. Trice laughed now and spoke up. "Reckon you'd best tell the Mexicans and Comanches that, too, Cap'n."

Manuel hissed in Judith's ear. "He is a bad man, that one. He is evil. Spanish people will not make trouble for the captain."

"Sh-sh-sh. He knows it."

Trice's voice always made her go tense and angered her. He was such a hateful, loathsome man, and he hated Johnny, and he had so shamefully witnessed. . . . He drawled out his words now and they were so contemptuous. They made a bid for laughter and got it from Hull Archer whose obedient whinny rose shrilly. Someday, she thought, someday this man and Johnny . . .

Unexpectedly, Nathaniel Butler, next to Trice the biggest man with the train, a serenely steady and unvocal man, a good, dependable man, roared out, "Will ye keep yer trap shet, Trice! Ain't nobody wants to hear yore views."

Johnny, who had been looking at Trice, flicked his eyes over to Nate Butler for a second, then he bent swiftly and plucked a dried blade of grass. To hide his grin, she thought. Butler never raised his voice but he had bellowed at Trice like an angry bull. When Johnny raised up again his face was sober. He stripped the grass blade down, then he rested an elbow on his knee and leaned forward, making each word he said distinct. "What I want every man here to understand is that nobody, nobody in this party, is to make trouble on his own. This train will make no trouble. Is that plain? We'll treat any Indians we meet friendly, unless they show they're hostile. If we meet up with Spanish troops, and we may farther on, we'll show 'em the same respect we'd show for United States troops. Understood?"

A ripple of movement flowed through the bunched men, as though a wind had bent them a little. They took quick looks at each other.

Johnny waited a moment, then went on. "Now. I'm aiming to do some trading with the first Indians we run into. They'll likely be Kiowas or Comanches. They've been friendly lately. But don't go getting the wind up first Indian you see. Don't go firing your gun off at your shadow. Some friendly Indian might take it unfriendly. I don't want any accidents or any incidents."

Some of the men began to nod and to speak up. "Makes sense. We don't commence no trouble, won't be none likely."

"Keerlessness starts a heap of trouble."

There was a letting down into laughter and some joshing. "Day'll take a coyote fer a Kioway, likely—first guard he has."

"Ben'll have to watch his trigger finger."

Then Josh Brand, who stood next to Trice, asked, "What have they got to trade, Cap'n?"

"Mules. Spanish mules."

Brand grunted. "We c'n damn shore use 'em."

"Yes."

Judith saw Bullitt Trice nudge Hull Archer, and the boy shuffled nervously and cleared his throat. Then he said, "Them Osages up ahead, Cap'n?"

Johnny's head swiveled slowly on his neck. His voice was flat, dead quiet. "Why?"

"Well, looks like . . ."

But Trice took it away from him. "Ain't seen 'em the last day or two. Come to think of it—" he moved a little and the great black coil of his whip loosened, "come to think of it, I ain't seen the Beaver since you got your roan horse back."

Well, he'd said it. He'd flung it right in Johnny's face. Her stomach squeezed. Now. Now, it was coming. He'd pushed too far. He didn't know about Shelley, but he'd noticed about the Beaver. He'd got Johnny boxed in. And dear Lord, he could cut Johnny in two with that bullwhip before he could take two steps! She closed her eyes, squeezed them tight and waited, without taking a conscious breath.

Silence lay still and heavy and for so long that she had to lift her lids again. What were they doing?

Parley was standing directly across from Trice, turned a little sideways, his gun resting easily across his arm. Judith's hand went up to her mouth. Parley's gun, as if by accident and carelessly, was pointed at Trice, and his finger was on the trigger. Her eyes fled around the group, then.

Legette was at the back. His gun was ready, too.

Asa Baldwin and Jesse, together, had stepped back. Asa's gun was loose, like Parley's. Judith swallowed. It was all right. It was all right. Nate Butler moved, now, and Ben Spring. No guns up, but leaving a line of fire clear. Trice and his three friends, knotted, stood alone.

Johnny waited and waited and waited and Judith thought her knees would buckle under her. Wasn't he ever going to speak? Was he just going to stand there? She put a hand behind her to find some kind of support and Manuel gripped it. "Cabrón!" he hissed.

Without hurry, with exaggerated slowness even, Johnny moved then. He took his boot off the wagon hub and straightened up, so slowly, so achingly slowly that he seemed to go up and up toweringly tall. He stood away from the wagon and his own gun, hidden till now by the slope of his body, looked casual and innocent leaning against the hub. Still without hurry he reached for it, ran his hand down the long barrel, caressed the gleaming stock, then stood it on the ground in front of him and crooked an arm over it. He held Trice's gaze steadily and he spoke in that same dead-flat, level voice. "Want to make something of it, Trice?"

Nobody moved. Nobody said a word.

He gave Trice plenty of time, then he flipped his gun up, swiveled on his heel and bit off a curt dismissal. "That's all. Meeting's over."

There was a smothered oath and a drift of uncertain movement, then one by one, or drawn into little groups of two or three, the men shifted about and began to melt slowly away. Craig and Brand and Hull Archer followed Bullitt Trice, who stalked stiffly, coiling his whip as he went. The very set of his shoulders showed how balked he had been and how furious it had made him.

Judith let her breath go out. She felt dazed and limp, and still smothery and breathless, and still horribly scared. And her shift was stuck to her in her own sweat. She pulled her hand loose from Manuel's and fanned the bosom of her dress.

He was chattering like a monkey. *"Ay, qué hombrón,* Señora! Qué hombrón, the capitán! Bálgame Dios, Señora, but he is the brave one! You see him? You see him call the bluff, no?"

The relief, the fading fear made her suddenly cross, cross with all men, the whole breed, that could draw whips and guns and then just stand there and glare at each other and scare the living daylights out of a body. "Oh, hush," she said, "just hush!"

Manuel's brows went up and his mouth went down and his voice was pained. "Señora?"

She waved him away impatiently and he went, looking back at her a time or two, his face showing his puzzlement and mystification. Then he shrugged, shouted to Legette, and loped off to meet him.

Johnny was calling for Parley and Jesse. "Want to see both of you."

Judith eased down on the wagon tongue. She would just sit awhile, until her knees felt as if they had bones instead of jelly in them. She would just sit and rest a minute, and then she supposed Legette would build a fire, and she and he would cook, and they would all eat, and then it would be dark and they would all sleep, and in the morning they would wake and roll on again. Well . . . well . . . She smoothed her hair and tucked a pin tighter and she smoothed her skirt and she sat up straighter. She looked about.

Legette was coming up with his arms full of firewood, Manuel trailing him. Johnny and Parley and Jesse were squatted nearby. Johnny looked up as the Negro dumped the wood. "Build the fire, Legette, but wait a bit to cook."

The Negro said Yes, sir, and set about lighting the fire.

At a distance, Trice and his friends had stopped. Talking, she supposed, still talking. Trice glanced around, then took something from his shirt and showed it to the other three. It looked like a piece of paper but from here she couldn't tell. They all bent together a moment, then broke apart. Hull Archer's cackling laughter rose, Trice clapped him on the back, and the group moved on.

She'd mend that shirt of Johnny's, she thought, pushing herself up. If they had to wait to cook, it would be a good time to get it done. She'd been meaning to do it for several days. He was hard on shirts. She'd brought a dozen new-made linseys for him, but he ripped out seams as if they'd never been stitched and tore off the tails to swab his gun or bind a cut or even keep the sweat out of his eyes if he'd forgot his bandanna; and he had a positive gift for embrangling himself with limbs and scrub. He usually left part of his shirt behind.

She pushed her campstool nearer the fire. She felt a little chilly. The sun has gone, she told herself, not admitting to nerves. She studied the long rent across the shoulder of the shirt. It was a clean tear and wouldn't need patching. She would stitch it, double and back, then overwhip the edges to hold.

The men moved closer to the fire, too. Jesse Cooper took out a clay pipe he sometimes smoked and Parley bit off a quid and set to softening it. With his heel, Johnny hitched his saddle over and sat on it, swung his hands between his doubled knees. He rubbed the knuckles and sucked on one he had barked. "I've not named to you," he said then, "the Beaver has turned back."

Parley nodded. "Figgered he had."

Startled, Jesse Cooper dropped his pipe. "Turned back? What for? Wasn't he supposed to go all the way? Who's going to scout?"

"I am," Johnny said shortly. "That's what I want to talk to you about. You'd best know the plain facts. The Beaver took Shelley's scalp and I harangued him about it, which didn't set good with him. Said," Johnny looked at Parley and grinned wryly, "said if his brother had no faith in him, he'd best skedaddle. Words to that effect."

Parley settled the patch over his blind eye, but his good eye was twinkling. "Reckon it unsettled his pride a right smart."

"I don't know what the hell you're talking about," Jesse said, staring at both of them. "You said that Osage took Shelley's scalp. How do you know?"

Parley snorted.

"Why, Jesse," Johnny said, "he brought it to me. Like any good warrior. Trophy for avenging his brother's honor."

"Good God! They're nothing but heathens!"

Judith's needle hung hoveringly, then was set firmly to stitching again. But she had glanced at Jesse Cooper and seen that his face was beaded with sweat and appeared a little gray. She knew he was feeling sick, as she had felt the night the Beaver had brought the scalp, but surely he could see, too, that Johnny had done what was right about it. Even not used to such things, he ought to see it took a lot of nerve for Johnny to risk the touchy temper of the only man that knew the way across the prairies, but he'd done it, chanced it and lost the man.

"You didn't tell him to kill Shelley, did you, Jonathan?" Jesse asked.

Johnny gazed at him reflectively. "I wouldn't of thought you'd had to ask that, Jesse."

"Fer God's sake," Parley exploded, "ain't ye got no sense at all, Jesse? Johnny jist telled him . . ."

Johnny waved him quiet. "My fault, too. Jesse don't know about these things. Stealing a man's horse takes his honor, Jesse. Only way he can get it back is recover his horse or kill his enemy. Him or one of his relatives. Way an Indian looks at it, leastways. I told the Beaver to get my roan back, but I was tired and mad and didn't think to tell him to leave Shelley alone. Just told him get my horse back. The Osage did what he's used to doing and takes pride in. He got his brother's horse back and killed his enemy for him and recovered his honor. One way of speaking, I didn't have no right to harangue him about it. But I had the good of the train to think of, so I had to insult the Beaver. And it was an insult, make no mistake about it. He had a right to expect praise. Back in his village there'd have been a feast and dancing and he'd have been a hero."

"Yes. Well . . ." Jesse fingered the bowl of his pipe, "this ain't back in his village."

"Ye dang fool!" Parley burst out, "cain't ye see that's why Johnny done what he did? Ye cain't have a Injun actin' all Injun round a bunch of white men. Whaddya think would've happened if e'er one of them men'd seed Shelley's skulp? One o' their own kilt by a damn Osage! It'd of wrecked this here voyage, is what it'd done."

Jesse bit down on his pipestem and growled, "All right, all right. Let's get on with it."

Johnny sat up straighter. "It's done and he's gone and no mending it. Now. I don't make no bones that him being gone is going to be troublesome, but if I didn't figure I could steer us right I'd turn back tomorrow. I can get us where we're going by compass. Trouble is, a compass don't tell you the waterholes and the dry scrapes and the bad going."

"You know where the worst of 'em is at," Parley said. "Beaver went over the map with you last winter."

Johnny nodded. "But that ain't saying they're pinpointed."

"How serious you make it?" Jesse Cooper asked.

"Hell," Parley said, spitting the word out with a huge mouthful of tobacco juice, "hit ain't serious. Johnny don't need the Beaver all that bad."

"Parley's right," Johnny said, "in a way. We can get along, but it'll be feeling the country out, and," he added, "likely I'll get us into some places we'd do better not to get into."

"Whatever ye git us into," Parley said loyally, "ye'll damn shore git us out of. I ain't wearied."

Judith's heart swelled. You could count on Parley, she thought, you could always count on Parley. She wondered if Johnny wasn't wishing he'd made Parley second in command. But there was Jesse's twenty years hauling freight back home. This wasn't back home, though, and he did get the wind up so easily. But it had been a miracle the way he'd got the wagons through the Timbers, and no harm to them except what could be mended, and with full loads. Nothing had had to be cached. If he just wasn't so cautious and old-maidy. She turned the seam and began doubling back. He ought to be more like Johnny. She paused. There. That was what she'd expected. That was the way he'd appeared at first. Oh, he was a good man, but he acted lately as if he had a pain somewhere, and as if he didn't think too highly of . . . well, much of anything. Wore a sort of sour look. Trip-sick, she wondered? Maybe she ought to try to cheer him out of it.

The men were silent. The night was coming on and camp sounds seemed very loud. A horse whiffled the dust from his nostrils. A knot of wood clunked on a fire down the line and a man's laugh exploded. An owl whimpered down by the creek and there was a splash. Somebody was filling a water bucket. An insect set up a dry drone. A mug or plate, something metal, was dropped and clattered against a stone.

The men by the fire talked on, but now she wasn't really listening. She heard scraps of words. "No real dry scrape, just a little dryer'n we been used to."

". . . lucky with the season. May git water the hull way."

"We got the droughty country ahead of us."

"Just have to see."

Johnny got the jug of whisky and all three took a drink. "Becknell said he thought his time had come. Said he was lost. Didn't have no idea where he was. No water for two days and all the animals going loco. . . . Cimarron cutoff . . ."

"We ain't goin' that way."

They kept talking, having another swig occasionally. Judith finished her mending and she folded the shirt and laid it in her lap. Her chill had passed. She was warm and, somehow, comforted. Nothing could be very bad with these three deciding and leading. Nothing would ever flurry them. Jesse, a little, maybe—but not Parley or Johnny. They'd be like rocks, no matter what.

From a little fire near the picket line Manuel's guitar twanged and presently he began to sing.

> *They rise, the mountains, like a cloud;*
> *Blue, the mountains, bluer than the skies;*
> *Light of my eyes, hope of my soul,*
> *The mountains . . .*

Judith smiled. Everything sounds homey tonight, she thought . . . all the sounds of the camp, they're real homey tonight.

14

FOLLOWING the False Washita they had been making a little northing but now they crossed the headwaters of the stream and turned
due west.

Since the Beaver had turned back, Johnny seldom rode with the wagons.
He was ahead, with the Indians, scouting the way. Mindful of her determination to cheer Jesse Cooper if she could, Judith took to riding oftener
beside him.

She rode almost entirely these days, rarely making use of the wagon. She
felt too good. On her horse she was part of the moving forward. In the
wagon she just sat. She couldn't remember ever in her life feeling better
than she did now. She'd thinned down a little—she knew that from her
skirts—but she liked her stomach lean and she liked the feeling of being
as limber as a switch. She liked the way her skin had tightened up and
was browning. She was almost the color, she thought, of a well-baked bis-
cuit. She liked eating with a big appetite and enjoying every bite of food
she put in her mouth. She liked the way her muscles had hardened, in
her arms and in her legs. And she liked the way at night she was tired,
but just pleasantly tired, not, as in the beginning, full spent and drained.
She liked the good comfort of the bed, and going to sleep at once and
sleeping without a dream until the morning bustle waked her.

And she loved, she just plain loved, this new freedom of riding astride.
She would never have asked Johnny. But she did hate that woman's saddle
and when Manuel had brought her horse the other morning and she had
looked at it with loathing again—her knee crooked around that horn grew
paralyzed by noon every day—she had burst out in spite of herself. "I *don't*
see why women can't ride sensibly, as men do!"

"They can," Johnny had said, grinning at her, adding, "out here on the
prairies."

"Could I?" she had been eager. "Could I, Johnny? My skirts are full
enough. It wouldn't be immodest."

"Good Lord, honey," he had said, "this is no pleasure jaunt. Ride comfortable."

He had scrummaged out a saddle for her and it was marvelous what a difference it made.

Jesse Cooper had been amazed when she rode up beside him, and maybe a little embarrassed, drawing his eyes away. It irked her when he said, stiffly, "I wouldn't have thought Jonathan . . ."

"He allowed it. He suggested it, in fact. Why," she added vexedly, "do you persist in calling him Jonathan?"

"It's his name."

"Not even his mother used it."

"I always have."

As if, she thought crossly, ways could *never* be changed. But being vexed with Jesse wasn't cheering him. She set about making pleasant talk with him.

Most days she was successful. As the habit of having her ride with him grew on him, he got into the way of telling her long stories about home, when he and Johnny were boys together. She learned about Johnny's father and mother and his sisters and brothers, and she heard other names and places he had never mentioned. She loved these stories and she deliberately drew Jesse out to tell them. Johnny talked so little about himself. She had a fond, sentimental feeling for the little boy he had been.

But some days Jesse was glum and rode the hours out without a word. When she found him in his glum mood, she left him alone.

He was glum the day they passed through the prairie dog town. They'd come into a stretch of low, ridgy land which had dwarf shin oak and plum bush scattered over it when all at once they were in the midst of acres and acres of small mounds laid out in streets. "What are they?" Jesse had asked.

"Prairie dogs," she said, scooting back to the wagon for a gun.

The small, squirrel-like animals stood in front of their doors and barked at the invaders, and lost their lives by hundreds. The men shot and shot and shot, and Judith shot, too.

"Why're you killing them?" Jesse asked. "They're too little to harm a body."

"Good gracious, Jesse," she said, "they're good to eat!"

"Dogs?"

"They're not really dogs. They're more like . . . well, they're good to eat. We can use the meat."

She didn't know whether he touched them, brown and crisp and juicy and roasted that night, and she didn't care. They tasted wonderful to her.

Johnny was fretted because they hadn't met any Indians yet and because he had to tell Parley and Jesse that night they were coming up to a dry scrape. "Not bad," he said, "less than thirty miles of it, but we'll have to make it through without stopping. It's real dry. We got any extry kegs, Parley?"

"Several."

"Good. We been carrying a keg of water to a wagon but fill up all we got tonight. And ration the hands tomorrow. They'll get thirsty but them damned mules are going to drop like flies." He fidgeted fretfully. "Dammit! Where are them Kiowas and Comanches? I'd looked to meet 'em fifty miles back."

Not even Parley could say anything hopeful. The mules were in bad shape and a dry scrape would just about finish them. But nobody could conjure up Indians out of nothing.

"Ain't seed no sign?" Parley asked.

"Nary 'un." Johnny had more learning than most, but he also had a way of dropping into the speech of the country. It had bothered Judith at first, when they were newly married, but listening now she thought it fitted him like a suit of buckskins. And it occurred to her that she, herself, had got into the way of speaking less properly and of thinking more comfortably. She let it go, easily and without shock. She sort of liked to hear Johnny say nary 'un, which she knew was a contraction of never a one, but how stupid to say it that way.

What they came to the next morning, what Johnny had scouted ahead, was an immense sand plain. There was no growth of any kind on it, nothing but sand and one hour after the sun rose a glitter that almost blinded. And there was a hot west wind that drifted skitters of the sand into the eyes and the throat, and made dustdevils across the endless plain.

They strung out across it, the hard labor of this day's travel evident immediately, Johnny and Jesse and Parley everywhere at once, exhorting, swearing, yelling, encouraging. The grit dragged at the great, wide tires of the wagons and the gaunted mules, stung by the whips, had to pull harder than they had ever pulled. And they were not the strong, fresh mules that had pulled through the Timbers. They were already worn out. When a mule fell, unable to rise again, he was unhitched and another was brought from the remuda. The fallen mule was left for Manuel to deal with. If the animal could recover, Manuel got him on his feet and drove him with the herd. If he could not rise he was left.

Far this side of famishment, there was enough of the discomfort of thirst to make the men nervy and cantankerous. Some, and you could have predicted them Judith thought, abided by the rules of a cup of water every three hours and sweated and dried out and suffered in patience.

Some, and they could have been predicted, too, complained and pled, saying they couldn't stand it. Hull Archer was one of the most importuning, and Craig and Brand made trouble. Sometimes William Day went the full three hours, sometimes he didn't. You could never tell about William Day. Bullitt Trice never even claimed his cup when it was due him. It was as though he meant to show everybody he was better than the captain who took his cup when it came time. Johnny allowed him his will once. The next time he said, "You don't get two cups, Trice. Missing one don't entitle you to two."

"Have I asked for two, Cap'n?"

"Don't skip the next one."

"I don't get as thirsty as some."

"I said, don't skip the next one, Trice."

Judith made a point of going the full three hours herself, though Parley scolded her. "Don't suffer yourself," he said. "This ain't no scrape. Save yer thirst fer the real thing."

"I'm no thirstier than the men."

"You're the captain's wife."

"More reason for me to abide by the rules."

Late in the afternoon they came to a place where the surface was harder, more packed, and Johnny was riding with Judith, slack in his saddle, half asleep.

Bullitt Trice rode up. "How much further we going today, Cap'n?"

Johnny roused. "To water."

"You got any notion where it's at?"

"I have."

"If these mules ain't give water soon they're done."

"They'll have to be done."

"You'll have none when you stop."

"We'll see."

Trice touched his hat in mock respect and rode away.

"How much farther is it, Johnny?" Judith asked.

He measured the sun. "How long we been rolling? Twelve hours?"

"About."

"Another five, then—six, maybe."

Her lips were cracked and painful but she made them stretch into a grin. "That's heartening. And it won't be so perishing when the sun goes."

In the event, it was seventeen hours and thirty miles they made, a long, punishing, grueling haul. They lost twelve mules and four horses and Hull

Archer finished the day in a wagon, vomiting the rum he had nipped between water rations. But at moonrise, again in ridgy, brush-grown land, they came to a gravelly dry wash with one hole of water, sweet, clean, clear water. It was fed by an underground stream and it was cold and there was plenty of it.

They came also to a fire already going and the Osages around it, with meat sizzling and roasting. But better than that, the Osages had news. There were Indians ahead. Johnny leaned forward in his saddle. When he spoke his voice was a croak. "Mules?" he asked.

Suard was the spokesman. He nodded. "Plenty mules."

Parley had come up and he and Johnny exchanged a long look. It said this had been a close call, but it was over and done, and their luck still held. It said all they meant to say of a risk taken and won.

Judith got off her horse without help, but when she tried to walk she had trouble with her legs. If that, she thought, bracing them, hadn't been a real dry scrape she didn't care if she never saw one, Parley or no Parley. It was all the dry scrape she ever wanted to experience.

15

SHE HAD THOUGHT she might be scared when they met up with
Plains Indians. She had heard a lot about Comanches and Kiowas,
and some of the tales had been gruesome enough to give anybody the
horrors. She had heard, too, that they were magnificent warriors, proud of
their horses all decked out with Spanish trappings, proud of their own male
handsomeness, and proud of their roving, prowling skills in war and
thievery. She'd heard also they were touchy and tricky and couldn't be
trusted; they'd appear friendly and suddenly turn hostile.

She *was* excited, and a little nervous, when the band of Indians hove
into view over the low ridge. She watched them come with her heart beating a little faster than usual. But eight weeks on the road had given her a
reassuring knowledge of the toughness and hardness of their own men.
She didn't believe there was a band of Indians anywhere that could stampede them. Johnny had warned them again to keep their shirts on and
make no incidents. But he had also posted them skillfully and seen to it
they were ready. "Parley will go with me to make talk. If there's trouble,"
he said, "he'll give the signal. But not a shot, you hear, unless you see
Parley's hat hit the ground. No matter what happens. They sometimes
like to show off, make out they're fierce."

But no one, Judith thought as they came closer, could have been frightened of these Indians. To begin with it was a small band, not more than a
hundred all together. And it was mostly squaws and children. They were
led by an old fat man, and there were no handsome braves or magnificent
horses. There were perhaps twenty men in the party and they were all
beginning to wither with age. The whole crew was ragged and poor looking and fairly dirty. Parley grunted. "In bad need of a swap, Johnny.
Ain't got nothin'."

Johnny nodded.

"Where are their mules?" Judith asked.

"Out of sight. They'll bring 'em up when they get ready to trade."

The Indians came on slowly, and quietly except for the hordes of dogs that yipped about them. The old fat man at their head rode as if he was asleep. At the foot of the slope, however, he pulled his horse up and straightened himself and in spite of his fat and in spite of his shabbiness there was great dignity in the way he waited for Johnny and Parley and Manuel to approach him. "Let's go," Johnny said and they walked forward.

There was a short colloquy as Manuel found out if the old man understood Spanish—most Comanches did—and told Johnny, "Poquito, Señor . . . a little."

Johnny then made a set speech of welcome, which Manuel translated, the old man answered briefly and heaved himself off his horse. It was taken, the other old men dismounted, and Johnny brought them all into the camp. The women and children were left to make shift for themselves. They sprawled over the hillside to wait.

The men were fed and pipes were smoked, all at leisure, and then the talk began. The old man was Tabba-quena. "Ietan," he said, which was to say Comanche—Ietan chief, in fact.

It took a long time, but Judith had watched her husband make trades with the Osages back home and she knew he had not only as much patience as this Comanche but as much caution, as much knowledge of the ritual, and more shrewdness. He honored the slow tradition of the swap, never insulting the old man by so much as the blink of an eye with his knowledge of their desperate need for goods. He needed mules just as desperately, but he would have done it anyhow. He had genuine respect for Indian ways.

When the old man admitted finally he might have *mulas para* swap, perhaps—with a vague wave of his hand—a few, maybe, he couldn't say how many, and there were a few things his people might desire, he couldn't say about that, either, Parley got up and sort of melted away. A little later the men posted about were going about their own affairs. One of the old men moved off, too, and before long Comanche lodges were springing up all over the slope. Within minutes the empty ridge-side was spread with slim, painted wigwams and a village of women and children and a few old men had taken root on the soil. The swap had been set up.

And now Parley put Johnny's men to setting out goods—blankets, calicoes, stroudings, beads, mirrors, needles, awls, kettles, crockery, and a little brassware.

The mules were brought up, and Judith's eyes opened wide. A few? She had never seen such a drove. There were at least three hundred! "They've been raiding for about a month," Johnny said. "That's where the men are now. On another raid. They bring 'em back here to hide out."

"Where do they raid? Where do they get them?" she wanted to know.

"Spanish villages."

"And drive them here? All that distance?"

"Honey," he grinned, "I'm glad to tell you it ain't so very far now. Three hundred miles or so . . . not much more'n that."

"To Santa Fe, Johnny? Are we that near?" She couldn't believe it. Well over halfway, then . . . oh, two thirds of the way!

"Not exactly," he admitted. "It's that to the mountains. We got to twist around in them some before we get to Santa Fe. But," he touched her arm, "we're getting there."

They were indeed! She felt as if they could soar on wings the rest of the way. More than halfway! More than halfway!

"Stay by the wagon," Johnny said, "and Legette'll be close by if you need him."

She opened her mouth to ask why she would need him, then closed it. Johnny always knew best. She got out her knitting and stationed herself on her campstool, fluttery with happiness and bubbly with joy and excitement.

She learned why she might have need of Legette within an hour.

Their lodges set up, the squaws and children came flocking around the wagons. The men warded them off and they gathered about Judith, making mouths of astonishment at her swift-traveling needles. She smiled at them and showed them the stocking she was making. They touched the wool and fingered it, giggled, touched the needles and said small things to each other. It was impossible to work while they were holding the yarn and interfering with the needles, so she tried to show them, slowly, how it was done. She made a stitch and threw the thread, but one of the younger women snatched at the stocking and ripped it from the needles. When she saw that the wool raveled, she had found an amusing game. She cried out and taking both hands quickly reduced the stocking to a mound of tangled, raveled yarn. Judith watched in dismay, but she was afraid to protest, afraid she might cause the incident Johnny wanted to avoid. She allowed the destruction and forced herself to smile.

There was one woman, she noticed, who did not crowd about, but kept her distance. She was grotesquely tattooed and she looked even poorer and more ragged than the others. She hung about, but she did not crowd and she did not join in the giggling laughter. She was also so pregnant that her skirt was hoisted up over her huge belly almost to her knees.

Judith had no time to notice more. The squaws, through with the yarn, gathered in closer and began to finger her hair and her collar and her skirts. She fended them off as best she could, her dismay growing. Their hands were so dirty, and they smelled so terrible, and she didn't doubt for a minute they had lice. She tried to stand, thinking to get into the wagon, but they pushed her down. Judith began to be frightened now, but she endured until a haggish old woman flipped up her skirt and peered under it, gigglingly. Fear overcame caution, then, and she slapped the old woman's hands away. "Leave me alone," she snapped, "and get away from me! Take your filthy hands off of me! Get away!"

The women closed in on her angrily. Their dark, dirty faces were thrust near hers and they muttered at her. Their hands felt of her and hurt as they poked and prodded, and one woman clawed her nails across Judith's neck. Panic rose in her and though she twisted and turned she could not escape the ring of crowding women. She felt as though she were going to be drowned in them, trampled down, and suddenly she had enough of it. She bawled for Legette. "Get these hussies off of me! I won't have this!"

Legette came running, laying about roughly, yelling in the fractured Spanish he had acquired from Manuel. "Es Señora del capitán! El capitán mucho mad you bother the Señora. No es bueno. No swap aqui. Git! Scamper. Get away from the Señora!"

He distracted them and Judith ordered her clothing and hair and picked up her raveled yarn.

It was the last sensible thing she remembered, for the Indian women began to swarm admiringly over the black man. With eyes bugging from amazement, Judith saw them climb over him, stroking his glossy black skin, rubbing his nose and hair, fingering his ears and mouth, examining his hands, clawing at his shirt.

Legette, also taken by surprise, was trying valiantly to defend himself, squirming and twisting, shoving and pushing, but a swarm of flying ants wouldn't have been more resistless. Where one woman was pushed away, another closed in, her hands creeping and lingering, her eyes rounding, her nose rubbing the sleek black skin. At his back, at the same time, they were lifting his shirt, thrusting their hands under it, poking at him and prodding and giggling.

Judith saw one young squaw wet her finger with spittle and rub it over Legette's check to see if the black came off. She held up a finger in awe, and then her hands were busy again, in the most private, the most personal places.

Judith fled, then, to find Johnny or Parley or Jesse or anybody to help.

The Negro couldn't afford to defend himself to the hurt of the women.

The first man she saw was Bullitt Trice. She shouted at him, "Go help Legette! Quick!"

Trice swung around. "He in trouble?"

She pointed. "The squaws are after him!"

The square, hulking, spraddle-legged man looked and when he had seen bellowed with laughter. He said, coarsely, "Looks like they're aiming to rape him in broad daylight."

But he did go to Legette's rescue and though he took care not to touch them he did crack his long whip about the women until he had driven them away. From the safety of Asa Baldwin's wagon, next to hers, she watched. The women weren't angry, apparently. They withdrew laughing and giggling and making gestures Judith did not understand. Trice guffawed at them and even Legette laughed. "Wish it was me," Trice said, "they was so mad after. You'll be right busy tonight, man."

Legette said something and they went away, and Judith went back to her own wagon. She stripped all of her clothing off and inspected herself for lice. Then she washed all over and put on clean garments. She combed her hair and combed it, inspecting the comb minutely each time, fearful of finding vermin. Nothing. It looked as if she'd escaped that humiliation.

She did her hair up and sat on the side of the bunk. In spite of the whole outhousy aspect of the incident, she couldn't help giggling. Who would have dreamed those squaws would be so excited by a black man? He must have been the first Negro they'd ever seen. And how wild it had set them. She thought about the seeking, creeping, crawling, feeling hands and the pressing noses and faces, the lit eyes, the rubbing bodies. Good gracious, she did believe they would have . . . right before her . . . if Legette would have . . . Well!

When Johnny came he was tired but he told her he'd done well, trading. "Got fifty good mules, all young and strong. Better'n I thought to do." He was stripping off his own clothes. "They was out of everything. Needing a swap bad. Honey, lay me out some clean clothes, will you?"

"Now?" she asked. "It's almost night."

"I know. And I wish I could go straight to bed, but old Tabba-quena's having a feast and I've got to go."

"Well," she said firmly, "I'm not going!"

"Honey," he laughed, "you *can't* go. It wouldn't be fitten."

It wasn't until he had gone, telling her that Nate Butler and Jesse would be in camp, that she took in his meaning. And knew why he'd set down in the ledger, not asking her to do it, a debit against his pay for almost every man with the train "for sundry articles." They'd bought beads and mirrors and shells and needles and tobacco to pay for a night's bed with a squaw.

She was shocked, of course, and her face flamed up, but what horrified her was that she wasn't as horrified as she thought she ought to be. It *was* outrageous, and it *was* indecent, and it *was* lewd and obscene, and she ought to feel properly outraged and insulted that Johnny allowed it with her so near, and not only allowed it but sanctioned it with his own presence. It was plain vulgar for a bunch of men to traipse off to bed down with a bunch of dirty squaws! She tried to work up a good case of indignation but, well . . . she'd been a wife for a year now. She knew a little more about the nature of men than she had when she and the other women of the Mission had bewailed the morals of the traders at Three Forks. Not, she told herself, that she condoned this night's business but . . . well, goodness, how was Johnny going to stop it? What could he do? Men being what they were, and these muleskinners having been eight weeks on the trail, and these the first women . . . It would be admirable of them not to want one of these Indian squaws, but it would hardly be natural, under the circumstances.

But Johnny wasn't to think for a second, she thought as she went to bed, that she didn't disapprove. She would be icy and moral and if he wanted *her* favors this night he would be refused! She owed that much to all wives!

She had a long time to wait and every minute of it was filled with the sounds of revelry from the Indian camp. Men whooped and yelled and laughed and the drums beat and a fiddle scraped and from time to time she even heard Manuel's guitar. Every dratted one of them, she thought, flouncing, except Nate Butler and Jesse and she didn't notice the small contempt with which she paired them—Nate was too stolid and Jesse was too squeamish.

As the time dragged on she waxed angry and waned forlorn, alternately. He didn't need to stay all this long. Not that she believed for a second that he . . . no, of course not. But he didn't have to linger on. He had to stay for the feast and some of the dancing . . . but, she scrubbed her eyes, he didn't have to *enjoy* it! And he was, or he would come. They'd told her at the mission, when she'd said she was going to marry him, that he was half Indian, and she wouldn't be happy with him. But she was, and he wasn't, only he *did* like Indians, and he did like Indian ways, and he was up there on that ridge now having a wonderful time and she was down here in bed all by herself, and why didn't he come on home where he belonged?

She wept a little and fretted some more and finally went to sleep. She waked when he came in, still laughing, not tracking very well. He came to bed and caught her in his arms and she was too glad to have him, warm and hungry for her, beside her again. It was too late when she remembered she meant to be icy and moral and refusing. "That Legette," he said, turning over to sleep, "that Legette. There's going to be several mulattoes amongst the Comanches next spring."

"Just hush," she said, "just hush," in an effort to be stern, but even that was ruined when she collapsed into giggles.

There was another episode with overtones of tragedy, and comedy, which had to be played out yet.

The teams were hitched and the train was preparing to pull out when the tattooed squaw crept up to Judith and twitched her skirt. Remembering the onslaught of squaws the day before, Judith turned on her angrily. "What do you want?"

The woman's Spanish was halting, as if she had to search for it. She had to speak very slowly. "You go to Santa Fe?"

"Yes. We go to Santa Fe."

"You will pass San Miguel?"

"I don't know."

"It is a small village on the way."

"If it is on the way, I suppose we will pass through it."

The woman kept her eyes lowered and one tattooed hand fingered her slovenly, ragged skirt. "If you are there, will you ask about an old man?"

Her Spanish was difficult for Judith to understand, but by listening carefully she was able to make it out. "Why?" she asked.

"He is my father. He is José López. He is a sheepherder for the Montoya family. Señora?" She would not yet raise her eyes.

Judith stared at the woman so distorted with her pregnancy, so disfigured with tattoo marks. "You are Spanish?" she asked, slowly, unbelievingly.

"Sí, Señora. I am the daughter of José López."

"But you are with these Indians . . ."

"Sí, Señora . . . but I am Spanish."

"You were taken by them? By these Comanches?"

"By Apaches first, Señora. Traded to Comanches."

"How long?"

The woman shrugged. "I do not know, Señora. I have forgotten."

The shrug was so typically Spanish, Judith had seen Manuel do it a thousand times, she was suddenly convinced, and suddenly galvanized. "If you are Spanish," she said firmly, "then you must come with us. We will take you home to your father. My husband can arrange it for you. You are a prisoner? My husband will buy you from the old chief."

The woman backed away in great agitation, looking badly frightened, and she broke into an explosive, sputtering language Judith could not understand. She shook her head. "I don't know what you are saying. But it can be arranged. I will find my husband. I will tell him. We can delay our departure until he has talked with the chief. Please do not worry. It will be all right. We will take you to your father."

The woman twitched at her skirt and sputtered again. Manuel was bringing her horse up and Judith called to him. "Manuel, please translate! This poor woman is Spanish. She is from San Miguel. We must buy her. We must take her home."

The woman was slowly inching away now, one hand covering her mouth, her eyes rounded with fear. Manuel spoke to her and she shook her head. Then she stopped and exploded into the sputtering tongue again. Manuel was asking questions, that was evident, and she was answering. He spoke at length and she listened. She spoke again, then Manuel laughed. "Señora, you have frightened her out of her wits. She does not wish to return to San Miguel. She is afraid you will make her go."

"Make her? But doesn't she want to go home? She is a captive. She is Spanish. Surely she wants to return to her own people! Surely she wants to leave these Comanches."

Manuel replied, with the same shoulder-lifting gesture, "Señora, no. These are her people, now. She is Comanche. She has a husband and children. She does not wish to return to San Miguel. She does not wish to see her father."

"Then for heaven's sake what does she want? She said find an old man . . . José López."

"Sí, Señora. It is simple. She only wishes to know if her father is living."

Stunned, Judith gazed at him. "And that's all? She just wants to know if he is living? She doesn't want to see him? She doesn't want us to take a message? She doesn't want to go back?"

"No, Señora. She only wishes to know if her father is living."

"Well, good Lord, Manuel, if we found him how were we to let *her* know? We'll never see the woman again."

Manuel laughed. "She is a stupid woman, Señora. Your husband is a trader. She believed you would be passing this way again, sometime— one year, two year, three, it did not matter. One day you would pass and Tabba-quena's band would meet you. She would learn. All Comancheros, which are all she knows of traders, and all Indians meet one time, an- other time, on the prairie."

Judith, dazed, pondered this. "But then . . . why didn't she ask some Comanchero before? She could have learned about her father years ago."

Manuel spoke to the woman. She answered him. "She says she did not think of it before."

It made no sense to Judith. "But why think of it now?"

Manuel was patient. "Señora, I have tell you, she is a stupid woman. A poor, ignorant muchacha when the Apaches take her, with not much mind. The Indians have had her a long time."

"Well, I don't understand . . . was it because she heard we were going to Santa Fe? She mentioned that."

"Quién sabe? Perhaps."

"Well . . . tell her . . ."

"Do not bother, Señora. I will ask about the old man. What I learn I will pass on to some Comanchero in Santa Fe. One day it will reach her."

He spoke to the woman again, she replied, nodded, looked askant at Judith, and waddled off. Judith watched her go. "I felt so sorry for her," she said. "I thought . . . I cannot understand. How can she be happy to stay with this band of Comanches?"

"But she is Comanche herself, now, Señora. Her husband is Comanche. Her children are Comanche."

"But she remembers! She remembered her father's name! Why doesn't she want to see him?"

"There does not have to be a reason. What could it matter, the reason? It would change nothing. She thought of her father. Something made her think of him. She had a wish to know if he is living. It does not mean she wishes to see him, or that she wishes to return to him. She only wishes to know if he still lives."

Never in her life had Judith felt more hopelessly bewildered. "What good would that do her, Manuel?"

"I do not know, Señora."

"But wouldn't you *like* to know?"

He smiled at her. "No, Señora. What good would that do *me?*"

The shout to move out came down the line and Manuel helped her on her horse. She gathered up the reins and kneed her mare into a walk. She hadn't the slightest idea what the whole thing had been about. But being Spanish, as the woman was Spanish, Manuel had been quite certain.

The comedy came later, when they had made night camp. Manuel brought her a new Spanish list for studying. She glanced at it. She had progressed far. There were no longer words and phrases, there were entire sentences. Manuel said she had an ear for the language. "When you are in Santa Fe, Señora," he said, "it will be as though you were born there."

That wasn't so, but she knew she would not have difficulty understanding or being understood.

She remembered an early list. *Alma de mi alma.* "Manuel," she said, "you have a señorita in Santa Fe?"

"Señora?"

"You are betrothed, perhaps?"

"But, *no*, Señora!" He seemed horrified.

"Manuel," she was stern, "when we crossed the Deep Fork, all those weeks ago, you gave me a list of Spanish words. At the bottom was soul of my soul. You are not in love?"

"Ay de mi!" he lamented, striking his forehead, "did I do that? I was not thinking, Señora!"

"You were thinking," Judith said, "of your own señorita. Come now, Manuel. Were you not?"

"Ah, Señora, I was thinking of all the señoritas. They are so many in Santa Fe. And they are so beautiful. Señora, wait until you see the señoritas in Santa Fe . . . the most languishing eyes, the most perfect complexions, the most graceful figures . . ." he swooned with his own eloquence, "and how they can dance!"

"Oh, bosh," Judith said, "and nonsense!" She chucked the Spanish list on the ground. "Go picket your mules."

And she had nursed such a romantic notion of him!

He was a Lothario, a Don Juan, who breathed *alma de mi alma* into the ear of any señorita who would listen!

16

AFTER the encounter with the Comanches they turned a little south-westerly. Here they found many gravelly, bright-flowing streams with rich bottoms, lined all along with white oak, black walnut, mulberry and pecans. Asa Baldwin had rich materials with which to make his wagon repairs. With no trouble they made their fifteen or twenty miles a day. Through these oases Judith felt they merely loafed along.

There was muffled laughter concerning the feats of the black man. Some said three, some said five, some went as high as ten, Indian women he had lain with that fateful night. Judith heard the snickers and the quickly hushed words when she was near. But she knew.

And if she hadn't known, Jesse Cooper would have told her. "Debauch-ery," he said, when she rode beside him, "plain debauchery. Jonathan shouldn't have allowed it." His mouth was thin and straight.

"Don't be a fool," she said.

"It was an insult to you!"

"It was nothing of the kind."

"You surely didn't approve!"

"Of course not. But men are men. Johnny has got sense enough to know that."

"For God's sake, Judith . . ." His face was twisted and his eyes implored her.

"Jesse! Face the facts. We're taking a train to Santa Fe. These men have got to get it there for us. You want him to make trouble with them?"

"It was weak of him," he muttered.

Oh, Lord, he was so stubborn, and so righteous. "It was practical."

She dropped back feeling that a hopeless rift was forming between Johnny and his second in command. The man didn't belong here in the West. He was too grooved in the ways of the East. He didn't understand this country, and he didn't want to understand it. He didn't want to change. He didn't want to let go and be loose and easy, like Johnny. The ways he knew were best . . . the old Kentucky ways. Well, Johnny grew up with Kentucky ways, but he'd forgot them. He'd left them behind. The ways that settled Kentucky were fifty years late, now. It took a new man for a new country, one that could leave off the old. Johnny could leave it, but Jesse couldn't. All he could do was remember.

Buffalo were a little scarce now, but Suard and Crowbait and Ba'tiste brought in antelope and partridges and grouse. They fed well, the train. But a pest descended on them. Black gnats swarmed and they attacked not only the faces and hands but they contrived, somehow, to crawl beneath the clothing, onto the body itself, and all the uncovered parts. They were very small, but they fastened themselves upon humans, mules, and horses, and they bit and gouged and gorged and they made themselves merry and fat. "What in heaven's name is this beastly insect, Johnny?" Judith asked, slapping at a swarm about her face.

"Buffalo gnat," he said, "and I'm right pleased to see 'em. Means there's a herd close by. We need the meat."

"Well, I don't need these bugs! They're driving me wild!"

"'Twon't be for long."

He left her and rode far out ahead of the train. She made do with catching up to Jesse. "It's a strange land, isn't it, Jesse?"

"Strange to the point of disbelieving," he said.

They rode silently for a while. "You must not judge him, Jesse."

"I don't. He's the boss."

"Don't try figuring what you would have done, Jesse. He's . . . he's . . ."

Jesse's voice was flat and dry. "He's tough and he's hard and he's changed."

"He has to be! Don't you understand that, Jesse? He *has* to be!"

"Sure. I know that. Forget it. I don't hold it against him."

She felt furious with him. "What difference would it make if you did? But I think you do!"

"I don't. Believe me, I don't. I'd of let the horse go. I wouldn't of risked it. But I wouldn't of started out to Santa Fe, either. He's got more guts than I've got."

"What are you talking about? What horse do you mean?"

"His roan. Shelley was killed because of that roan."

"Oh, good gracious, Jesse, that was weeks ago! You aren't still holding that against him?" She had been talking about the Comanche camp, and she was aghast that he should still be brooding about Shelley.

"Can't seem to get it off my mind," he admitted.

"Well, you'll have to. You know the straight of it, and it can't be helped."

He shook his head and settled into a glum silence.

The afternoon was half gone when they came up with the herd of buffalo that had caused the epidemic of gnats. "This is a real herd," Johnny said when Judith joined him.

She was awed by its size. There was no way of guessing how big it was. It was like a big black river, so wide you couldn't see across, pouring endlessly from the north and out of sight already to the south. Thousands and thousands and thousands, maybe a million, she thought, but you'd never know—there was no end to them. "They'll be hours passing," Johnny said, "so we might as well camp."

All hands were turned out to hunt when the camp had been secured. They were in a long, flat stretch again and wood was scarce. Judith wandered about salvaging every piece she could find. It wasn't much and it wasn't worth much, either. She supposed they would come pretty soon to burning buffalo chips. She wasn't looking forward to that, but Johnny had said they made a hot fire, though they burnt up fast.

She had offered to cook that night, so Legette could hunt, too, and she had her fire going when the stranger came up. But the wood was as worthless as she'd thought it would be, taking its time to catch and smoking as if it had been waterlogged. She frowned over it and poked at it and wished for some kindling slivers. She was just no hand, she told herself, with a fire. She never had been and she never would be.

Squatted by the fire, fanning it with her skirts, she didn't notice the stranger until he spoke. She jumped as if she'd been poked and almost toppled into the blaze. "Don't you know enough," she burst out angrily, "not to come up on a body suddenly? You'll get a bullet in your ribs some day doing that."

"In my trade, ma'am," the man said softly, "it'd be more likely I'd git one if I give notice."

He and his outfit were startling enough, she thought, without sneaking up on a person. He was riding one horse and leading another. Both were brushy and shabby and rough. The pack animal carried the man's possessions and she'd never seen such a motley collection—a patchy and balding buffalo robe, a frayed blanket, an iron pot, half a dozen beaver skins, six steel traps, a dented and broken tin coffeepot, a bundle of dried branches (which she'd like to have herself right now), and the unskinned head of a deer. He didn't look to have any food except the deerhead.

"You can hobble your horses over there with ours," she said. You didn't ever turn a traveler away from your fire. Whatever he looked to be, and this man looked a renegade, when a stranger rode up out of the weather and out of nowhere, you made him welcome. "The drover will show you where." Manuel had got buffalo hunting out of his system back in the glady valley. "Unless," Judith added, "you mean to join my husband and his men."

"Thankee, ma'am, I'm some used up an' jist as soon not do no huntin' fer the time." His voice was very deep and a little husky. He used it quietly. "I'll jist hopple my brutes."

Judith fanned her apron at a stream of smoke. "This wood makes the meanest fire!"

"Hit's sand-choked, ma'am." The man untied the parcel of twigs and handed them down to her. "Why I allus carry these. They'll git ye started."

She took them, nodding at him. "There'll be coffee pretty soon."

"Hit'll be welcome, ma'am." He touched his old hat and left.

She wondered about him, who he was and where he'd come from and what he was doing and where he was going, but it wasn't her place to ask questions. He was a big man, bigger, she guessed, than Trice or Nate Butler, bigger maybe than Legette. He would range tall, too, for his legs had hung well below the belly of his mustang. He rode *up* on his horse, like an Indian, and without a saddle. He was ugly and shabby and shaggy and he had large, shallow eyes that were strangely pale in his dark face. And either he or the deerhead was as rancid as a pot of last year's bear grease.

When he came back he was without his hat and his hair showed greasy and tangled and coarse and black. Everything he had on was made of buckskin, his shirt, breeches and moccasins, and so old she wondered how they held together. An old gun was slung over his shoulder and his powder horn and pouch hung in front. None of this was unusual. Parley Wade wore old, filthy buckskins, too, and smelled like a billygoat. But there was a peculiar note in the grimy stock the man wore around his neck, that had long since curled into a rope. The buckle had been lost and he'd tied it with a deerstring.

When he came closer she saw that his face was badly pockmarked. At some time he'd had smallpox, then.

He made himself comfortable and she gave him coffee, then she paid him no more mind. It was growing late and she had bread to make and meat to fry and the fire was still troublesome. With it so pesky, she'd be pushed to have a meal ready when Johnny came.

"Ma'am," he said from behind her, "if ye wouldn't take it amiss I'd like to fix yer fire fer ye."

"Take it amiss!" she said, "I just wish to heaven you would! I can't abide a smoky fire."

He laughed the way Johnny did, she thought, sort of chuckly, deep down in his chest. He made no fuss over the fire, just did a few things, moved a piece of wood here, raked a little, turned another piece up-end, but the blaze began to grow and the smoke ceased. "Hit's got to git air," he explained. "Won't burn 'thout a draft." He sat back on his heels and watched it a moment, then nodded. "She'll do, now." He squinted up at her. "Would ye like me to cook that thar deerhead, ma'am? 'Twouldn't take long. Fine eatin', roasted."

"Why, yes," she said, "if you want."

He dug a trench under the coals and then, to her dismay, buried the head, still unskinned and raked the coals over it. "Thar. Ain't nothin' more to it. C'n jist fergit it till time to eat."

"But you didn't skin it!"

"No need. Skin'll come off easy when it's done. Slide it off when ye eat."

Well, she thought, she'd tried almost everything. The roasting would make the meat clean, she knew, and she supposed you *could* skin your meat as you ate it.

Johnny showed no surprise at the presence of a stranger when he came in. "Howdy," he said, "my name's Johnny Fowler."

The big stranger held out a ham-sized paw. "Knowed who ye was. Heared of ye. Up on the Missouri. Ain't never crossed yer trail afore but I'm pleased to. Heared ye was takin' a cargo to Santy Fee."

Johnny grunted. "Sit. Legette," he bawled over his shoulder, "bring a jug."

It still amazed Judith that in a country of such vast distances, with, you'd think, such meager lines of communication, you couldn't make a move without everybody within a thousand miles knowing about it.

After his first, deep, thirsty swig, the man swiped his mouth and said, "I'm Joe Britt."

"Joe Britt," Johnny repeated, then nodded. "Sure . . . the trapper. Worked mostly with Manuel Lisa."

"An' my pa afore me. Lisa's dead now, reckon ye know."

"Heard it last summer in St. Louis. Who's heading up the Company?"

Joe Britt shrugged. "Don't know as they got e'er head. Drips, I'd reckon. Me an' him don't gee. I ain't with the Company no more."

Johnny eyed him speculatively. "Going a loner?"

"Goin' a loner."

Johnny slapped his knees and stood. "Well, now, I'm nigh famished. My wife fed you yet?"

"Not yit," the trapper chuckled, his vast belly shaking. "I'm aimin' to feed her when that deerhead gits done."

"You got a deerhead roasting?"

"Right under them coals. Yer woman ain't sartin she'll hanker fer it, though." He laughed again.

Johnny joined him. "She don't know prairie fixin's. Her first trip."

"Jedged it was." He looked at Judith with friendly conspiracy, saying nothing about her smoky fire.

She grinned at him. "You aren't going to stump me. I'll eat your deerhead or any other prairie fixings you cook up."

"Spunky, ain't she?" Britt said.

"Spunky as a bear cub," Johnny agreed.

Judith caught the easiness between the two men now. They had met and measured and they liked what they had measured. They belonged to the same big fraternity . . . men who had roved the country pure and new and loved it and loved the way they lived on it and settled their own bones into it with a brash sureness, and held it in awe and feared and revered it, and took it into their bloodstreams. Joe Britt was kin to Johnny Fowler in all the ways that counted.

The good talk came when their bellies were full and the jug still flowed and old Parley drifted up and pipe smoke curled. "I mind the time," Britt would begin, and a tale of amazing dimensions would follow.

"I recollect," Parley would say, a prelude to one of his own adventures.

"I remember," Johnny would say, "it was on Bird Creek . . ."

But it was Britt who talked most. They gave him his right. He'd been the farthest, seen the most, done the most. He told about his father. "Married into the Kioways. Raised me up amongst 'em. I'm half Kioway myself. Ain't been with 'em much, though, since I was a chap. Now, he was a trapper, my pa. I'm cute, an' I c'n ketch plews, but I don't shine like he done. Never see the beat of him. Floated two thousand down the Platte in a bullboat one season."

"All his'n?" Parley asked.

"All his'n," Britt said, but his eyes were twinkling. "He had a woman amongst the Shoshones, too. But his joints got stiff an' he went with Lisa, an' Lisa prized him more'n any trapper he had. I l'arned from him," he finished, simply.

When he went on his talk was dredged with names and places—the Yellowstone, the Platte, the Niobrara, the Sweetwater, the Wind and the

Green; the old Missouri Company, the American, the Northwesters, the Rocky Mountain, Pratt, Cabanne, the Chouteaus, John Jacob Astor, McKenzie, Fontenelle, the Sublettes, General Ashley—the fur places and the fur people and the fur trade.

"I'm headin' fer the high parks," Britt said. He took a twig and made marks in the sand. "Thar," he said, "thar is whar the old Arkansas boils down outen the mountains. Clean up an' up from thar is the big country. Up through them big rocks an' passes, up to the Bayou Salade. Ever seed the Salade?"

"No," Johnny said, regret heavy in his voice, "no, I've never."

"Ye've missed it, lad. Hit's the onliest place in the world so sweet an' purty. Hard to git into but when ye git thar, ye don't ever want to leave. High an' green an' crossed over with little creeks an' streams, an' the grass up to yer brute's belly. Gits cold up thar, cause she's high, but they's beaver an' they's grass an' they's timber to shelter. Sightliest place on earth. Oh, they's plenty other parks. Commence at Taos, thar, an' foller up. Hit's all purty."

He smoked and talked and made marks in the sand. "Off thar is the peak they're commencin' to call Pike's. Don't go messin' with the Peak, lad, less'n ye mean bizness. She's spread an' thick an' humpy an' dangerous. She's a tough old lady. They's a trail runs right thar, though. Goes past St. Vrain's an' the Vasquez an' passes over Laramie to the Green. Now, man, thar's ye a river. An' thar's ye some country. Injuns been ridin' that trail since time begun. Oldest trail I know."

He hauled up and Johnny handed him the jug. "But ye're headin' fer Santy Fee. Ain't got no interest in the Green." He drew in the sand again. "Fust ye'll see of the mountains is the Spanish Peaks, the Huajatollas." Judith took no offense that he had forgotten her when he went on. "Injuns call 'em the Breasts of the World. Do look a mite like a woman's tits at that—young one, kind of sharp an' p'inted. Huerfano country, that is. Headwaters fer the Huerfano an' Cochara an' Ganeros. Spanish country. They's a trail heads up over the Medano Pass—tough one an' ain't many uses it an' I'd bypass it if I was you. I'd try the Mosca or the Poncha."

"Man," Johnny said, laughing ruefully, "you've forgot. I can't head for them passes. I got wagons to get through. I got to head for Pecos and San Miguel."

The trapper's lit eyes dulled. "Yeah. I did fergit. Ye're tied to the flat lands. I feel sorry fer ye. Hit's jist ploddin'."

As if he had a fever, he talked on. He knew every high park in the mountains, the Bayou Salade, the San Luis, the South Park, the Saguache, the

Uncompaghre country. He knew Taos and Santa Fe, he knew the Mora, Truchas and Chimayo country. He knew the whole Sangre de Cristos range.

"Where," Johnny asked, finally, "is the best place for me to go? When I get these wagons to Santa Fe, where is the closest and best place?"

The trapper grinned and puffed on his old pipe. "Depends. Depends. Some says the San Luis, some says the Saguache. They both got beaver, plenty of beaver."

Johnny puffed on his own pipe. "I ain't asking where you're headed."

Joe Britt grinned. "An' I wouldn't say, if you did. I got my own places. I wouldn't tell ye of 'em. I bin trappin' too many years to steer ye to one of my own places."

"Wouldn't expect you to."

"No. But I'm a halfbreed an' I don't mind sayin' I got my ins with the Utes an' Shoshones. That don't give nothin' away fer they trap all over. But I'll tell ye this, lad, I'll tell ye this. If ye want to ketch beaver, head north of Taos into the San Luis. That's what I'd do. Hit's not my country. Mine is richer, an' I don't mind sayin' so, but ye'll make out fine in the San Luis."

Johnny shoved the jug at the trapper. "Drink up. There's plenty."

Joe Britt drank long again. "I got a powerful thirst. Hit's good likker. No, sir, ye wouldn't go wrong to head fer the San Luis."

"I wouldn't be surprised," Johnny said, casually. "Expect that's where I'd better head." As if in afterthought, he added, "Utes like the Saguache, don't they?"

"Not allus," the great head wagged, "not allus. They . . . hey! Hey, you tryin' to git my secret places outen me? Tryin' to git me drunk so's I'll talk?" He waggled his finger in Johnny's face. "Let me tell you something, boy. Old Joe Britt ain't ever been so drunk he'd tell his secrets. Ye cain't git him that drunk."

"Didn't figure to," Johnny laughed. "Joe, I'm no greenhorn. I'm new to this country, but I know Utes trap the upper Arkansas and the Shoshones trap the Snake."

Joe Britt peered at him. "Ye're cute, lad, ye're real cute."

"And from here," Johnny went on, "you're heading for the upper Arkansas. Wouldn't make sense, this far south, not to. Britt," he leaned forward, "you've got six traps. You've got no possibles. How about traveling with me and scouting?"

"Ain't lookin' fer no scout's job."

"I pay ten a month and found. You can outfit right in Santa Fe."

"Don't need to. Ain't never needed nothin' but my traps an' my brutes. Whut ye need a scout fer? Why ain't ye got one?"

"That's my business. I can get along without one, but we'll move faster with one. I want to move fast."

"Well . . . reckon ye know whut ye're doin'."

"I wouldn't own this train if I didn't, and I own it lock, stock and barrel. Will you swap?"

The trapper fingered his chin. "I wouldn't go no further'n Santy Fee. Ye understand?"

"Don't need you any farther."

"Ye wouldn't be askin' me to take ye on into the up-country?"

"I've said I wouldn't."

The trapper, who was becoming very drunk, belched hugely and sighed. "I dunno. Well, all right. You done seed fer yerself. I ain't even got the necessaries fer a season. Need to git holt of some money, somehow. I'll do it, Johnny."

Numbed with drowsiness, Judith stumbled to bed. But when Johnny came, she roused. "You took advantage of him, Johnny. You got him drunk."

"Honey," he said, his voice a little thick, "don't you know he didn't stumble on us by accident? He was needing a job and looking for a job and he's likely been trailing us since we crossed the Spanish line."

"Oh." She raised up on an elbow. "You trust him, Johnny?"

"Sure. Sure, I trust him." He pulled off his boots. "Anybody could trust him. He don't get paid till we get to Santa Fe."

17

THE WAGONS rolled on.

The routine of every day was now so familiar that Judith had forgotten what any other life was like. You rose and washed and dressed and ate and hooked up and stretched out and moved on. You nooned in the blazing heat, on cold food, you dozed a little, then you hooked up and rolled again. When the sun dipped below the earth line, you halted, formed up, unhitched, unpacked grub boxes, cooked, ate, set guards, and turned in for the night. It was dreary and deadly in its monotony, but nobody, she least of all, wanted the monotony disturbed. The monotony was its own security. As long as there was monotony, there were no disasters. They kept eating up the slow miles, ten today, fifteen tomorrow, but every mile advanced, a mile behind them.

Now, every man knew his job every hour of every day. They were trail-weary and glummer, but they were more effective. Now Judith could look about each morning when the wagons were ready to move out and place each man. Today O'Toole and Wash Craig were riding flank. Hull Archer would be trailing and would be eating dust all day. Tomorrow, William Day and Ben Spring would ride flank and Legette would take the tail. The hunters, Suard and Crowbait and Ba'tiste, were always fanned out, watching for game and riding guard.

Once she hadn't known these men. They had been question marks to her. Now she knew them too well. A wagon train, she thought, was like a family or a small settlement. It had its gossip, its rumors, its quarrels, its small cliques, its ups and its downs. One thing was everlastingly true. They were bound together by a common goal and they could not escape each other. Inevitably they knew every ache, pain, grudge and disgruntlement a neighbor had, and had to put up with it.

Some men had worn well—Nate Butler and O'Toole and Ben Spring and, increasingly, William Day. You had to give Bullitt Trice credit, too. He was a malcontent but he never slacked his work, and he kept Brand and Wash Craig and Hull Archer in line. The towers of strength remained now, as when they had first taken their departure, old Parley and Asa Baldwin and Legette and Manuel. Jesse Cooper fell somewhere in between. He had his good days and his bad. He showed the erosion of the journey, but his knowledge of loaded wagons was invaluable. He had never failed to get them through.

Joe Britt was in a category all to himself. Everybody liked him. He was a jovial, genial, cheerful companion to them all.

They moved now along a depression with a low ridge lying north of them, brushy with shin oak and plum bush, and a desert of sand to the south. The road was mixed. From hour to hour it changed. One hour it was nothing but sand. The next it was sand and mesquite and shin oak and the bluffy land of the first mesas. When they hit these places there was a desert floor of sage, pear cactus, and scrawny greasewood. It all tilted west, lifted slightly and rose, imperceptibly, toward the mountains.

Johnny rode out ahead every day now. He got the train rolling every morning, setting scouts, flankers and drags. Once under way, he rode off. The train was Jesse's job, then.

Joe Britt rode with Johnny. Like him, Britt wanted to be free of the wagons. He wanted his nose pointed ahead, free and ranging. He bedded with Parley's crew and Trice and his gang had made him their hero. At night Judith could hear the loud talk and the laughter.

"He tells them his tales of trapping, Johnny."

"Sure. Why not? They're meaning to trap, too, most of 'em."

"Wash Craig said today he wished they could cut loose from the wagons. Said he wished they could just follow Joe Britt to the mountains."

"You know, honey," Johnny said, "I sort of wish I could, too."

"Johnny!"

"Ah, honey, the wagons are so slow. He'll never lead 'em there," he added. "He don't want a crew."

Judith was troubled about Jesse Cooper, too. He had grown thinner and thinner and his face had become more worn. His mouth was often tight and his eyes were shadowed. The heat, of course, was bad, but she was afraid he wasn't well. One day she asked him. "Jesse, aren't you feeling well?"

"Sure." There was real surprise in his voice. "Sure, I feel fine. Why?"

"You don't look fine. You've lost weight. You're thinning down too much."

"I don't think so," he said slowly. "I'd not noticed, leastways."

She rode nearer and reached to touch his arm. "Jesse. We can't have you coming down sick. If you're ailing, say so. We need you too bad."

She was astonished when he swerved his horse away. "Don't do that," he said, "don't touch me! Don't . . ." He broke off, then continued bitterly, "I'd of done better to stayed in Kentucky. There's nothing but grief for me here . . ." He broke off again, kicked his horse up and rode ahead of her.

She let him go for a spell, then caught him up again. "Now, that's just not so, Jesse. Johnny trusts you and he needs you. If you're sick . . ."

He turned on her. "For God's sake, leave me alone! What I'm sick of nothing in your black medicine satchel will cure!"

"Well, good gracious," she said indignantly, "there's no call to be so violent. I only meant . . ."

"I know what you meant. You think one of your blue pills will cure anything a man's got."

"It will, oftener than you'd think."

He glared at her, then softened and smiled. "Oughtn't to've busted loose on you. I'm sorry. Not your fault. And I'll take one of your blue pills if you want. Might do some good at that."

"It can't *hurt*," she said, appeased. She didn't know what was bothering him now, but a good purge never did harm to anybody.

They jogged peacefully along.

At the same startled moment both saw the lone horseman at the top of the sandy ridge. He was poised there, watching them, but he was too far away to make out clearly. There was merely a horse and a figure astride of it. Before they could recover, he had wheeled and disappeared. Judith looked quickly at Jesse. "Indian?"

"Don't know." He shook his head, puzzling his brows. "Acted queer to be one of ours. Why would one of them sit there and look on? Way his legs hung so long, though, he wasn't using stirrups. Britt rides that way, but Britt would've hulked bigger on the horse. He makes his horse look small. Don't know . . ."

"What should we do?" There had been nothing to fear from the Comanches, she reminded herself. One lone Indian, if it was an Indian, didn't mean they were going to be attacked. But her breath was a little short, just the same.

"Well, Johnny . . ."

"Johnny's not here!"

"No." He brooded another moment. "Just trying to think if I ought to halt the wagons. Don't see how it could have been anything but an Indian. Could be scouting for a band of 'em." He made his decision. "I'll

ride on—see what I can see. Better find out. You turn back and tell Parley."
He kicked his horse up.

Judith called after him, "Jesse, take care!"

She wheeled about and galloped back to the train. Parley was driving
the lead wagon that day, to rest himself he said. Said his old bones got
almighty weary of being pounded in a saddle day after day. He batted
his hat back in exasperation when Judith told him Jesse had ridden out
ahead. "Now, whut'd he do *that* fur?"

"If that was a hostile Indian, Parley, it'd be best to know."

"How's he gonna tell? By gittin' his skin shot full of arrers? Johnny an'
Britt wouldn't of missed a strange Injun. They'd o' been back here 'fore
you could bat yer eye. Likely," he added, heaving himself more comfortably
on the seat, "likely 'twas one o' the Osages."

"Jesse didn't think so. Aren't you going to do anything, Parley?"

"Do what, fer instance?"

"Halt the train or alert the men, or *something*?" Parley took this news
mighty casually, but after all he didn't know everything. She couldn't
help feeling they ought to make ready for . . . well, for whatever happened.

"No," Parley said firmly, "I ain't gonna halt these wagons. If you ain't
noticed, missy, the skies is threatenin' an' a storm is brewin'. I'm aimin'
to hustle these wagons right along in the hopes we c'n git out of this draw
'fore she breaks. I'd a sight ruther face hostiles, which they ain't the least
chance of, than git caught in the mess we'd be in bogged down. An' the
men is ready. They're allus ready. But if you're itchin' to do something
real bad, ride back to the tail an' tell Manuel to close up a mite. Don't go
skeerin' the pants offen him, either, with no talk of Injuns. Likely that
pack o' mules has done got weather-skittish an' he's havin' his troubles
with 'em. Ye want somethin' to do so all-fired bad, ye c'n give him a hand
with 'em."

"You needn't act so uppity," Judith snapped. "I noticed the weather
clouds some time ago."

"Hit's a pity Jesse never. Now, scamper. I'm gonna commence pushin'
these critters." He hauled in on the lines and cracked his whip. "Git,
honey. I'm aimin' to blister . . ."

But she was racing away, feeling guilty. She'd noticed the clouds. That
was true. But she hadn't noticed how swiftly they were rolling up and
how black they were turning, and she hadn't noticed the wind blowing
up. It was coming in gusts, skittering and whirling sand before it, tumbling the dried weeds into flying balls, beginning to crack the canvas

wagon sheets. Lord, it was going to blow, and it was going to pour, and they were caught in this draw! Parley would make a good run for it, but there might not be time. She'd never seen a flash flood but she'd heard of them and she knew a wall of raging water could bowl their wagons over as if they had been children's toys.

Hull Archer had drawn the tail today and been sulky about it. He still looked sulky, but he was working. He was having to work. The herd had nosed the storm and had laid their ears back and were making trouble. Manuel was circling and driving on one side, Archer on the other. Both were busier than a woman making soap.

"Can you close up a little?" Judith shouted at the Mexican. "Parley said close up."

Manuel didn't bother to answer, he just shook his head and pointed at the skittish animals.

Judith drifted back to guard the rear. They looked pretty panicky. They milled and huddled, not liking close quarters now, instinct driving them to break free. Almost anything, she thought anxiously, could make them stampede, the shape they were in. All three of them, Manuel and Archer on the edges and herself in back, had to cut and wheel and circle and chase. The pack mules were the worst, their loads fretting them, though goodness knew the whole drove was nervy enough. She hadn't time to give more than a quick look now and then at the sky, and she had completely forgotten the lone Indian. She had all she could do hazing breakouts back in line.

It was, of all things, a tumbleweed that set them off finally, and of all the animals, her own horse that shied at it, stood on his hind feet, whinnied and squealed like a stuck pig, pawed the air, bucked half a dozen times, then broke loose into a hard run. She sawed the lines and yelled at him, but he'd bolted and was out of control. All she could do was hang on.

A sound like rolling thunder caught up with her and she knew the whole herd had bolted behind her. She risked a quick look over her shoulder and saw them, riders already fanning out from the train in pursuit. This fool horse! It only took him, getting the wind up over a bunch of dry weeds, to set them all off! They'd scatter over the whole prairie, and the storm would keep driving them, and it might take days to round them up! She'd never been so mad at a dumb creature in her life! Her bonnet bounced over her eyes. She nudged it up but it flopped again. She tore it off and threw it away. The wind caught her hair immediately, tore it loose from its pins and streamed it like a bright banner behind her. But she was set now, without hindrance, to ride this mustang out.

As far as she could tell he wasn't tiring yet, but she might be able to draw him around, a little at a time, and circle him into heading back in the right direction. She began trying to swing him to the left. He felt the bit, but instead of answering to it he bulled his nose down and stiffened his neck. She thought he was going to pull her arms loose from the sockets. Exasperated, and with no time to coddle him, she braced in the stirrups and took another half-hitch on the reins. She had to get his head up and turn him, and he had to learn he couldn't take the bit in his teeth when he chose. She hauled back, putting her hard leg muscles into it and her hard, lean belly, and she sawed till he broke his gait. Dratted stiff-necked, tough-mouthed animal, she scolded at him, spook at a tumbleweed, bolt at a shadow, start a stampede!

She had his head coming up now and she hung on without giving him an inch of slack. Her hands were losing their feeling and the knuckles showed white against the brown skin, but she didn't notice. This fool animal was going to answer to the bit and he was going to swing wide and he was going to take her back where she wanted to go! His head gave a little more and she took another half-wrap on the lines and hauled hard. Suddenly the battle was over. The head came all the way up, tossed against the hurting bit, and the long running stride jolted into a faltering trot.

Judith swung him around and began talking to him, patting him, soothing him. "There, now. There, now, boy. Steady now. Steady. Nothing to be afraid of. Nothing to fret about. Whoa, now, whoa. Be easy. Be easy." He was lathered and she bent around to see if she'd torn his mouth. No blood. She didn't know whether to be glad he was tough-mouthed or not. He'd have been easier to bring up if he wasn't, but his mouth could have been ruined, too.

Well. Well! She took a deep breath and let her arms go slack. Quite a run they'd had, quite a run. Her stomach muscles were as quavery as a bowl of jelly and her arms felt like ropes. Soon as this jackrabbit got his wind back, though . . . she looked up sharply. What in heaven's name was Bullitt Trice doing pounding her way as if something was after him? Somebody had cut the herd off to the right and they were black dots on the prairie. Why wasn't he with them?

She kicked her horse up, but hearing the other horse running, he began to sunfish and prance and wheel. Judith waved violently at Trice and screamed at him to keep back. "You'll set my horse off again! Keep back!"

But Trice just whipped up his horse and came pounding on. The next thing she knew Jupiter was off again, and she was once more sawing away.

It was only a short sprint. The mustang was too winded and he soon dropped into an easy lope that Trice had no trouble catching. "Why didn't you keep back?" Judith yelled when he came alongside. "Don't you know better than to come up to a bolted horse?"

She wasn't at all prepared for what the man did. Closing in, he swept her from the mustang's back and held her tightly cradled until his horse jogged to a standstill. When she got over being surprised she was furious. The idiot had nearly jerked her head off her neck, he'd nearly broken her ribs, and he'd nearly suffocated her in his sweaty old shirt. She fought to free herself.

"Now, ma'am," he was saying, "just be easy. Just be easy. No harm has come to you."

"Let me go, you stupid lout!" She beat at his chest. "Let me go! Of course no harm has come to me!"

"Now, Miz Fowler . . ."

But his hold had loosened a little and she squirmed quickly and slid to the ground. He was out of the saddle instantly, coming toward her. She faced him, her chest heaving, and tears of rage streaming down her face. "Why didn't you keep back! I had my horse under control! What got into you? No one but a fool would come pounding up to a scared horse! And what do you mean dragging me off my horse? What crazy notion have you got into your head?"

Her hair was hanging, wildly windblown, around her shoulders and to her waist. She gave it no thought except to brush it out of her eyes.

Trice took two more steps toward her, his small, close-set eyes squinting, a grin stretching his mouth. "My, but you're pretty when you're mad."

"What are you doing here? You aren't needed. You had no business chasing off after me!" She could have hit him she was so angry.

"Well, now, when a pretty lady is in distress I'm not one to take thought of a bunch of stampeding mules, like the others."

"I wasn't in distress," she snapped at him. "Do you think I've never ridden a runaway horse before?"

"I didn't know, ma'am." His eyes roved over her. "It looked to me like you was having a right bad time of it. I didn't allow the captain would like his lady bucked off and her neck broke, mebbe."

She drew herself up and said coldly, "The captain himself taught me to ride. And I haven't taken a fall since the first time I mounted a horse."

Trice came nearer. He bent a little, bringing the flattened, obscene nostrils very close, the pig eyes, the wet mouth, almost in her face. His look shifted to her hair and slowly he touched it, pulled his hard, square hand through the long length of it. "You've got the prettiest hair," he said, almost crooningly, "the prettiest hair I ever seen."

She knocked his hand away. "Get away from me!"

The wet mouth was drooling a little spittle at one corner. "Now, ma'am, you're so kind to Mr. Cooper with your favors, ain't you got none for Trice?"

She hit him hard across the face, and was then blinded as a fork of brilliant lightning leaped and sizzled suddenly all around them. The thunderclap was deafening and shook the earth. The storm! she thought, the storm! Fat drops of rain were splattering. She ran for Jupiter and was up and lashing him with the reins. She had to run for it. She had to get back to the train! The train was in the draw!

There wasn't much run left in the mustang but he gave her what he had. Even so it seemed to take an eternity, and the first spattering drops had turned to a sheeting downpour before she came over the last rise and could see the wagons. She had to wipe her eyes, then, and peer, but she went limp with relief. They were canting up the slope. Parley had made it.

Nearer, she saw it wasn't all made yet. The slope was greasy with the sluicing rain and the teams were pulling hard. Parley had set William Day driving in his place and he was pounding and shouting the length of the train. "Keep 'em movin'! Keep 'em movin'! One falter an' they'll bog! Keep 'em movin'!"

He spared her one short comment when she came up. "Ye look like a drownded rat." But his old, experienced eyes saw in one glance she'd come to no harm. He barked at her. "Git in that wagon an' take the lines an' let Day on the wheelhorse. We're short-handed on account o' that stampede you set off!"

Her eye was experienced, too. She saw they were without Legette and Ben Spring and O'Toole and, of course, Manuel and Hull Archer. She didn't bother to answer Parley, to bite back at him. She raced up to the wagon, ranged as close as she could get, gathered herself, and leaped from Jupiter's back. Day couldn't pull up to let her clamber over the wheel. She took the lines and Day walked the tongue to the wheelhorse.

Later, she didn't know how they kept the wagons moving, but they did. So slowly that it sometimes seemed as though the wheels turned by inches, they crept up the slope until finally all four wagons were atop the low ridge. They halted and she turned about and looked down where they'd been. The draw was a dry creek bed and already a stream was flowing. Not more than hub-deep, maybe, but rising every second. She began to shake and her teeth chattered against each other. She was cold, cold, and she was wet to the skin, and her arms ached and her hands were numb, and if nobody cared she was going to be sick to her stomach. She dropped the lines.

Parley came up with a blanket. He reached it to her and she wrapped it about herself, and then he held up his arms and she lowered herself into them. She didn't know why she was crying, or why Parley was carrying her, but she was, and he was, and then she was in her own wagon and it was warm and dry and safe, and Parley was helping her out of her wet shoes and he was rubbing her hair dry, and he was making her drink some whisky, and he was talking to her soothingly. "Thar, now, honey, thar. Ye been a good, brave girl, but it's all over now 'cept waitin' out the storm. Ye kin take yer clothes off an' wrop in some blankets an' jist set. Take a sip more, now. Hit'll warm ye. Wish I could hot it up fer ye but they'll be no fires tonight. One more sip, now, fer old Parley. Ye're Parley's bonnie little lass an' ye've fit a runaway critter an' a evil man an' a storm an' ye driv a wagon up a goddamned slidy ridge, an' ye've . . . another sip, now. Jist one more. Jist one more."

Ah, but it was good to feel warmth returning. He held a blanket and turned his head and she stripped out of her wet clothing and clutched the blanket about her. Parley let down the bunk and fussed with the pillows. She sat on its edge and felt wonderful, the good heat of the whisky spreading all through her. She laughed at Parley. "You're like an old hen fussing over a lone chick."

"Never mind," he said, "never mind. Git in this bed an' kiver to yer chin." He peered at her anxiously. "Is that chill passin'?"

"Passed," she said. "See? My teeth have quit chattering."

"Reckon ye won't come down with the pneumony, then."

"Probably won't even take the sniffles. Parley, how'd you know Trice was . . . was offensive out there?"

"Know Trice," he said shortly. "Would of rid after him if that danged Jesse'd been whur he belonged an' I hadn't to stay with the wagons." He was tucking her in and piling on more blankets.

"You're going to bury me," she protested, "that's enough. Has Jesse come in?"

"Not yit."

"I hope he's not run into trouble."

"He's not." Parley was positive. "Might drown hisself, but that's all."

She laughed. "Try to make Johnny come change his clothes when he gets in, Parley, will you?"

"Try," he nodded. "I got things to do now. Ye git hungry ye'll jist have to scrabble in yer grub box, honey. Won't be no cookin' this evenin'." He peered out before letting himself down on the step. "Godamighty, whut a sight! Looks like war had broke out over the hull danged prairie. Don't stick yer nose out fer nothin', sweetheart, a bolt of lightnin' 'll nip it right off."

He was gone.

She wanted to see. She worked herself up from under Parley's swaddling and propped herself with pillows. Then she raised the wagon sheet a couple of inches and put her eye to the slit. Both eyes widened with wonderment. She'd heard the thunder raising a continuous tumult, but she'd had no idea what was actually going on outside. For one thing, it had got very dark, as if night were coming ahead of its time. But the darkness was incessantly lit with the lightning, blue forked tongues of lightning and whole skyfuls of flames and streaked lances. Every kind of lightning she'd ever seen, and some she hadn't, was playing around in the sky out there. It sure did look like war had broken out over the whole danged prairie! She'd never seen a war, but a night battle must look just like this . . . guns blazing and shooting fire all over the sky, and it must sound like this, cracking and booming and rattling and rolling. The rain was slashing down and the wind was up, hard and fast and tearing. Golly Moses, what a night to be out in! And there were so many out in it— Johnny and Joe Britt and Jesse Cooper, and the hands that had chased after the stampede, and some of the men here, trying to get the teams unhitched and picketed. She could see them struggling. And the mules were scared and made it no easier.

She was almost blinded, suddenly, by a brilliant glare, and blinked, and then watched, unbelieving, as a ball of fire rolled about the backs of the mules. Then she was stunned and deafened by the crash of the thunder. That hit, she thought, clapping her hands over her ears instinctively, that killed those mules. She scrabbled out of her coverings and kneeled, thrusting the canvas up to see. The men, too? Were any of the men struck, too? She heard them shouting, but perversely the lightning, having struck, now chose to play about dimly. It seemed a long time before the darkness was lit up enough for her to see, and it lasted only long enough for her to tell that some mules were down . . . two, no three . . . but no men . . . unless that rock, or was it a log . . . or a man? "Parley!" she screamed, "Parley!" But the wind tore her voice away.

She crouched and watched. Men were sloshing about again, now, but they weren't carrying anybody to shelter. And the rock, or log, was still there. And one of the mules had struggled up. There was another bright streak, and she flinched, but there was no ball of fire. In the flare she saw two horsemen, shapeless under blanket shelters, coming. Johnny! And Joe Britt! Oh, thank heaven, thank heaven! Johnny threw himself off his horse and bellowed over the thunder, "Get these mules away from the wagons! They're wet and they're drawing the lightning! Get your backs into it! Quick!"

There was a swift, drumming tattoo on the canvas roof and she looked up quickly. Hail! She hoped . . . but it had already grown to a clamoring hammer, and it was already tearing the canvas, and the rain and the big stones were already pelting through. She scrambled to set pots and buckets under the leaks, but she hadn't enough, as the rents grew, and she had to dash about finding the worst drips. They were like knives, she thought, ripping the canvas. If the sheets on the freight wagons were being damaged as badly, the goods would get wet and that meant unloading and spreading and drying, *if* the rain ever let up!

The hailstorm passed on quickly and the great clattering on the roof became again the solid beat of rain.

Judith stood in the middle of the floor and looked at the pots of drip and the melting stores and the puddles soaking into the bed and more rain streaming through the holes, and she thought of the cold, wet, miserable camp they must make tonight, and the men still out in this cloudburst, wet to their skins, sloshing about, and more men out on the prairie just as wet, chasing a drove of stampeded animals. Suddenly she began to laugh. If they weren't the worst bedraggled passel of folks that had ever ridden this way, they came close to it! But the worst was over—it had to be.

She climbed on her damp bunk and dozed, and when she woke the storm had died away. All was quiet and the wagon was lit with the sun. She peered out. It was low on the earthline and red and swollen, but it was alone, not a cloud in the sky. How serene and beautiful and peaceful the whole world was, now. How clean and scrubbed.

"Judith?" It was Johnny calling. "You awake?"

"I'm awake!"

"Dress and come out. Hot coffee!"

She poked her head out the back. "How'd you make hot coffee?"

He waved at a small fire. "Buffalo chips, and a goods box chopped up. Legette's got a piece of meat right hot, too. It'll be on the rare side, but better than nothing."

She dressed quickly and went out. Legette's black and grinning face shone at her. "When did you get back, Legette?"

"A little bit ago. When the storm had passed, ma'am." He handed her a plate with a great slab of smoking meat on it and a mug of steaming coffee.

"Manuel sent him in," Johnny said, "to say they'd weathered the storm. Nobody hurt. Eat up, honey. You need hot food after what you've been through."

She grinned at him. "How do you know what I've been through?"

"Parley told me."

From his curtness, and from the grim line of his mouth, she guessed that Parley had also told him that Trice had made trouble. She began to eat. Nobody could have foreseen that, she told herself, nobody. And Johnny would have to handle it the way he thought best. Maybe he'd tell her, and maybe he wouldn't. But he couldn't have one of his hands molesting his wife. She knew that. She guessed he would order Trice to stay away from her. How Trice would take that, she didn't know, but however Trice took it, Johnny could take care of that, too. They had never discussed it; he had never warned her or advised her concerning her deportment with the hands; but not being blind he would have seen that she had her own seemly idea of how to conduct herself. She had been friendly with them all, but she had not made friends with any of them, saving, perhaps, Manuel and Legette and Jesse Cooper.

"Have you eaten?" she asked him now.

He nodded.

She finished and told Legette the meat had been good and the coffee better. It was a miracle, she thought, the difference hot food made in the way you felt. "How much damage?" she asked Johnny.

"Two mules killed, all the wagon sheets torn, and most of the goods pretty wet. Could be a lot worse."

"I reckon," she said, the word he and Parley used so much coming easily to her tongue, and unnoticed, "I reckon we'll make and mend tomorrow, then."

"Yes. We'll not move tomorrow."

They smiled easily at each other, partners in an unwanted necessity. He didn't like delays, and she didn't like delays because he didn't like them. "Jesse come in yet?" she asked.

"About thirty minutes ago. Tuckered out. I don't know what got into him. Fool thing to do—ride out by himself that way."

"That's what Parley said." She felt a little guilty herself. "Jesse thought he ought to find out about the Indian."

"Could've got himself into a mess of trouble. Ought to've remembered that's what we've got flankers out for, and me and Joe ahead."

"You knew about the Indian?"

"Sure. I dunno," he rubbed his chin, "Jesse's not acting right. Something's wrong with him."

"I think so, too. I'm going to give him a blue mass pill tonight." She said it with determination.

"That'll fix his guts," Johnny laughed, "but I don't know as it'll help his judgment." He stood and stretched. "Well, we come out of it pretty good, all 'round. Funny, isn't it, how that much rain can run off in such a hurry? Sand's almost dry already."

"Was a little while there," she said, laughing, too, "when that bolt hit the mules and could have hit one of the men, I didn't know but what we'd come to the end of the trail."

"Just God's mercy, that," Johnny said. "I was just riding up, and when I saw that ball of fire I made sure I'd find two or three men dead. Just a mercy."

Her hands were loose-folded in her lap and she felt like that all over, slack and idle and lazy and good. "Was the Indian one of those Comanches?" she asked, almost as idly.

"Why, no. It was the Beaver. He showed himself several days ago." Johnny chuckled, and she knew he liked it that the Osage hadn't turned back after all. "He won't come in, and I've not talked to him, but he's let himself be seen lately. Reckon," he added, "he's been trailing us all the way."

Parley knew, she thought. But Jesse didn't. She made her hands stay still although they wanted to pluck at her skirt. "You didn't want Jesse to know?" she asked.

He looked uncomfortable. "Not 'specially. Not unless the Beaver makes up his mind to come in again. No need. Figured Jesse didn't have much use for him, after what happened. Might set him off, or something."

It might, she thought . . . it just might.

18

THE HUGE, bulky, pot-bellied trapper poked a finger at the map. "This is the dry plains, now, an' ye got to bear north. Commencin' today."

Johnny and Parley were studying the map, too. "I don't like it," Johnny said. "It takes us out of our latitude."

"Whut's latitude? Ye aim to git to Santy Fee, don't ye?"

"Sure."

"Then fergit latitude. Ye got to head north here, north by west. Ye don't, ye'll wind up in the staked plains an' God help ye if ye git mixed up thar."

"Bad?"

"Like the seventh circle of hell."

Johnny stared at him. "When did you ever read Dante?"

"Who?"

"Dante—the seventh circle of hell."

"Oh, that. Hit was a sayin' of my pa's. He was a man of l'arnin'. I cain't read. Never l'arnt. But them staked plains is fierce, an' no mistake."

"The map," Johnny said, "shows 'em pretty well to the south of us."

"Ye aim," Joe Britt said with contempt, "to b'lieve a man that's been over the kintry, or yer map?"

"I dunno." Johnny pulled at his chin. "To bear north now will take us pretty near the Canadian canyons. Don't know but what I'd as soon risk the plains."

"Ye'll bear west 'fore ye hit the Canadian. Come out by the Tucumcari Mound. Onliest way to git through here."

"How about water?"

"They's ponds. Some's brackish, but they're all wet." He waited a moment, then hitched up his pants and spat. "When ye make up yer mind, let me know. I'll lead ye." And he strode away.

Judith watched him go with mixed feelings. She didn't like him as well as she had. He and Bullitt Trice had become great friends. He rode out with Johnny every day, and the train made every landfall he predicted;

but in camp he and Trice were forever together. Any man, she reflected, that could like Bullitt Trice that much, could bellow so enormously at his crude jokes, could abide his spraddling, swaggering ways, had something suspect in him. But it didn't seem to bother Johnny. He was only bothered by this northing they had to make.

"Where we at?" Parley asked.

Johnny's lean brown finger pointed. "Here."

They were nearing the hundred and second meridian.

"That them staked plains down there?"

"That's them."

"Look purty fur south of us to me," Parley said.

"This map ain't the most reliable there is," Johnny said.

"Yeah, but the Beaver marked them plains fer ye."

"He's been this way once. He could be wrong. Indians can follow their nose, but when it comes to maps . . ."

"Well, yep," Parley admitted, "they ain't no great shakes. Hell, I wish that dumned Osage'd come on in an' talk!"

Johnny sighed and rolled up the map. "He'll come in when he's ready. Not before."

"Ye ain't had a word with him yit?"

"Not a word. Not that first word. Fact is, I've not even seen him since Jesse got the wind up the day of the storm. May have turned back, for all I know."

"Ain't likely. He's follered this far, 'tain't likely he'd turn back, now. He's jist bidin' his time."

"What for?" Judith asked.

Both men raised their shoulders. Both men shook their heads. "Who knows," Parley said, "why a Injun does whut he does?"

Johnny put his map in his pouch and looked down the train. "All right," he said, "let's roll."

Judith made a quick change in her plans for the day. Parley, to rest himself again, was going to be driving her wagon. "Tie Jupiter to the back, Parley. I'll ride with you."

They rode in silence for an hour, shoulders rubbing together as the wagon jolted, Parley speaking to the mules once in a while. He didn't hurry her. It was one of the good things about Parley. He knew she had something on her mind, but he gave her her time and didn't rush her.

Joe Britt was right about one thing, she thought. This was dry country, real, bona fide dry country. Without furniture, it was featureless. Mile after slow mile it flung out ahead of them, with no swells, no billows, no rises, no ridges, no valleys, nothing but a level floor, straight, dull, drab, and full of sand. Only the wind was at home here. It blew incessantly, sometimes strongly, sometimes fitfully and almost playfully. But they had this desolate land to cross, it lay in the way, and it was only two weeks, three maybe, to the mountains, and another two weeks to Santa Fe. You had to endure it, she thought, you had to endure it, because the mountains lay just ahead, not very far now.

She waited until the train was strung out and the mules had settled from their first friskiness into a slow, steady pulling. Until Parley had filled his cheek with tobacco and slumped into a graceless, sack-easiness beside her. "Why?" she asked then, "why is the Beaver trailing the train?"

Parley kept his eyes on the lead mules. "Whut makes ye think I know?"

"You know."

He flicked her a look. "He's jist keepin' a eye on the boy. He nearabout worships Johnny."

"He can't do so simple a thing as to come into camp and join the train again, can he?" She was vexed and her voice showed it.

"Ain't no use quarrelin' with a Injun's ways," Parley said.

"Then why doesn't Johnny seek *him* out and make his peace?"

"Ain't no use quarrelin' with Johnny's ways, neither."

"Oh, good gracious," she said, suddenly put out with the ways of all men, "there's that Indian, riding out there just out of sight, doing no good and being no help. All Johnny has to do is find him and bring him into camp."

"'Tain't that simple," Parley said. "The Beaver has let Johnny see him a time or two so's he'd know he was around. But he ain't ever got close enough to talk, an' if he don't want to, ain't no way Johnny c'n make him. Suits him, he'll come in. Don't, he won't. Might suit him tomorrer. Might not ever."

"Hmmmph."

She didn't say, and he didn't say, what both knew was really troubling . . . this sense of unease and discomfort over this north angling. And that they were all, Johnny, herself, Parley, and even Jesse and to some extent Legette and Manuel, feeling it. You couldn't, she thought, put your finger on it. And it might be they'd got so used to Johnny's liking for as much straight westing as he could get that any time his compass had to shift it affected them all. They were the ones that had heard it the oftenest—nine weeks of nights, now—listened to that hammering west, west, west. That drive had got inside them all and was driving them.

The men felt it less, being used to a little north here and a little south there, satisfied they were heading, generally, west.

It wasn't, she told herself, that they *really* distrusted Joe Britt. Why would they? Johnny had said it—"he don't get paid till we get to Santa Fe." But if you pinned them all down, and each had to own the truth, she believed they'd all admit to feelings prickled and awry. And it hadn't helped hers any for Johnny to mumble in his sleep last night, something he'd never done before, "Don't ever forget he's half Kioway."

"But I *do* wish," she muttered, "he'd come in."

"Hit'd be handy," Parley agreed.

For three days they hauled over the flat wasteland and it was heavy hauling. The only change in the dullness all around them was in the ponds that loomed up once in a while. Ahead of time, it was impossible to tell whether they were mirages or actual ponds. Sometimes they turned into mirrored, shimmering deceptions, but as often as not, and as foretold by Joe Britt, they became real water, shallow lakes dimpled on the surface of the flat earth. It was always warm, sometimes brackish, often muddied by buffaloes, but it was water and it was wet and it took away from everyone the fear and dread of a dry scrape like the Cimarron cutoff.

Most of the three days Judith stayed with her wagon. This was so unlike her that Johnny finally eyed her with suspicion. "Feeling bad, honey?"

"Sort of no-good," she admitted, "a little headachy, and my back and legs . . . it amounts to nothing. The heat, likely. It don't use me well." She smiled at him.

He nodded. "It's punishing," and mopped his own sweat-studded face. "Best for you to stay under the canvas, I guess. Sun could give you a stroke."

"And when it's gone you freeze to death," she said. "Nights are real chilly."

"Getting into high country," he said. "You'd be surprised if I told you what the altitude is here."

"How can it be high? It's as flat as the floor of a house."

"Long slow climb," he said, "up since . . ." he thought a moment, "since the Canadian. We're nigh four thousand feet right now."

"What's the altitude at home?"

"Four hundred."

"But we've not climbed a real hill since we left!"

He was as pleased as a boy at her astonishment and took time to show her, with his inclined hand, how gradual the climb had been. "Passes understanding, don't it? But the whole land tilts down towards the Mississippi. Can't tell it from day to day, but you're climbing till you get to the mountains."

She did feel sort of no-good and headachy, and her back did hurt a little, and her legs, but mostly she just felt languid and like a roast of meat skewered and turning before a hot fire. She'd thought the Territory was hot, after New England, but there'd never been heat like this. It was steamy and smothery, but this was like having the juices baked out of you, all day every day that ball of orange fire in the sky and that blasting, burning west wind in your face. Your lips cracked and your skin peeled and even your eyes dried out. You couldn't, she thought, cry a tear if your life depended on it. Then just as soon as the ball of fire was gone, the minute it sank out of sight, a chill that crept into your bones to the marrow itself fell on you from the same sky that had basted you in your own sweat all day. Unfriendly land, and unfriendly sky. She'd be glad when they'd passed it behind them. Fit only for beasts and wild Indians, and even Indians, she guessed, had better sense than to have truck with this kind of country. It took something that couldn't think to inhabit it. What it was like in the winter made her shudder to think—blizzards and six-foot snows and death, with a thousand miles of flats to spread themselves over and nothing, not one blessed thing to stop them. Even God forsook it, she thought, even God. And just passing through was making everybody, Asa and Nate Butler and Ben Spring, the men whose nerves were made of steel, edgy and nervy. They didn't like it. They didn't like it at all.

The afternoon of their third day in the flats the sand grew so bleached it was almost white and there were greenish scabs in patches that looked like gangrenous sores. Hit-or-miss at first, only here and there, they became more common until by the time they made night camp the whole land was encrusted with them. "What are they, Johnny?" Judith asked.

"Salt pools," he said, "dried up. The water'll be bad tonight. Drink from the keg."

The waterhole was only a small leak from a dried pond and it was the worst they had yet encountered. It was slimy and green-crusted and wallowed. The stock swilled the water down but the men couldn't stomach it. "It's salt," they said.

"Drink it," Johnny told them, "it ain't too salt yet."

He came back to the wagon and Judith forgot salt pools and grumbling men and the north track they were making. Johnny was shaking with a chill. "Been feeling queer since noon," he said, "and now I'm chilling . . ."

Quick fright stabbed at her. "Why didn't you come in straightaway? You know better than to be so foolish, Johnny."

"Nothing," he said, "nothing. Too much sun, maybe."

"I'll let down the bed."

"No. Get some blankets. I'll wrap up by the fire."

She heard her voice grow shrill. "Buffalo chips won't make enough fire! We haven't seen a piece of wood in three days."

He was taken with a fit of shuddering but he controlled it. "Tell Legette to chop up a goods box."

Oh, he was so mulish and stubborn! There was no budging him when he set his head. She set Legette busy with his ax and went for blankets and her medicine satchel. Her heart was held in a vise, tight and hard and gripping.

He wouldn't lie down, but he clutched the blankets around him and he took the medicines she gave him—quinine and a potion made from an herb that soothed fever. She boiled rice for him and chopped meat into it, and she seasoned it with hot red pepper. When he made a wry face over it she said, "Eat it. Don't give me trouble, Johnny, it'll do you good."

"It'll burn my insides out," he grumbled, but he ate it down and then, drowsy, his chill subsided, he stretched out to sleep. She felt his forehead and sighed. He was sweating.

Parley and Jesse came up.

"He all right?" Parley said.

"For now," she said. "He's got a touch of the sun. But his fever's broke and he's sweating."

"Good."

Jesse sat on the wagon step. "The men is wearyin', Judith."

"Oh, God's name, Jesse, they'll just have to worry."

"They got the wind up, like they done in the Timbers."

"They got over it then, they can get over it now."

"It's different, now."

"How's it different? They got the wind up then, they've got the wind up now." She swiveled toward Parley. "Have they got to know Johnny's sick?"

"Depends how sick he is an' how long it lasts. How much you know about sunsickness, honey?" the old man said.

"Not much," she admitted, "but I've seen it. One of the mission sisters had it, on the boat—down the Arkansas. Dr. Palmer called it heat prostration." Her teeth worried her lower lip. "She was . . . well, she was mighty sick."

"I seen a man struck down once," Jesse said. "He went clean out of his head . . . dreamt he was burning in hell, the fever was so hot. Before he died."

Parley glared at him and then said, contemptuously, "He warn't Johnny Fowler. Johnny's got a tetch of sun. Hit *might*," he added with emphasis, making the probability seem remote, "hit might do him up some, give him a chill an' fever a day or two, keep him in the wagon outta the sun—that's all."

"And I've got remedies," Judith said strongly. "I know what Dr. Palmer used and I've got them. I know how to tend him. It's heartening that the fever's down so soon. Sister Cleaver's didn't break for five days." She wasn't going to *let* Johnny be bad sick! He *wouldn't* go out of his head! He wouldn't burn up with fever! She wouldn't let him!

"Suppose he loses his powers . . ." Jesse was querulous again.

"His powers fer whut?" Parley said.

"For . . . for deciding things. What if he gets too sick . . ."

"To lead this train? Is that whut ye're thinkin'?"

"That feller I seen, he didn't even know his own wife—towards the last." It was miserably said, but said.

"Ye wantin' to lead yerself? Is that what ye're calculatin'?" Parley said shrewdly.

Jesse turned toward him with genuine puzzlement on his face. "How could you think it?" He made a vehement gesture of denial. "My God, no! It's the *last* thing I'd want! I wouldn't know how to commence. And we're in the awfullest country I ever seen! What I'm a wearying about is . . . he named me second. I ain't wishing to be first. I just want to keep on being second, without nothing happening. Don't want Jonathan . . ."

"Ye c'n save yer wearyin', then. Ain't nothin' gonna happen to Johnny. If it does, I'll save ye the trouble o' bein' first. I'll git these wagons to Santy Fee myself."

Jesse tucked his chin down. "I'd want to do what was right."

"So would I, but they ain't gonna be no call fer it. You git on, now, an' pass out the word Johnny's et somethin' don't set good. That'll pass fer tonight an' take keer o' tomorrer when he's got to ride a wagon. My opinion, he'll be on that roan ag'in the next day."

Jesse got up slowly from the wagon step, but Judith stopped him. "What men are grumbling? Trice's crew?"

"Mostly," he nodded, "but they're all wearing down and getting edgy. Ben Spring and William Day had words a little while ago."

"Come to anything?" Parley asked.

"No. Butler stepped in . . . stopped 'em. I reckon," he said, rubbing his hand tiredly over his face, "it's Trice has started the whisper Jonathan has lost his way . . . don't know where he's going."

"With Trice's good friend, Joe Britt, leading?" Judith asked, measuring her sarcasm acidly. "Why don't Britt stop the whisper?"

Jesse looked at her and shook his head. "Don't reckon he's heard it yet. I'll get on, then."

"I'll git on, too," Parley said briskly, "an' stop that whisperin'."

Judith watched them go. Nate Butler had to step in and stop a fight between two men. Parley had to go and stop a whisper that was news to him but Jesse had heard. Jesse ought to have handled both, at once, and firmly. Well, she hadn't time to worry over Jesse. Whatever was ailing him would just have to right itself its own way. Thank God, she thought, wheeling about to her own work, for Parley.

Johnny slept reasonably well, waking a few times and stirring restlessly, but she kept him quiet enough, mostly with fairly stiff whisky toddies. She wanted him to rest but she didn't want him logged with an opium pill.

In the morning he had no fever but she knew that was no real test. Fever was at its lowest in the early hours. They wouldn't know till later in the day if it was going to come back. "How do you feel?" she asked, taking him coffee.

"Queasy," he said. "What was that you kept pouring down me all night? Every time I waked up, you handed me another dose."

"Whisky," she laughed, "whisky and water."

"God!" He stared at her. "Then all I got this morning's the shakes from being drunk all night!"

"No. You didn't have enough for that."

"I had enough," he retorted, "I don't want no breakfast. Drink that coffee yourself and bring me some more whisky. It'll take it to settle my stummick. And don't put no water in this, hear?"

When he had downed it, she said cheerfully, "'Twon't hurt you to miss breakfast since you'll be riding in the wagon today."

He looked up at her. "Who says so?"

"I say so."

"Now, hold on a minute, just hold on . . . where're my boots?"

"Here."

He was struggling up. She gave him a hand and he looked down at his wobbly legs, surprised, and snorted. "Fool things're as weak as a kitten's."

"To be expected," she said. "Fever does that to you, don't you recollect?"

"I've not ever had a fever. Never been sick a day in my life."

"You had all I ever want to see you have," she said, "when the Blade cut you up in that knife fight."

"Oh," he said sheepishly, "I'd forgot that." He grinned ruefully. "Legs was right wobbly then, too, wasn't they?"

"Right wobbly," she agreed. "Best I remember, first day you were out of bed you held on to a chair to walk across the room."

"I never," he growled.

She laughed. "No matter."

He appealed to her seriously. "Best I don't get in the sun today, huh?"

"You can't risk it, Johnny. Far as I can tell yet, all you've got is a light touch. If you stay out of the sun you'll probably be all right tomorrow. But you get out in it and it's certain to bring the fever back."

He nodded. "I know enough about it to know that. I'll ride the wagon. Send Legette for Parley and Jesse . . . and Joe Britt, honey. And tell him to hurry. Sun's almost up."

"Yes. Parley and Jesse know, Johnny, but Parley thought the hands had better think it was something you'd eaten."

"And that'll make 'em parky enough," he admitted. "Hands are like horses one way. They spook easy."

She watched him lean against the wagon to wait for the three men. He always leaned like that, against anything that would prop him up. Habit of a lifetime, she guessed, and it stood him well now. You'd never know his legs were wobbly. He looked casual and easy and brown and hard and strong. His face wasn't peaked and his eyes were clear. He was going to be fine, she thought, tenderness for him softening her. He was going to be fine. She set her bonnet on her head, bringing its strings under her chin. He looked the way he always looked, except that time he'd fevered so long after the knife fight with the Blade. He'd been white enough then, and thin as a strap. They'd never mentioned that fight since, she remembered, never. When he was well and they married they didn't say they wouldn't talk about it, they just never did. Her fingers stopped knotting the bonnet strings. Why, they'd named it this morning . . . just a little while ago! And she was the one who'd named it first, and teased Johnny about the way he'd had to push a chair to walk. What had got into her? She never would even let herself think about that fight, but she'd named it and passed it over and Johnny had laughed . . . She finished the knot under her chin with a neat bow. It just went to show, she thought, how worried you could be without knowing it. She'd thought she wasn't the least bit put out about Johnny this morning . . . but she must have been, more than she'd known. She'd never have mentioned that dreadful time, otherwise. She'd been too taken with concern for Johnny to know what she was doing.

Parley and Jesse came up, Joe Britt trailing them. "Feelin' better, boy?" Parley asked.

"Feelin' a heap better," Johnny said, and he put heartiness in his voice. "She," nodding at Judith, "is a good doctor."

"It's a relief to hear it, Jonathan," Jesse Cooper said.

He's the one, Judith thought, noting his drawn face and red-veined, sleepless eyes, he's the one needs doctoring. He hadn't shaved lately, not for a week she guessed, and the stubble he was raising gave him a peculiarly disheveled and unkempt look. Jesse wouldn't look his best in a beard, she thought.

Joe Britt was laughing and his belly shook with it. "I could've told ye," he said, "that antelope'd give ye the squirts, Johnny. Never eat it, myself. I'm strictly a buffler man."

"I mean to stick to it myself," Johnny said, with false wryness, "from now on. I'm going to sit today," he went on, "till they ease off. Joe, how far'd you go beyond that hole where I turned back yesterday?"

"Not fur. Nother hour, mebbe."

"Find anything?"

"Not a damn thing. I take it hard, Johnny, these ponds is turnin' up dry. They was full last time I was this way."

"A wetter season," Johnny said, easily. "Let's do it this way, Joe. Take Suard with you today. Make a wide circle beyond that waterhole . . . ten, fifteen miles on past it. Send Suard back to wait for us there. If you find better water we'll push on . . . till dark if there's need. If you don't, we'll have to make do with that one."

"Wisht I could promise ye . . ." Britt began.

"Save your wind, Joe. It's a dry year, is all. Move on out, now."

When he had gone, Johnny eased down on his haunches. "This is the last day of this north heading," he said. "Wherever we make night camp tonight, we strike west tomorrow. We're nearing the Canadian. I don't mean to get boxed in by those Canadian canyons."

"Britt know that?" Parley asked.

"He knows it."

"Agreeable with him?"

"He thinks we'd do better to go on half a day further, but he's agreeable."

"Good. We'll pull out when ye're ready."

"Fifteen minutes."

It was nearer half an hour before they moved. The men didn't hustle the way they had done in the earlier days of the journey. They didn't care any longer who was all-set first, and nobody made bets. They made ready stolidly and for the most part silently, except for the usual curses directed at the mules. They were all, Judith thought, getting tired. They were all weary of this journey. They were all wanting to see the end of it. They'd had enough of mules and wagons and prairies and sour water-holes and heat and sand and wind. They wanted the sight of a mountain and they wanted to see houses again and people they hadn't journeyed six hundred miles with. They wanted to sleep in a real bed and eat some-thing besides wild meat and they wanted to visit a tavern and they wanted to look at a pretty girl. They wanted to reach the end of this Santa Fe Road!

Me too, she thought, climbing up over the wheel, taking her place on the wagon seat beside Johnny. Me too. But all in good time, all in good time. He'll get us there.

At the head, Jesse waited. Johnny lifted his hand and Jesse roared the all-set. Nine weeks had not dulled the tingle of this moment for Judith. Everything had been done; the camp had been broken; all loose things had been stowed; the mules had been hitched; every man was in his place. The signal had been given. Then there was this long pause, the leader's hand still lifted. He watched and waited. A man there settled his hat more firmly. Another wedged a foot tighter in the stirrup. Another shifted the grip on his whiphandle. A man on a wagon hauled his reins closer. Another made sure his gun was tight against the saddle. Then all, all of them, every manjack of them, including Judith, gave that last wiggling squirm of the seat to find comfort. All set.

The leader dropped his hand, whirled his horse, and cried "Roll 'em!" The whips cracked, the mules plunged and heaved, the drivers shouted, and the great wheels turned, an inch, two inches, half round, then they were rolling. Judith's pulse, accelerated during the moment of wait, evened out again. It got into you, she thought, this moving on every day, this rolling out the land under your wheels. If you had to wait over a day in the same camp place, it was tedious. You wanted to be moving on. You didn't know whether you were pulled by the end of the road that waited, or pushed by the place you'd come from, but when you got used to moving there was magic every morning when the wheels began to roll.

She raised her eyes from the turning wheels and looked far ahead. A speck in the vastness, Joe Britt was riding there and rapidly disappearing. She looked for Suard and couldn't find him, started to say something to Johnny and didn't. Suard was ahead of Britt, likely, already out of sight. She watched a moment longer, then the wind raised a dust and the speck was curtained out.

19

T HEY hadn't ignored the warnings, Judith thought later. No, they'd noticed them, but they hadn't read them right. They'd been uneasy enough and they'd been puzzled, but they still hadn't seen plain.

When Suard wasn't waiting at the waterhole, Johnny studied about it. "He was to wait for us here. I know I made that clear to Britt. I told him he was to circle ahead but no matter what he found he was to send Suard back to wait for us here—so's we'd know whether to keep moving or to stop."

Judith told that she had only seen Britt, riding alone, that morning.

"Don't mean nothing," Johnny said. "Suard likely fanned out. No use two men riding side by side."

Only Parley had come up to ponder it with him. Jesse and the hands were unhitching the mules and taking them to water.

"Hit's a miserable waterhole, Johnny," Parley said, eying it. "Worse'n that'n last night."

"I know it." He was curt and short.

They had pressed on without nooning to reach this hole. Johnny knew it was foul—he'd tested it yesterday—but it wasn't too salt for the animals and if they had to make their night camp here it would do for coffee. The kegs had six inches of drinking water in them.

He looked at the sun. It was only two hours past midday. "Hate to night it here," he said. "Lot of traveling time left. Can't think where Suard's got to, though. Dammit, he was supposed to meet us here!"

Parley was philosophical. "He ain't part Injun fer nothin', Johnny. He's notional. A buck antelope'd send him chasin'."

Johnny beat the dust off his hat and clapped it, impatiently, back on his head. "That's right. He ain't half Indian . . ." Then he stared into the distance and repeated, more slowly, "he ain't half Indian for nothing."

Judith waited silently. He had to make a choice. They would either camp here for the night, this early, and waste the rest of the day, or they would move on. He watched the mules at the waterhole. He was thinking, she guessed, that with the animals watered they might risk a dry camp, if that's what it came to. He was remembering six inches of good water in each keg, a little more or a little less, and he was weighing it against thirst. She could almost see his mind adding and subtracting— six inches of water, eight kegs, eighteen men if the Osages came in, fifteen if they didn't, but Suard likely would. Night camp and morning. How dry would they be?

The decision was made in another way, however. Nate Butler came up, quiet and unexcited as was his way. "There's a carcass in that hole, Cap'n," he said.

Johnny swore and went to see for himself.

When he came back he said, shortly, "We'll hitch and roll. Water's useless to us."

They ate and moved on. Johnny's shoulder rubbed hers with the sway of the wagon. He looked tired and worried. Surreptitiously she managed a feel of his wrist. He was still cool. He said to her, finally, "I could swear that carcass wasn't there yesterday. I tested that hole. It was brackish and a little salt, but it wasn't stinking and foul. Don't see how I could've missed it."

"Maybe," she said, "you were too feverish to take notice."

"I wasn't that feverish," he said. "It had to be there, though. I just missed it. But the stink . . ." He shrugged. "A carcass don't just walk into a hole . . ." He broke off then and looked again into a distance she couldn't penetrate.

An hour later there was a crack off to the right . . . nothing much, just a crack in the hard, baked surface of the earth. It ran out before it reached their road, twisted and snaked up close, but ran out. There wasn't even a jolt to the wagons. Judith looked at it interestedly and followed it out and thought it was like a crack in a layer of cake—one of her ribbon cakes. She'd turned out many a layer that was hot and thick and whole and had it split, suddenly, all across like that. She'd never known what caused it. Too much shortening, likely. But the earth didn't have too much shortening. She turned to speak to Johnny and found him staring at the crack, too. Whatever she'd meant to say dried in her mouth. Johnny didn't look as though he'd appreciate being spoken to.

Before long they were in a web of cracks. They ran out in all directions, no reason to their trend. It was as if some great spider had spun them out of his entrails to trap them. The cracks weren't deep, rarely more than a foot, but they went crisscrossing every which way and the wagons were jolting over them constantly. No sooner had one been passed than another lay in their path. Sometimes a wagon stalled and it took belly-pulling and curses and whiplashing to get it free. A half hour of it made Johnny pull up. "I don't like this. I'm going ahead."

Without a word, Judith took the lines. He oughtn't to be in the sun; it might do him harm and bring his fever back. But as well as he, she knew he had to risk it. And she had to let him. He was the owner and leader. Every man on the train was in his hire, and none responsible but him. He couldn't sit here in a wagon and guard his health.

Uneasiness sat like a great black crow on her. What could they mean, these cracks? Hadn't they turned north in time? Were they, after all, getting into the staked plains? Hadn't they come far enough north soon enough? Did that maze of canyons cross the whole west?

Legette came up to help her with the wagon and she turned the reins over to him. Worried, anxious, she watched the cracks until they became so regular, so much a part of the scenery, neither worse nor better but forever a part of the outlook, that they lost their uniqueness. Any danger, she thought wonderingly, loses its fret when it becomes usual. And the cracks had become usual. When she looked, they were there. Between jolts she began to doze, to rouse at the roughness, then doze again.

The sun was an hour from the earthline when they halted. Judith, rousing again, saw Johnny and Jesse Cooper ride forward. Then they got off their horses and walked on a few steps. "What is it?" she asked Legette.

"Don't know, ma'am. Captain just stopped."

She sat, looking about. The wagons were drawn up in a shallow saucer, Johnny and Jesse standing on its farthest rim. Limned against the sky they simply stood there, their heads bent as if they were looking down. As still as statues, they made no movement of hands or feet or body. Mostly the hands had dismounted and were resting in the only shade available, the shadows of the wagons. A few, Nate Butler, Parley Wade, Bullitt Trice, walked ahead to join Johnny and Jesse. Then they stood, a line formed against the sky, their heads bent, too.

"What *is* it?" she said fretfully. "I'm going to see."

She saw the great canyon of the Canadian, and gazed in utter bewilderment at the desolate, sublime and awesome sight stretched before them.

They stood on the rim of a high cliff which fell away to the floor where the river, red and swift, flowed below them. For miles beyond the canyon the land was broken into pinnacles and cornices, crevices, more cliffs, pillars, columns, all eaten out of the red earth and standing isolated or tumbled together into a wild and fantastic disorder. It was like nothing they had ever seen before. It was chaos in space, as if the land had suffered a mighty convulsion and had writhed under it into these grotesque sculptures, then settled, frozen forever into the writhen shapes.

It was magnificent and beautiful and terrible and frightening. The sun, late and lambent, stained the peaks and pinnacles every shade of purple and rose and coral and changed so swiftly the eye could not catch and hold the colors.

"My God!" Jesse Cooper breathed.

And that said it all, Judith thought. That was all there was to say. There was too much of it.

She focused on one pinnacle that was bulky at its base, slimming to a blunted needle at the top, and she moved her eyes from level to level of color, from the deep purple root, to lilac, to rose, to palest pink. Then the sun dyed the top a bleeding crimson. So beautiful, so beautiful, but so raw, too, and so stark and so desolate. There was no vegetation save some stunted bushes on the lip of the chasm. Beyond was nothing but hard, red, rocklike earth, scoured by time and the endless scrubbing of water, into this barren, upheaved, eroded, formed but somehow formless, nightmare. This, she thought, is the way the planet looked before life began, and man was never meant to be here to look upon it. It was not man's world. It would not support him. The valleys of the moon couldn't be more lifeless. Looking at it, you had either to pray, she thought, or curse.

Parley Wade was cursing, steadily, fluently and inspiredly. He broke off to go ambling about, studying the ground.

The men were straggling up. Noisy on the way, speaking to each other, they were made speechless when they reached the rim of the canyon. Stunned, they gazed across the vast, tumbled area.

"He ain't been here, Johnny," Parley said. "Ain't no tracks but our'n."

Johnny turned his back on the canyon and walked away from the lip. Judith followed. She didn't want to look any longer. She didn't want to see it, ever, again. Johnny said, "He veered off down a wash about two miles back. It was too narrow and rough for the wagons. I figured he was making a sashay and would circle 'round. Held on straight. And Suard's not been with him all day. Not been but one set of tracks."

Judith studied the faces of the two men as they pondered the situation. Serious, she thought, even sober, Parley's face still reddened up with what was left of his anger, Johnny's beginning to have that still, withdrawn, impassive look. But there was no fear on either face; there wasn't even the puzzlement and uneasiness of earlier in the day. They had come to something real, now. They had come to the Canadian canyons and Joe Britt had led them there.

"What do you make of it?" Parley said.

"I make he's led us astray."

Parley's head clipped a nod down. Neither man bothered to wonder why. They stood against a fact, a thing done, and the reasons were bootless now. Johnny didn't waste time cursing himself for trusting Joe Britt and Parley didn't waste time blaming him. It was done, and their job now was to undo it, without harm or injury if they could, taking the harm or injury if they couldn't.

Johnny swung around and called the men to him. "You've seen where Britt's led us. For what purpose, I don't know, but it'll be balked whatever it is." He made no apology. His apology would be leading them safely out of here. He did not explain what he meant to do. He only said, "There's a crack two miles back, deepens into a feeder ravine. We'll backtrack to it. Make night camp there."

Trice was grinning and fooling with his whip, playing it out and dragging it in. "Water there, Cap'n?" he said.

"Likely not. There's drinking and cooking water in the kegs."

Trice's whip cracked suddenly and by the toe of Parley's boot a small cloud of dust rose. Judith jerked, unable to control the reflex at the sharp rifle report of the whip. Hull Archer whinnied and Jesse Cooper jumped, but nobody else made a sound, nobody else moved. When the dust settled, a little, scaly creature six inches from Parley's toe was without its head. Trice had neatly sliced it off. Everybody looked at it, and beside her Judith heard Legette made a sound in his throat. She touched him to reassure him. He must have felt that whip on his own back again. Her hand said it wouldn't, ever, know a lash again.

Parley looked at the lizard, then kicked it away. She didn't know whether he meant it or not, but he sent it in Trice's direction.

Trice coiled in his whip. "If the water in them kegs is that hogwash was at the last waterhole, Cap'n, reckon we'd ruther go dry."

"I said it was *drinking* water, Trice," Johnny said, "but suit yourselves. Move out, now."

At its head the feeder canyon was little more than a dry wash, a scooped and shallow fissure. They made their camp above it, but near. Watching Johnny ride down it, Judith saw that it deepened sharply a little farther on, for he was lost to sight very soon, the walls of the canyon rising higher than his head and shoulders.

An hour later he was back. "No water," he said. "Dry as a bone far as I went."

"Britt went further?" Parley said, and it was more of a statement than a question.

Johnny nodded. "Where's Jesse?"

"Lyin' down. Says he don't feel good. Want him?"

"No, leave him be. Don't mean to count on him for nothing but the wagons any more. Whatever's gone wrong with him, he still knows how to get a loaded wagon over a bad place, but his judgment's gone about everything else. He'd have lost the track through those cracks a dozen times today if I hadn't been with him. Not," he grinned, "that they led anywhere, but just the same . . ." He scrubbed his hands together and glanced about as if looking for the fire.

He might be chilling, Judith thought quickly, probably is. She said, "Can we spare a goods box, Johnny? There's nothing else to burn."

"Out of buffalo chips?"

"Plumb out."

Parley chuckled. "She's commencin' to talk like folks, ain't she?"

Johnny drew a blanket around his shoulders and folded onto the ground. "No goods boxes," he said, "have to make do with a cold camp tonight."

Judith set out meat and a pot of beans, and dished them up and handed them round. "The bread's finished," she said, "you'll have to use meat for a sop."

They wolfed the food down.

The sun had gone and the cold was rising. Judith brought her cape and wrapped it about her and sat with her own plate, eating more slowly than the men. She wished they could have a fire, to cheer as well as to warm. With fire, you could stand almost anything. Without it this landscape was cold and dreary. Well, she told herself sensibly, don't look at it.

Johnny spun his empty plate across to Legette. "You set a strong guard around the stock?" he asked Parley.

"Manuel hisself," Parley said, "an' Legette to pair with him soon as Judith c'n spare him . . . an' Butler an' Ben Spring."

They were all men, she thought, Parley and Johnny trusted. "I don't need Legette," she said, "we'll not waste water washing up tonight."

"Good. Better go now, Legette." Johnny looked up at the black man. "Take care. Extra care."

"Yes, sir."

Judith heaped a plate and gave it to the Negro. "Manuel's supper," she said, "and tell him I've still not got any chili peppers for his frijoles."

Legette smiled. "He will grumble."

"Which won't keep him from eating hearty."

When he had gone, Johnny unsheathed his knife and sliced a splinter of wood from the grub box and began shaving it down in fine threads. Judith watched the thin, hairlike curls drop. Parley knew his ways as well as she did, better because his knowledge went back farther and for a longer time, but they both knew the whittling went with the thinking Johnny Fowler was doing right now. And both of them waited, and said nothing. He was looking now at the reasons for this thing Joe Britt had done, what they might have been and why. Now was the time to consider them and weigh them and make some guard against them. Now he was asking why and why and why!

The knife was very sharp, razor-edged, and it peeled the shavings down as thin as a fingernail. "He didn't take nothing?" he asked.

"Nary a thing," Parley said. "I made sartin. Figgered he'd took some of the traps. Ain't none missin', nor none of the goods."

The blade sheared slowly but steadily. "It was him put that carcass in the waterhole."

"Shore."

"So's we'd move on here."

Parley, folded beside him, stirred the shavings with a forefinger, and left them swirled when he withdrew the finger. "Them canyons," he said slowly, "'d hide a right smart o' Kioways."

Johnny flicked him a look. "I was thinking it."

He needn't have said it, Judith thought. Parley would know it. They'd been together so long. The grooves of their brains, she thought, must be exactly alike. They didn't need speech. What they were both doing was thinking out loud. But what cheered her was, it was making sense to her. There'd been a time when the half phrases they used hadn't. She was learning, she thought . . . she was learning.

The splinter was thinning now, and sharpening.

"Trice in it?" Johnny said.

"Ain't showed his hand yit."

Johnny studied the splinter, ran his thumb down it, found a rough spot and set to work to smooth it. When it suited him, he sheathed his knife. He turned the splinter, now a needle, over and over, then tossed it to Judith. "Reckon you can knit with it?"

She caught it in her lap. It was as smooth as silk. "Yes," she said, "it'll never snag."

Parley stirred. "I thought to set William Day at yon end. Me in the middle. You, this end."

Johnny nodded and looked around. "Coming dark."

Suddenly Judith wanted light. "Can I bring a candle, Johnny?"

He stretched and yawned. "Sure. Why not? Break out a keg of rum, Parley. Serve 'em a pint around."

Parley pushed himself up off the ground, but he lingered, pulling his beard. "When'd ye see the Beaver, Johnny?"

"Not since we turned north."

Parley grunted. "Rid fast to git here ahead o' ye."

For the first time Johnny showed impatience. "I'd rather," he said, "he'd saved us the fifty miles."

"Ain't fixed his mind to meddle yit," Parley said.

Judith brought the candle, already lit, and set it in the sand. Its light was feeble but it was heartening and soft and yellow. "That beard of yours," she said to Parley, "is scant enough without you pulling at it."

"I'm aimin'," he drawled, "to shave it off right soon."

"You won't have to," she retorted, "you'll have it clawed off."

"She's gittin' impydint," he growled to Johnny, then added, as if there'd been no interruption, "ye're sartin he ain't made away with Suard?"

"No, he's not. Suard never rode with him today at all. Britt never told him what I'd said. Suard fanned out and hunted, same as usual. If he's not run up on the Beaver, he'll be in."

Parley nodded. "Way I figger it. I'll git the rum."

When he'd gone, Johnny rolled onto his back, pillowed his arms under his head, and stared at the darkening sky. Judith dug out her knitting. This was, she remembered, the last stocking of the ninth pair. It matched a smaller one she'd finished, and made the third pair she had done for Manuel. She'd stocked Johnny and Parley some time since.

She waited to see if he wanted to sleep. When his eyes stayed open, she said, "You feel all right, Johnny?"

"Feel all right."

"Feverish?"

"No." He sat up, grinning at her, "Done had the fever scared out of me."

She smiled. Johnny, scared, was something she was certain she'd never see.

Parley shuffled up a little later, the rum keg on his shoulder. He lowered it. "Now, ain't this cheerful!"

He poured two mugs.

Judith put down her knitting. "Pour me one."

Parley's beard dropped. "Honey, you don't want rum. Hit's strong medicine."

"Pour me one."

"I tell ye . . ." he scrambled up, "I got a leetle wine in my chest. I'll git it fer ye."

"I don't want wine. Pour me a mug of that rum."

"Hit'll addle ye!"

"I'd like to be a little addled."

"Pour her a mug," Johnny said, laughing. "I'd like to see her a little addled. Maybe she won't say I told you so, then."

She gave him a quick look. "I wouldn't ever."

"You never liked him, did you?"

"Not lately," she admitted. "But, Johnny, I never did . . ."

"I know you didn't."

Scowling with disapproval, Parley handed her a full mug of the rum. "Be easy," he warned her.

But Johnny had thrown her off. She gulped it like water, then clutched her throat, gasping. "My word and honor!"

"I told you," Parley said. "I done told ye so."

Johnny whooped at Parley's unconscious parroting, and when she had her breath back, Judith giggled. "You told me. I'll be careful, now."

Johnny lifted his own mug. "Here's to my map and compass," he said, "may I never forsake them again."

It was as near an admission of error and apology as he would ever come.

They were suddenly gay, talking all at once, interrupting each other, laughing, chuckling, happy in their own company. We three, Judith thought, sipping at her drink, we three. She had the feeling all care had been slipped from her shoulders. These were her men and they loved her and she loved them. Johnny and Parley filled their mugs again but, only halfgone, she thought she'd better make do with one.

It was like a party, she thought, like a gay, lovely party. Only never at any party had the stars been so near and so bright and so . . . she peered, so tipsy. She could not make them stay put. One very bright star insisted on making a wheel of itself going, when she looked and tried to fix it, into circles of many smaller stars. She pointed. "Johnny, that star has been drinking rum."

Parley beat the ground. "Ain't she the beatin'est?"

Johnny moved his blanket to sit beside her. "Honey, even the stars know they've got to get out of their track once in a while."

Since they had got out of their track, this struck Judith as the funniest remark in the world. But everything Johnny and Parley said was funny. They were the two wittiest men she knew. She felt all doubled up with well-being and pleasure and joy. She peered in her mug. "It's empty."

"So it is. But you can't have any more."

She leaned against Johnny. "Why? Am I tipsy?"

"A little," he said, "a little. But it becomes you."

She drew his head down and kissed him. "Johnny Fowler . . ." and could not finish. She was all feeling and no words.

She put her head on his shoulder. It was such a fine, strong, steadying shoulder. She was blissfully at peace, the fret of Britt and the Canadian canyons lulled. She wanted this lovely night never to end. She wanted it to stretch out forever.

She shifted her head to watch the candleflame. When small puffs of air touched it, the flame staggered a little, as she would, she thought gigglingly, if she tried to walk, and it pointed up in a tongue and smoked. But when the breeze passed it lowered again into a nice fat gold globe. How beautiful it was and how splendid she had thought of a candle tonight.

She looked up. The stars were gold, too, and very big and close and friendly-looking. If you could shake the tree that held them, she thought, they'd drop like ripe plums in your apron. She laughed at her own invention and sighed. Such a sweet interval of peace could not last. Soon, she supposed, they must stir and she must go to bed; Johnny and Parley must watch out the night. She was already growing a little heavy-eyed.

The report of the gun was shattering in the stillness, it was so sharp and so sudden and so unexpected. She saw a stab of flame beyond the candlelight and she heard a high whine. She heard someone shout, "Injuns! Injuns!"

The shoulder pillowing her head went stiff, then threw her off roughly. Johnny was on his feet. "No," he said, so softly it was almost a whisper, "no . . . not this time of night!"

Again the cry of Indians was raised.

Parley was up, also. "That's Archer," he said.

"No! By God, no!" Johnny's voice was loud and strong. "It's a trap!"

Then he was running and thundering as he ran, "Jesse! Asa! The corral!"

The rum left Judith abruptly and she was cold and scared.

20

I T W A S Parley who scrambled to douse the candle and who hustled her behind the wagon. "Not inside, honey," he hissed in her ear, "them sideboards ain't bulletproof an' Injuns shoot high. Git down here in back."

Confused and unable to see in the dark she stumbled. "What is it? What's happening?"

"Mebbe nothin'. Mebbe jist the boys seein' their shadders. But you stay put right here. Don't git the wind up an' go wanderin' about."

He shoved her onto the floor of the slight declivity. "Lie thar. Don't go pokin' your head up, no matter whut happens."

"Where are you going?"

"I'm a goin' to help Johnny, whur ye think? Make me no trouble."

She shivered. It was dreadfully cold. "Go ahead. But I wish I had a gun."

She heard a laugh growl in his throat and then he was gone.

When he was gone it seemed so dreadfully dark and she was so alone and she was so cold and she didn't know what was happening. Everything was buzzing around in her head, guns shooting, men shouting, feet pounding . . . "Over there, I seen him!"

"Here, this side!"

"Gimme a gun, mine's jammed!"

"Where's the ca'tridges? Quick?"

"Git down, you fool!"

"God, there must be a hundred of 'em!" That was Trice's bellow. She couldn't mistake it.

And Hull Archer screeching like an Indian himself, just screeching and making a noise.

Suddenly she was very sick. She squirmed around and clawed up the far lip of the shallow gully, retched, and her stomach emptied itself. When it was over she sat, shuddering, and thought that rum wasn't as nice coming up as it was going down. She'd have no more traffic with the stuff. She groped for her skirt tail and wiped her face. She was damp with sweat and shivering cold all at the same time, and she'd lost her cape. Next time she'd listen to Parley. Next time she'd drink his wine. Her mouth was as sour and foul as a cow stall.

A volley of shots sent her flat onto the sand, just as flat as she could get, her arms outstretched and her face rubbed into it. There might not be a next time, she thought grimly. This was an Indian attack. They were after the rich cargo, she supposed, and they would kill everybody . . . She scoured her face against the sand and wished if she had to die Johnny could be beside her. She lay quite still and waited, and waited, and waited. The firing was more desultory and there seemed to be less yelling and shouting. Cautiously she raised her head, then inched her shoulders up until she could peer over the edge of the gully. She couldn't see much, no men running about now—they'd all taken cover, likely— lances of fire from gun barrels popping off, over here, then over there, and in the middle of the camp some guns blazing away pretty steadily. She didn't see any Indians, and come to think of it she couldn't hear any horses charging about, nor any yipping yelps. But then she'd never been in an Indian attack before. Maybe they were stealing up quietly. Maybe they had the whole camp encircled. Maybe the very next second . . . she jerked her head quickly to look over her shoulder. She felt awfully bare and naked lying in a ditch, no protection but its shallow banks. She'd feel a lot safer in the wagon, but Parley had said stay here. Why *hadn't* he given her a gun, she thought. She could shoot. Johnny had taught her. She could have killed *one* Indian before he. . . . She made her mind twist away from that thought. She wasn't going to be killed, she told herself stubbornly, Johnny wouldn't let her be killed! And he wouldn't be killed, either! No! But she added, please, Lord.

It couldn't have been very long, she knew that, for in crises time always passed swiftly though it seemed to stand still, but it seemed a long, long time she lay waiting. Finally she was so cold she was shaking all over, even her legs trembling as though she had an ague. She twisted and tugged at her skirt until it was free, then hoisted it up around her shoulders. Her behind, she thought, wasn't half as cold as her neck and arms— besides, there was still her petticoat to protect it. The skirt felt wonderfully warm and she huddled into it gratefully.

Every once in a while, when the shooting seemed to die down a little, she risked another peek over the bank. There was nothing to see but she felt better for looking. Then the firing would pick up again and she would flatten herself. There was some yelling over at the corral, more there than anywhere else now. She dug her forehead against the bank. Johnny, take care, please take care. She'd heard him at first, thundering his orders, but there'd been nothing since but pandemonium.

Quite suddenly the shots seemed all off to one side, around the head of the draw, and feet were pounding and the shouting had begun again. It seemed to her she was right in the path and she shrank against the sand and waited for an arrow in her back or a bullet in her head. They never came and as the noise drew away, she breathed again. What in God's name was happening now?

There was a slide of gravel near her and her heart ballooned into her throat again. She swung about. "Don't you dare come near me! Don't . . ."

"Señora?"

She wilted, weakly. "Manuel! You scared the living daylights out of me!"

"I did not mean to, Señora." He scrabbled closer. "Señor Parley . . ."

He loomed beside her and she clutched him. "What are you doing here? What's been going on at the corral?"

"Señor Parley send me, Señora . . ."

"Johnny! He's been hurt! He's killed!" She began scrambling up.

Manuel tugged her down. "No, Señora! No! The captain is safe, I swear it. He is not hurt. He is not killed. Señor Parley . . ."

Her hand still clutched her stomach where she felt something had hit her hard, but she let out her breath. "You're certain? You're very certain?"

"Señora, I swear it! With my own eyes I see him. With my own eyes I see he is safe."

She sat up straighter. "Then what are you doing here? Why aren't you out there with him?"

"Señora," the boy said patiently, "I try to tell you . . . three times I try to tell you. Señor Parley . . ."

"Parley's hurt! He's killed!"

The boy sighed. "No, Señora."

She sank back against the bank. "Oh, good. Wonderful! Are we standing them off, Manuel? How many are there? Are they Britt's Kioways?"

"We stand them off pretty good, Señora. Captain say not many Indians, say four, mebbe six, eight. They take some mulas and traps, is all. They take Legette, too. Those Indians come up ver' quiet, Señora, and they hit me over the head and I know nothing for a little while. When I can see something but stars, Señora, I see they put ropes on Legette and they take the traps and the mulas . . ."

"They took Legette?" Judith said, "the Indians took *Legette?* Why? Why would they do that? What would they want with him?"

"No, Señora . . . not the Indians. Joe Britt take Legette. Indians take

the traps and mulas and Joe Britt, he clonk Legette on the head and tie
him up and throw him on a mule . . ."

"Wait a minute," Judith said. "Joe Britt?"

"Sí, Señora, sí. Joe Britt and these Indians, they come up behind us,
me and Legette, Señora, very still. First I know, Señora, they go clonk on
Legette's head, then they tie him up . . ."

"What in God's name were *you* doing while they were going clonk on
Legette's head?"

"Señora," there was dignity in the boy's voice, "they are going clonk on
my head, too."

"Oh. Oh! You're hurt, Manuel?"

"Señora, I have try to tell you. Is why Señor Parley send me here. He
say," he added mournfully, "Manuel is no good for fight no more."

"I should think not! Here, let me look . . . but I can't see a thing in the
dark! How bad is it? Let me feel, Manuel."

"Is nothing." But he bent his head obediently. "Nada, Señora."

She felt him wince when her fingers found the gash, matted with hair
and blood. "Good gracious! Why, your head's laid wide open! What did
they hit you with?"

"I do not know, Señora. It make the sky go whirl about and many
stars to shoot."

"I'd think it. Something heavy, to cut like that . . . and it's bled a lot,
too, Manuel."

"Señora," he said, with some pride, "one does not get clonked on the head
without bleeding."

She felt anxious about the wound and wished for her satchel and its
salves and bandaging, but she could not help laughing. "Of course not,"
she said, "and it's a very good thing, really. The bleeding will clean the
wound and keep it from being very sore. We'll take care of it, Manuel.
Soon as they quit shooting out there. You're lucky they didn't take your
hair!"

Manuel snorted. "They would not dare!"

Judith was conscious of a lull in the firing, aware suddenly that as she
and Manuel had talked she had not had to strain to hear him, that there
was a queer sort of vacuum of silence. "I do believe . . ." she began, but
something went swish in the air, and whoosh, and thudded against the
wagon bed. "What was that?"

"Señora . . ."

There was another swish and whoosh and Judith heard the canvas of
the sheet rend. "Manuel! Those are arrows!"

He gave her a hard shove that flattened her. There was another singing swish, a thud, and her face was suddenly blasted with sand. She cried out and Manuel flung himself down beside her. "Señora! You are hurt?"

"Sand in my eyes," she muttered, "and in my mouth. Just sand."

"Thanks be to the mother of Jesus!"

She spat and spat and wiped with her dress tail and dug with her fists. "That last one . . ." she could see, mistily, now. She peered about and felt and found something. "God's name, Manuel, it's sticking right here in the sand. It just missed us!"

She snatched her hand away. She couldn't bear to touch it.

Feet came pounding near and she wheeled about.

"Judith?" It was Johnny. "All right?"

All right? All right? She sputtered in swift indignation, her teeth still gritty with sand, "They're shooting . . . they're shooting arrows at me!"

"Won't be no more. They're chased. Stay put, though." The last came drifting back. He was already running, leaving.

"Johnny!" she wailed.

Parley slid down beside her. "Whur's he goin'?"

"I don't know," she snapped at the old man, suddenly very angry. "I don't know where he's going and I don't know what's been happening except there's been a hell of a lot of shooting and yelling and flapping around and I've been lying in this sand for hours and I'm freezing to death and people have been shooting arrows at me and I'm sick to death of it! When is this shooting scrape going to end?"

"Done ended," Parley said, his chuckle growling up, "done ended." He laughed, then coughed, then cursed. "Dammit! I've done swallered my cud!"

She pounded him on the back and he belched suddenly and windily. "Quit that," he yelped at her, "ye're knockin' the breath outen me an' the cud's done gone. Ye cain't bring it up ag'in."

"I hope it makes you sick!"

"'Twon't. I've swallered too many. Whur's Manuel? I sent him along."

"Here, Señor."

"Good. Hit's over, honey. Done over. Not much of a scrape . . . mostly noise."

"There was plenty of that, all right! Now, I want to know exactly what's been going on!"

"Why, honey, that rapscallion Joe Britt an' a measly leetle passel o' Pawnees . . ."

"Pawnees! You mean Kioways, don't you?"

"Nope. Nary a Kioway amongst 'em. Jist a bunch o' ragtail, renegade Pawnees. They crep' up that canyon an' whomped Legette an' Manuel over the head an' made off with some mules an' traps. Laid out to git 'em all, but they misfiggered a mite. Archer couldn't hold his horses an' made the outcry too soon. Me an' Johnny an' the others got thar 'fore they could do their bizness way they'd planned."

"There was shooting," she said, "from all sides."

In the dark Parley's voice was drawly. "Mostly jist a confusion. Somebody raises a Injun cry ever'body jist naturally commences firin' off his shootin' iron, ever' direction at once. Wonder hadn't somebody hurt theirself."

"It wasn't confusion that shot those arrows into my wagon," Judith said grimly.

There was a silence. Breaking it there came, from far down the canyon, a high, piercing, ululating whistle. It was eerie and spooky, rising and falling, rising and falling, rapidly. It had a strange unearthly sound. Judith shivered and whispered, "What is that?"

Parley sighed. "Hit's the Pawnee whistle, honey."

It came again, from still farther away, then faded without echo.

"Why?" Judith asked.

"Reckon it's meant to put the fear o' God into ye."

"It does. It mortally does." She took hold of herself. They were gone. It was over. That whistle was probably only a last defiance. "Do we have any injured?"

"Well," Parley said, quietly, "they shot a few arrers over at the picket line, too, honey, and Jesse Cooper took one in the shoulder. Ye'll have to help us git it out, I reckon. That's all was hurt. Jist Jesse an' Manuel here." She heard him suck in his breath. "I hate to tell ye this, but they takened Legette with 'em."

"They're gone with him, then? They really got him? Manuel said so, but . . ."

"They got him. But, we'll . . ."

Manuel suddenly began to sob. "He was my frien' . . . Legette was my frien' . . ."

Judith heard Parley's feet shuffle and she knew he was uncomfortable, a little embarrassed by the Mexican boy's sobs. Likely, she thought, he was clawing at his beard. "Now, Manuel," he began.

The boy was beyond her reach but she said, soothingly, "We'll find him, Manuel. We'll find him. Captain Fowler won't let them keep him."

"Ye're durned buglin' tootin' he won't," Parley said stoutly. "Come day,

we're aimin' to git back ever'thing that renegade's took, an' that means
Legette, too, boy. Ye needn't to weary. Ye'll git yer friend back!"

Johnny shouted. "Parley! Meeting down by your wagon. Come on!"

"I'm a comin'," Parley yelled. "Hit's all right to git in the wagon now,
honey," he told Judith. "Fix up Manuel's head fer him. Johnny'll send
fer ye when he gits ready to take that arrer outta Jesse's shoulder."

A light flared up down the line and a dark huddle of men could be seen
around it. Somebody dragged a goods box out and set to work on it with
an ax . . . Nate Butler, she guessed, from the build and size of him, or
maybe Trice. No, that was Trice down at the end, near Archer and Craig
and Brand. Johnny was going to have a fire for Jesse, she guessed, and
light to see by when he took the arrow out. She'd never seen an arrow
wound. It wasn't going to be very pretty. But it couldn't be, she told herself, bracing her shoulders, it couldn't possibly be any worse than Tig
Vance's bear claw wounds.

She and Manuel groped their way into the wagon and she lit a candle
and set to work to wash and dress his head. He was patient and good,
making no outcry even when she took several stitches to close the cut.
She patted his shoulder when she had finished. "You are a very brave boy,
Manuel. Now, lie down on the bunk here and I'll give you a pill to make
you sleep."

He was interested. "One like you gave Señor Vance?"

"One exactly like it. It will ease the pain and make you sleep well."

His great dark eyes widened suddenly, alarmed. "But not to sleep so well
I don't wake again, Señora."

She laughed. "No. You'll wake in the morning. Es nada, Manuel, your
head. Nada. Just a little cut, all stitched up."

He looked doubtful and felt gingerly of the bandage. "Is a pretty good
clonk, Señora."

She covered him and fed him the opium pill. Then she checked over
her satchel and tore some more strips of bandaging and rolled them. It was
good she had brought as much old linen as she had. Without thinking how
it might be needed, she had known it would be. She looked at her pots of
salves and felt of the little bags of dried herbs. She had tried to anticipate
all their needs . . . fevers, burns, wounds, cuts, catarrhs. Whatever ail-
ments men had in settlements they were as likely to have on a journey, plus
a few more. She had been lavish with her supplies and there were plenty
of them.

There was nothing now to do but wait until she was sent for. She sat
down beside Manuel. He was already sleeping and she looked at the long,

curled-back lashes so like a girl's laid on the cheeks. They were still a little wet and pointed from his tears. She'd had to hurt him a lot, but he hadn't murmured. And he'd lost his friend. Poor boy . . . She drew the blanket closer under his chin. Poor, brave boy. Legette had been his closest friend, and the Pawnees and Joe Britt had taken him. But what for? Why? What on earth did they want with him? She couldn't make sense of it, but she had a troubled feeling, an uneasy feeling that went beyond the physical fact of his capture. It had to do . . . but she couldn't put her finger on it.

She could hear a rumble of talk from down the line but couldn't make out what was being said. She didn't try very hard. She was dreadfully tired all at once, and she felt limp and languid and drained. Once or twice she heard Johnny's voice, raised, and she thought he sounded angry. He would be, of course. That was natural. Not angry with the men, but angry over the attack and his losses. And once, at least, she heard Hull Archer's screech. She wondered if Johnny was angry with him. She was growing very sleepy. Her eyes felt as full of sand as they had when the Pawnee arrow had blinded her. Perhaps Archer had failed in some way . . . perhaps he'd been on guard . . .

Johnny never did send for her. He sent, instead, for the medicine satchel. Parley came for it. "Jesse don't want you to see it," he said.

She had drowsed off but she roused. "But why? I've seen as bad."

"Don't know, but Johnny give him his way. Gimme the satchel. An' whyn't ye git to bed now, honey? Ain't no need you settin' up. Git on to bed an' fergit yer first Injun scrape."

"What's Johnny been haranguing about down there?" She was only half interested. She was too painfully sleepy. It was an effort to speak.

"Nothin' to weary yerself about."

"I thought I heard Archer yelling."

She heard Parley answer but she didn't know what he said. She felt him roll a blanket about her and knew, dimly, he was lowering her to the wagon floor. She felt the good softness of a pillow under her head and she thought his scraggly old beard brushed her forehead and she thought she heard something about being braver than any man . . . but it sort of faded out and though she meant to say thank you she never did. She only sighed and gave the faintest, gentlest, little ladylike snore.

21

JOHNNY wakened her the next morning, shaking her and handing her, unbelievably, hot coffee.

It was so welcome, so steaming hot and strong and black and good that she asked no questions. Another goods box had been sacrificed, she supposed, but it did not matter. What mattered was this wonderful, marvelous, reviving hot drink. She clutched the mug and burned her tongue with the first long, greedy swallow. But she didn't even mind that. She kept sipping until she had half finished the mug. Then she surveyed her husband sitting on the foot of the bunk and noticed, for the first time, that Manuel had been moved and she was in her own bed. "I slept like a log," she laughed, "never even knew when you moved me."

"Didn't mean you to." He smiled. "I was real gentle." He touched her hand. "Judith, when I was a little tad, the best praise my mother ever gave me . . . about the only praise she ever had to give anybody . . . was to say, 'You done good.'" He looked at her and there was a gentleness and tenderness in his eyes she had rarely seen, a kind of devotion and respect new to him, and therefore new to her. She'd seen love there, many times, and humor with her, and the honest lust of a husband, the rightful pride of a husband, the infrequent anger and impatience of a husband . . . but this was different, this was a little humble, this was even, though it made her wonder, a little adoring. "I'm not any good with words," he went on, "you know that. I have a hard enough time saying what I think, let alone what I feel. The best thing I can think of to say right now is what Ma used to say, honey. 'You done good.'"

The quick tears pricked her eyes and she pressed the hand that held hers. "There was never anything nicer, Johnny." Because her tears embarrassed her and embarrassed him, her chin went up. "I don't know what else the wife of Johnny Fowler could have done."

He squeezed her hand and released it and she knew the tender moment had passed. With this man it would always pass quickly. But it went so deep, she thought, when it came, so newly and so unexpectedly, that it could never be forgotten. She drank from the mug again. "How's Manuel?"

"Good. He's got a headache this morning is all. He's mourning over the traps and mules we lost . . . and Legette."

"Yes." She sipped. "And Jesse? How's he?"

"Feverish. In a right smart pain. But he'll do. An arrow's bad to take out. Makes an ugly wound and hurts like hell. But he'll do."

"What got into him? Not to want me to help?"

Johnny shrugged. "I've no idea. Just kept saying he didn't want you to see it . . . didn't want you to watch. Thought it best to give him his way."

"Yes." She looked him over carefully. His face looked tired and a little drawn about the mouth. He was so brown she couldn't tell if he was pale, but his eyes were bloodshot. "Sleep any?" she asked.

"No. I'll sleep later."

She set the empty mug on the floor. "Johnny, I want to know. There's no need trying to hide anything from me. I know there's been something queer about all of this. That wasn't any ordinary Indian attack. Joe Britt was mixed up in it, and he's got Legette, and Hull Archer did something you didn't like. I'll be easier if you tell me."

He rubbed his hands together. "How much do you know?"

"I know Joe Britt led a little bunch of Pawnees up that canyon and surprised Manuel and Legette. I know they hit them over the head and made off with some mules and traps and Legette. That's all I know for certain. And there was a lot of shooting and milling around and a few arrows flying. What I want to know is the rest of it."

"Well," he said slowly, "that's about the size of it, actually. Best we can tell there wasn't but eight of the Pawnees. Archer claimed there was a whole band of 'em. Said they'd closed in all around us. Said he saw 'em, creeping up. Trice backed him up. Said he saw 'em. But nobody else could say for sure he ever saw an Indian. They just all shot. In every direction. At anything."

"When Archer gave the first alarm," Judith said, "you said no . . . you said something about a trap."

"Yes. Well . . . Indians don't attack in full force at night. They'll creep up and steal horses and mules, but they don't want any fight at night. It goes against their beliefs. There's evil spirits at night. I was looking for trouble at daylight."

"You thought Britt had met a whole band of Kioways down in the canyons, didn't you?"

"That's the way I figured it. Didn't see no reason for him leading us here, elsewise. I looked for trouble, real trouble, at daylight. So'd Parley."

"What happened?"

"When Archer made that outcry it took me a minute to get my bearings, but I knew right straight, then, I'd misfigured and what we had on our hands was a little party after the animals. Britt still had to be in on it, so that meant the traps, too. And on account of it being Archer that give the alarm, I couldn't help figuring him and Trice and the others, Craig and Brand, were mixed up in it."

"What did they say? Did you accuse them?"

"No. I didn't accuse 'em. I tried to pin 'em down to what they'd seen. Surprised me some they didn't light out during the fight. I didn't look to find 'em when it was over." He rubbed his chin. "Archer held out he'd seen Indians creeping up. Swore he had. Trice swore he had. Others owned up they hadn't. Trice is sore at Archer, though, about something. Shouldered him off last night and wouldn't talk with him."

"Why? Why do you think?"

"Parley thinks they'd made it up for Archer to sound the alarm and that he got the wind up and gave the outcry too soon. Before Britt had time to make off with all the mules and traps and get clean away. It's Parley's notion he was to make the outcry then to distract us so's we wouldn't follow. There's no pinning Archer down, though. He tells it the same way every time. Says he saw the Indians, says he made the outcry, says they were there. And Trice says he saw 'em. We didn't. None of the rest did. I make it there wasn't any save those down at the picket line."

"And Brand and Craig . . . ?"

"They don't own to seeing nothing. Said they just grabbed their guns and commenced firing wherever Archer pointed." He added dryly, "They made a right smart fuss of it."

"But you *do* think, you still think, Britt and Trice were in this together? And Trice's crew?"

"I do think it, yes. But something went wrong, or they wouldn't be here this morning. Me and Parley had it figured. Mistake we made was believing Britt had a band of Kioways hid out in the canyons and the trouble wouldn't come till daylight. We figured Britt was with the Kioways when he spotted the train. Figured he trailed us for some time, to see our strength. Joined us, then, on purpose, to lead us astray. Figured he wanted the goods. They're a pretty rich haul. Till last night we hadn't give too much thought to Trice's part."

She fingered the edge of the blanket. "What do you think, now?"

"I've told you. We was wrong in some ways. Britt didn't have no band of Kioways. I've got no idea what he told Trice, but all he had was a handful of poor, dirty, renegade Pawnees. Don't know whether he'd promised Trice to take the wagons and the goods, or whether Trice had talked him into settling for the mules and traps. About all he could hope to get with no more help than he had. But I'm certain Trice and his crew were supposed to make a diversion last night, which they did. What's got me studying is why Trice and his boys didn't light out. Why didn't they join Britt and the Pawnees? Why stick around the train?" He pulled at his ear. "It could be, since Britt didn't get but six mules and a dozen traps, Trice's changed his mind. But he wouldn't know that right off. Far as he knew last night, the plan had worked. I'm foxed. All I can come up with is, he's give it up. Decided to stick with the train."

"Trice do any fighting last night?" she asked.

"Oh, him and his boys all blazed away right steady. They didn't make no break to help us out at the corral, if that's what you mean." He bent for her mug. "Want some more coffee?"

She nodded.

When he had brought it, she studied the froth of bubbles on top. "You're going after Britt, aren't you?"

He glanced at the opening at the back of the wagon. "Just as soon as it's light enough to track. That won't be long, now."

"They went back down that canyon?" She blew on the hot drink.

"They went back down it, yes."

She blew on the coffee again, and didn't know why she said, "I was sick last night, Johnny. I lost all that rum."

"I was afraid it'd turn your stomach."

She made a face. "I'll never drink rum again. Here, hold this a minute." She shoved the mug in his hand and pushed herself up on the pillows. "Now." She took the coffee again.

He looked at the opening in the canvas again. "I'm going to have to go pretty soon, honey."

"Wait. Why'd Britt take Legette, Johnny?"

He brought his eyes back to her. "I've no idea. To sell, likely. He's a good strong nigger. Britt could get a fancy trade for him with some Indian." He moved restlessly.

She touched him. "Wait, Johnny. Parley said you saw that notice in the *Gazette*."

He gazed at her. "I did. Didn't know you had, though."

She nodded. "Yes. I brought some papers along, Johnny. I hadn't read

them. One of them had that notice about a runaway slave. Parley said you'd
seen it. Said for me to burn it."

"Did you?"

"I did. I did burn it. But, Johnny, I think Trice had seen that notice,
too."

More tense now, he asked, "What makes you think it?"

"I think I saw him show it to the others."

"What others?"

"You know . . . Brand and Craig and Archer."

"What day was that?"

"The day . . ." she knit her brows, "the day you and Parley and Jesse
stood them down."

"Oh, then. We was across the Spanish line, then. Legette's been safe
since then."

"Has he? Then why'd they take him?"

"Like I said," he said impatiently, "to sell to some Indian."

"Would that bring them as much," she asked slowly, "as to return him
to his owner?"

She watched as Johnny's mouth hung a little open, then closed and
thinned. "No," he said, "not near. They'd have to take it out in trade
where the other'd be cash. How sure are you?"

She spread her hands. "Not sure at all. How could I be? What I saw
was Trice . . . he took something out of his shirt and he showed it to the
others. They all looked. It appeared to be a paper of some kind. I didn't
think anything of it. They studied it and laughed. Then he put it back
in his shirt."

"Whyn't you tell me then?"

"How was I to know? I can't run to you with everything I see. It didn't
mean anything to me then."

"No. Sure. You're right." He stood. "Well, that explains it. Trice meant
to take him back."

She bent her neck to look up at him. "But when? Why did he wait till
now?"

"Because now is the first good chance he's had. He couldn't show his
hand sooner." He scrubbed his face with his hands. "God, I wish I had a
bath and a shave." He pulled the wagon sheet aside. "It's full day. I've got
to go. There's a little fire left, enough to heat you something to eat. And be
easy today, hear? Stay close. Give Jesse a look after a while."

She swung her feet to the floor. "Where's Manuel?"

"By the fire." He wheeled about. "I almost forgot. The Beaver came in last night."

She stopped midway of her movement. "Fine time *he* picked! Why didn't he come when he could do us some good?"

"I know, I know," he warned her off, "I said the same thing. He *did* try to warn us. He's been circling around out there in those canyons. Picked up Britt's trail and followed him till he saw him meet those Pawnees. Come in as quick as he could after that. Trouble was, he didn't know about that buffalo track up this canyon."

Carefully, holding her tongue because that Indian so outraged her that she didn't dare speak, Judith took the pins from her hair and shook it loose. "I'll never be clean again," she said, finally. "My hair is full of grit."

"Still pretty," Johnny said, touching it.

She ran the comb down its full length. "You and the Beaver," she said, "are going to take that canyon trail, aren't you?"

"Why," he said easily, "I guess we might."

"The two of you are going to take the trail that leads right to Joe Britt and those Pawnees." She didn't say it accusingly, only positively.

Johnny's easiness dropped from him. "Honey, they're my mules and my traps and Legette was hired by me. He's my job. I've got no right to ask anybody else to go after them."

She gave him a long, weighing look. "Of course, you can't." Then she turned about and bent over the lidded chest which held their personal belongings.

He waited, then asked, "What are you doing?"

"Why, nothing," she said, "nothing at all. I'm just going to put on a fresh dress." She swung about and shook it. "I was saving it for when I could have a bath, but I think I'd better . . . I think . . ." She wondered if she would be putting on a fresh dress at every crisis the rest of the way to Santa Fe. "Who's going to be left in charge of camp today?" Her face was serene and untroubled as she squared toward him.

His eyes widened in the barest instant of astonishment before he grinned. "Asa."

She slid the dress over her head. "Good. I'll mend that tear in the wagon sheet while you're gone."

He put his arms about her and swung her gently back and forth. "So there'll be no leaks?"

She kissed him, lightly. "So there'll be no leaks. May I have a fire tonight?"

He frowned. "Honey . . ."

"I know, there's no wood. But if I find some . . . ?"

"There's not any, but if you find some, yes."

She pulled away. "I'll have a hot supper for you."

He grinned again. "I'll be here to eat it."

Deviously, she had asked when he would be back. Deviously, he had answered. By suppertime.

"Take care." He gave her a gentle spank and went away.

Take care. It was he who had said it, but her heart echoed it. You take care, Johnny. I have no need. I am safe. You are the one. You take care. Take very good care.

22

WHEN THEY had gone the camp seemed not only very quiet and untenanted, it seemed also incredibly small and lonely and disoriented, with no sense of belonging on the immense Canadian plateau. It was like a small alien growth on the vast skin of the baked plain, a tiny irruption of such small moment it was not even an irritation. It was there, it gave no trouble, it would go, and nothing would be changed by it. Out of pocket, Judith thought, we are simply out of pocket here and the sooner we make haste to leave it behind the better it will be for us.

She sorted over in her mind the ways she could occupy herself this day. She didn't want time flapping around on her hands because then she'd think too much of the men probing around in those canyons looking for Joe Britt and his Pawnees and the mules and traps, and the kind of trap any one of them might run into. She'd see to Manuel's head again, of course, and to Jesse Cooper's shoulder. She'd mend the arrow split in the wagon sheet. She'd look about, perhaps explore the upper reaches of the draw, for wood. And she'd air clothing and blankets. One good thing could be said for this country—the air was so light and so dry and so bright that, save for ingrained dirt, it was as good as a washing to expose clothing and bedding to it. An hour of it gave things a fresh, sweet smell.

It was good, also, for wounds. They healed more quickly, with less tendency to suppurate. A barked knuckle on her hand several days before had neither swelled nor become sore. It made her wonder a little about salves and poultices. Perhaps a cut was best left to dry out. Johnny had once told her that the Osages never salved or bandaged a wound. They cleansed it with water and the crushed soap plant, drew out the poisons with various herbs, then leaving them dry and clean let them heal themselves.

She determined to try it when she looked at Manuel's head. He was young and he was healthy and he hadn't even a headache this morning. Without question he accepted her dictum that he was not to wear his hat today. He was to let the sun get to his wound. He came from a long line of sun lovers and it seemed sensible to him, since the sun was good for all things. "Sí, Señora. No hat."

"But don't bake all day in the sun, Manuel. Come lie under the wagon occasionally. And don't work too hard today."

"No, Señora. But Señor Asa and me, we have to sort the packs and put them together again. They break them open last night and scatter them."

"Good." She nodded. It was the kind of chore that would require attention but not too much physical effort, precisely the sort of job she would have chosen for him. She sent him away and went to see to Jesse.

He was flushed and feverish and she knew he must be uncomfortable, but when she laid her hand on his forehead it didn't feel terribly hot. He closed his eyes and rolled his head from under her palm, groaning softly. "Is there much pain, Jesse?" she asked.

He kept his head turned and his eyes closed. "It hurts," he admitted.

"It must," she said, and set about stripping the bandaging off. Over the wound it had stuck. Johnny hadn't plastered the salve on as thickly as he should. She dipped a basin of water from the drinking keg and as gently as possible began soaking the dried bandage free. "I'm sorry to have to hurt you again," she said, "but it won't be as bad as having the arrow out." She made talk to take his mind from what she was doing. "That must have been dreadful. I would have helped but you wouldn't let me."

He caught his lips in his teeth. "No sight for you to see."

"I tended Tig Vance, remember? An arrow couldn't be worse than those claw marks." The cloth was coming away nicely. She bent her head to look more closely.

"Oughtn't to had to tend Vance," he said, fretfully. "That wasn't no sight for you to see either. A woman's to be cherished, not exposed . . ."

"Hold still, Jesse, this is the last bit. Now. There." She straightened and his hand, which she thought must have been hovering nervously to stop her if she hurt too much, brushed her head and withdrew quickly. "I'll just bathe the edges and put more salve on and a clean bandage, and then I'll bother you no more."

He groaned a little again.

"I'm sorry." She was penitent. The wound didn't look all that bad but it must be more painful than it looked. "I'm being as easy as I can."

He threw his good arm up and flung it across his face, hiding his eyes. "Get on with it," he muttered, "get on with it and for God's sake leave me be. A man can stand just so much . . ."

She could have told him, she thought crossly, of men she'd seen who had stood much more—Brother Redfield, of the Mission, whose foot had gone putrid after an ax cut. Half of it had had to be cut away and the stump seared with a hot iron. He hadn't groaned and said he could stand just so much. Nor had Johnny when the Blade had split his arm from shoulder to elbow and laid it bare to the bone. Not even poor Tig Vance had claimed he couldn't stand it when his brains were oozing out. But she said nothing. She compressed her lips and got on with the job. Jesse was just naturally a grumpy, growly man.

She finished and considered him, still lying with his arm flung over his eyes. "You need a potion to cool your fever," she said. "I heated a little water over the coals Johnny left. It's tepid by now, but it'll have to do."

"No," he mumbled, "don't think I'm feverish . . ."

"You are," she said, "but. . . ." She touched his hand to be more certain.

To her surprise he closed his hand around hers and held as if clutching, as if hanging on, as if not wanting to let go, as a child would clutch and hold for comfort. She suffered it, pityingly. Poor Jesse. She felt such an ache of sadness for him.

For a long time now he had kept himself walled off from all of them, not joining the men at night, not seeking out anyone for company, rarely speaking unless spoken to and then only briefly. He looked so ill and shabby and unkempt and old, lying here. It wasn't only the arrow wound, she knew. Some kind of eating darkness was at work in him. He was fighting some festering feeling and it was not serving him well, and it had been going on for too long. But who could help him, if he couldn't help himself?

Part of her sadness lay in the thought that whatever he had expected from this journey, whatever his reasons were for undertaking it at Johnny's call, it hadn't worked for him as he must have believed it would, hoped it would. And she didn't think he deserved the disappointment. He was a good man. He must have expected something splendid and fine at the end of this journey. He must have hoped for so much. It didn't seem right that the heat and the thirst and the vastness and the loneliness and traveling should have sickened him as it had done. And he didn't look the kind of man it should have. But a man was what he was. Some strengthened, some weakened, and there was no telling how it would be until the time of trial was on them.

Some, like Johnny, were iron to begin with, strong in every way the land was going to use them. Asa Baldwin and old Parley were like that, too. They'd all been baptized in heat and thirst and vastness and loneliness and were no strangers to them. But they had had their first times, too, and come through. Some, like Nate Butler and Ben Spring and even William Day, the whichaway one, had taken their own baptisms well. Some, like Bullitt Trice and his friends, were perhaps as enduring as any man needed to be, but they were flawed and faulted and pulled awry.

But Jesse, poor Jesse . . . something had given way, something that didn't have the iron in it in the beginning. And now he had an arrow gash in his shoulder. She had the discrepant thought that it *would* be Jesse Cooper that stopped an arrow, out of the whole train, but she put it quickly aside. Jesse had stopped that arrow doing his duty. She hoped he would mend well and that he could pick up and last till they reached Santa Fe. Then he could go his own way and restore his soul and be rid of this wagon train and all its people and all its vexations. And be rid of the strange land, too, if that was what he wanted. She guessed he would like to go home. She guessed he wished he had never left it.

Absently she patted his hand. "Well, Jesse," she said, trying to comfort him, "it will be all right, I'm sure. Everything will be all right for you in time."

It distressed her to see the effect of her words, meant only to be cheering. The Adam's apple in the gaunt neck heaved convulsively, the parched lips quivered, the hand over his eyes clenched and the jaw went slack, then gritted tight. "No," he said, grinding the words out, "it won't ever be all right again. Nothing will ever be the same again." He uncovered his eyes and they beseeched her. In the beginning she had thought he had the kindest eyes, but now they were only anguished. "Judith . . . Judith. If only . . ." Then he shut his lips and his eyes again and shook his head. "I can't even tell you."

She released his hand and stood. "That's natural. None of us ever can. Isn't it strange we have only words to say what we feel? And they never do." She had never been a preachy person, not even in the days when she had been attached to the mission, but she did believe very strongly what she said next. "There's only One who can see in the human heart, Jesse. Just don't turn loose of His hand."

He made no answer. She studied him. "Jesse, can you walk? I'd feel better if you were nearer my wagon. You're halfway down the line here."

He shook his head. "No need."

"All right. I'll not trouble you. Rest, now, and sleep. One way or another I mean to see you have some good broth today. I may even," she added, meaning to be funny, to bring a smile if she could, "I may even risk Johnny's fury and chop up another box for a fire if I can't find wood."

She was appalled when he raised on his elbow suddenly and barked at her, "Jonathan! Jonathan! Oh, you're bound to him—you're wed to him, but such as you wasn't meant for the likes of him. No better'n a murderer, he's not, and no better'n them Osages he consorts with. You're too good for him! He's not done right by you!"

"Jesse!" she cried, horrified at the venom he was spitting out, "you must not say such things to me! You *must* not feel so, and you mustn't talk so!"

He gazed at her and she thought his eyes were a little glazed. He seemed to have to make an effort to focus them. Oh, it's the fever, she told herself, he's out of his head with the fever. He doesn't know what he's saying. As if to bear her out he brushed vaguely at his eyes, mumbled unintelligibly, scrubbed at his mouth and lowered himself to his pallet. "Go away," he said urgingly, "go away, before I forget."

Sick at heart, trembling, she was only too glad to go away. It made her ill to learn the harshness of his feeling, the extent of the barrier grown up between him and Johnny. To believe Johnny was a murderer! To believe he was savage! To believe he was callous to his own wife!

Her hands were still unsteady when she threaded the heavy needle to set about patching the wagon sheet. Oh, Jesse was sicker than she had known, the darkness was deeper and blacker, and the festering was fuller of pus. How could he come to this pass, to feel such things about his old friend? She couldn't think how they could manage if he wasn't able to control it. Johnny was troubled about Jesse. He knew Jesse hadn't taken Shelley's death too well, blamed him some, but there was no way he could have known how it had eaten away at Jesse . . . and she didn't want him to know. They had trouble enough on their hands without trouble between Jesse and Johnny and there would be, there certainly would be if Jesse forgot himself and said such things to Johnny. Johnny . . . no man, would stand for it.

She crawled onto the hub of the wagon wheel. She could reach the hole from there. No. Jesse must hold his tongue. He must look to his feelings and keep them reined in. He had hinted before that Johnny shouldn't have brought her on this journey, but what did he think she was to do? Johnny wasn't simply making a journey; he had sold out lock, stock and barrel. He was going west for good. Her place was with Johnny. Besides, it was not Jesse's affair and he mustn't make it any. He must surely be able to see for himself she wasn't the kind to sit home and wait, vapor and faint and have the megrims. He certainly knew she had had hardships most of her life, and risked far greater dangers when she had ventured, without Johnny, too, to the Territory with the mission. What possessed him to believe Johnny was not thoughtful of her?

The patching was cumbersome work. She couldn't get a purchase on the osnaburg, had to punch the big needle, like an awl, through the canvas, draw the thread, then bring the needle through again. It was awkward and slow and made more tedious because the arrow had torn through a patch she had put on after the hailstorm. She stretched to reach upward to the farthest edge of the slit.

A pair of hands closed round her waist. She was so startled she gave a small cry, jumped convulsively and pricked her thumb. "Johnny! See what you've done! I'm bleeding!" But she was awfully glad he had come back so early. She twisted around, a happy laugh bubbling up in her throat.

It choked off in a gasp. It was Bullitt Trice who grinned up at her, not Johnny. "Well, now, that's a pity, ain't it? I'm real sorry to make you prick your pretty finger. But I'm not your Johnny, ma'am."

"I can see you're not," she said waspishly, "and you can take your hands off me, Bullitt Trice. What do you mean? And what do you want?"

His grin widened. "Your temper is as prickly as your needle, ain't it, ma'am." He swung her down to the ground. "Just come quiet, ma'am. That's what I want."

She twitched to settle her skirts. "I'll do no such thing. I'll come nowhere with you. What do you take me for? What are you doing here? Why aren't you out helping track down Joe Britt?"

"Why, that I wouldn't need to do, ma'am," he said chuckling, "for I know right where he's at. You'll come easy, ma'am?"

"Come where? I'm going nowhere with you!"

"Yes, ma'am, you are." He took hold of her arm firmly. "Make me no trouble, ma'am, or I'll have to gag you."

"Gag me!" She gaped at him openmouthed. "Have you lost your mind? You wouldn't dare!" She was incensed. How dare he walk up and put his hands on her waist! How dare he assume she would go anywhere at all with him! How dare he . . . *gag?* Her mind slowed, felt stupid. Gag? And Joe Britt? He knew where he was? She bent away as the man leaned nearer and she smelled his ripe, rancid odor. "Get away, Trice!"

"Ma'am, I don't want to hurt you."

"Then turn me loose." She dug her heels in and tried to jerk free. His grip only tightened. "What do you want?"

"I just want you to come quiet. Come with me. You're coming, ma'am, for I mean to take you. I've not ever meant to leave you behind. But I don't want no trouble. Make me no trouble and nobody'll get hurt."

He led her a few steps. Suddenly she had a sense of overpowering evil and though she didn't mean to, didn't know she was doing it, she began screaming. She could hear a high voice somewhere, a piercingly, shriekingly high voice and it bothered her. She was fighting Trice, beating at his chest and squirming and kicking, and she was trying to scream, and all the time she couldn't, and this dreadful shouting noise was filling her ears and nobody could have heard her if she had screamed, for someone else was screaming so loud it would have drowned her voice out. She arched her back and she clawed and she kicked, then Trice's hand closed over her mouth and the screaming stopped. He thrust his thumb into the small of her back and pressed and it was agonizing. She hadn't known there was so tender a place back there. The pain made her feel faint. Oh, God, she thought, where is Johnny, where is Parley, where is help? This man meant harm to her, real harm; he had always meant harm to her and she had always known it and now the time had come and there was nobody to help her. Johnny was gone and Parley was gone and Legette was captured and Jesse was hurt and Asa and Manuel were at the corral.

Desperation gave her strength and she heaved again and struggled and Trice's hand slid a little and she bit deeply in its fleshy part. He cursed and flung her away, then he picked up his coiled whip and hit her across the shoulders with the heavy butt. It felled her to the ground, but she hardly felt it. She scrambled away, partly rolling, partly crawling, until Trice caught her and pulled her up again. "You've done it now," he growled, "here comes old mooncalf."

Like an old man Jesse was coming toward them, bent to favor his wound, stooped to its pain, coddling it, but coming with his gun across his good arm. He had the stock steadied under the arm, the barrel raised, his finger on the trigger. Thank God, oh, thank God! Jesse had heard her!

He fumbled along, one foot dragging, his head cocked, peering, as if he couldn't see them clearly.

Trice needed only one hand to hold her tightly. With the other he gripped the handle of his whip. Why, Trice doesn't have a gun, she thought, and wondered, and then suddenly she knew why. He didn't need his gun. His whip was enough. "Jesse!" she cried, "go back! Go back! His whip, Jesse, his whip!" The last wailed off diminishingly, for Trice clouted her again.

Jesse was very near now.

She stuffed her fist against her mouth. He was dazed with the fever. He was walking like a man in his sleep. He hadn't heard her. He couldn't hear anything except whatever voices in his head were speaking to him. He stumbled and dragged and his head hung, but he came on.

"Jesse," she said, trying once more to warn him.

"Shut up," Trice said.

Jesse halted finally and stood weaving uncertainly, squinting, turning his head to listen, shaking it, fuzzily peering and blinking.

Trice was snaking out his whip, playing it out easily, lazily.

Judith moaned, almost inaudibly.

He heard it, though. Jesse's head tilted and he smiled. He heard what he had been listening for. "I'm coming, Judith. I hear you. You need me, don't you, Judith?" He took another step.

Trice said, "That's far enough, mister. Don't come no closer."

Jesse's face contorted with anger. "Don't tell me what to do! I'll kill you!"

Trice taunted him. "Whenever you're ready, Jesse, whenever you're ready. You just try it." He was crouched, his knees bent a little, the long whip snaked out, its tip dragging the sand.

"Turn her loose, Jonathan," Jesse cried, "turn her loose! She called for me, didn't you hear? It's *me* she wants now! She's learned about you! She's finished with you! She knows who loves her best. You hear me, Jonathan? Turn her loose or I'll kill you!"

Trice's mouth gaped. "Godamighty, he thinks I'm the captain!"

Judith thought she would die that second, that very moment. Her heart stopped and lunged and hurt and she thought it would never beat again. He is insane! He is in delirium! And he's spread before Trice his hatred and his obsession . . . and what have I done, what have I done, in my ignorance and blindness. God forgive me for not seeing . . . forgive my blindness!

Jesse's voice was low and pleading now. "Judith. You are my love, aren't you? You won't go with Jonathan, will you? God meant you for me, Judith. He meant for me to save you from him. He is a vile and evil man, Judith, not fit to touch you. He has done things . . . I heard . . . at the trading post, I heard . . . and he is no better than a murderer, the same as if he'd taken Shelley's scalp himself. He sent that Osage. He told him to get his horse back, and he didn't care when he took the poor man's scalp . . ." The words were low but piercingly plain.

"Jesse," Judith pled, trying to penetrate his delirium, "please, Jesse. Go back."

Trice's laugh ran out foully. "Now, ain't that a revelation? Ain't it, just, though? The pure Miz Fowler ain't so pure after all. And the pure Captain Fowler ain't so pure, neither. The pure Miz Fowler has got her husband's friend hot after her, and the pure Captain had old Shelley killed.

Git back, Cooper! I ain't wanting to hurt you, but I'll have to. Git back and shut up, now."

Jesse took another slow step.

"Jesse," she breathed.

His head cocked foolishly to hear her, he smiled, pleased at the sound of her voice. "I'll save you," he mumbled, "I'll save you." He brought his gun up.

Trice's whip cracked and the gun was cut from Jesse's arm and fell uselessly at his feet. He came on, not missing it, clucking and mumbling and muttering. The whip cracked again and numb with horror Judith saw Jesse's face fall apart, split as though it had been seamed and the seams had given way. She saw the blood gush and fill until there was nothing but blood where there had been nose and eyes and mouth. Jesse screamed, covered his mutilation with his hands, staggered, and fell.

She started to him, but Trice clutched her. "That's what *your* screaming done. Now, git moving."

"You've killed him!"

"Naw. I've got nothing ag'in *him*. He ain't but a pore fool. But he wouldn't quit so he'll have to carry my scar. Now, git moving, Miz Fowler." He hustled her toward the head of the draw, shoving her, pushing her, sometimes dragging her. "I got no more time to waste."

The canyon, which began as such a shallow, saucered little scoop, deepened rapidly, dropping steeply down and down toward the river so far below. Its floor was unexpectedly broken and rugged, gullied by swift waters and eaten and eroded into pyramids and pillars of the rock-hard earth. Judith made her way between them, harried by Trice. "Git on, git on. Hurry."

It was difficult to keep her footing, but like one drugged, too benumbed yet by shock to feel, she did her best, struggling, reeling a little, stumbling, never quite falling but never very far from it, Trice behind her hurrying and urging her. "Git on. Git on. There's horses part way down, but we got to git there. Hurry."

She did not even feel afraid, now. Fear was frozen in her, too. And she could not think. Automatically she braced against the strong pull of the down-tilting ramp; she propped against the studs of red earth; but she did not see the floor or the pillars, she did not know she touched them. All she could see was the ruin of Jesse's face, the red, gushing split seam that had been opened before her eyes.

They came, finally, to a plateau of sorts, a bench that leveled off for a stretch. Trice reached for her arm and stopped her. "Horses is just beyond. You can rest a spell now."

Choking for breath, half blinded by sweat, the muscles in her legs ropy and quivering, she hauled up against the canyon wall. She spread her arms against it and pushed her back into it and tried to make the bones of her knees lock against their buckling. She closed her eyes and let her head fall back. It was so hot, so hot, and so bright. She hadn't known humans could bear such heat as was caught and boxed down in this high-walled canyon. It was like being in a furnace, one of the furnaces at the saltworks, stoked until the hearth was red. The sun poured down into the crack in the earth and there was nothing at all to cool it.

Trice's hand rubbing her arm brought her back to her senses and brought feeling back into her. She was stung and filled with loathing. Loathing poured through her in such a flooding gush that she felt swollen with it, as if her skin couldn't hold it, and even her mouth tasted sour with it. His hand was hot through the thin stuff of her sleeve and it was thick and puffy with flesh and she could have vomited that it should touch her. She jerked against it and spoke for the first time since his bullwhip had spoken. "Take your hand away, Trice." The intensity of her feeling made her voice sound thick, like beaten cream.

He mocked her, mincingly, " 'Take your hand away, Trice.' "

She looked at him and her revulsion made her nostrils flare. He was the most obscene man, the most brutish man, she had ever known. He was almost not human. She had seen dogs with more decent instincts.

His manner changed abruptly. Always toward her he had been wheedling, a little fawning, persuasive, sometimes charged with veiled threat, but never, not even today, losing a show of good temper. He had hit her and he had shoved her and he had yelled at her but he had not yet been violently angry. Now his eyes slitted and he snarled at her. "You hate and despise me, don't you? You hate and despise for me to touch you. I'm not good enough to lay a finger on you. I'm not even good enough to look at you, or to speak to you. Your husband said that. Said keep my distance from you. I'm worse'n a snake to you. You draw your skirts aside to keep from being dirtied by me. What is it? My smell? You don't like it, Miz Fowler? That old rogue, Parley Wade, he can put his arm around you and he can smooth your hair and he can even touch his mouth to your face. I've seen him. And you don't care. He's as dirty a old man as I ever seen. He smells higher than me. We all smell ripe nowadays, Miz Fowler. Jesse, he smells right ripe, though likely you ain't noticed it. And the captain, that sent the Osage back to do his dirty work for him, he ain't as lily pure as he was the day we left Three Forks. We all sweat the same, lady, and there ain't no grades to sweat. It makes us all smell pretty much the same. It's a leveling thing, so you needn't flinch from mine."

Without warning he gave her a hard shove which sent her reeling and stumbling. She tried to keep her balance but he had pushed too hard and the floor of the bench was too broken. She staggered first to her knees then lost all balance and rolled over and over, fetching up bruised and shaken, her hair falling down, against a monstrous pillar of the hard red earth. She was hurt and the breath was almost knocked from her but she minded most the dreadful indignity. She could have wept to be sprawled there at his feet while he stood over her and laughed. "Look at you now! Groveling there in the dirt. You ain't such a fine lady yourself, now, are you? You're might' near as filthy as me. Your hair hanging down in your eyes. You look like what you are, ma'am. A slut! A slut wet down in her own sweat which don't stink too good, either. Making eyes at old Parley Wade! Making eyes at pore old mooncalf Jesse! Making eyes at me! Undressing yourself in front of me, like you didn't have no notion I was in them bushes. Heating a man up then pretending ain't nothing happened. Keep your distance. Play the fine lady to fool your man. Draw off and don't foller through. Could of been we'd of enjoyed this journey a heap more if you hadn't. But old Jesse was sightlier, wasn't he? And easier to handle. Not so much man. When old Jesse got to panting for you he just groaned. Not me, ma'am. Not me. What Bullitt Trice wants, he takes, and he's been wanting you a long time."

He stood over her, his laughter ringing out, his heavy legs spraddled and his thumbs tucked in his belt. "Want to try screaming some more? Go ahead. Ain't nobody to hear. I tapped old Asa on the head and the Mex and you seen the shape Jesse's in. Ain't nobody gonna foller till Bullitt Trice has put several miles betwixt hisself and this puking dry camp."

Cold fear settled over her as he spoke. "What are you going to do?" She had meant to speak strongly, but her voice came out dry and whispery.

"Scared to death, ain't you? You got no call to be. Treat old Trice right and no harm'll come to you. Treat him bad and he's a rattlesnake. You better give heed to him. Now, git up from there. We got to be traveling."

She pulled up by the rocklike pillar. She was sore in so many places and beginning to be stiff and her mind felt as bruised and banged about as her body. Instinctively, without thought, she arranged her bodice and straightened her skirt and made an effort to tuck up her hair.

Trice, watching her shaking hands with amusement, said, "That's it. You look a sight, ma'am. Neaten yourself up."

The pins had scattered and she found only three. She coiled her knot and fixed them in place. Having made a lady's gestures she stood straighter and faced Trice. "Where are you taking me?"

"Down below. Plumb down below."

The sharp edge of fear had not left her—this man was one to be afraid of—but scorn and anger were returning and pouring their strength into her veins. "What have I got to do with all this," she said. "Where do I fit into your plans?"

He leaned lazily against the canyon wall. He hawked and deliberately spit the obscene load of his throat at her feet. "Where do you fit in, Miz Fowler?" He pushed away from the wall suddenly and shoved his dirt-scabbed, foul-breathed face close to hers. "I'll tell you where you fit in! There is some of us has got sick and tired of this wagon train and sick and tired of the captain and sick and tired of the whole goddamned journey. We aim to leave out. We're for the mountains. If we was at sea, I reckon you could call this a mutiny, except we ain't at sea. And we ain't aiming to saddle ourselves with them heavy wagons and we ain't trying to take over the running of things. We just aim to take what we need and leave out on our own. We're being real kind to the captain. We could of burnt his wagons and his goods, but we never. We're just taking his traps and some of his mules and his guide and his nigger and his woman. We're leaving him what he values most. But you come in because I want you in. I've a fancy for you."

Her mind seized on his mention of the Negro. "You've got Legette, then?"

"Sure, we've got him. You ought to've seen to your fire better the day you burnt the paper. Part of it never burnt. Part of it blowed away and it was me found it. Easy to figure the notice meant the nigger. Wouldn't of thought of it without, though, him being already serving you when I come. Just takened it the captain owned him. Shame on the both of you, aiding and abetting a runaway slave, Miz Fowler. It's ag'in the law, didn't you know? Now, being a law-abiding person, I aim to see his rightful owner gets him back."

"What you aim to see," she said, "is that you are five hundred dollars richer."

"Yes, ma'am, I do. I don't miss much, ma'am. Not in the way of turning Bullitt Trice a good trick."

"My husband," she said, making herself look straight into the close-set, blood-shot eyes, "will kill you. You know that, don't you?"

"No, ma'am, he won't. For he's not ever gonna catch up to us. Joe Britt is the only one knows his way through them canyons. *Your husband,*" he stressed the words, "will lose hisself before he's been mixed up in 'em an hour."

He doesn't know, she thought, the first hopeful thing there had been to think, why, he doesn't know the Beaver came in last night. He doesn't know Johnny and the Beaver are down in the canyons right now. He thinks Johnny is floundering around alone. Clever Johnny, to keep the knowledge of the Beaver's return from this man, to let him believe he had nothing to fear down in the canyons. She saw the reason for Trice's hurry now. He was afraid only of being followed from the camp, that Asa or Manuel might rouse. She wondered why he hadn't killed them and then thought, he may have. He may have lied about tapping them on the head. And he may have killed Jesse, too. "I suppose," she said slowly, "Joe Britt is going to lead you to the mountains."

"Just as straight as we can go. Straight to old Joe Britt's high parks, and no fooling with wagons."

She didn't know why she was making this talk, except that she had a reluctance to move on. There wasn't much hope anybody would follow down this canyon, but until she was taken into that great, broken maze by the river her tracks were at least clearer. "Seems to me," she said, "you'd have done better to stick with the captain. You'd have drawn your wages in Santa Fe and had a good stake for trapping. What you made would have been profit, then. Now, you've got to split with Joe Britt."

Her mind was beginning to fit the pieces together. If she was compelled to go on it still wasn't hopeless. The Beaver knew Joe Britt's hiding place. He'd tracked him there. Johnny was with the Beaver. They'd find her. She'd be as well off there as here.

Trice was laughing. "No, ma'am, I ain't that foolish. I ain't aiming to split with Joe Britt. When he's served his purpose, we'll dispose of him."

"You and Josh Brand and Wash Craig and Hull Archer?"

"Me and Hull. No need splitting four ways if two'll do, is they?"

A chill ran down her spine. The man was totally depraved. She controlled a shudder. "You're very clever, Trice."

"Yes, ma'am, and I'm clever enough to know we've been jawing long enough. Git moving, now."

"Wait . . ."

"No more waiting."

"Trice, I can't go any farther . . . . I'm too exhausted . . ."

"You'll go just as far as I say. There ain't no questions about that." He swung around and took her chin in his hand, holding it hard and keeping her face forced toward him. His small pig eyes roved over it, searched it, then he flung her off. "A-a-agh," he said, spitting in derision, "what do I want to look at your face for. I've seen the mother-naked whole of you, all the bare-assed whole! You've got no secrets from me, Miz Fowler."

Her hand darted out and rang against his cheek. It was a hard blow and his head snapped back. He put up his hand and rubbed the smart. She went scrabbling back up the ramp but he pounced from behind and grabbed her, pinioned her hands behind her back. "That'll be all of that," he growled, "that'll be just about all of that. Now you git going, miss, you git going before I whomp you one. And you'll pay for that lick tonight. I promise you'll pay for it, proper."

He twisted her arm and the pain sent all thought of defiance out of her mind. He would as soon break her arm as not.

A little farther on a section of the wall jutted out prominently. "The horses is behind that," Trice said, "though I ort to make you walk."

She trudged on, in the full sun now, her head bent, trying to find a path and keep her footing, her eyes spotting from the hard, brilliant glare. A pinnacle rose in her way and she made a bend around it, her hand bracing against it. Trice was behind her, waiting until she had found her way beyond the upthrust spear of earth. It was very still. There was nothing in this dead canyon to make a noise except her voice and Trice's.

There was no warning at all, no slide of gravel, no shadow crossing the path, no rustle of clothing, nothing, just stillness and hot glare and sweat and sore feet and a shoulder, bruised by Trice's whip, beginning to ache, and weariness and a faint, sickish feeling. She would be glad when they reached the horses. She would ride faster toward more trouble, but at least she would ride, not walk. When she reached that angle, just there ahead, her feet wouldn't have to stumble over this dreadful ground any more. Just a little farther . . .

Out of the hot, bright stillness a rifle spoke.

She stopped deadstill, not knowing what to do, and waited for whatever was going to happen next. There was no place to hide and she was too tired and too sore to find it had there been one. She thought she might be going to be killed now. Earlier she had guessed that Trice's gun was with his horse but he could break her neck with his whip. She waited, dull with heat and weariness, for his shout or his shove or the crack of his whip. He had been her enemy, her danger, for so long—the morning itself had been forever—that she had no thought of danger from any other direction. Whatever the shot meant, Trice was her danger.

Sweat ran in her eyes and she smeared it away with her sleeve and wondered sluggishly if brains roasted inside one's skull turned brown or gray. She waited and her eyes found her shadow and she had the foolish thought that her shadow was moving while she stood still, moving back and forth in a strange swaying pattern. It made her smile and she knew, vaguely, the smile was silly and she tried to make her lips be firm.

Horses were coming. She heard the ring of a shoe against hard dirt and the soft sluff of their slide in the sand. Horses. She tried to steady her mind. Whose horses? Trice's? Joe Britt's? The Pawnees?

Then, singing hopefully and exultantly through her mind, bringing her head up, stopping her weaving, came the beloved name, Johnny . . . Johnny.

But it was the Osage who rode out from behind the angle, leading two horses. He rode slowly and he was like something carved from this hard, red earth itself, as still, as frozen, as passionless, his eyes fixed on her but offering her nothing. Dark, sifted with dust, sweat-wet, he came on. She forced herself to stand proudly. This man, too, was her enemy. He had never liked her, and she had never liked him. But he meant her no harm. He only hated her because she had taken his brother from him. She could meet his hatred with her own. It was as strong, and she was the victor, she sat in the driver's seat, because Johnny was hers.

The Beaver stopped beside her and pointed with the barrel of his gun. "He is dead."

She turned slowly about to look where the Osage pointed. Trice was sprawled on the canyon floor, his heavy legs bent strangely, his arms flung out, and the whip, his great, heavy, threatening bullwhip, folded across him where it had fallen. It lay coiled on his chest like some huge snake taken to his bosom, like some sacrifice hugged to him and betraying him. It had no life except through him. It was as dead as the hand that had wielded it.

Her sigh was soft as a feather. That nightmare, at least, was over.

The Osage swung the near horse around for her to mount. When she was seated, his eyes met hers directly. When he spoke it did not surprise her that it was in her own tongue. Better than most Indians he understood and spoke English well. But he hated all things white, save Johnny Fowler, and he used the white man's language only when he had to. He knew her knowledge of his tongue was fumbling and uncertain. He wanted her to hear what he had to say, hear it plainly and make no mistake in her understanding. "My brother's wife," he said slowly, holding her eyes, "makes him much trouble."

She gathered up the reins and gave the horse the feel of her hand. Well, and perhaps she did, but she was too tired and too sore and too bruised to talk about it. Her great weariness, she thought, was her great ally for otherwise she might have quarreled with this Indian. She only nodded mutely. She wanted to get out of this baking canyon; she wanted to get out of her torn and sweated clothing; she wanted to wash the dirt of Trice off her skin, and she wanted to soothe her aches and bruises with ointments. She wanted to lie on her own bed and close her eyes.

"My brother's wife," the Indian repeated, "makes him much trouble. My brother's Osage wife would not make him so much trouble."

Her temper flared instantly and she said bluntly, "Your brother's Osage wife be damned."

She saw the face which was usually so controlled, so emotionless and impassive, show horror briefly before the discipline of a lifetime could restore control. She shouldn't have, she thought, she shouldn't have . . . but she was too angry. She kicked the horse into motion, guided him around the spear of upthrust earth and set him into the climb. She did not look back to see if the Osage followed.

23

THAT wasn't the end of it.

She had known it wouldn't be. She had known it was anger and pride and some instinctive sense of precious honor that had moved her, made her refuse the wound the Osage had given. But she had known that later it would thrust and hurt. Only later he would not know. He wouldn't see. Though she had been betrayed into one angry outburst she had her own kind of discipline and she had her own kind of control. She had had to make it equal to the Indian's.

She never once doubted the truth of what he had said. Osages did lie, when it suited them, and they were very clever, shrewd liars; but about this thing she knew intuitively there had been no need to lie. It explained too much. Johnny's past with the Osages had always been a little bit shrouded with mystery, more a mystery of feeling than one of fact, for he had actually told her much about it. He had told her happily, pleased that she asked, about his long hunts with them, about their habits and customs and their village ways, their ceremonies and their rituals and their beliefs. He had never avoided discussing such things with her. And he had never minded her knowing that he greatly admired them and that he thought their way of life sensible and good, even beautiful, for them. But from the day she had confessed to herself that she loved Johnny Fowler she had sensed that there was more than this to his great attachment to them.

She had sensed an abiding responsibility, even an obligation, in him that went deeper than friendliness and liking. All the traders had that much. Nathaniel Pryor had friendliness and liking. Auguste Chouteau had them. Colonel Arbuckle at Fort Smith had them and, beyond, compassion. But Johnny Fowler had a deep river of something more. In her ignorance, and in its obscurity, she felt that it was a sense of family with them, a tenderness that bespoke things shared, such things as only family living engenders . . . the common stored fund of small knowledges that meant so much, the humors and oddities, the dangers passed and the griefs cried over together, the joys sung and the excitements prickled skin to skin, the kind of closeness that made a glance speak eloquently. You didn't come by such knowledges through friendliness and liking, or even compassion, only. You came by it through love, and you came by the love through some tie that generated love. This, she guessed now, was what had always made her a little uncomfortable when she thought of Johnny's past with the Osages. No, she didn't doubt at all that Johnny Fowler had at sometime had an Osage wife. It explained the obscurity and her discomfort too well.

But that wasn't to say he had an Osage wife right now, she told herself, now at the same time he had Judith Fowler to wife. Nothing could make her believe that Johnny Fowler had maintained an Indian woman in the Osage village during the year she had been married to him. Men did, she knew. She knew white traders who with equanimity kept two separate households and had two families of children. But Johnny had not done this. She knew it. And part of the pain of the whole wound was that this conviction could not be based entirely on an honest feeling that he loved her too much.

There was a certain Indian agent she knew, a man of learning and a gentleman in his habits. He had come to the Territory ahead of his wife and children, leaving them in the east for a year until he determined whether a suitable life could be made for them in the rough new country, and whether his position would be permanent and warrant their removal. During that year he had formed an attachment with an Indian woman. When he had concluded his wife and children would not suffer on the frontier, he had sent for them and Judith remembered the pleasant, comfortable, charming home in which she had been a guest many times. His way with his wife was loving and tender and thoughtful. But he went regularly to be with his Indian wife, he provided more than her needs, and he was deeply attached to the children she bore him. Love could be compartmented apparently, even with an honorable man, though she did not know how.

It was like applying vinegar to a cut to acknowledge it, but she could not be comforted with a half-truth. She was certain Johnny had put away his Osage wife, in part perhaps for love of her. She thought she could lay claim to that much. But it had something to do, also, and this was intuitive again, with the Beaver himself. There was some bond between him and Johnny that had been forged more strongly than any chance linking could have done. She thought, now, that perhaps Johnny's Osage wife may have been the Beaver's sister. But whatever it was that bound them together it was both tragic and grand, simple and elemental and as complex as all simple and elemental things always are. And, she was just as strongly convinced, this thing between Johnny and the Beaver had also to do with that knife fight of his with the Blade. Like the many strands of a cobweb, all converging toward a center, making an intricate but perfectly traceable pattern, she knew the duel was the hub, the center, the heart, that would explain and give meaning to Johnny and the Beaver and perhaps the whole of his Osage past.

What was a special torment to her, though, as she lay awake that night thinking and probing, crying a little, worrying, trying not to feel pity for herself, was the wonder whether there had been children or not. There had been seven years of Johnny's life as an Osage trader before she knew him, eight years before he loved her. She could not honestly say she believed him to be better or worse than any other young man and during those years he had been young and lusty and hearty and free. Though the people of the mission deplored the customs of the rough, undisciplined frontier, there was no ignoring them, and few men lived there long without taking an Indian woman. For one thing it made life much simpler, much more comfortable, much easier, and an Indian marriage was not legal or binding, not really a marriage in their minds. They scattered their seed freely and the halfbreed population of the Territory increased heavily each year. Some men cared for these fruits of their lusts and provided for them, even recognized them and had them schooled and insured their future. Others ignored them and left them to the care of the mother's people. Not the least of the ironies inherent in the conditions was the fact that to a people considered savage and heathen a child was a whole soul, held dear, and always welcome.

Had there, she asked herself for the hundredth tormenting time, been children? Were there, now, in that Osage village Johnny had so loved, small, slightly darker images of Johnny Fowler? Did he see them when he went there? Did he care for them? Had he provided for them?

Oh, it was wounding and bruising and hurtful to know you hadn't been first, but you didn't think too much about it because it wasn't sensible. You had to suppose, in some dark cave-corner of your mind, that if a man was twenty-seven years old when you married him he was not without experience. If you were realistic you knew there were few exceptions to that and you could not quite believe your own lusty man, in his peculiar situation and circumstances, was one of them.

But what was like twisting the knife in the stabbed heart was the thought that this child you were certain now you were going to bear, if

Trice's knocking about didn't cause you to lose it, would not be first—that out on that prairie, even though now left behind, there might be young halfbrothers and sisters, bronzer and with darker hair and with slanter eyes, that your child's father, their father, too, had held and cuddled and petted and fondled and loved. There had been certain knowledge only a few days, but in those few days she had learned, to her awed wonder, that you felt a joy so intense and so immense that it was as if the whole vast canopy of sky must lift to give it room. She thought it must be unique to the first child, to the first seeding and conceiving, and she coveted it fiercely for that child, from his father as well as his mother.

She turned carefully in bed. She could learn the truth. She could bully old Parley into telling, or she could go straightway to Johnny and demand to know. She didn't think he would lie to her. But she wasn't certain she wanted to know. It would be a solace if there were none. But how could she support the knowledge if there were? And what would it do to her and to Johnny, the living wound, kept forever sore by her demand and his answer? It was strange, she thought, that one could be more hurt for a child's sake than for one's self. All new to the fierce jealousy of the creator for his creation, she could lie in the dark and wonder.

It was good, she thought, they would lie over another day. She was almost sure that all was well with her and the child. By now she could almost discount danger. But a day without the jolting of horse or wagon would be helpful. Except for this deep concern, she had only surface scratches, cuts and bruises, and one very sore, stiff shoulder where Trice had clouted her with the butt of his whip. She would be easy with herself tomorow but she could stir about.

It had been a disastrous day.

The casualties, counted grimly, had been Trice, Jesse Cooper and Joe Britt killed: Asa Baldwin cut on the head and Manuel, injured over injury, badly hurt. He had been concussed and still lay unconscious. Whether he would live or not they did not yet know.

The pieces of the day had been sorted out and put together, like a patchwork quilt, Judith thought.

Johnny had asked the Beaver for explicit directions through the maze of canyons to Joe Britt's hideaway. He had even drawn a crude map for himself so he could not go wrong. He had then ordered the Osage to trail Bullitt Trice. Johnny had believed, it appeared, that Trice would make an attempt to circle around to the camp. He didn't think the man would be satisfied with the half success of Joe Britt and the Pawnees. He thought he would make one more effort to get the rest of the pack mules and traps.

He had warned Asa to expect it. And Asa had made the work of sorting the traps to keep him and Manuel near the animals. Not once, not once, and he cursed himself for it, his face gray and pallid still, had he thought there might be danger to Judith. It wasn't enough for him that she had been saved. He felt bitterly at fault that he hadn't taken more thought, that through his blame she had been frightened and hurt and threatened. "What more could you have done?" she asked, not to comfort so much as to recall his practical planning. "You set the other Osages to watch Brand and Craig and Archer, and they were not to let them join Trice or return to camp. There was only Trice to deal with, and Asa and the Beaver and Manuel to deal with him. What I want to know," she added, a little acid creeping into her voice, "is where the Beaver was when Trice was threatening me and killing Jesse."

The Osage wasn't there to ask. He had gone away again. They all pondered it and could come to only one conclusion. He had lost Trice, somehow, somewhere, and it was simply God's mercy he had found him again in time to save Judith. What else was there to think?

Having set his Indians to watch the suspect men, Johnny had taken Parley and Nate Butler and Ben Spring with him into the canyons. Before reaching the hideaway they had been joined by Suard and Ba'tiste and Crowbait who said the three men they had been detailed to watch had gone directly to the spot where Joe Britt waited. They had seen and they knew.

It was a cave, of sorts, Joe Britt had chosen, an eating away of the base of a pillar of the red earth. In itself it was not defensible for it was shallow and open across the front, but its approach was so tortuous that left to himself Johnny knew he would never have found it. If the Osage hadn't trailed Joe Britt here and remembered it he would have lost the way a dozen times over.

There was a quick, short fight. Josh Brand, Wash Craig and Hull Archer surrendered and when Johnny came up he found Joe Britt killed. Legette had shot him. Behind the pinnacle they found only the horses the men had been riding. They never saw a Pawnee. At some time, probably much earlier, they had slipped away taking the mules and traps.

Brand, Craig and Archer wanted nothing better than to rejoin the train. They had had enough of mutiny. With one voice they blamed Bullitt Trice for the whole thing. It was his notion from the beginning. He was the one planned it and talked all of them, even Joe Britt, into it. But it was Britt, they said, had stood out against taking over the whole train. He'd have nothing to do, he said, with stealing the wagons and goods and killing off all that wouldn't go peaceably. "He made his own terms," Josh Brand said, "about that. Said he'd go fer takin' the mules an' traps an' enough possibles to git us to the mountains but that's all. Said it was too risky 'thout you could travel light an' fast an' you couldn't do it with wagons. Him an' Trice argied days about it. Trice give in fer he needed him to guide us."

Johnny didn't bother to ask why they had joined Trice's plan. Their reasons didn't interest him. He told them coldly, "You'd never have lived to reach the mountains. Trice would have rid himself of you. He's too greedy."

Brand and Craig nodded sheepishly, as if they had given it some thought themselves. Only Archer, the hero worshiper, stood up for Trice. "He wouldn't of. He ain't that kind."

None of them knew that Trice was dead but Brand and Craig were eagerly ready to forsake him. Johnny thought Archer would cleave to him, but that was of little importance. He brought them all back to camp with him. "Will you take them on again?" Judith asked.

"Yes," he said, "but it's a bitter pill. I'd turn 'em out, for they deserve it, but I need 'em too bad now. We still have got to get to Santa Fe."

Legette had a gash in his head which hadn't been tended but he had not been mistreated. His glossy black skin was a little gray from weariness and hunger but he was so pleased to be back with his people that he beamed happiness in all directions. He told how in the middle of the fight, which had caught them by surprise because Joe Britt didn't believe anybody could find it but the ones that knew the way, there was so much confusion he'd been able to lay his hand on a gun. "Why'd you pick Britt to shoot, Legette?" Johnny asked.

"He was the leader, sir," Legette said simply, "and I thought the others might give up if he was killed. And they were the captain's own men." His face lit with a happy grin. "It would have been a mutiny of one, sir, to take over the captain's duty of punishment to them."

His precise, tutored English made them all laugh. It fell so strangely on their ears, used to the slovenly language of the frontier, and was even more strange coming as it did from the coal-black man. Judith wondered again about his past. Who had taught him? What had he been besides a slave? How, like Lucifer, had he fallen from favor? Why had he run away?

Asa was telling that when he roused, he had found Manuel first. "I don't hear as good as I used to," he said, "and I never knew what hit me. Don't know how long I laid there but best I could tell it warn't more than half a hour. I made certain Manuel was alive, then I seen to the horses and mules. To see if any had been took. None had, so I hefted Manuel and brung him to camp for the missus to tend."

There he had found Jesse Cooper, in his terrible mutilation, still breathing but only barely. "A dretful worry it was, sir," he said in his flat, level voice.

Judith thought she had never heard anything stripped more cleanly to its bare bones of meaning. A dreadful worry! Two dying men, as far as he knew, on his hands and he couldn't find her.

He hadn't panicked, however. He was distraught only to know what he ought to do, tend the injured or search for Miz Fowler. He saw tracks leading into the draw and in his slow way he concluded someone had come for her. Someone had been hurt down in the draw, maybe. She had gone to help. He didn't think about harm to her. He didn't think she had been compelled. So his duty appeared plain to him. Do what he could for Jesse and Manuel. Believing she had her medicine satchel with her, and too timid to believe he had the right to search for it in her wagon if she didn't, he had gone to his own wagon and found a shirt of his own to tear into bandaging. "Don't know why," he said, "I picked Manuel to tend first. Mebbe because I knowed him best. But I done it and I got him fixed up and I laid him on a blanket and kivered him ag'in the chill. Jesse," he added starkly, "was gone when I got to him. Had done breathed his last."

He was laid out now, Judith thought, just as cold, just as stiff, just as dead, as Bullitt Trice and Joe Britt, who lay nearby. They all would lie the night, to be buried on the morrow. She wondered if there would be an auction of their effects and thought she could not bear it if there was. Among Jesse's possessions were those small things he had bought of Tig Vance's. To be sold again? No. No.

Judith's piece of patchwork began where Asa's left off, for when she had ridden up out of the draw she had found him sitting stoically beside the corpse of Jesse Cooper, full of blame that he hadn't tended him first. "It would not have mattered," she comforted him. "Trice had killed him." She had looked to Manuel, seen that Asa had done well, and that all that was left to her was to wash and bandage Asa's own head. Then she had gone to see to herself.

Johnny had found her, curled on her bunk, a small, sore, sad little bundle. Her lower lip was swollen from Trice's backhanded clout and her eyes were swollen from weeping and she shook from the pile on pile of shock and trouble. But she was not hysterical. Battered as she was she had control of herself and her young face was still screwed to courage. She didn't rail at him or screech or flinch or shrink. She didn't gaze at him with hatred or fling angry blame at him. This was what broke his heart. He could have stood hysterics better. He felt so bitterly at fault himself that he would have welcomed a tirade. It was so much more than he had bargained for, to put her through so much. But, wordless, as he nearly always was under strong emotion, he simply gathered her up and held her. He couldn't know it was the wisest thing he might have done. It warmed her and comforted her and reassured her and restored her to sanity. It almost made the day and the night before seem a nightmare, a haunted, dreadful dream, but over now and behind and she herself awake and safe and secure. Like a child she loosed the wails that had been stopped up so long, loudly and gustily, and felt better for making the loud noise.

And now it was night and she was drowsy and all had been said, and all had been done that could be done.

They pampered her the next day, all of them. It's as if, she thought, they know the special reason I need a little pampering, but she knew they did not. No one knew it yet but herself. But if she moved Legette or old Parley was beside her instantly, to fetch or carry, to give her an arm to lean on, to peer at her anxiously, and to fret lest she overtire herself.

Ben Spring and William Day took the stock to the river to drink and they brought back kegs of water so she could bathe if she liked, or have unlimited coffee, or have Legette wash out some clothing for her. "Likely git 'em dirtier than they air, though," Ben Spring said shyly. "Don't look like that Canadian runs clear no place. Jist as silty here as it was back in Arkansas."

She was moved by all of the attention and a little fretted. They were saying, as best they could, that she had come to be very dear to them and they were glad she had come to no harm. They were trying also, she believed, to speak of admiration and respect. She had little truck with false modesty, deeming it indulgence and luxury. She knew she had behaved very well. The Osage might say she had caused Johnny trouble but she had caused him only the trouble any woman, solitary in a community of men, would cause by the laws of nature. She was the only woman handy so Trice had fixed his eyes on her. But he would have fixed them just as greedily on a Comanche squaw. Jesse Cooper was a little different, but he would never have believed he loved her, she was convinced, had they not been thrown together in this isolation.

She didn't load any guilt on her shoulders about Trice. He was an evil man and evil was bound to come to him. She didn't load an unusual load of guilt on her shoulders about Jesse. With Jesse her sin had been ignorance and a degree of carelessness, but it was the kind of carelessness that comes of perfect innocence. It simply had not occurred to her that men fell in love with the wives of their friends.

What guilt she felt she did not try to unload on Johnny. She didn't tell him what she had learned about Jesse. He was dead. Let Johnny mourn him as an old friend, grievously and puzzlingly sick of late, but still his good friend. That horse couldn't be ridden again . . . no need saddling him.

The attentions of the men fretted her because she strongly believed in staying on your legs and making them work. The time for lying quietly had passed for her with the night. What her body needed now was gentle exercise. She'd seen too many people take to their bed and die, while others, feeling sick to death, had kept going and lived. She never stayed in bed if she could help it. But the men came near compelling it.

She did not, however, go to the gravesides for the services Johnny held over the dead men. That was a harrowing she could not face, not even for decency's sake and one which, mercifully, she did not need to face. No one expected it of her.

Hesitantly she had asked Johnny if he meant to sell the men's effects. "I've not got much heart for it," he'd said.

"Then don't. Give them away, or send them back to their people."

He had seemed glad to agree. "They didn't die naturally like Vance," he said.

She considered the circumstances that made a man's death from a bear's claws natural and came to terms with them. He had not been shot to death nor clove by a bullwhip. The distinction had to do.

Late in the afternoon she sat by the fire which Johnny had provided by recklessly sacrificing old wagon pieces he had been saving. "I'll not have you cold tonight," he'd said.

"What if we lose a wagon in a dry scrape for lack of mending wood?"

"We'll lose it."

She watched the low blaze and thought how a wagon journey was made up, really, of only two parts—moving on and nighting. In the daytime the wheels turned and the miles were eaten up and there wasn't much talk nor much of anything else if all went well. It was just getting forward, rolling on. Camp time came and the fires were built and food was cooked and things were said. She thought of all the nights and all the fires and all the things that had been said and the things that had happened, the decisions taken, the guards and watches set, the alarms and the quick and sudden frights. It would almost be true, she thought, to say that the life of a train, the pulse of a journey, was in its night fires. Whatever happened in the day, almost always the night had hatched it. Bullitt Trice and Joe Britt had laid the plans for their mutiny around night fires. Shelley ran away when a night fire burned low. The Beaver brought his scalp back when another night fire was in embers. But good things had happened, too. Manuel's guitar had sung for them most often when flames flared high, and William Day's fiddle had scraped and there had been rum for the men and they had jigged and flung their hoedowns from their heels.

And this child of hers, this child, had been conceived as a fire sent its thin-traced smoke toward night stars in a night sky. She smiled to think it would be born in Spanish territory. Never mind, she thought to it, never mind. You began in a lovely glady valley.

24

W HAT they had to do was very simple.

They had to track back over their path to the point of their northing. From there their way was west, not by south or by north, but due west, as Johnny's map had indicated all the time. "And I ought," he said grimly, "to've believed it. Five days northing, two days laid over, five days back is the time we've lost. And a good man, to say nothing of mules and traps. It's a bitter learning."

"You couldn't know," Judith said. "Britt made it seem right."

"I could've believed my instincts," he said. "I never liked that northing. It went against the grain. And I could've remembered Britt was half Kioway. And I could've paid more heed to Trice. Slack. That's what I was. And it's cost us dear and like to've cost us dearer."

She could have reminded him that no man was all wise, not even Johnny Fowler. No man could make wise judgments every time, wise decisions all the time. Nor did he have the gift of total prophecy. But she didn't, because this was the most he had said about the disaster and the most he was likely to say. It was much for him and brought on, she knew, because he still shuddered over the threat to her and was still lashing himself about it. Let it rest, she thought, let it rest.

Inexplicably, when they broke camp to leave the Canadian canyons the Beaver appeared and took his place at the head of the column. He rode up from the draw and said nothing to anybody. There was pride in his bearing, however, and he took the lead as if he had the right. Johnny grunted, seeing him. "Figures I've had my comeuppance. Now he'll come out of the sulks."

"Where's he been?" Judith asked.

"Lord knows. Looks like he's been fasting. Gaunted down some. Been purifying himself probably."

"He's too notional and unpredictable to put your dependence in," she said shortly.

The sight of the Osage bruised her afresh. She was trying to put down resentment and hurt against him, and against Johnny. She wasn't, she had concluded, going to have any spleen or any dramatics about what the Indian had told her. She couldn't see that any good would come of it except to relieve her of some stormy feelings. She was female enough to wish angrily to confront Johnny and accuse him, to have that satisfaction, to rant at him and lacerate him as she had been lacerated. But they had their life to live out and the danger of quarrels, though they disburdened, was that things said in hot anger were like words graven in stone. There was no taking them back; they were there permanently, never to be rubbed out or forgotten. You couldn't mend the damage they had done, or put new flesh on their scars. The most you could do with them was walk away and never look at them again.

She had no intention of breaking with Johnny Fowler. However wounded she was by his past his present belonged to her and she meant to keep it. She had forfeited some of her own integrity as the cost of her love. It had been a big price to pay and almost impossible for her, but she had done it. She had taken him for better or for worse until death parted them. Since that was irrevocably so, it would serve neither of them well for her to raise a wall between them. Far better, she had decided, far, far better that she batten down this further cost inside her own heart. A woman was made with room inside her for tucking away many unwanted and unneeded things. She wasn't yet certain a man was.

But the Osage made it no easier for her.

"If he sticks," Johnny said, moving his horse ahead to give the starting signal, "it'll be a godsend."

That was it, she sighed, that was it. Johnny still needed him.

The Beaver stuck. He kept himself distant and he made his own camps, but each morning he was there to lead them. He led them a longer, ambling way back to their old road but they fetched up sixty miles farther west. When Johnny verified the latitude and distance he was jubilant. "Four days made up!" he said, "and a easy road and good water. I tell you, he's good! You know," he added thoughtfully, "wouldn't surprise me a bit if all those weeks he was gone from the train he wasn't riding plumb to Santa Fe. To make certain of the road."

"He was somewhere," Judith admitted. "I don't like the look of him, though. He's growing dreadfully thin. He looks ill to me."

"Ah, he knows what he's doing," Johnny scoffed. "Indians can gaunt down thin as a latigo strap and come to no harm. He's making some kind of medicine for himself. He's all right."

"I hope so."

For all they were short-handed they had made good time. Trying to show their change of heart Brand and Craig worked twice as hard as they had ever done before, and even Archer quit grousing. He had squalled like a scalded cat over Trice's death, but the man in the grave his grief had ended and he took to Johnny with the same doglike faithfulness. Give Hull Archer somebody to follow, Judith thought, and he'll follow with no discrimination. With Manuel ailing he had to take over the herd and though he did not contrive particularly well, he contrived doggedly.

She noted, with some melancholy, that poor old Jesse was hardly missed. Parley stepped in and Legette stepped in and the ranks closed without gap. He might never have been with them.

The man it was hard to supplant, whose place it took two men to fill, was Trice. Evil as he had been, he had also been the best muleskinner of the lot and whatever his failings one good thing could be said of him; he had never shirked his work. Judith guessed he had loved the power of it. If he couldn't drive men, he could drive mules. But they were a better found company without him. There was harmony and a pulling drive now that the dissident element was gone.

And they were nearing the end of their road.

On the third day after they had found their latitude again they were aware of a changing scene. The plains were swelling with a roll and billow again, and there was sparse grass, clumpy and scattered and almost dry, but enough of it to change the color of the long look from dun to a pale, whitish green. It was good to see grass again and to see color on the land. Occasionally the level was broken with a mesa which stood up with low height but with sharp break. At first these troubled Judith. She was afraid they were too far south and might be coming into the dreaded Llano Estacado. But Johnny shook his head. He'd talked with the Osage. "They get no worse. And mostly we can pass 'em. He's got us marked through."

They began to see about this time also a growth that puzzled Judith. It was small, dwarfish, stunted and gnarled, black-green in color. Hardly trees, she thought, but what kind of bushes? The first day they appeared there were only a few to be seen, two dozen perhaps, the entire day and there were none near their night camp. But the next day there were more and more of them and they were perceptibly larger than the ones seen the day before. Manuel was riding in her wagon that day. He was slowly growing better but they dared not risk his riding a horse yet. By midmorning when the whole land was dotted with the clumpish trees, Judith called him from the bunk. "What are they?"

His grin was happy. "Piñons, Señora. They are piñons, the tree of my country. We burn the wood and eat the nuts. We could not do without the piñon tree."

She raised her brows. Nuts? Wood? "They're pretty small."

"Not in my country, Señora. They grow pretty big there. Here, of course," his shoulders lifted eloquently, expressing his disdain of this nothingness, "one could not expect them to grow well."

When they made night camp she looked closely and found them a variant of a cedar, an evergreen, twisted by wind and sand and altitude into something darker and more deformed. The wood burned resinously and gave off an acrid, piney, penetrating odor that she found pleasant. "I like it," she told Manuel.

He laughed. "Sí, Señora. Is good. Is the first thing you will smell in Santa Fe. Is the smell of Santa Fe. And the little smokes, you will always see them there. And burritos bringing the piñon on their backs from the mountains. Piñons and burritos, Señora, and the little so-wide streets and dobe houses, and my people. Is Santa Fe, Señora."

She thought it sounded pleasant.

Another change was rain. After so long a dry time, no drop of moisture since the bad storm, it was wonderful to have rain again. It was peculiar that it came every day at the same time, though. The morning would be bright, the air light and piercingly dry. Shortly after the nooning there would be clouds, coming from nowhere, and the rain would pour for thirty minutes or so, then it would pass on and the sun would shine as brightly as before. "The rainy season, Señora," Manuel explained. "Always in July and August it is so. The good rains."

One day they passed the Tucumcari mound, a tumulus that stood alone, looking very like one of their own wagons, rounded at the ends, flattened a little on top. It looked unimportant, but when Johnny took a sight and said it was almost five thousand feet in altitude Judith viewed it with more respect. When they had passed the mound Manuel took to riding as much as possible on the wagon seat and he seemed taut and straining, forever searching ahead. But his head ached if he exerted himself and he still tired quickly. When he complained one morning of the pain in his head Judith sent him to doze in the bunk.

Shortly afterward she noticed a bank of clouds looming ahead, lying low on the horizon. It was a solid dark bank, purplish but hazed, and it stretched across their front save for a little piece in the south. It was an undulating bank, higher in places than in others, with an odd white line along its top. She watched it thinking it must be a storm bank, but after an hour of watching when it remained exactly the same, no change, no movement in it, no shifting about as all weather banks did, she grew puzzled. No storm bank she had ever seen had kept its identical shape for so long. Wind broke it up and played about with it and roughed and re-shaped it.

Manuel wakened and climbed back to the seat beside her and she gave him the lines. He yawned and she knew he felt dull and sluggish. Day-time sleep often made her feel the same. He glanced ahead automatically, then she felt him stiffen. Suddenly he rose up from the seat and cried out loudly, and she clutched at him, frightened, afraid he had lost his reason. They had watched carefully for signs of derangement. Two head wounds were enough to derange a stronger mentality than Manuel's. He shook off her hand and pointed excitedly. "They are there! They are there! My heart, my soul, the light of my eyes! Señora, they are there!"

"What's there, Manuel? In God's name, what is it?" If he grew violent she must call Johnny.

Tears were raining down the boy's cheeks and he was sobbing, still on his feet, the reins dropped and forgotten. She recovered them.

"The mountains, Señora, the mountains, the mountains! See? There?"

"Manuel, I see no mountains. Where?"

"But there, Señora. Ahead of us. They looked like that from behind when I was leaving. Like clouds. I looked back all the time, Señora. And that is the way they looked. One day when I looked they were not there. Ay de mi, that I should ever have left them!"

She wept with him, for joy that they had been recovered. She patted his arm. "But you are home again, Manuel. You are truly home again now. You can see the mountains."

That loom of clouds, she thought, the mountains. She had listened for so long to stories about the Sangre de Cristos she couldn't believe it. Johnny was forever quoting Becknell about how towering they were, how grand. And Joe Britt had described them. "Snows on their tops the year round. High, high peaks, like Truchas and old Baldy. Real mountains, the Sangre de Cristos."

"Why are they called the blood of Christ?" she asked Manuel.

He had no idea, he had never heard, they had simply always been the Sangre de Cristos.

"How far?" she asked. "How far, now, Manuel?"

He lifted his shoulders. "I do not know. It is just there. Not far."

That night Johnny was more explicit. "We are making for San Miguel," he said. "Five days at most . . . four, if we have luck."

"And from there, Johnny?"

He shrugged.

"Ten days?" she said. "To Santa Fe?"

"At the outside." He grinned. "You getting anxious?"

She grinned back at him. When they got to Santa Fe and when Johnny had rented a store on the square (but they called it a plaza in Santa Fe) and when they had got settled into one of Manuel's dobe houses, she had something to tell him. Something, she believed, that would delight him and make him glad. But not until then. She had made up her mind about that. Not until then. Sometime in August. "Aren't you?" she asked.

"I couldn't tell you," he admitted. "I just couldn't tell you how anxious I am to get there."

And now the mountains were towering and the wagons were winding around among the foothills. The hillocks and mounds and sudden sharp peaks, none of them seeming high, were covered all over with piñon, the reddish earth showing underneath. Johnny's sextant showed they were at an unbelievable altitude of five thousand four hundred feet. They had been crawling, Judith thought, like a flea up the flank of a sleeping dog, since the day they left Three Forks, a fraction of an inch at a time, never knowing it, never feeling it. Becknell had told Johnny, she remembered, that the air in Santa Fe was so thin and rarefied that until you got used to it it made your breath short and sometimes gave you a headache. But she had never felt finer in her life. They had come so slowly, she guessed, that they had grown accustomed to altitude gradually. "But we have fifteen hundred feet more these next few days," Johnny warned her. "The Santa Fe plateau is nearly seven thousand feet."

And yet the mountains towered. They were majestic, grand, snow-mantled, high and magnificent. Nobody had ever yet put into words what they actually were, she thought. Going by boat when she had adventured to the Territory she had never seen real mountains before. She couldn't get enough of them. She filled her eyes with them and was exalted by them. If you lived, she thought, where you looked on them every day, if each time you raised your eyes you saw them, lifted high and noble and pure before you, you could not hold a mean thought in your mind, you could not do a mean act. They would not permit it.

But her exaltation tumbled. Men did. However grand, however noble their surroundings, where men lived there was meanness. Not this side the portals of heaven was perfection achieved. She guessed that if you lived where you looked on these great peaks and valleys you grew used to them until the day came when you didn't even see them. They came to be neither noble nor pure. They came to be simply there. Something you saw all the time. Your neighbor's wash was more meaningful than the mountains.

They had come now to a valley bordering a clear and rushing and sparkling stream. Judith called it a brook. Johnny called it a creek. With affronted dignity, Manuel said it was the Pecos River. The valley was neither glady nor green and it was broken by arroyos and mounds and the queerly peaked hills. They followed an old cart road that led to San Miguel, the ford. The water of the river was a delight to Judith who expected to have another wash all over in it. But one toe dabbled in it sent shock all over her. Here in the last week of July it was icy cold. "Comes down from the peaks, I reckon," Johnny said, laughing at her shivers. She had to make do with a quick rinse of her face and hands.

A day or two later they were looping around the foot of a hillock, expecting at any moment to come upon the village, when they met an old shepherd. More to make talk than from the need of information Johnny asked, in his fractured Spanish, "How far to San Miguel, friend?"

The old man was as brown as an ancient leather book binding and as fragile. He looked as though he might shatter if handled roughly. "Oh," he said, pointing with his chin, "está cerquita. Ahora está usted allá." Which was to say, it is close by. You will soon be there.

Johnny laughed. "Manuel said it was close by four days ago. They have no idea of distance."

"Why did he point with his chin, Johnny?" Judith asked.

"I've got no idea. Ask Manuel."

Manuel was amazed that she had not seen for herself. "But his hands were not free, Señora. He wore a serape."

Elementary, she thought, amused. You cut a hole in a blanket and stuck your head through. Your hands were not free, so you pointed with your chin.

They came into San Miguel just before nightfall on a Saturday. Judith was a little prepared for it because Manuel had talked so much to her. When she saw the cluster of low, flat-roofed, strangely boxlike houses straddling the river she was glad she had listened so often. She might otherwise have thought it dingy and ugly and squalid. But she knew, because he had told her, that these houses were made of adobe bricks, and that adobe was a mixture of the native earth and straw, muddled and shaped, then stacked into walls when dry. He had told her how, when the adobes had been stacked so high, a plaster of the same earth was put on both sides of the walls, inside and out, and patted with the hands until it was smooth and the corners rounded. He had said they left their roofs flat, sloping them very gently. "Is not much rain," he explained.

They laid on poles first, then filled the spaces with small branches. Lastly they spread over a layer of soil. She had thought it odd and not a very sensible way to build. Surely the rains must melt a mud house away. "But no, Señora, they are strong houses. One must mend the plaster on the outside, naturally. And there may be a small leak from the roof sometimes." He said this as if it did not matter. One was not inconvenienced by it at all. It was a thing to be expected, and one did not permit oneself to be troubled by a small leak. "Is a good house for here, Señora. Cool, you will see, when the sun is hot and warm when the snow blows. You will see. Is good house."

They looked very small, she thought, those mud houses of San Miguel, and so nearly the color of the earth all about that they seemed to grow out of it as naturally as the piñons and ocatillo and chamisa. There were the little smokes, all coming from corners of the houses, no visible chimneys on the outside. Beside almost every door was a great string of big red peppers—the chilis Manuel had so missed.

Pole corrals were scattered about. There seemed no logical plan for their placement, nor much logic in the way they were built. But in some fashion they seemed right and natural, too, as if they had grown where they found their need to grow. There were dogs about, and ponies, and a great many tobacco-brown children. More slowly a few adults, hearing the noise of the lumbering wagons, stood in the doorways. The young men were excited, chattering together and pointing at las carretas. The older ones were somber and contained, the older women drawing their black rebozos over their heads. Judith's heart beat up with excitement. They were the first people, the first civilized people, she had seen in three months.

Manuel rode flying by. He had insisted on riding this day, and Judith's mouth twitched seeing him giving himself airs now, showing his importance to his countrypeople. He, Manuel García, was attached to these great carretas. He had a position of trust with the captain of this Americano caravan. He amounted to something. He made his horse sidle and prance a little, and he shooed the dogs and children out of the way with style and flourish.

Over eight hundred miles, Judith thought, across the prairies, from one world into another. And this was the first village, the first town. They had not yet come to Santa Fe but they had come, in reality, to the end of that long, uninhabited road. Here were people—Spanish people, true, and strange people—but people with a civilized way of life, a recognizable religion, living in a recognizable town. She felt a tremendous sense of accomplishment.

"We'll lay over tomorrow," Johnny said. "I have to let the alcalde see my papers and we'll do some trading tomorrow."

"On Sunday?" she asked, shaking out her skirts.

"Their Sabbath ends with the Mass," he said chuckling. "You want me to find a room for you? Want to get out of the wagon for a night?"

She looked about at the strange houses, nothing of home in them to her. She looked at the wagon, so known to her she could lay her hand on anything she needed in pitch-dark. It was old-looking now, grayed by the weather and the winds and pitted by the sands and repaired and mended here and there. There were two splintered gouges on one side, where Pawnee arrows had thudded heavily, and the osnaburg was patched, one patch flapping loosely and fraying at the end. She touched the wheel and smiled at her husband. "I believe I'll stay home," she said and did not think it odd she should say it just that way.

He nodded. "We'll ford the creek then and bed down for the night on the far side."

It was strange that night to hear the stir of people about. There was a baile, jumped up she guessed on the spur of the moment, for the men. Johnny could not go. He would be closeted with the alcalde. And he did not much want her to go without him. "Might be a fight," he said.

She didn't care, but Manuel was disappointed. She knew he wanted to show her off, his Americano Señora. *He* would have been her escort, he assured her, in the captain's absence. *He* would have protected her. "I'm sure you would," she told him, "but I am truly tired. But," she added, trying to make amends, "I will go to church with you in the morning. There is a church here, isn't there?"

"Por supuesto, Señora. There is always a church. Here is San Miguel del Bado."

Saint Michael of the Ford. "Good. We shall attend."

His eyes flashed but he knitted his brows warningly. "The Mass will be very early, Señora."

"No matter."

"Sí. I will come."

"Manuel," she stayed him. "You will find the Comanche woman's father? José López?" It seemed another lifetime since the Comanche captive had pled with her to find her father.

Manuel drew himself up proudly. "Señora, I have already made the inquiries. The man is dead." His attitude said plainly that he had carried this responsibility conscientiously. He had not forgotten.

"Are there no other relatives?" she asked.

"A brother. He does not remember her."

"Well." She turned away. "We have done as she wanted. You will see that some trader, Comanchero, passes on the word?"

"Sí, Señora. Consider it accomplished."

"In the morning, then."

"In the morning, Señora."

It was sad, she thought, but it was all the woman had wanted—just to know if her father was living. In some roundabout way, a year from now, two years, some passing trader would let the word fall, José López had died. She wondered if the woman would give the news more than a moment's thought. And the brother . . . she had been taken captive, probably, when he was too small to remember her. She guessed it hadn't meant much to him, to learn that he had a sister among the Comanches. How could it, if he could not remember her? It was as well, she thought now, the woman had not wished to come with them. There was no family waiting for her here.

Manuel came for her just as the sun rose the following morning.

The service was shocking to her. The interior of the small mud church was whitewashed so high and hung about were pictures so odd to her, so weirdly painted, in such a sad state of repair, that she could make nothing of them. They were, she supposed, sacred paintings, some perhaps from Mexico or even Spain, but they were horrid to her inexperienced eye. The Christ was bloody and agonized, as, her mind reminded her he must have been, but surely not so . . . not so dreadfully . . . She passed on quickly to a carved wooden figure set into a niche . . . another Christ, elongated painfully, the splintered beard draggled and stained. A leak in the mud roof, doubtless. Some of the paintings were crudely framed. Others hung frayed and tattered from their tackings.

There was not a chair, not a pew, not a bench in the entire building. The floor was earth, hard-packed and shiny from use, and black-shawled women knelt on it and black-haired men stood about, heads bowed, hands folded, praying. Apprehensive, Judith kept to the back and Manuel stayed beside her. She was surprised when she spied O'Toole leaning against a wall. Irish and Catholic, of course, she thought. But they had never known. He had not ever said a word.

A noise, not music to her ears but obviously meant to be, began, coming from an alcove near the altar. Two lank-haired men emerged, one with a fiddle, the other with a guitar. From these instruments they drew whining, scraping sounds, like those she had heard from across the river at the baile last night. She was startled and thought it impossible that the same music should be played here in church, by the same men, as was played at the dance last night. She looked quickly at Manuel but his eyes were piously fixed on the altar and his lips were moving as he silently said his devotions.

A priest—she judged he was a priest—entered, followed by a man in a long black robe carrying things. A Catholic service would have been strange to her in any circumstances. Here, it took on the aspect of a mummer's play. It could not be meant for a church service. It was a pantomime of some sort. But the people, kneeling and standing, were all devout. There was nothing strange about it to them.

The priest made his genuflection and catching up a brush from his acolyte he wandered about among the congregation, flicking his brush in the basin of water the black-robed man carried, whisking it over the heads of the worshipers. He stopped short of Judith and studied her so shrewdly she wondered if she were improperly garbed. Nervously she felt of her bonnet, fingered her skirts. Some decision made, the priest flipped a drop of water in her direction and passed on, returning to the altar. The business of the Mass began, but he went too fast for her Latin and spoke too low for her to hear anyhow. It was all over in less than an hour.

The people streamed out and instantly the whole village took on the air of a fiesta. They had dutifully gone to church, been absolved, and now they could turn to the pleasure of bargaining and buying and trading with these Americanos who had so unexpectedly come among them. Judith saw the priest strolling toward the building Johnny had taken to display his goods in, a chupar fuming violently from his mouth.

Well, she told herself, if there are no Presbyterians in Santa Fe I shall simply have to make my devotions to myself. I don't think I can ever grow used to this!

It was a long day and for a part of it she wandered about trying her Spanish on the children and on such of the women as weren't at the store trading. Mostly they were old, left behind. They replied to her courteously but shyly. She took some pride in the fact they understood her at all, though she thought her pronunciation must be atrocious. She had modeled it after Manuel's and she did not know if he spoke correct Spanish or not. It amused her to think how it would sound if some foreigner learned his English from Parley, say. For all she knew she was abusing the Spanish language just as badly. But she didn't much think so.

She wearied in the afternoon and went across the bridge to the camp. She slept awhile, then rose to wash her face in the stream, and sat on watching what must surely be the most foolish pair of birds in the world. They were water birds of some sort, though tiny and grayly brown. One bird stood on a stone which thrust up out of the water, kept its little clawed feet perfectly dry, but it squatted and bent ceaselessly, never stopping the perpetual motion of squatting and rising, squatting and rising. The other bird moved constantly, too, but in diving and fluttering for long periods of time under the water, coming up eventually with something in its beak, tripping back to the bird on the stone and giving the food over. This little female, Judith thought, with amusement, is about as badly spoiled as a woman could be. The male, for it had to be the male doing such yeoman service, was literally drowning himself to feed her. And all she did was stoop and rise, stoop and rise, once in a while when he was gone too long, squawking impatiently.

Old Parley crossed and came over and she looked up at him to share her amusement. One glance at his time-beaten old face told her he was troubled, deeply troubled.

She collected herself, for whatever troubled him now concerned them—herself and Johnny. "Johnny?" she asked. "Something's happened?"

"No. No," he said, but the gentleness of his voice struck fear into her. "But I got to talk to ye, honey. I'm afeared he'll die elsewise."

25

ORDINARILY Parley had the same capacity as Johnny and the Indians for hiding his emotions. His face could be inscrutable when there was real trouble. You would never know by Parley's face when he was afraid. He met fear with a countenance as bland as a baby's, as smoothed and as innocent and as untelling. But he was no good at hiding loving concern. When his mind was full of worry for her or for Johnny or for anyone he loved, his forehead would furrow as if it had been plowed and his wayward old eyebrows would pucker together and his sweet old eyes would darken with pain. They were dark now and ambered with hurt.

He came to sit beside her and he took her hand. She waited stilly and not impatiently. If Johnny was all right, it couldn't be too bad. Parley smoothed her hand and she felt the roughness of his. The palm had hard cakes of calluses and the skin was cracked and split and broken. She thought what it would do to a skein of silk thread, then let the thought drift away. That hand, which served her and Johnny so faithfully, could have split a dozen skeins of the finest silk for all of her.

When he looked at her finally there was a film of moisture over his eyes. "It's the Beaver, honey. I'd not tell ye this, I'd not trouble ye, but I'm afeared he'll die. He's awful sick an' he's skeered to death."

Her stomach squeezed. So. She wasn't through with the Osage yet. She hadn't felt the last of the pain he had stored up for her. There was more to come. "Tell it," she said. "Why is he sick? What is he scared of?"

"He says you . . . he says you . . ." But the old man couldn't go on. He faltered and looked at her pleadingly.

"Yes. What does he say I did?"

Gathering his courage the old man plunged. "He says he told you 'bout Johnny's Osage woman. He says you put a curse on her. Honey, I know ye was mad, but whut made ye? Didn't ye know if ye put a curse on a dead Injun they got to wander? They ain't got no home then. Cain't git to whur they belong. They're like ha'nts, walkin' the land, mournin' an' wailin'. They's no rest fer 'em till the curse is raised. What come over ye?"

She felt totally bewildered. "I don't know what you're talking about! I didn't put a curse on her. Surely you know that. I wouldn't know a curse if I met one in the road. Witches went with Salem, Parley. I'm no witch to go about putting curses on people."

"He says ye did."

A sternness came into her and made her know that now was the time, that now this thing must be set straight, all of it. There was no turning back now. The mystery must be pierced, the last ignorance taught, the last cost paid. "I want you to tell me," she said, "about Johnny and the Beaver. I want to know what this is all about."

"All of it?"

"All of it."

So he told her. He told her how it had been when Johnny had first come to the Territory, a lanky beanpole lad, strong and sandy-haired and blue-eyed and loving the new land and taking to its ways like a duck takes to water. "Like a duck takes to water," old Parley repeated, "fer if ever they was a bein' made fer a special place, Johnny was made fer the Territory. He'd got bones to fit it, honey, an' skin to fit it an' marrer to fit it an' guts to fit it. Hit couldn't tame him an' he couldn't tame it, an' they fit an' they was rejoicin' betwixt 'em, the lad an' the land. An' the Osages," he added, nodding, "an' the Osages. Like he'd been borned amongst 'em. Ah, but he was the bonny, bonny lad them days, honey. I wish ye could of knowed him. The mornin' star warn't no brighter. No brighter. I wish ye could of knowed him then."

It made her sad. She said, "I wish I could have known him then too, Parley."

He was immediately repentant. "Aw, honey, ye've got the best of Johnny Fowler. I didn't mean ye didn't. He was jist green an' limber an' full o' juice them days, joyful like. A man'd like him best, mebbe, fer he'd be ready fer a romp. But likely you wouldn't o' keered fer him at all. He'd of been too brash to suit ye."

She put a mechanically cheerful smile on her face. "I doubt it. I think I would have liked him. Go on, Parley."

More slowly he continued. He told about the long hunts and the young men dances and the feasting and the flute playing and the old man ceremonies and the singing and then, more slowly still, he told her, finally, about Pretty Bird. "Two year he'd been in the Territory then. Two year, an' amongst the Osages most of the time." He stopped.

Pretty Bird, she thought, Pretty Bird. There had to be this, too. She must have a name so lovely it was like the singing of the bird that had given her the name. *"Was* she pretty, Parley?"

His old eyes pled with her and she knew. He didn't need to tell her. She had been pretty. She had been more than that. She had been beautiful and exquisite in the way some Indian girls could be, small-boned, delicate, honey-skinned, sloe-eyed, sweet-mouthed. She took the knife to the hilt, and it didn't kill. She waited.

"Well," Parley said flatly, "they was married. The Injun way, mind, which ain't much of a way cordin' to some whites . . . not legal . . ."

"Don't," she cried, "don't tell me that. It was a marriage!"

Parley bent his head. He loved her so much. He hated what he was doing to her. But he had to confess. "It was a marriage. He didn't jist take her, which he could of. He paid fer her with horses, the Osage way."

He would have, she thought anguished, he would have. For, God help her, he had loved her. He had loved her!

Parley held her hand tight but he flattened the other hand against the sandy creek bank. "They didn't have long, honey. A year. Jist one year. He never brung her to the post. Not that he was ashamed of her, mind ye. He warn't. He jist liked to think of her whur she belonged. He jist wanted to think of her thar, waitin'. Waitin' fer him."

A year, she thought, her heart quickening. One year. It shouldn't matter. It shouldn't matter at all, but it did. Over and done with, she calculated quickly, four years before she ever knew him! The relief was blessed and sweet. Over and done with, and nothing to do with her!

"Jist one year, honey," old Parley was saying. "Then they was that massacree . . . ye've heared of it . . . when the Blade led the Cherokees ag'in Claymore's village."

She nodded. It had been before her time but she had heard of it. The men of the village had been away on their long hunt. Only women and children and ancients had been left in the village. Suddenly the Cherokees had descended in swarms and they had murdered ruthlessly all that couldn't get away into the hills. They had taken captive but few.

"She was killed," Parley said.

Judith sat very still. Johnny's Osage wife had been killed in that Cherokee massacre. "Who did it?" she asked, but already she knew.

"The Blade. Honey, she was the sister of Suard's woman . . . the old Suard. Ye've heared Johnny tell of him. They was as close as brothers. This 'un is his boy that's with us now."

"Yes."

"Well. Suard's woman an' kids got away into the hills safe, but Pretty
Bird was too clumsy . . . she was near her time an' heavy . . . an' that
devil got her. Johnny an' Suard rid out soon as they heared an' they found
her." Parley's voice was as bleak as winter. "He'd cut her open an' took
the young'un an' stuck it like a pig. An' he'd flung it down aside of her.
Hit was a leetle gal baby, pretty as Pretty Bird herself, jist ready to be
birthed, leetle fingernails an' toenails already shaped, black hair on its
head, even leetle eyelashes to its eyes, an' fat as a leetle pig, all crinkled
over with fat . . ."

She hadn't known she was crying but her face was all wet and she
couldn't see. "Poor Johnny. Poor, poor Johnny . . ."

Parley waited a while, then he went on. "He'd mangled Pretty Bird's
face with his blade and he'd cut off her . . . cut off . . ."

She put up her hands. "Please!"

"All right," he said quietly. And then, "The way the Beaver comes into
this is that just four year later the Blade led another massacree of Cherokees. You was in the country then an' you knowed about it."

She lifted her head. "The hunt?"

"The hunt. Johnny was with 'em. You recollect the hull Osage village
had went. They'd killed plenty buffalo. The young warriors wanted to
count coup ag'in the Pawnee. Johnny was off huntin' wild mustangs. The
Blade follered an' hid out, made his play. They wasn't nobody in camp
but women an' children an' old folks ag'in. That was his way. Ketch 'em
'thout their menfolks. Made it look like a big victory. Bring back a heap
of skulps. An' women an' young men captives. An' it went in the books,"
he said bitterly, "it all went in the books as big Cherokee victories.
Victories! Where's the man couldn't call it a victory ag'in women an'
children? Ag'in the Injuns they was pushin' out of their own lands! Ah,
sure, honey, the Osages raided an' depredated. Sure they did. But why
wouldn't they? They was bein' pushed right out of their own lands. They
was bein' shoved off the lands that'd been theirs since time commenced.
How come the Cherokees had any right to it? Their land laid back east.
How come they left it? How come they give it over to the government?
An' how come 'em to have ary rights to Osage land? How come the government to have any right to it? Who's to sell an' who's to give an Injun's
land? Who's to know what they think about it an' feel about it? The little
old people of the Osages lived in the Arkansas Territory as fur back as
memory went, then suddenly here come Cherokees an' Creeks an' Choctaws an' whites. How come? Who give 'em the right?"

"Parley," she recalled him.

"Sure. Sure. Well, after the massacree, the Blade done the same to the Beaver's woman he'd done to Johnny's. Left his mark in the same way with his knife. 'Twarn't pretty. An' Johnny takened the blame in hisself. He said it wouldn't o' happened if he'd done whut he ort to've done, gone fer the Blade before. But he never, then, fer he allowed the law had come to the Territory with the military. God knows how come Will Bradford to let them Cherokees past Fort Smith. He even give 'em powder! But they was allus favorites of the government. They was so slick and so smooth an' so smart. They knowed enough to pretend they was white . . . but they allus had their eye on Osage land. They wanted all of it. They whined an' complained till they got it. An' when they was trouble, the government allus taken their side. The Osages was troublemakers. The Cherokees was saints. But they never belonged west of the Mississippi! Their land laid east and if they give it up, it never entitled 'em to Osage land."

"Parley," Judith said again.

"Yes. Johnny had been workin' with Will Bradford at the fort to git the Osages to abide by the law. Tryin' to git 'em to quit raidin' an' depredatin' the Cherokees. They was the dearlings of the government an' ever' time the Osages raided an' depredated they lost some more land to the Cherokees. He seed the way the wind was blowing, an' he wanted the Osages to quit raidin' an' depredatin' so's to save their lands. But, honey," the old man cried, "how ye gonna tell Injuns! How ye gonna tell 'em the land they've lived on all their lives an' counted their own, how ye gonna tell 'em ever' time they make a quill scratch on a piece o' paper they've give up another million acres of land? They don't know nothin' 'bout land. Nobody owns land but Wah-kon-tah, an' Wah-kon-tah has been good to Osages an' let 'em live an' hunt there. Ah, Goddamn Thomas Jefferson an' his notion to resettle the eastern Injuns out here! The trouble he's made! The trouble they've made!"

"Parley. Parley, please!"

"Yer pardon, love. Well, Johnny figgered he ort to let the Blade go an' let the government have its way with him." The old voice grew bitter. "They never done that first thing to him. They never took him in. They never exampled him. They jist let him go free to kill ag'in. An' he killed the Beaver's woman. So Johnny faulted hisself an' he takened it on hisself to set things right. He fit the Blade an' you know the rest."

Ah, yes, she knew the rest. She certainly did know the rest. She remembered, wincingly, how arrogantly and smugly and ignorantly she had begged him to let the law take care of the Blade. She remembered how she had threatened him if he fought the man. She had said she wouldn't marry him if he killed the Blade. She had said it would be murder, and no marriage was big enough to hold murder. Murder! He had tried the law and the law had done nothing. Another Osage girl had been murdered because of his patience. "He didn't tell me," she cried, "he didn't tell me."

"He was jist tryin' to save ye," old Parley said.

Yes, and he had expected her to have faith in him, to trust him. Shame raked her and made her feel sore. It wasn't his way to justify himself. Whatever he did he had his own reasons and to him they were good enough and just and sufficient. If you loved somebody, in his thinking, you believed in them and you didn't have to know why. How, she wondered, anguished, had he kept on loving her when she had failed him so? For she hadn't taken him on faith, or accepted him in trust. And she had felt so right, so certain. She, Judith, knew so well what was good and just, for him as well as for herself. In the end she had been forced to her knees by love, though she shrank from what she felt was her own betrayal of herself, and all she had done was closet in her heart his purpose against the Blade, hating it, but knowing she must take it if she was to have his love. When it was done and she had gone to him he hadn't asked her reasons for change. He had just caught her to him and called her his love. Ah, he put the lightest chains on you, loose and easy, that left you room to yourself. He didn't invade anywhere, nor tighten, or demand. He *believed* and she should have believed, too.

Parley said, "Well, that's the way of it. It's nothin' to do with you an' all to do with yer man. But the Beaver is sick an' he's worse skeered. Not fer hisself. God, he don't keer fer hisself but he's skeered fer Pretty Bird. He's been doin' whut he knowed to do to git shet of the curse, fastin' an' makin' his own medicine. But he's skeered it's done no good an' Pretty Bird is wanderin' without no place to go. He would of turned back but he had to git Johnny to here first. Now, he aims to go, but he'll die 'fore he gits home."

She fixed her mind on the scene with the Osage. "What I said when he told me, Parley, was 'your brother's Osage wife be damned.' I shouldn't have. But he did make me angry and I just blurted it out. I saw him look queer, go all over queer in his face, but I didn't think. . . ."

" 'Course ye never, an' don't think I ain't berated him proper fer tellin' ye. Hit was mean of him. Johnny'd a wanted ye to know, he'd a told ye."

"Why didn't he?"

"Why, honey, it's plain. He loved ye too good. Said he never aimed ye to know ye warn't the first one. Said fur as he meant it, he'd not ever loved nobody else now."

Her eyes pricked suddenly and her breath caught. She was forced to her knees again by love, Johnny's love . . . his dear, dear love for her.

Parley patted her hand and pushed himself up. "Well, if that's all ye said, he'd not told me, hit c'n be righted. He warn't never a mission Injun, as well ye know, but he's been around them missionaries enough to know about damnation. That's whut's skeered the wits outen him. Git yer medicine satchel an' bring it, an' ye'll have to fool him a leetle. 'Twon't do no good to tell him ye didn't mean to damn her to eternity. He wouldn't believe ye. Got his own notions. Ye'll have to make out ye're takin' the curse off."

She mopped her eyes, nodding her head. "Of course I will. Of course I will."

As the sun went down, as earnestly as she had ever done anything in her life, she went through a strange ritual, making it up as she went along, uttering stray Latin phrases and incantations, plastering the Beaver with poultices here and there, letting some blood from a vein in his arm, dosing him with steaming potions. His eyes glittering with hope he followed every move she made, listened intently, but she made certain the garbled abracadabra that came from her lips could not be understood. It was so impressive that it satisfied him, however. She knew when he began to think this woman of Johnny Fowler's made a very big medicine, and it must be very powerful, for she saw respect come into his eyes, and bent over him she could see strength flowing back into him, as he put his mind at ease.

She didn't think it odd that when she had finished she herself felt cleansed and relieved and washed with a blessed peace. Hate was gone from her, and doubt, and she felt like a child, innocent again and good.

26

THERE WAS an episode of minor importance the following morning as they made ready to go on their way. But as usual with such events the edge of sorrow touched it, the gray fringe of tragedy.

The wagons were loaded, the teams hitched, the men were in their places, when there wandered out from the nearest hut a queer, wild figure, a young woman with long, matted, hanging hair, garbed in a strange long garment so threadbare a summer zephyr would have whipped it in pieces from her thin, angular body.

Without purpose, in an odd, jerky, disjointed gait, she went down the line. The people standing about suddenly drew in their breath, hissed together and pulled back. They were afraid of this one. Judith's own breath drew in when she saw her close, for there was madness in the woman's eyes. She made a weaving, hopping way past the wagons, searching the face of each man she passed, muttering to herself. She stopped a moment beside each man, who stared uneasily down at her, and peered up at him, then shaking her head she moved on.

She grew bolder as she moved and they could hear what she was saying but it was a bad mixture of broken English and Spanish. "Is not my Joe. Is not my Joe. Americanos, but is not my Joe." She lapsed into Spanish then and began to weep.

Manuel nudged Judith, his eyes rounded fearfully. "Taos girl. Is crazy, that one."

"What is she looking for?"

His shoulders lifted. "They say Americano have her sometime. Bring her here. Go away. Say he be back. No come. She look for him all the time. Think every American know about her man."

The train lingered, waiting for Johnny who was having his papers back from the alcalde. The girl wandered, in her queer hopping walk, up and down the line. She stopped finally beside Judith's wagon and tilted to look up. She spoke to Manuel. "You see my Joe? You Spanish, you see him? He come back. He say he come back. You see him, huh? He tell you he come back?"

Mutely Manuel shook his head.

Judith felt pity for the girl. She said, "We have not seen your Joe, Señorita. We have not seen him. He does not travel with us."

The girl twitched a shoulder high, threw her hair back, and made to move away. But Legette rode up. "Ma'am, Captain Fowler said to tell you . . ."

Judith never heard the rest of Johnny's message, for the Indian girl flung herself at Legette's stirrup and clawed at it, screaming, "Is my Joe! Is Joe! Is Joe come back!"

Horror ripped sickeningly through Judith. This thing about the black man again . . . what was it? Why did Indian women go so mad over him?

Every man down the line turned to look at the screaming, clawing, climbing girl. She was trying frantically to get up on the horse with the man who had suddenly become her Joe to her. She was raking Legette's leg with her hands and scrambling in queer, disjointed jerks. When the old robe fell aside in one especially desperate convulsion, Judith saw, with shock, that her feet were loosely hobbled.

Legette, frozen, sat like a statue on his horse, his black satiny face gone ashy and his eyes almost bulging from his head. The woman's screams rose and fell. "Is Joe! Is my Joe! Joe! Joe! Is Joe come back!"

She's gone completely mad, Judith thought, appalled, gone violent and dangerous. She saw Legette's tongue lick out, and his eyes rolled whitely as he looked at her in appeal. She was galvanized. "I'll get the captain . . ."

But he was coming. He and the alcalde had emerged from the store building and hearing the commotion, sensing trouble, had broken into a run. There was a short, wild struggle before they could subdue the girl. "What's it all about?" Johnny asked, his breath coming fast.

The alcalde was having his hands full hanging on to the woman but he managed to pant, "This one is a lunatic, Señor. Was a man in Taos one time . . . name of Joe Britt. She was his . . . his esposa. He brought her here with him. Went off and left her. She grieved until she lost her reason. Looks for him constantly." He broke into rapid Spanish and hauled the woman away. But her weeping was heartbreaking. She had found Joe again and they were taking her from him.

The wagons moved and San Miguel was left behind. But they were all subdued, shaken by the episode. It was as though the ghost of Joe Britt had walked among them. It was the purest coincidence, the least likely of happenings, but it was uncanny and it had the touch of the supernatural in it. It sent a shiver down the back and a quick look over the shoulder and a wish to cross fingers and say a swift prayer.

When they stopped that night, still beside the Pecos, and the night work was done and the fires were blazing and the hands were singing, William Day's fiddle scraping, Legette approached Judith and Johnny, who were alone by their own fire. "Sir," he said to Johnny, "I am troubled by this thing that occurred today."

"No need to be, Legette. It was unfortunate, that's all. She's been looking for Joe Britt a long time and she was ready to mistake the most likely man for him. Just happened to pick on you."

"But it *was* me she picked, sir. Me. And I am the man who killed him. It's like in some weird way she knew, and I must take his place."

"No, no. You've been brooding. You were the biggest man, and Britt was darker than most of us. Your dark skin fitted in her mixed-up mind. That's all."

"It's as if some kind of burden was laid on me, sir."

Johnny motioned impatiently. "Now, that's foolish. He wouldn't ever have come back to her. You know that, don't you? Britt's kind don't. He was done with her."

Legette's hands wove together restlessly. "But now she thinks he *did* come back, sir. And we know he won't. Not ever. I'm not sorry I shot him, sir. It's not that. And likely you're right, he wouldn't have come back anyhow. But that poor woman . . . that poor woman . . ."

"Well, there's nothing can be done about it."

Legette stood before them, his glossy black color not yet fully recovered. "Maybe . . . is she a slave, sir? Does someone own her?"

"I've no idea. They probably make her do some light work for her keep."

Legette moistened his lips. "She was tied."

"For her own good, I'd think. Keep her from straying, coming to harm."

"How far are we from Santa Fe now, sir?"

"Twenty-five miles, two, two and a half days maybe. Why?"

"There would be time for me to ride back, if the captain would permit it . . . bargain for her . . . buy her."

Johnny's head lifted sharply. "Damnation, man, what do you want with her? She's mad, stark, staring mad! You saw her! What good would a mad woman be to you? How could she serve you?"

Legette shook his head. "I don't want her to serve me. I don't expect her to do any good for me. But I've been tied, sir . . ."

Never thinking to learn his past, never asking, they heard it now.

Briefly he told them. Black, born black into slavery on a sugar plantation in Louisiana, but given by some whimsical or relenting God an excellent mind, he had been early trained for house duty and spared the labor of the fields. He had been set aside as a companion and servant for the young son of his master, given to this young son. He had been tutored. He had been taught the skills his young master would need of him. He had been valet, waiter, barber, hunting companion, he had even learned figures so as to ease the boy's way when he took over running the plantation. What he had done finally, and in innocence, was to love a brown girl the boy fancied for himself. Vindictive because the girl preferred Legette, the boy had had him whipped and turned into the fields. "I wouldn't have minded the work," he said, "but I was to be treated like a prisoner. Every night I was tied and I worked with chains on my legs and I knew it would be for the rest of my life. I made a chance and ran away." His voice quickened now. "I have no money, sir, you know that. But you were kind enough to give me a contract to pay me in Santa Fe. If you would lend me, advance me, on it? If they want money for her, I could bargain."

They looked at each other, appalled by the story, moved to a dreadful sense of shame for the white owner, moved also to a strange humility. Johnny cleared his throat. "It's not because you killed Joe Britt, then?"

"Not altogether, though that plays some part, yes, sir. Looks as if I was singled out, some way. But her ankles were raw where she'd worked against the straps. It'd be hard for me to forget."

"She would be a terrible burden to you."

Legette shook his head. "No, sir. Chains are a burden, sir, and a whip on your back and starvation. But that poor harmless woman a burden? No, sir." His head bent and he fumbled his thumbs. "I've been thinking about it all day. I could take her back to Taos and maybe she'd be comfortable with her people again and know I'm not Joe Britt."

"If she wasn't?" Johnny asked, "if she never knew the difference?"

"Then I'd just take care of her, sir. The best I could."

Judith felt torn apart. She couldn't bear for Legette to sacrifice himself for a mad woman. He was coming now to the promise of his life, the best it could give him. He was in Spanish territory and he was free and he would have his wages and he could make of his life what he wanted to make of it. He could never have dreamed of the chance that was his now. And he was still young and strong. To throw it all away, burden himself with a mad Indian woman, for the rest of her life certainly and perhaps for his, was madness itself. And it wasn't fair! It wasn't fair! But she could understand, also, why he must. His life gained, he must gain another's.

He couldn't, if he ever meant to live in peace with himself, leave Joe Britt's cast-off behind, thongs about her ankles.

Johnny studied his spread hands a long, long time. "All right," he said then, "I'll get your money."

There was nothing else to do, she knew. This was the way it had to be.

Johnny returned and handed a money pouch into the Negro's hands. "That's all of it, Legette. That's your wages to Santa Fe. Maybe they'll give her to you and you won't need to use any of it, but if you do, bargain shrewdly, will you? You'll need as much of it as you can hang on to to get started in Santa Fe."

Legette's face cleared. "Thank you, sir. I'll be watchful. And I'll rejoin you the day after tomorrow."

When he had gone Johnny laid on another log of piñon wood. The resin sputtered and crackled and Judith went around the fire to draw near to him. He put his arm about her shoulder and pulled her close. "A man don't know," he said slowly, "when he decides a thing, just one simple thing, what can come of it, where it's going to lead, how many are going to be drawn into it, and maybe hurt and damaged. If I'd sent Joe Britt about his business . . ."

She pressed his hand. "You can't go back. It's water over the dam."

Under her head his chest lifted with a long breath taken. "Yes. Yes. It's water over the dam now."

The log dropped and the sparks blew up and his lips brushed softly against her temple. "He will be all right," she murmured, "Legette will be all right."

27

THEY FOLLOWED the river as far as the pueblo of the Pecos, but they left it there for it went home into the high places above and they must now turn to the great Sangre de Cristos.

From here it was dragging; the climb sharpened but the wagons were still slow and heavy. From the time they had sighted the towering mountain range it had loomed ahead and to the right. Now, through its foothills, they were hauling up even and then, almost by inches, they were putting it a little behind.

They had to spend one full day double-hitching up the pass, the last long ramp before they reached the plateau. But it was the last punishment, they told themselves, it was the last back-breaking, mule-killing, perishing hill they'd have to haul. Tomorrow they'd reach the city. Tomorrow they'd unhitch the blasted, long-eared critters for the last time and they'd turn their backs forever on all wagons or anything else that moved on wheels. "I feel," old Parley said, rubbing his back, "like I'd hauled them pesky contrivances ever' damned foot of the way by myself."

They all felt the same.

With no warning they came upon their first sight of the plain. They had been, as usual, winding slowly through the hills, piñons growing up thickly on all sides and hiding the long view, when suddenly they topped a rise and there it was, laid all clear and unobstructed before them.

No one gave an order to halt. No one signaled, no one shouted for a breather. They just stopped, as if what they saw ordered them and compelled them to wait, to look and to try, if they could, to take it in. Judith plucked at Manuel's sleeve and they rode a little apart. He was in raptures, but she signed him to silence.

Spread all before her was the enormous sweep and range of the Santa Fe plateau. She looked and looked, trying to adjust herself to its compass. She had come more than eight hundred miles across the prairies and plains, she thought. Distance was not new to her. For days at a time they had rolled across the flatlands where there was an immensity of land

and sky as far as the eye could see. But boundless distance, she thought now, diminishes itself. It runs into nothing for there is nothing to measure it by. But this vast plain was like a great saucer, the most enormous saucer in the world, tipped up on all sides and limited by mountains and hills. Its extent was lengthened and widened and opened by its limits.

Straight ahead, but purpled by distance, was another great range of mountains, as regal as the Sangre de Cristos but serried and jagged and saw-toothed. The sun hung over them now and flamed their clean profiles with gold. She looked a question at Manuel. "The Jemez, Señora."

Southward the plain was broken by one single tremendous mountain that lay humped like a giant turtle asleep, with smaller mountains, like a hatch of smaller turtles, slumbering around it. "The Sandias," Manuel whispered.

To the north rose broken hills, a penciled cart road crawling across their flanks. "The road to Taos," Manuel said. "And there where those cottonwoods are, Señora, is the river and the city."

She heard him, but she didn't look yet. Her eyes swept round the whole circle of hills and mountains and came back to rest on the vast basin itself. Color, she thought, color—the rawest and the boldest mingled with the softest and the mellowest. Red and gold and black and apricot and pink and blue and green. Blaze and glitter and fire and flash. Angles and shadows and glare. Space and lightness and height and radiance. But not grace, she thought, and not suppleness, not yielding and not pliant. Stark, rigid, formed, harsh, gaunt, angular. If you took oils and a brush, she thought, and painted the highest sky your canvas would hold and if you used the boldest blue you could mix, you'd have this Santa Fe sky. If you painted the golden plain as deep as you could push it and dabbed it with tar-pitch green, studded it with butter-yellow here and there, you'd have the floor of this Santa Fe basin. If you pointed your brush and gave it teeth and sawed it around the saucer you'd have these Santa Fe mountains. And if you put nothing human there, nothing at all, you'd have the punished, disciplined cruelty of this Santa Fe emptiness. It was beautiful, she thought, magnificent and splendid. And it was merciless, indifferent, and unfeeling, and the lonesomest lie of land she had ever looked upon. It blew a cold wind on her soul.

She shivered away the coldness and caught at Manuel's hand quickly. But it wasn't empty. You could put human life on the canvas. There were people here. Manuel's people were here. And there had been people here long before Manuel's people had come. There had always been peo-

ple here, as far back as anybody knew. Time before history, as far as man
knew, the Indians had been here.

And where there were people there were roofs and walls and fires. There
was warmth and cheer and eating and sleeping and sighing and laughing
and loving and birthing and dying. Contained as the land was, prisoned
by the mountains, formed and angled as it was, fixed, people could not be
contained and formed and angled and fixed. They lived daily, and in
living pushed back the great beetling shoulders of the mountains and filled
the great cruel void of the plain. You couldn't take too much of this into
yourself, she thought, or it would wither you and seep away your essence.
In some measure, it must be ignored, while at the same time it was used.
Show yourself vulnerable to it, she thought, and it would eat you up. It
would take a special valor for anybody with his nerve ends near the skin
to live here. It was too magnificent and it was too indifferent.

She followed the line of cottonwood trees that traced the river. It was
the only tender green to be seen. Down there, still mostly hidden, was the
city, a very old one. In it were the little dobe houses, rosy-glowed with
sun. She pondered how men had wrested the substance of their homes from
this stark land, shoveled it up and re-formed it, given it their own notions
of form, muddled it and mixed it and shaped it, stacked it and plastered
it and rounded the corners softly. Perhaps, she thought, because there were
so few softnesses here. Hands patted the plaster on and left their prints
to dry. Hands built small corner fireplaces and hewed down piñons and
built fires. And the little smokes braved up to haze the light, clear air, and
to tell that men were here. Men planted corn and peach trees and beans
and chilis, and gathered them, and made them into food, forcing the raw
earth to feed them. Men built churches and places of government and
markets. And men built a city.

Down there, covered by the cottonwoods, were narrow, so-wide streets
with the little burros ambling along them. There was a governor, there
were soldiers, there were priests, and there were black-rebozoed women and
black-hatted old men. There were paint-faced young women and cat-
graceful young men. There were merchants and clerks and herders and
officials and husbandmen. There were dogs and goats and fowls and
ponies and all the clutter men made at their living on the earth. But there
was not emptiness there. How valiant of them, she thought, to put something human on this vast canvas.

She swung her horse about and cantered him to where Johnny waited.
When she came up, he grinned at her. "What do you think?"

"I think," she said, "you would either die miserably in this place or learn to love it very much."

His face sobered and he searched her eyes. Then he smiled. "You won't die."

She smiled back at him. "No. I won't die."

He wheeled and gave the signal to start, then he caught her up and rode out ahead with her, down and down the long ramp that led into the city.

They did not speak together now. There was no need. They knew each other so well. Judith sighed, restingly, contentedly. This was so much her place, so much her home, here beside her husband. She had a queer moment of remembering . . . some blathering nonsense when they first left Three Forks about what a husband was and how a woman should know him. It was so simple. A husband was the man you had married and lived with, and you knew him just as simply.

You began to know him at once, with the most elemental things. You learned that he slept lightly and kicked the blankets off at night. You learned that he wanted his coffee very hot, that he liked milk very cold, that he liked meat of any kind, cooked any way, but couldn't abide vegetables. That, like a child, he had a sweet tooth for pies and puddings but had no special fondness for one against another. You learned that he liked a linen shirt soft and nothing provoked him more than stiffening ironed into one. You learned that he was the most disorderly man that ever entered the door of a house, but that he never saw your own disorder either. You learned that he rarely praised you, but that neither was he often cross with you. He didn't talk much, but his hand, touching quickly, said all you wanted him to say in tenderness and concern. You learned that your own hand could make him tremble and that your eyes, troubled, could trouble him deeply.

And because you loved him you slowly changed your own ways. You'd always liked covers tucked firmly about your feet, but now you kicked them loose yourself. You'd grown to like them easy. You'd never wanted your coffee boiling, but you couldn't abide it tepid any more. You'd always liked garden-fresh vegetables better than meat, but they were bland and insipid to you now. His slipshod speech, no better than his neighbors', had grated on you at first. But you picked it up and not only talked it now but thought it.

She grinned. You just made yourself over, to know a man. You just grew into his ways. You just lost yourself in him, and found yourself whole. You were hurt by him, and you hurt him. You went through things together and you stood by him and he stood by you. You just slowly, without thinking much about it, began to talk like him and act a little like him and look a little like him, until before you knew it you were thinking like him, and you had his same pride and most of his same wants and purposes and you couldn't remember when you hadn't.

Once your name was Lowell. Now it was Fowler. It was that simple . . . and it was that profound.

She turned to look back up the line. "We'll make an entrance with a flourish," Johnny had said, ordering all hands to spit and polish.

The Beaver came next, immediately behind her and Johnny, his Osages flanking him. They were gorgeous and regal, carelessly graceful and splendid, their eagle feathers spinning, their bridles jingling, their fine blankets draped, their chests bare. Parley and Legette and Manuel came next, spruced and combed and clean, new buckskins for Parley and Legette, ruffles for Manuel.

And the hands, the men, cracking their whips and riding very tall and bulked and strong, grinning with their pleasure, already leaned toward señoritas and bailes and faro games and tequila. The mules were curried with red tassels hung from harnesses and yellow flowers strung on their ears. They looked, somehow, dapper and dandy.

In the lead wagon, so that she could see Legette, was his wild girl. There were no hobbles on her feet now and her mumbling and clinging and clawing had ended. Judith herself had washed the girl when Legette had brought her in, and combed the long tangled hair into smooth braids and dressed her decently in clean calico. She had proved docile and contented as long as she could see Legette; when he was out of sight her eyes grew anxious and she became restless and fidgety. It would take a time, Judith thought, for the girl to get over the fear that her Joe might leave her again. What a care Legette had loaded onto himself there. She shook her head. But who knows what freedom means to a man that has never been free. Perhaps the burden and the care and the unshackling of another had to be added before the full sense of freedom could be felt. It was his concern, she thought, only and wholly his, to do with what he could. She let it go.

Behind, the other wagons lumbered squawkingly, but they were solid and promising and exciting, loaded with cargo, bringing gifts to Cathay. Ah, she thought, they *were* making a flourishing entrance. All the dust and all the sweat and all the evidences of haul and pull and double hitch and dry scrape and Pawnee arrows and mutinies and death were gone. They were an Americano caravan, making its proud entrance, and her own heart rose in choking pride for what they had done.

She squirmed about and wiggled for a firmer seat. The side-saddle had a different feeling. She looked to make certain her habit covered her ankle and set her small, plumed hat, packed carefully away for this moment, more securely on her head. She braced her shoulders back and held them there, very straight, very erect. She held her reins correctly, her hands properly gloved, and she did not allow her eyes to wander as the first dobe house came into view.

But she saw it and her pulse quickened. There it was, now, the first house. And this voyage to Santa Fe was ended. On the second day of August, 1823, they were here.

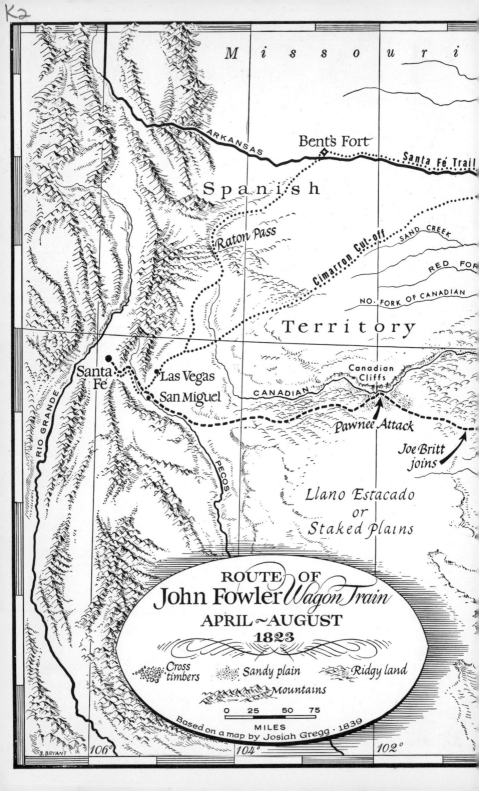

K2

M i s s o u r i

ARKANSAS

Bent's Fort

Santa Fé Trail

S p a n i s h

Raton Pass

Cimarron Cut-off

SAND CREEK

RED FOR

NO. FORK OF CANADIAN

T e r r i t o r y

Santa Fé

Las Vegas
San Miguel

CANADIAN

Canadian
Cliffs

Pawnee Attack

Joe Britt
joins

RIO GRANDE

PECOS

Llano Estacado
or
Staked Plains

ROUTE OF
John Fowler *Wagon Train*
APRIL ~ AUGUST
1823

Cross
timbers   Sandy plain   Ridgy land

Mountains

0   25   50   75
MILES

Based on a map by Josiah Gregg · 1839

S. BRYANT   106°   104°   102°